A KINGDOM OF CROWNS AND DAGGERS

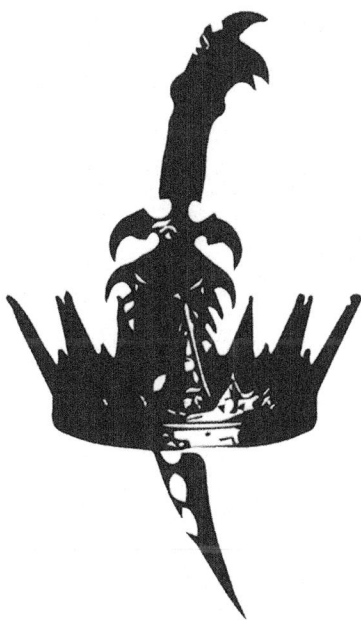

K.A KNIGHT

ERIN O'KANE

A Kingdom of Crowns and Daggers

Written by K.A. Knight and Erin O'Kane.
Edited By Jess from Elemental Editing and Proofreading.
Proofreading by Norma's Nook.
Formatted by The Nutty Formatter.
Art by Annteya
Cover and art by Moonstruck Cover Design & Photography

READER CONSIDERATIONS

This is a dark book not meant for anybody under the ages of 18. Content includes: explicit sex, explicit violence, stalking, murder, torture, dubious consent and much more.

THESAURUS

Stumbler - One of rich or noble birth, called this due to their slow, almost stumbling steps everywhere. Never in a rush.

Lowers - Those from the lower ranks and lands.

Palanquin - Wooden transport for people or food, hand carried.

Queen Mother - The previous king's wife, cannot lead the nation but still holds the title, takes on "mother" when passed.

Daggers - Assassin and thief guild located in the Lowers.

DRESHA

KING'S MONUMENT

MOONSHADOW

THE LOWERS

FORT

LANIDE RIVER

BLACKSMITH

CHRIST CHURCH MARKET

FISHING WHARF

FLOATING SLUMS

BLEEDING SEA

IMPERIAL MOUNTAIN

TEMPLE

StormHallow Province

TUNDRA PROVINCE

TUNDRA PASS

GRAND MARKET

RIVER SHADE PROVINCE

FLAME STRAND PROVINCE

MINES

MINER QUARTERS

MINES

...EN PROVINCE

CAIRN PROVINCE

WHITHORN PROVINCE

MERCHANT DOCKS

HUNTING

LAKE HOUSE

THRONE ROO

SCHOLARS

CONCUBINE
PALACE

SCHOOL

SERVANT
QUARTERS

GUARDS
BUNKER

STABLES

WESTERN GATE

MAIN GATE

QUEENS PALACE

WINDFALL HALL

WATERFALL

HEALERS HOUSE

TEMPLE

FREY HALL

QUEEN MOTHERS PALACE

GARDENS

KITCHENS

ENHOUSE

EASTERN GATE

MOONSHADOW

CHAPTER
ONE

ALYX

He's going to die, which is a shame since the robe he is wearing is of good quality and will soon be ruined by bloodstains. I watch as they circle him, their gleaming knives poised and ready to attack. Sucking the remaining meat from the chicken bone, I take shelter from the rain on a wooden barrel hidden under the awning on the back of the blacksmith's, one arm pressed against my knee and the other holding my precious food.

The sky is a muddy grey as the heavens pour down their frustration, turning the hard clay dirt of the Lowers into a slippery, muddy mess. The robed male slips in it now, not quite falling before barely managing to stay upright. His eyes, a bright cerulean blue that we don't tend to see in the Lowers, dart between his attackers as they circle him.

The fool. He should have known better than to head down the alleys back here. I'm safe because they know who I am. They don't bother trying to assault me, but even the people from the Lowers avoid alleys such as this for this exact reason—the bandits who hide and wait for their next meal.

They are lazy mongrels if you ask me.

While some of our work may share a few similarities, they use half the effort my family and I employ. They just lie in wait and attack, without planning or a perfect escape. What they do doesn't require skill. They just kill and pillage—the heathens. Where is the sense of justice or pride in their work? They have none, and that's the difference between us.

We may have the same ultimate task, which is stealing from the rich, but they give us thieves and assassins a bad name. Honestly, I don't know why we haven't done anything about them.

The Daggers have a clear code, however, and it isn't my job to intervene.

Even if I jump in and save him now, I would only be painting a target on my own back. The cloaked fool wandered down here, and he will pay for it with his life. From where I'm sitting, his face is concealed behind a silk face mask, his head covered by the cloak's dark hood that falls luxuriously down to his booted feet, the fabric clean and rich. He's taller than most of the seven bandits surrounding him. Compared to his simple yet clearly high-quality robe, they are practically in rags. Their once white shirts are now tattered and stained brown, and their pants fair no better. All are male, some of them boasting scars from their previous attacks, and one is even missing an eye. They range in ages, from barely past their fifteenth name day to as old as to their fortieth, yet they all have the hard glint in their eyes that everyone in the Lowers has.

They are determined and angry. It's what keeps us all alive and surviving in this shithole when most others would die—like the noble who was foolish enough to come here alone.

Dropping the empty bone to the ground for the strays, I sit back and sling one mud-stained leg over the other. The sleek black cotton of my suit keeps me warm as the chilly wind blows in from the mountains in the north. My hood is down, as is my face guard since I was eating. Thanks to my outer cloak, all of the weapons hanging from my hips, arms, and thighs are concealed, but my bright orange hair is hard to hide, even with my hood up, and it ends up hanging down to my waist in wet curls. Despite being in the shadows, I have no doubt that my green eyes are sparkling, taking in every detail.

I'm like a beacon in the night, yet they pay me no mind, too entranced by their prey.

"I want no trouble," the man in the cloak calls, his voice calm and his accent eloquent. His soft, clean palms are held up in a signal of peace. I want to laugh at the absurdity of it, especially when paired with how well spoken he is. He's definitely a noble; it's in the lilt of his voice. The knowledge of his own worth gives him an air of pompous self-righteousness, as though he is better than everyone else.

"Well, that's a shame because we do," one of the older men retorts, brandishing a rusty knife. It might look tarnished, but it's wicked enough to gut the noble. He's clearly the leader, and although short and skinny, he carries an air of authority that would quickly put you right. It's not his stature or attitude that would make you think twice about crossing this man, but his cruel, dark eyes— the eyes of a killer.

I know the look well, and it's an easy one for me to recognise— after all, I carry the same look in mine.

"Here, take this and leave," the rich stranger commands, his voice ringing out as if he's truly expecting them to listen, throwing down a ring of coins like candy thrown to children on summer solstice. We all watch them sink into the muddy ground, tarnishing the polished gold, and I can't fight my smirk.

What a fool. All he's succeeded in doing is showing his foe where he keeps his money, which makes him an even easier target than he was previously.

"Oh, we will." The leader grins, menace sparkling in his dark eyes. "That and more."

With an unspoken signal, they attack as one, leaping forward to catch their prey by surprise.

The nobleman is fast for a stumbler, the name we've given to the upper classes on account of the slow way they all seem to move, never in a hurry to get anywhere. Jumping back, he dodges the initial swinging blades, but he's hopelessly outnumbered against them and has no weapon. My interest is piqued by the stranger, and as I watch, one of the attackers slices through his robe. What a waste. Blood blooms from the cut on his arm, seeming to awaken something in the noble. His bright eyes narrow in anger, and he grits his teeth and smashes his head into the bandits, surprising all of us.

This one has fire, which is unusual for someone from higher families.

Call it boredom or intuition, but I feel compelled to do something. Sighing, I stand and bark, "Enough. Leave him."

Throwing my outer cloak back, I meet all their surprised gazes as I pull out my sword. "Or go through me. Either way, I don't care which option you pick."

"You're protecting noble scum," one spits, clearly able to tell that I'm one of them, yet also not recognising who I am.

I arch a brow at him and notice that another hurries over to the leader. "That's Alyx," he murmurs, but he's not quiet enough so that no one else hears.

Rookie mistake. Now everyone knows, and the atmosphere shifts. Fear flashes in some of their eyes, but not the leader's. Sure, I'm almost positive that I see fear in his expression, but it's quickly covered up by the pure disgust he shoots my way. His men all look to him now, and he knows he's going to have to do something to assert his authority.

Everything is on a carefully balanced scale here, including his tentative leadership. One wrong move and it will fall, and he knows that.

Scowling, he pins me with a sour glare. "Then she should know better than to protect a stumbler."

"It's true, he's a stumbler, but I said enough. Walk away," I command, swinging my sword with an effortless flick of my wrist to show them I mean what I say. "Or don't. It's been a while since I had a good stretch."

Males like him can't resist the challenge, and I knew that if I got involved, I'd be fighting at least one of them. They are bandits, they don't care about right or wrong, and now they have a chance to prove they are stronger than an assassin, one of the great Daggers.

Grinning widely and showing me teeth as rotten as his soul, he chuckles. "Let's put the rumours of the great assassin to the test, shall we?" the leader sneers, the nobleman forgotten. "Get her."

"It's your death." I shrug nonchalantly, adrenaline flooding my body as I prepare for what I do best and duck the first two males coming at me. With a spin, I slice and bring my sword up to block an incoming knife. One howls as he stumbles away with a cut across his neck thanks to my quick movements—he didn't even see it coming. Smirking at the one with his knife pressed to my sword, I throw my head into his, taking him by surprise and knocking him backward just as arms wrap around me from behind. When they lift me into the air, I use the momentum and flip us, landing on my knees in the mud before pushing up and slicing with my blade.

It's a warning shot. The man's shirt flutters away as he watches me, wide-eyed, before I turn and see another running towards me with a war cry. Jumping to my feet, I sprint towards him, only to throw myself to my knees in the mud, bend backwards, and slide through his open legs. Coming up behind him, I bring the pommel of my sword down on his head before he even has a chance to realise what's happened. He crumples onto the wet, slick ground as I race to the nearest wooden wall. Running up it, I use my momentum to flip over the man chasing me, landing behind him. They aren't about to stop, and they certainly aren't just trying to injure me. These are kill shots, so I give up warning them. Wrapping an arm over his shoulder, I use my other arm to swipe my sword across his neck. He has a split second to realise what happened as he turns, attempting to cover the killing blow with his hands. I knock him to the ground with a kick to die like the dog he is.

Swinging my sword, the bloody tip bright in the darkness, I face the remaining bunch. "Still want to play?" I call mockingly as I move my legs into a defensive position and gesture for them to come at me with my free hand. They race at me at once, and I grip my sword with both hands. That's the problem with these bandits: they don't know how to work as a unit or coordinate their attacks.

As I meet the first of them, my sword hits his blade and snaps it. When the broken metal flings up into the air, catching the light as it reaches its peak and begins to fall again, I bring my leg up and kick. My timing is perfect and hits the shard where I wanted, and I watch as it flies towards one of the other men. It buries in his chest with a satisfying thud before he falls back.

The nobleman grabs for one of the men coming towards me, but I slam the flat of my sword into him and spin, kicking his chest until he stumbles back into the mud with a grunt. "Don't get in my way," I snap. "Stay down." I quickly fling myself back into the fray.

I make quick work of the two that circle me. Feinting left and then diving at the one on the right, I run him through with my sword so he falls hard, blood seeping through his hands as he attempts to hold his guts inside his body. Turning to the other, I leap into the air and slice down, watching his head fall from his body and roll through the mud towards the final bandit. It's poetic, really, and way too easy for me. I'm not even out of breath. I would have thought they would be harder to kill when this is their job.

I grin at the leader as his nostrils flare, dirt sprayed across his face and body. I feel it dripping down me as well, coating my body and hair, and I'm sure that along with blood, it's even smeared along my face. Fighting in the dirt is always messy and my favourite type, since I was never allowed to before.

"Come on then." My tone is impatient, but I'm relishing the chance to do this. However, he glances at the nobleman one last time before turning and hightailing it out of the alley.

Rolling my eyes, I sigh at his cowardice and slide the hilt of a dagger into my palm. I flick my wrist, watching the blade sail through the air, feeling grimly amused as it hits the fleeing man so hard it pins his body to the side of a wooden house. As I stroll over, I notice that one of the earlier men I incapacitated is trying to get to his feet. Bringing my sword down with a casual movement, I end his life. When I reach the now dead leader of the bandits, I press my knee to his body and pluck my dagger free. Wiping it on his pants, I slide it back into place before grabbing the coins in the leather pouch at his hip and shoving them into my pocket. I remove my knee and step back to avoid being hit by the body as it falls to the ground, now that it's no longer being held up.

Turning back, I see at least one of the bandits has fled, but the others lie in broken parts around the nobleman, who is watching me with wide eyes.

I stroll back over to him, and he kneels there, watching me. His once pristine cloak is covered in mud, the arm cut away and barely hanging on by a few threads.

"Thank you," the man says, reaching up for me like I will help him to his feet.

I crouch instead, using the tip of my bloody blade to lift the golden, shiny chain from his neck, holding it between us as I meet his blue eyes surrounded by long lashes. "You are a fool for wearing such things here." I cut the chain away and catch the chunk of warm gold in my waiting hand. "My fee for saving you," I say by way of explanation and pocket it. Standing, I tug my hood up and prepare to leave. "Go home, rich man, where you belong. I will not save you a second time, you moron."

CHAPTER
TWO

JOHA

I have never been called a moron in my entire existence. Truthfully, I am not even sure what the strange word means, but as I watch the retreating form of the female who saved me, I realise two things.

One, I want to know what it means.

Two, she is unlike anyone I have ever met.

Stumbling to my feet, I slip in the mud for a moment before catching my balance. I'm glad she's facing the other way as I wobble, my cloak almost falling off in the process. Securing it while ignoring the tattered arm, I clear my throat and call out, "Wait!"

I hurry after her, stepping over the fallen bodies and cursing myself for my own stupidity. I thought I had hidden my station well, but apparently, I was wrong. It has been too long since I have been over the walls of the palace and in our lands. I had not realised the depths of despair and ruin it had fallen into and how I would stand out so much amongst them. That is exactly why I ventured here in the first place, and if not for the amber-haired beauty, I would be dead.

When I manage to catch her at the corner of a building, I grip her arm to get her to stop. What I did not anticipate, however, was how she would react to this. She spins in a move too quick for my eyes to follow and slams me into the wooden building. I have to smother every instinct to fight back and remain meek and dumb, continuing to pretend to be the person everyone thinks I am.

This woman and the bandits called me a stumbler. The look on her face as she spoke about it makes me think that whatever that is, it is not a good thing.

For a moment, I get a good look at her face. It's shaped like a heart, pale, and dusted with the same coloured freckles as her hair. Her skin looks soft and perfect, not marred at all, unlike most from the lower part of our lands. I have the insane urge to reach out and brush my fingers against her skin to see if it's really as soft as it looks. I manage to catch myself, though, as I would likely lose my hand for touching her again. After what I just saw her do to those bandits, it would be easy for her to take my life. Knowing this should make me fearful, but instead, I continue to stare at her, noticing how her unruly, curly hair is slipping out from beneath her hood, the colour reminding me of burning flames, warmth, and home.

Her eyes shine like the finest jewels of the king's crown.

Her lips are full and pursed in fury, and they are the palest shade of pink, as if run across by the berries from the south. She is remarkable, and more beautiful than most court ladies that flock to me, yet unlike them, she watches me with barely controlled anger and annoyance.

When her voice comes, it is silken and contains a familiar lilt, yet her words are coarse and crude. "Fuck off, rich man. Touch me again and I will take your hand like your soldiers did to my family."

She departs, plunging into the crowds beyond the alley. I stumble after her, my heart racing even though I am not sure why.

Maybe it's because no one has ever spoken to me that way before. No, no one has ever spoken to their king that way before.

They bow and scrape, never letting a foul word cross their lips in my presence. Even my enemies hide their threats behind perfect, thinly veiled complaints.

Not her. No, she told me exactly what she thought of me. I am a fool. She was right.

I search the masses of the market beyond. This was my original destination before I got lost, following what appeared to be a starving child into an alley in hopes that I could help him. Of course, I realise now that it was all a ruse to lead me into the trap the bandits contrived.

Many are cloaked thanks to the poor weather, yet they look nothing like mine. These are tattered and patched, made from dark, dull colours so as not to stand out. Wherever she is, she blends in perfectly, knowing the back streets far better than I do. Turning away with a sigh, I reach up and rest my fingers over my throat where her blade was poised. It would have been so easy for her to end me, and given the fact that I got her dragged into a fight, some might think it would have been justified.

The bandit in charge had spoken of an assassin, and at first, I had not realised that he was speaking about her. However, she seemed to have the attitude and fighting skills to back it up.

Who was this woman?

Just then, I hear the toll of the bells from the palace, letting me know the change of guards is about to happen. I must hurry back before they come to wake and dress me for the day. I can just imagine their panic at finding my chambers empty.

I may be king of these lands, but I am as much of a servant as those who work for me, trapped in my own palace—a puppet king.

For one moment this evening, though, I felt alive with those emerald eyes peering at me, and as I hurry through the streets to the palace, they are all I can think of.

No one bothers me on my hurried journey back, but as I

approach and the western hidden gate slams open, I know I've been caught. The light at the guard station frames the huge, hulking silhouette of my personal guard. "You are in trouble, my king."

His voice is like shifting boulders, and I grin as I push my hood back and step in beside him, flashing him a wink. "Don't be so uptight, Orion."

"We are not friends right now," he says, looking around to make sure that no one is nearby to overhear us. "You left without me. That is not allowed—"

I know that when it comes down to it, *this* is what upsets him the most—not that I snuck out, but the fact that I did not take him with me.

"Which is exactly why I did it." I clap his shoulder to lessen the blow, trying to make light of it. He is the only one I trust here, but I have not been alone since birth. My every move is watched and monitored. I am escorted to my rooms to sleep, and they wash me and dress me. I am *always* with someone. I needed to see what has become of my father's lands and be alone. The reports I was being given from my stepmother did not add up, and I knew that the only way I would get the truth was to find out for myself.

"My king." Orion sighs in that disappointed way of his that I hate. Many would think he was years older than me, not that we are the same age. I guess protecting me ages him, or it could be because he's one of the largest men I've ever met.

"I am back now, safe and sound. Let us go before they find out." I move through the familiar palace, every inch of which I have explored. Orion follows me, stern and annoyed as always, but he does not stop me.

"You will be the death of me, Joha," he mutters as we reach the king's palace. We wait as servants rush from the building to fetch water for my morning bath, the palanquins of food stopping before the doors.

"Do not be a moron," I whisper over my shoulder as we wait for the perfect moment.

He blinks in confusion, taken aback by my comment. "Do you even know what that means, my king?"

"Not a clue." I grin widely. "Follow me."

I run to the wall, leaping and catching the railing. I roll over it effortlessly, landing on my feet and slipping silently into my rooms. Orion is right behind me, silent despite his size. He is the best warrior we have and just so happens to be my best friend.

As I shed my cloak, he picks it up, his face darkening as he finds the cut in the garment. Holding it up, he waits until I meet his gaze. "Is it not enough to have threats and enemies in every corner of your life, but you must also seek out danger as well?"

"Orion, I had to see the state of my kingdom. They are my people," I reply seriously. "Now, let us get ready for another boring day of meetings and bowing and scraping."

"You are the king," he says with that same stern frown he has had since childhood.

He was always the serious one, whereas I was always jovial and playful. His comment quickly brings me back down from my high.

"We both know it's in name only," I state bitterly, the familiar sense of hopelessness falling over me.

"Your Majesty," the court servers call through the sliding doors separating my rooms from the hallway, giving the illusion of privacy. "Your bath is ready. Shall we wait to serve your food?"

"I am coming," I call loudly, watching their shadows back away. My choices are limited, and it makes me bitter. For a moment, I wonder what freedom I would have known had I not been born into a throne—a position many covet and would kill to obtain.

"Puppet king," I murmur, shaking my head in disgust.

CHAPTER

THREE

CRUX

With my legs slung sideways across the wooden chair I have dubbed my throne, I narrow my eyes on the man before me. "Are my little rats telling me that Alyx, *my* Alyx, was seen defending a nobleman in Christ Church?"

The sly man swallows hard, his beady eyes dropping to the slick stone before him. The lanterns glow brightly from their fixings on the wall, spread evenly around the circular room we use for meetings. I can hear the jubilant laughter of those coming back after a successful night of thieving, heading into the handmade bar to celebrate or to the traders' stalls to sell their goods. The last thing anyone wants to do after thieving is keep whatever they just stole. If they sell it as soon as possible, it gets the suspicion off them. The traders all know what they buy is stolen, but they can't afford to turn down something that will make them fast money.

All the thieves are mine, and down here, under the lands of

Dresha, lies a whole other world—a world I created, and one I am the ruler of.

My Daggers.

Everyone forgot about the tunnels running under their precious city or thought they were disgusting and useless since their sewage flows through some. That just made them perfect for us, though, becoming our safe haven that no one dares to venture near. Those who have been rejected and shunned by the world above now have somewhere to go, and it's our sanctuary.

I am the thief king or, as many of them call me, devil.

If I am the devil, then Alyx is my reaper, my collector of souls.

"Yes, my king, I am sure of it. We were listening in the market." There are different types of people who serve me and live down here in our little family—assassins, thieves, and rats. We need them all to survive. My little rats tell me all the secrets. They overhear everything, looked down on by everyone so much that they become invisible. "We saw it."

"Leave," I grumble, my eyes going far away. They don't protest, scurrying away like the rodents they are named after. Everyone knows not to mess with me when I'm in a mood like this.

Alyx wouldn't protect a nobleman without a reason. I *know* there will be an explanation behind her unusual actions. I shall have to ask her when she returns.

As if my thoughts conjure her, I see her familiar silhouette as she drops onto one of the stone bridges from the entrance above, and I watch as she prowls right towards me.

As usual, the air in my lungs freezes at her mere presence, and my heart skips a beat as she tears down her hood and mask, letting me see the face I know better than my own. I don't have dreams often, but when I do, she's in every single one of them.

She bows mockingly before me, her eyes glistening with mirth. "My king."

Rolling my eyes, I lean back. "My little rats tell me you saved a nobleman in the market at Christ Church."

Straightening, she heads my way, throwing herself across my lap. My hands reach for her automatically, uncaring about the dried blood and mud flaking across her. I would bathe in it to touch her, but I pretend to be disgusted by it. Nose wrinkling, I hide my action by plucking at her cloak. "You are filthy."

"Just the way you like me." She winks, making my chest tighten and my brain start to play out various scenarios of helping her get clean. I force myself to focus as she lifts a pouch and a solid gold necklace from one of her pockets. "Taken as a fee from said nobleman." She grins widely. "I was bored."

"Of course you were." I sigh, fingering the gold and weighing the sizable piece of jewellery. "This is far too unique to sell around here, so you may as well keep it."

Grinning, she slides the necklace around her neck, letting it fall against her black leather corset. "As my king orders." She leans in and kisses my cheek. "I'm going to bathe and sleep."

She takes off, leaving just like she entered my life—as a whirlwind.

My hands are clenched into fists to maintain the heat and feel of her body as I swallow and watch her go, wondering if she knows how much she affects me. What would she do if I kissed her? I may be the king of assassins, but I'm like a child shaking with fear when it comes to telling her how I feel. Instead, I sit here and wonder if, after all these years, she feels the same way I do.

She is the reason my heart beats.

Does Alyx love me the way I love her?

Could she ever?

Once more, I am too cautious to ask her, afraid of losing the only good thing in my life since I found her in a bloodstained dress seven years ago.

CHAPTER

FOUR

ORION

I watch my king's rigid back as his people bow, almost prostrating themselves as they pass him. They may be unable to meet his eyes, but as soon as they believe he is out of earshot, the whispers begin. Here, in the palace, I have learned rumours are more dangerous than swords. Many people have been brought down with just a handful of words, their lives destroyed and families torn apart.

One would expect civility in the glittering throng of leaders, but if anything, they are more feral—poisoning, knives in the back, taxes, and word games that lead to death. It is all the norm, and it is much more dangerous here than in the Lowers.

My king knows that all too well.

His usual posse follows him, his two advisors dressed in their bland, grey, shapeless robes and square hats. Behind them are the king's soldiers in purple armour and matching purple hats, the royal feather standing tall and straight from the tops marking them as one of the highest ranks. At the back of the procession are the king's scholars in long, flowing white robes, and it is then I understand his need for space.

Ever since Joha was young, he was destined to inherit the throne, and despite his lineage, he was groomed for it. He had lessons every hour of the day until he couldn't even think straight and could quote facts about the kingdom's laws in his sleep. He cannot step one foot out of line. He must glide across the rough-hewn stone of the paths to the council chambers, his head tilted back at the perfect angle despite the heavy crown he bears. His purple robes swirl around him, tied at the front in a bow. Instead of the sword I know he wishes for, he clutches a book. Jewels drip from every inch of him down to his black, soft-soled, pointed shoes.

I walk behind him to the left, where I will always remain. My silver armour embezzled with the king's symbol—a wolf—is shown proudly. My longsword is sheathed at my hip as I stomp after him. I will never forget the honour of this position, and despite the old king's requests—may he rest in peace—Joha chose me to lead his protection. In spite of my young age and his father's insistence on choosing a general, the former king bowed to his son's wishes.

It was his last act of kindness for his son before he died.

I know Joha misses him greatly, despite the fact that they were never overly close. A bizarre, archaic rule imposed centuries ago insists that a cool distance is expected amongst the royal family, even from a father to his heir. He doesn't speak of his father often, but he reminds me more and more of him every day.

He was a good king, but Joha will be a *great* king.

Despite the façade he shows everyone else, his intelligence hidden in his shrewd gaze, his passion for his people comes through in every act, even when he can't always show it.

The path through the palace to where the council meets daily is not a short walk, but it gives Joha time to prepare himself as we pass Deajul Hall, where his throne sits.

"Your Majesty." The cool, soft voice makes us still, and Joha turns, spotting the Queen Mother and her ensemble coming from the direction of her palace, which is just past Windfall Hall and set amongst the greenery there. I feel my stomach sink, knowing it's a feeling that will be echoed in Joha. In a small act of rebellion, he makes her cover the distance between them rather than meeting her halfway as is expected.

Even small interactions like that are governed by laws.

Her brown eyes narrow slightly, not missing his silent slight, but they quickly soften. She has an audience to play to after all. Her hands are clasped perfectly in front of her pink robes, making her look graceful as she floats around the palace as royal ladies must. A sunshade decorated with a hand-painted wolf is held above her by one of her many ladies-in-waiting. A whole line of them moves perfectly in sync behind her, ready to attend to her every need. Unlike when I first met the queen, lines now surround her eyes and mouth, betraying her age despite the many lotions she demands from far and wide.

She was barely older than Joha when the former king married her. She is from one of the oldest families in our nation, so it was a marriage of political advancement, a move that I'm sure Joha despises.

He never knew his mother, but the one who replaced her is anything but motherly. She is like the beasts that hide in burrows in the mountain. Get too close and they will strike. She was trained to be queen, her family counting on it and the prestige it would bring to their lands. The old king bowed to the council's pressure to remarry, and the fool actually loved the woman heading towards Joha now. Right up until his death, he was completely oblivious to the anger and resentment growing between his wife and son.

She knew that without an heir, Joha would inherit the throne— the throne she so badly wants to sit on. Her own child could be controlled, but not Joha, or so she thought. So did I, yet here we are. He sits upon that gilded seat, but she is still very much in charge.

When she stops the perfect distance from us, Joha bows deeply, almost touching the floor as is expected. "Queen Mother," he says formally as we all bow with him, not rising until he does. Despite him being king and leading this nation, the queen is above him and everyone knows it, which is why he keeps calling himself the puppet king. She pulls his strings, leading in the only way possible for her.

By law, a female cannot lead the nation, but this one seeks to.

Her eyes are sharp, and every inch of her is perfectly made up, as a lady should be. She drips in jewels, and a crown is perched on her perfect coils. Her ladies back away, still bowing, to give the illusion of privacy while remaining close if the Queen Mother needs anything. I ignore their giggles and looks when they glance at me. Either I disgust them since I am nothing like the clean-shaven nobles many lust after and are taken by or they are curious, wanting a walk on the wild side. Everyone within these walls, even ladies-in-waiting, wants something, so they think if they get close to me, they will get close to the king.

The king has no bride and no queen yet, and many are desperate for it to be them. He always says he will not fall into the same trap as his father, but he must marry. That is the law, but he is taking his time, and I respect that. I don't wish to see my friend even more unhappy by being tied to one of the rich, stuck-up women he is presented with daily.

"Your Majesty, I hear the council is discussing plans to redevelop the Tundra Province today."

"Are they?" He chuckles, his expression a little vacant, one I know he has practiced many times. "I am sure you know more than I do, Queen Mother."

"Yes, indeed." She frowns, her eyes skimming over his expression. She is waiting for more, but when she does not get it, I see her irritation flare. "Well, I will allow you to take your leave and attend the meeting. Just remember, Your Majesty, that my family hails from just south of there."

"Like I could forget, Queen Mother." He bows again, a sign of respect I know he detests. "I shall take my leave."

She watches him turn and, as all royals do, walk slowly towards the chambers of Windfall Hall, where the council meets daily and awaits him now. They do not rush. They do not show emotion. They do not break protocol.

They are to be perfect in every way.

A perfect leader to inspire our lands.

If only Joha would believe he is capable of what I know he is. He has so much more power than he thinks. He just needs the belief that he can do it.

Following him closely, I keep my eyes on my king, wishing I could help him in this battle he faces.

One most know nothing about, fought for the soul of our lands and the heart of our king.

CHAPTER
FIVE

JOHA

The droning of my advisors' voices is enough to lull me to sleep, especially considering how tired I am. It was a long night, and my adrenaline from sneaking out of the palace and almost losing my life has finally faded, leaving me bone weary. The seemingly endless meeting and the monotonous tones of the haughty males around me does not help with this matter, and I have to fight to stay awake.

I should be paying attention, since they are discussing my kingdom and where to invest money in our lands. It's an important matter, and usually, despite how I would fake ignorance, I would make mental notes of everything said.

Not today.

Currently, sitting in my large, throne-like chair, I lean against one side and sit at a jaunty angle, my left leg crossed over my right. I stare at my nails as if contemplating a hangnail.

The conversation goes on around me, and honestly, I believe they forget I am here most of the time, which is exactly how I like it to be.

These meetings might be boring, but they are important, and I need to be present to hear the decisions made about the kingdom.

My kingdom.

Despite what they think about me, I do care. They will never see that side, however, not while the Queen Mother lives.

She is the one truly in control here and has somehow managed to convince most of the advisors and scholars to listen to her. They say I'm simple and that these decisions are best made by them, but they don't know that I take note of everything said or that I understand every undermining decision they make, all to enforce their power and fill their pockets

The former queen may appear like a perfect Queen Mother to guide her departed husband's son, yet she is dangerous. She already had her claws in everyone before my father died, and since I took the throne, she has only grown in power. I have seen what happens to those who don't agree with her, and I know my life would be forfeit if I ever became difficult and attempted to challenge her, which is why I play up to their vision of me.

Sadly, it is easy enough to do. They all assume I am nothing more than a puppet and have no opinion on what happens in the kingdom. This makes them believe I am weak, pliable, and easily manipulated. I have no power either way, so at least by playing along, I can still be involved and know what's happening in my kingdom. If the other options are death or imprisonment, then I know which option I will choose.

Even if some days it is so hard I wish to scream and rage, I do not. I play the long game.

I lounge in my chair, my eyes skimming over the familiar meeting room. It is long and thin, only made more so by the dark wall-to-wall bookshelves that are packed with heavy tomes. Most of the books are filled with the laws and history of the kingdom, something that I find fascinating, yet I have to pretend otherwise. The long meeting table we sit at is made of ash, the wood highly polished and gleaming under the lanterns strategically bolted around the room. A large bay window takes up most of the far wall, and I often find my gaze drawn to it and the view of my lands beyond.

Here in Windfall Hall, we are gifted with views over the stone wall that separates the palace from the city beyond. To my left, I see the different provinces, each split and named after the nobles that lead them. From Storm Hallow all the way to Whithorn. Dividing the middle of our lands is the Lanide River, which separates those provinces from the Lowers, as the nobles aptly named them—the lands our workers and normal folk inhabit, the streets I visited just the night prior.

One side boasts wealth, ornate houses constructed with the finest stone, and the most beautiful trees offering shade, while the other boasts the will to survive.

Beyond it all is the Bleeding Sea, the dark, churning water separating our lands from those beyond. My eyes follow the waves for a moment, watching a merchant ship find its way to the docks before I sigh and turn away.

When I do allow my mind to wander, I think of how much good we could do in the city instead of sitting here debating things that do not matter.

However, today, everything is different.

My advisors and scholars are the same as usual, wearing their rich robes in different styles to mark each provenance. Only the purple sash they wear makes them stand out as members of my council—that and their haughty expressions. The meeting room has not changed. Everything is still in its place from the last time we were here. No, the change isn't anything in this room. At least, nothing I can see.

Today, I do not have to fake being distracted. I should be listening to them talk about the benefits of developing the already prosperous Tundra Province, all while pretending to be lost in thought.

Instead, I do not need to pretend to be lost because all that I can think about is the woman with piercing green eyes and shocking red hair that not even she could tame.

My mind replays our interaction and how she took out those bandits without breaking a sweat.

She saved my life.

Alyx.

I overheard one of the bandits hiss her name to the leader before the fight broke out. They appeared surprised and impressed, meaning they knew of her, so she must have a reputation. After seeing her fight, I am not surprised.

Absentmindedly, I realise that my hand is at my throat again, missing the comforting weight of my necklace. It was my father's, something passed down to me, and I had not taken it off since he died. She took it as 'payment' for saving my life. After what I had seen, I was not going to argue about it. It was stupid wearing it into the city anyway. The absence of the weight is a constant reminder of what could have happened.

My chest feels tight every time she appears in my mind, which happens to be almost constantly since I encountered her. I have to see her again. Someone like her, with her knowledge of the city and the criminal underworld, is exactly what I need. Where I am tethered to the castle like a dog tied to a tree, she has insider information that I need. We could make a difference to this kingdom by working together.

She is the secret weapon I have been searching for.

Perhaps I am just a naïve moron with his head in the clouds, dreaming of a better world. However, after what I saw last night and the state my city has fallen into, I know I have to do something.

The king and the assassin.

One of my advisors chuckles as if he can see into my thoughts, and I quickly tune back into the room. They are not discussing me or my wishful thinking. Instead, they are discussing revamping the upper market in the Tundra Province—a market that was only built two years ago and is deemed one of the best places in the region to shop. It is nothing like the muddy ramshackle of Christ Church at our very door.

Anger boils in my gut once more, and before I realise what I'm doing, I'm leaning forward and addressing the table, drawing every eye to me.

"Should we not be investing this money into the city itself? I—" I manage to stop myself from blurting out that I'd seen where our citizens live. Clearing my throat, I try once more. "I have heard that people in the city are suffering, especially around the market area. Bandits lie in wait to mug and kill, and the conditions they have to live in are—"

"Where did you hear this, Your Majesty?" Advisor Ruik asks lightly, cutting me off mid-sentence. As a noble from the family Rivershade, the same family as the Queen Mother, he has always been bolder than most. His brown hair is greying at his temples, and his mouth is twisted in an unfriendly expression, but his eyes, so much like the Queen Mother's, give me pause.

They are cruel.

No one would usually dare to cut me off, even my advisors, and it takes me aback for a moment. That is when I see the tension around his eyes and shoulders. A quick glance around the table confirms that my other advisors are wearing the same expression. I have made them nervous by asking questions they don't want to answer. I must have asked too quickly and too out of the blue, and they are now wondering if I'm going to cause them problems in passing the motion they are proposing.

I do not wish to tip my hand, so I must relent.

"Oh. I must have overheard it from someone in court." Smiling, I shrug and wave off the question, playing up to their opinion of me.

I obviously convince them, as they all let out sighs of relief and Ruik smiles at me like I'm a simpleton—a condescending smile that has my hands gripping my chair tightly. "Your Majesty, I can assure you that the city is fine. I have seen it myself. The people are happy and thriving under your rule. However, the Tundra

Province would really benefit from the redevelopment of the market."

Liar.

He is a liar, and he has the gall to do it right to my face, expecting that I will just smile and agree. The relaxed set of his shoulders and crinkles around his eyes just prove how sure he is that he's in control here. It sparks an anger inside me that I've not felt for a long time. It's a wild, untamable anger that moves like a wildfire, turning everything to ash in its path.

I want to stand up, slam my hands on the table, and make sure that every single one of the puffed-up males in the room is paying attention. I have *been* there. I saw the conditions my citizens live in with my own eyes, and that was only a tiny portion of the city. His assurances mean nothing to me, especially now that I know for sure that the reports I am being fed are false.

However, calling them out on their lies is not an option and would only destroy the persona I've created. Shattering the illusion that I am just a dumb puppet to be manipulated would put me in danger and cause them to act differently around me.

Sucking in both my anger and pride, I give them what they want. My smile feels bitter as I press a hand against my chest.

"Well, that is reassuring to hear!"

Leaning back in my chair, I beam at them, waiting until they turn their attention back to their conversation before I allow myself to plot. The only person still watching me is Orion, and as I glance over my shoulder, I see the giant of a man observing me with a frown, his arms crossed over his chest.

I will have to explain everything to him later, but for now, I face forward and stare out the window. They have already made up their minds about the market, so I don't fight it when my mind returns to Alyx.

Who is she truly? Is she from the Lowers?

What must have happened to a female to make her an assassin?

Once again, I can feel myself struggling against sleep, a loud yawn escaping me. Pressing a hand against my mouth, I take a deep breath and find Advisor Ruik's narrowed eyes on me.

"Are we keeping you awake, Your Majesty?"

He's annoyed that I interrupted him. However, he has just given me the perfect excuse to leave. There is nothing more I can do here, especially when there is something very important that I could be doing.

"Actually, yes, I am most tired today. I believe I shall retire." Standing, I smile brightly at the others around the table as they hurry to get to their feet. "You have everything under control here, yes?"

They have already made up their minds thanks to the Queen Mother whispering in their ears, so my contribution is neither wanted nor needed. They do seem surprised by my abruptness, but not enough to stop me, nodding at my comment.

"Then I bid you all farewell."

Bowing, they mutter their goodbyes, but I do not stick around to hear them. I leave the room with Orion on my heels, my other guards meeting us in the hallway. They dutifully follow behind me without question, even though I know they will wonder why I left the meeting early. The journey back to my chambers within the king's palace is short, and thankfully we don't come across anyone. Once we reach my chambers, Orion barks an order, and the guards depart, stationing themselves outside as usual.

As soon as the door is shut and I know it is just Orion and me, I hurry over to the wardrobe and start pulling out different clothing. I will need something that will help me blend in, ideally dark and dirty. Unfortunately, a king doesn't have much need for garments like that.

My guard and best friend looks at me like I have lost my mind. "Your Majesty, what—"

"Orion, we need to go," I tell him, rushing to the other side of the room as I search my chest of drawers, still not finding anything of use.

I have all the money in the kingdom, and yet I do not have an outfit.

"Go?" His voice is sharp, and when I turn around, I see his hands hovering over his weapons, as though he is looking for a threat. "What do you mean?"

I finally let my true smile pull at my lips.

"There is someone we need to find. Someone who can help us win this war."

CHAPTER
SIX

ALYX

Staring up at the stone ceiling, I frown at the small hole there. It hasn't always been there—it only happened recently and was thanks to someone deciding that they wanted to be the top assassin in the Daggers. They thought they would gain that spot by taking me out, foolish male. I always sleep lightly. I presented his head to Crux's people the very next day as proof of my victory.

It turns out that assassins are the targets of other assassins more often than you would think. None of Crux's lot would dare take out a hit on me, not when they know they have no hope in completing it alive. We have a code. Even the underworld has rules. We don't hunt our own, not unless they have broken that code. Besides, Crux would kill them if they so much as looked at me wrong. He's very protective, that best friend of mine.

Nope, these are foreign assassins from other lands trying to take me out. The worst thing is, I have no idea who keeps putting out the hit because they all keep killing themselves with the cyanide pills clenched between their back teeth before I can interrogate them.

One hard bite down and they are dead.

Although, before one died, he decided to take a chunk out of my ceiling with a wayward dagger. If anything, I'm more annoyed by the damage than the attempt on my life. In this line of work, you'd be a fool to expect a long, comfortable life.

Looking around my room, I don't bother to hold back the small, smug smile that tugs at my lips. My life might not end up being long, but it's pretty damn comfortable. For someone living in the Lowers, I have it good. Although it's set in the tunnels under the city, I managed to make it homey and warm. The room has a lock from one of the best locksmiths in the city, giving me some semblance of security. Sure, it wouldn't keep Crux out, but no one else would even dare to try. My double bed takes up about a third of the space, while the rest of the room is richly furnished with polished wooden furniture and a couch made with exotic fabrics that cost more than double what the average worker in the Lowers would earn in a year. The stone walls have been covered in paintings and stolen tapestries, the curved walls reaching the peak where my stolen chandelier hangs.

Sure, there aren't windows, but after years of living here, I'm used to being underground. I've worked my ass off for this, and I enjoy every exuberant moment of it.

The sun has risen, and I can feel my eyes drooping, tired from another night of stalking the city. As I lie back on my bed and stare at that damn hole, my eyes getting heavier by the second, my mind begins to wander. While it meanders through the events of last night, I keep getting stuck on one particular image—crystal-clear blue eyes staring up at me with shock and awe.

Why I keep coming back to this, I don't know, and it's driving me crazy. What do I care about some haughty noble who moronically walked into the wrong side of the city? The only reason I helped him in the first place was because I was bored and he intrigued me. It's as simple as that. The. Only. Fucking. Reason.

Then why does the image of that damn noble's eyes keep coming back to me? Every time I try not to think of them, there they are again just a second later, taunting me.

I finally realise that this isn't going to work, so I give in and let myself think of the stumbler. He was handsome, from what I saw of his face, in a polished way you don't see much of in the city. Even if it wasn't for his poor excuse of a disguise, which did nothing to hide his wealth, a child could tell he wasn't from our part of the city. He didn't carry the hardened expression and distrust like the rest of us do. This kingdom would eat him up and spit him out. Only the tough survive. There's no such thing as kindness here.

There was something about him though. I can't put my finger on it, but he carried a naïve sense of trust that drew me to him. Stumblers rarely come into the city, not the Lowers at least, and certainly not during the night, yet there he was, blindly stumbling into one of the roughest areas. Did he think he wasn't in danger?

Snorting at the thought, I shake my head and let my eyes close. I need to get some sleep. I'm exhausted, and I have a job tomorrow. Forcing myself to relax into the mattress, I take a deep breath and allow fatigue to wash over me, pulling me into a deep sleep.

The last thing I think of are the noble's blue eyes.

I HAVE no idea how long I've been asleep for, but I don't think it's been long since my head is still thick with the fuzziness of sleep. My whole body protests at the very thought of getting up, aching from a night of fighting. Why am I even awake?

The bed shifts slightly, finally pulling me from my slumber, my body stiffening for a moment as I realise I'm no longer alone in my room. I force myself to relax into the mattress as various scenarios run through my mind. The best time to assassinate an assassin is when they are at their most vulnerable, and no one is more vulnerable than when they are asleep. By pretending to sleep, I gain a handful of precious seconds to make my plan. I'd been sleeping on my front, so I must have rolled over at some point, and my arms are wrapped around my pillow. As gently as I can, I slide a dagger from the hidden pocket in the mattress, conveniently placed under my pillow. Many people think I'm mad for sleeping with a dagger, but I've not survived this long without a reason. I'm always prepared.

Wrapping my fist around the hilt, I prepare to spring up, attempting to work out the position of the stranger crawling up my bed. Any second now, they'll practically be straddling me—a position that, while not impossible to get out of, will put me at a further disadvantage.

If I'm going to act, it has to be now.

I spring into action, twisting like a pinwheel and raising my dagger in an upward motion. It's only in that moment that I realise who is climbing into my bed—Crux.

Gasping, I attempt to yank my arm away, but my aim was too true and is still heading straight for his jugular.

Thankfully for my best friend, he has lightning-quick reflexes and manages to pull back before being caught by the blade. Raising a brow, he looks at my shocked expression and then the blade in my hand.

"Whoa. Calm down, Red." His crooked grin only ignites my anger. "Are you trying to kill me so you can take my throne?"

He makes no mention of the fact that I'm sleeping with a blade, but I'm sure he probably has several dotted about his bedside. You can't be too careful in this industry.

His familiar drawl has me relaxing, my heartbeat slowing even as adrenaline still pumps through me. His dark eyes watch me carefully while his plump pink lips smile lazily. His right brow arches, making the scar that cuts through it more visible. As usual, his dark, shoulder-length hair is scruffy, and he has day-old stubble marking his jaw. He tries to hide it, but he's handsome in a rough way. His once noble nose is crooked thanks to one too many fights, and I have to stop myself from reaching out to trace the line of it.

"You shouldn't sneak up on an assassin when they are sleeping," I scold, hitting him across the head with a pillow.

Of course, Crux just laughs and steals it from me, climbing farther up the bed. Throwing the pillow back down, he lies on his side, resting his head on his hand as he looks up at me, that stupid grin still splitting his face.

"I'm serious." I know it's pointless arguing with him, but I can't seem to stop myself. "I could have killed you."

"Probably, but I'd have made you work for it." Shrugging as if we aren't talking about his death, he drops his smile, but I still see humour in his eyes. "I didn't want to wake you."

"Well, you did."

Snorting a laugh, he makes himself comfortable, pulling the discarded blanket over himself and lifting one of his arms in invitation. "Alright, grumpy. Come back to sleep."

Blinking at how blasé he is about this whole situation, I shake my head after a moment. "You really think I can sleep after you just scared the crap out of me?"

"Alyx, lie down and go to sleep." There's an order in his voice devoid of humour.

As it has started to recently, my body hums to life at his dark tone, and I do as he instructs.

His arms wrap around me, and my body comes alive as he breathes in my scent. I'm not sure when things started to change between us. We've always been friends, and he's had my back through everything. However, in the last year or so, I've started to notice the way he watches me when he thinks I'm not paying attention, not to mention these little cuddles we've been having.

They seemed to start out of nowhere, but now I miss him when he's not crawling in my bed to wrap his arms around me. It's easy to think that he's got feelings for me, but things have always stayed friendly between us, and I have to think that is intentional on his part. Sure, I flirt with him, kissing his cheek and making suggestive jokes, but nothing has ever gone any further. I don't know when I started thinking of him as more than my friend and how my breath is literally taken away when I watch him spar, his movements so smooth and fluid. When we're pressed against each other like this, I want more of him against me, more skin, more of *him*.

Of course, nothing ever can or will happen between us. In his mind, I'm sure I will always be the young girl he helped when she was in danger and that I'm imagining any looks he might send my way. There are no illusions that he's remained celibate while waiting for me, and even just the thought makes my eyes roll. He's fucked more women than either of us could ever count.

Besides, he's the king of the underworld down here, and his kingdom means everything to him. He built this sanctuary, and he's not about to give it all up for me.

"I can practically hear your mind turning," he comments sluggishly, his arms tightening around my middle. "Whatever it is, worry about it tomorrow."

He's asking for the impossible, but as I allow myself to relax against his warm body, his tight embrace and his rhythmic breathing start to lull me to sleep.

This time it's not blue eyes I fall asleep thinking of, but his dark ones.

CHAPTER
SEVEN

JOHA

"**Y**our Majesty," Orion hisses, hurrying after me. His steps are loud on the packed dirt road as we head away from the palace, the shadow of the castle and the Imperial Mountains cooling our backs. It was hard to hide Orion's hulking form or for me to get him to agree to come, but when I simply informed him I would go alone, he relented. After borrowing two kitchen servants' cloaks, I almost look the part this time as we move deeper into the Lowers. I make sure to hide my jewellery, but Orion will not cover his sword. He did, however, cover his armour, which is something.

His hard eyes coupled with his square, scarred face has many moving out of our path as we cut our way through the Lowers. "Do not call me that here," I remind him, "unless you wish to be mobbed."

"Joha," he snaps instead, catching my arm. "What are you doing?"

Covering his hand, I lean in. "Trust me, brother," I beg, my eyebrows raised. He has always looked out for me, both as a friend and my guard, so I understand why he is concerned by this.

When he sighs reluctantly and releases my arm, I grin, tightening my cloak to ensure nothing shows underneath. "I have a plan." That is all I will tell him. I know he will try to convince me this is a bad, reckless idea, and maybe it is, but I have to do something. This needs to be done. I cannot continue to live like this, and neither can our people, as evidenced by the ruins and starvation surrounding me.

Children run around half-clothed, messy, and begging for food. Men fight others for scraps of bread, and women sell their bodies to dress their children. It must change. While the Lowers struggle to survive, the nobles thrive with feasts, banquets, parties, and opulence. It will only continue this way unless I can do something about it. I know most think of me as a useless king, but I never wanted to be. I want to change it all, which is exactly why I am here, potentially risking my life for the betterment of my people like a true king, searching for the woman with the emerald eyes and bright hair.

Alyx.

If I am to save our lands and people, then it all depends on that female assassin—one who cannot be bought. I need someone who's willing to get their hands dirty.

I need someone to look like a pawn while playing a queen.

First, I must find her, and surprisingly, assassins are not easy to find. I check the alley where we met, but there are only some stray animals fighting over bones. The bodies of the bandits are gone, which surprises me. Next, I move into Christ Church Market. It's packed to the edges with stalls selling clothes, food, alcohol, and even weapons. Each stall is made of leftover wood, some from old ships or houses, with their wares hastily carved into the knotted timber. Some have dirty, stained tents above them to protect them from the elements, but many do not.

There is no reason or sense to the layout of the market, and they are crammed together with people screaming and fighting to get through. It's a thriving place for pickpockets, many of which I see moving through the crowd and stealing from the oblivious. Tugging one of my coin pouches closer, I make sure to keep my eyes sharp as I manoeuvre through the activity. My eyes track everyone, searching for the brightness in the dullness.

Orion cuts a path behind us, protecting my back, for which I am eternally grateful.

"Sir, how about a genuine amethyst necklace for your woman?"

"Miss, how about a new shawl?"

"Take a look at our newest delivery of berries, straight from the field!"

The noise is overwhelming compared to the quiet serenity of the palace, where nobody raises their voice nor grabs anyone, and I have to force myself to relax and blend in. I cannot afford to cause a scene. I am here for a reason, but it simply seems like my reason is not here.

Where else could I find an assassin?

After searching for a while without luck, I find myself on the outskirts of Christ Church, wandering the streets aimlessly in hopes she will appear. Is this her hunting ground? I can feel Orion's confusion and frustration as time passes. It won't be long before I am found missing, and I must be back before then. At that moment, I watch two men slink down the side of a wooden house with the front door askew. They seem to be tailing a man dragging a wooden cart who's talking to a soldier.

Perfect.

I hurry after them, and when they duck into an alley, I follow them. "Excuse me," I call loudly.

They spin in shock. Their faces are filthy, covered in dirt that looks days old. Their clothes have many holes and hang from their skinny frames, and their rancid smell makes my nose twitch even from here. Their hair is shorn and uneven, but their eyes are sharp and intelligent. A disguise maybe?

"I am looking for a woman," I say when they simply stare.

The one on the left chuckles. "You are in the wrong place for women. Go to the brothels near the river."

I can't contain my blush, and when my words come, I stammer. "Ah, not like that. She is an assassin. How do I find her?"

That gets their attention. Their eyes sharpen, and they stand taller, making me realise they were hunched. Are these assassins? It is hard to tell. Where Alyx looked put together and clean, they are the opposite.

"The Daggers? You do not find them; they will find you," the one on the right replies ominously.

"Come, my—Joha." Orion snarls. "These little rats know nothing."

The men in question grin and scurry away like the rats Orion called them, and I peer up at his stern face in confusion. "Little rats?"

"It's what they are called in the Lowers. They spy and report back, moving unseen and unwanted, but beware of their teeth." His eyes drop to me, though they don't stay on me for long, busy scanning the area. "Why are you seeking an assassin, Joha?" I hesitate, and he sighs. "Assassins are not to be played with. The Daggers—"

"So you know them?"

"The Daggers are paid killers located in the Lowers. They practically run these streets. They venture into noble land when paid, and even though they are looked down upon, many pay for their services. Are you planning to do so?" he demands.

"In a way," I admit, walking so we do not look odd.

"Joha," he admonishes. "You—"

"Stop," I command before he lectures me. "I am not asking your opinion. You promised to trust me, so trust me."

"I am worried about you, Joha," he whispers as we walk side by side. "I have been since your father's death when you took the throne."

"You worry too much, old friend," I reply with a coy smile, pretending the mention of my father's death doesn't cause my heart to kick painfully in my chest. "Now, where do you think we'll find these Daggers?"

It is only then that I realise we have traversed down empty roads, and when the noise of a rock being kicked assaults my ears, we both turn. Standing behind us, feet away, are four men dressed in all black. One has a familiar cloak on, and I perk up, even as Orion places his arm before me and pulls his sword. "Stay behind me, Joha."

"Hand over your money and we will let you live," one in the middle calls. I cannot see their faces due to the hoods and masks, but the voice sounds distinctly male.

"Very well." I pull out my pouch and ignore Orion as I step closer. "If you tell me where to find Alyx, you can have all my money."

Another chuckles. "We will just take it."

"See him?" I nod at Orion, who is double their size. "He will kill you first, so save yourself the trouble and take the money for services rendered. Where do I find Alyx of the Daggers?"

One of them pulls his mask down and grins. "You want to find Alyx?"

I nod eagerly as the others chuckle.

"Fine, we'll tell you. She will eat you alive, noble." His hand darts for the money, but I step back. "Find her at the tavern by the docks. She is hunting."

Throwing the pouch to him, I watch his arm dart out and catch it effortlessly. "Good luck, noble. You will need it, even with the big man." They fade back into the shadows as effortlessly as they appeared.

Smiling brightly, I turn to Orion. "To the docks!"

"You are going to get us killed, Joha." He sighs but does not try to stop me as he tucks his sword away.

"Only you, my friend, only you," I tease.

THE DOCKS ARE VERY different from what I imagined. I do not leave the palace often, but Father took me with him to greet some dignitaries from the Rising Sun Islands once. The docks, however, were on the other side of the Lanide River, which splits the Lowers from the other provinces where the nobles reside.

That side of the docks gleamed with brand-new warships and ferries, and it was so bright and colourful, it was like a celebration. The taverns there overflowed with nobles and riches, and the shops sparkled with jewels and delicacies. The road is even made of stone, leading right to the peaceful blue water of our bay.

Here, on this side of the river, the docks are very different indeed.

It's another stark reminder of the split in our lands. The port on this side is an old, floating wooden dock with smaller ships, mainly fishing vessels, in dire need of repair. Men throw barrels of fish and nets from the boats to the dock, the fragrant smell of fish, sewage, and mouldy food assaulting my senses.

The shops here are boarded up, but I see flames inside, indicating people live there. The one bright spot here is the tavern. No wonder they did not tell me a name. It is the only one in business. It looks to be built over the river, and it's at least four stories of towering dark wood with windows cut out on each level. A wooden sign, hand painted with a naked mermaid and a ship blowing in the ocean breeze, hangs above the open doorway spewing laughter, music, and frivolity.

Tables are spread across the street and docks, overflowing with people. Some are passed out, some are eating, and some are drinking. It is a shock for the senses. I see men and women touching, flirting, and dancing, breaking every law we have in the palace. There is no careful distance here, no courtly bows and conversation.

This place exudes life in its filthiest and barest form.

I like it.

It is then I see a concealed merchant vessel at the far end of the dock. The men working on it and the flag give it away. I do not understand why it is hidden, but I watch two men in silk cloaks disembark, their faces hidden as they hurry towards the tavern, clearly trying to hide.

They shine so brightly with wealth, I am surprised a bandit does not appear.

However, someone else does.

Alyx slinks from the shadows, wearing the same, skintight black suit as the other day, only this time I see the brown harness hugging her bust, overflowing with weapons. Her sword hangs at her side, the one she saved me with and also used to steal from me. Hanging around her throat is my father's necklace, my necklace, as if to dare anyone to try and take it from her.

Her bright hair is plaited back and hanging over her left shoulder as her blazing eyes search the road she crosses, following the two rich men silently. Boots with silver latches reach her knees as she splashes through puddles without a care.

My breathing stops, and my heart skips as I watch her slink from shadow to shadow, her targets none the wiser. A cruel but amusing plan comes to mind.

"Alyx!" I yell rather uncouthly.

She turns, as do her marks, her eyes narrowing at her name.

CHAPTER

EIGHT

ALYX

I stare at the tattered, cloaked man until he pushes it back, revealing one of the most handsome faces I have ever seen in my entire life. He has the face of a noble, with brightly glowing skin, a clean-shaven jaw, and familiar, vivid blue eyes surrounded by long black lashes. His hair is as black as the shadows I inhabit and slicked back into a plait I see trailing down his back—another sign of his worth and status because the higher you are, the longer it is. I see jewels threaded through it, which is another sure sign.

His nose is straight and perfect, his cheekbones are high and sharp, and when he smiles at me, a dimple appears in each cheek, giving him a youthful appearance.

"Alyx," he calls again.

I look over my shoulder to see my marks eyeing me before running away. Fuck! I glare back at the man, recognising the voice if not the face.

He is the one I saved in the alley, so why is he here now?

He does not belong here, that is for sure, and standing at his side is a hulking man.

He is almost cruel looking, with deep, sharp eyebrows and dark eyes. His dark hair is shaved nearly down to his scalp, showing one ear with the tip cut off. A few scars decorate his square, strong face that leads into a bushy brown beard and plump lips. I cannot see what he is wearing, as a matching cloak hides his body, but it's a tad too short, which makes me believe he stole it.

The sword at his side is unmistakable though, as is the clear intention in his eyes.

This man is dangerous. Good, so am I.

I glance back to see my marks escaping, and frustration fills me again. I waited for their ship for a whole month. An entire month of my life has been wasted, and I lost two years' worth of coin, all because of the smiling fool and his massive friend.

He waves like he's unsure if I can see him, and I feel my nostrils flare in annoyance. I might have spared him the other day, but I won't today. One way or another, I'm getting paid. I cannot go home empty-handed.

I storm over, and the man at his side places his hand on his sword, clearly sensing my intent, but the clueless noble simply smiles wider, right up until I grab him.

Snarling in annoyance, I slam the familiar man into the wall of a house, and when the big man leaps at me, I kick out, throwing him back to the other side of the road. My blade comes up, and I press it to the rich man's throat as I pull my sword with the other and point it at the bigger man, who's climbing to his feet and heading my way.

"One wrong move and he's dead," I warn the bigger man before turning to the man I saved. "You fool, you ruined my hunt."

"I apologize," he says, but he is smiling too widely and looking too happy.

Did he do it on purpose?

"I have killed for less," I warn, though he does not seem fazed by my blade at his throat.

43

"He is foolish, that is for sure. Here, take this for your troubles." The big man thrusts a pouch forward.

I grab it before he can move, but I keep my blade in place. "Now, why are you searching for me, stumbler?"

There is only one reason a man like this comes calling, and like all the other rich men, he will die if he ever touches me.

"I have a proposition." He relaxes like we are sitting in a tavern, talking over beer.

"Not interested." I pull my dagger away and point at the burly man since he seems smarter. He's probably a paid protector, since the noble clearly needs one. "Keep him away from me or I will gut him." I turn and stride away, hoping to catch my marks. I can still rectify this hunt.

"Wait, Alyx," the man calls.

"Joha, stop," the burly man warns, yet I hear them both hurrying after me.

Rolling my eyes, I walk into the alley next to the tavern, the river to the back of us. More than one body has been dumped in there, and tonight, I might just add two more. Leaping up, I catch the edge of the tavern's second story railing and hang in wait.

They don't keep me waiting long, and when the two shadows appear below me, I drop, landing right behind them. The big man whirls, but my sword is already at his throat, knowing he is the most dangerous of the two. "I warned you," I tell him.

"I implore you to listen," the noble, Joha, begs.

"I am not a subject you implore or command." I raise an eyebrow without looking away.

"Then how about a contract? That is what assassins take, is it not? The Daggers?"

Sighing, I remove my blade. "Go home, nobleman, you don't belong here. I do not want your money."

For a moment, his eyes drop to my necklace, the one I stole from him. "I cost you your hunt, so I will pay the sum you were owed if you listen to my proposal. If you wish to say no after, I will go. I give you my word." He covers his chest as if that actually works.

"Your word means nothing to me."

"His word is everything," the bulky man roars, and when he opens his mouth to say something else, he swallows, and Joha glares.

"Just listen, that is all." He holds out a pouch. "And this is yours. I'm sure it will cover your sum from tonight and more."

Leaning back into the wall, I cross my arms. "Has anyone ever told you that you're very annoying?"

"No," he admits brazenly, and strangely, I believe him. "Not to my face at least."

"Fine." I hold my hand out. "I will listen, and then you will leave or I'll wear that pretty face as a mask."

He grins. "You think I am pretty?"

"Money, now," I snarl. The fool hands it over. A worse man would run with it now, a better man would be grateful, but I linger between. "You have one minute."

"I want to offer you a contract. I have enemies—"

"Shocking," I interrupt with a smirk.

"There have been multiple attempts on my life. More than that, someone is actively working to bring me down. I need someone from outside—someone who can come in and find who it is."

"And kill them?" I query.

"If it comes to it. If not, I will ruin them," he replies. "I need someone I can trust, someone capable who cannot be paid, like a soldier."

"What do I get in return for sorting through your noble house's shit?"

"Who said it was a noble house?" He grins. "To do this job, you will need to go undercover and pretend to be my queen. My future bride. A lady."

"The queen?" I chuckle. "Good joke." I start to push away when he parts his cloak, showing me the royal purple robes underneath. I look at the burly man, who shows me his armour.

Only two people wear that.

I have heard enough tales of the young puppet king and his dog. I should have known, but in my defence, I never expected to find them here.

He is even more foolish than I thought.

"You're the king?" I hiss, swinging around. "You're a fool for coming down here."

"You've called me that before. I am starting to think it is a compliment. I had no choice. You're clearly capable, but you are beautiful enough to fulfil the role. No one would suspect a lady is an assassin in their midst. I will pay you whatever you wish, more than you would earn in three lifetimes. You may have anything you ask for if you find my enemies and help me stop them."

"And pretend to be your new queen?" I snort, looking him up and down.

It's crazy but tempting. The money I could earn would set us up for life. I could give back to the Lowers and help those who are struggling, not to mention sticking it to some nobles would be nice, but still. "No thanks, go back to your palace, my king," I mock.

"Anything you want," he says urgently. "Name it."

"I don't think she would be capable, Your Majesty." The big man snorts.

I know he's winding me up, but it's starting to work. Grinding my teeth, I look between them, scarcely believing I am asking this. "When do I need to decide?"

"Before daybreak, come to the western gate of the palace. We will be waiting, and we can discuss everything then," Joha replies. "This is Orion, my bodyguard. You can trust him."

"I trust no one, and neither should you," I tell him, eyeing them both. Surely this isn't real, and if it is, how foolish would I have to be to walk into Moonshadow Palace, a place known for its backstabbing and murder?

The rich are worse than the poor—I know since I serve most of them. However, gaining access to the palace, people, and the records there might get me something I have always wanted—the truth about what happened.

I would get paid and get my revenge in one go.

All I would have to do is pretend to be this foolish king's queen-to-be. How hard can that be?

"Until then," I say, unsure if I will take it. I need to think.

"I will see you then," Joha calls, but I don't look back as I slink into the shadows. His pouch rattles at my hip, reminding me he is good at paying his debts and keeping his word, at least for now. I am no fool to think the king won't double-cross me at the end to silence me and keep his throne safe, but I am good at disappearing, and with him paying me anything I want, I could go anywhere and be anything.

The only question is, do I want to?

It feels as if fate has once again flipped its hand and drawn me another path, if only I am strong enough to take it.

CHAPTER
NINE

ORION

I'm seething.

In fact, I'm so furious that I can barely look at Joha, who whistles happily at my side, oblivious to my inner turmoil.

The journey back to the palace is uneventful despite the number of eyes on us the whole time. Little rats watch our every move, reporting back to their master. We'll be lucky if the whole city doesn't know that their king was stumbling amongst them by tomorrow morning. The consequences if the Queen Mother finds out are beyond thinking about, but I know for sure that my life would be forfeit.

Losing my life for my king isn't what enrages me though. If I'm put to death, who is going to look out for him then? He'll have no one. That's something I cannot allow.

We get back to the palace in silence, the king realising that I need some time to decompress. Making sure we're not being tailed or watched, I sneak us back into the palace grounds. It's disturbingly easy, something I'm going to rectify later. The guards are going to feel the brunt of my anger, which is probably something I should feel bad about, but I don't. If Joha can just walk out without anyone noticing, then anyone could just wander in, especially if they are trained in stealth.

As I lead him through the maze of the palace grounds, I feel his eyes on my back, but he says nothing. We have to be careful. We ditched our stolen cloaks at the gate. If anyone saw the king dressed so casually, it would only raise suspicions, and everything that happens in the palace gets back to the Queen Mother.

Stupid. So fucking stupid.

What was he thinking? If he'd told me his plan before we left, I never would have let him leave, which is exactly why he didn't tell me. He only fed me enough snippets of information to gain my help. He's sneaky and far smarter than anyone gives him credit for, which is how he managed to use my weaknesses against me.

However, it's not just Joha that I'm angry at, but myself. How could I let him convince me to waltz into the Lowers and speak with an assassin of all people? My job is to protect him from people like her, not enable the meeting.

How did he even meet an assassin in the first place?

No, I don't want to know. Just the thought of it is giving me palpitations, and I don't fancy adding images of Joha stumbling around the Lowers with an assassin to my list of nightmares.

My duty to the Crown is everything, but it goes deeper than that. Joha is my king, and I will protect him with my life, but as my best friend, I want to make sure he flourishes in every aspect. Seeing how unhappy he is breaks my heart, and I don't know how to fix that. He's family to me, and not being able to help him makes me feel useless, which is why I let him talk me into this ridiculous plan today. His eyes lit up in a way I'd not seen since before his father died, excitement pulsing from him. That and the fact that I knew he would find a way to go with or without me. He's already proven that he's able to sneak from the palace without attracting attention, something I'm begrudgingly proud of—not that I'll ever tell him that.

I'm sure that part of his excitement is that she's a woman who isn't bowing and scraping or trying to get into his good graces. From what we saw of her, I could tell she was beautiful, and the danger she offers was probably a huge thrill for him. She's unobtainable, making her the perfect challenge. Joha is far smarter than he lets anyone believe, but I know my friend, and a pretty face can influence his actions. He wouldn't be that foolish though, would he?

Marriage. That's what he's proposed to her.

Anger surges within me again as we finally make it to the king's palace and can let our guards drop a little. He's offered an assassin a crown and for her to pose as his queen. We have no idea who this woman is, and while his explanations made sense with his unique sense of logic, no sane person would hand this sort of power to someone whose career is killing people like us. She'll learn secrets that could topple the monarchy, and we have no guarantee that she won't sell the information to the highest bidder.

Entering Joha's private chambers, I inspect it for danger before gesturing for him to enter, slamming the doors behind me. My body is tense and ready to fight, and from the looks he keeps sending my way, Joha is obviously expecting me to explode. No, I'm going to stay professional. I'm going to be the best guard he's ever had and will stick to him like fucking glue. He's not going to get away from me for a second.

"I think you're about to blow a vein in your forehead. It's pulsing," he calls out, his voice deceptively light. When I retreat to my usual spot and say nothing, he rolls his eyes. "Are you going to ignore me for the rest of the day?"

That's all I need to break my vow of silence. Hands balling at my sides, I stride over to him, forcing myself to hold back and not throttle him like I want to. "What were you thinking?" I demand through clenched teeth.

"That didn't take much," he comments with a snort. "We need

someone in the palace who is on our side. Someone who can pass as a noble but has the skills to move silently through the palace and keep tabs on what's happening behind my back."

Grabbing onto the doorframe, I squeeze until it groans beneath my fists. "Then you train one of the noble's daughters—someone we can trust, Joha. She's an assassin! What makes you think she won't just turn on you and slaughter you in your sleep?"

All pretence of amusement flees his expression, his eyes hooded and brow furrowed as he meets my glare. "It will take too long to train someone. We have to act now—"

"Why?" I cut him off, demanding the answer. Releasing the doorframe, I gesture wide to show my confusion. "What's the sudden rush?"

His face flushes with anger, an expression I don't see often. "Because the attempts on my life are getting more and more frequent. Because if I have to pretend to be an airhead for one day longer, I might just do Queen Mother a favour and throw myself off the Imperial Mountains!"

I'm shocked by the outburst, and I realise that it's not anger I see on his face, but desperation. I've never seen him like this before, and I don't know how to react. He's been struggling for a while, but he's so strong that I never realised that it had gotten so bad for him.

I am a failure.

I'm supposed to be his best friend, and I missed how much this has been weighing on him.

"Joha . . ."

Realising what he just admitted, he seems to deflate before my eyes, releasing a long breath. He scrubs his hands over his face and huffs out a sigh. "Don't worry. I'm not really going to do it. I just . . . Something has to change, Orion."

The vulnerability in his voice breaks something within me. He's sharing this with me because he trusts me, and I need to make sure I don't break that trust by messing this up. Rubbing a hand over the stubble of my shaved head, I feel the anger drain from me, replaced by reluctant acceptance.

Joha is no fool, despite what everyone else thinks. I know his mind works ten times faster than most. He will have thought this through, so if he thinks this can work . . .

"You really think she's the person to do it?"

Joha meets my eyes, his gaze steady and sure. "Yes."

"Fine." I can't believe I'm agreeing to this. It seems that it's going to happen either way, so I might as well help him so he doesn't get himself killed. "Tell me everything about this plan of yours, and I mean everything."

His eyes light up despite my lack of enthusiasm, and he gestures for me to follow him to the large wooden dining table in his adjoining chamber. The walls here are covered in windows that look out to the Imperial Mountains, and half of the table is covered in books and scrolls. Taking the seat at the head of the table, he waits for me to sit next to him and leans forward eagerly.

"I first met her when she saved me from some bandits."

I groan loudly as he grins. Of course. Bandits, because what else could possibly make this story worse than it already is?

Wincing, I gesture for him to continue, bracing myself for more truths.

It's going to be an uncomfortable few weeks.

CHAPTER
TEN

CRUX

Pacing the length of my room, I barely notice the little rat nervously waiting for me to dismiss him, his eyes tracking my movements worriedly. Honestly, I forgot he was even there, so lost in my own frantic thoughts. Each step is agitated and full of pent-up anger and frustration.

This can't be happening.

What the fuck is going on with Alyx? The things I've been hearing recently are so unlike her that the delusional part of my brain tells me the rumours must be about someone else. My Alyx wouldn't get herself twisted up in this sort of mess. She would talk to me. What I'm hearing, however, it's like I don't even know her.

My room is just down the hall from Alyx's, but I don't tend to spend much time here. It's got a few stolen paintings on the wall, but it's nothing like hers. This room is where I come when I need to get away from everyone else or to grab a few hours of sleep. Sleep doesn't come easily these days, and when I can, I slip into Alyx's bed and wrap my arms around her. In those sleepy moments, I can pretend that we're together like we should be. Occasionally, I think I see longing in her eyes, but it's gone in a moment. A braver man might bite the bullet and ask her if she feels the same way, but I won't risk losing her, so I keep my mouth shut.

Everyone knows not to bother me when I'm in my room. I've made the consequences very clear, so when this little rat knocked on my door, quivering with fear, I knew something had happened. I run the information he told me through my mind over and over, taking it apart and examining it from each angle, looking for possible reasons Alyx might do this.

"Your . . ." The warble in the rat's voice grates on me.

Stopping mid-stride, I spin on my heel and pin the weasely man with a look. "You're absolutely sure about what you heard?" I stalk towards him, my anger making each step rough and powerful. Stopping in front of the rat, I lower so I can stare directly into his face. "If I find out this isn't true, I will hunt you down and gut you like a rodent."

It might be harsh, but I didn't get to where I am now by being nice to everyone. I may look after my own people, but I won't tolerate liars.

With impossibly wide eyes, he swallows his fear with an audible gulp and nods so frantically that he's going to make himself dizzy. "Y-Yes, sir. I heard it myself and followed the stumblers back to the castle. It was the k-king."

Shit. That was not what I wanted to hear.

"Leave."

Dismissed, he doesn't waste time, practically throwing himself out the door. Finally on my own, I resume my pacing, running a hand through my messy hair. It probably looks worse than it usually does thanks to my agitated movements, but that's the least of my problems right now.

· · ·

THERE'S a light knock on my door, and before I can roar at whoever it is to leave me the fuck alone, the door opens, and someone slides quietly inside. Only one person would dare enter my room without permission—Alyx.

Turning around, I see her glance back over her shoulder with a wry smile, amusement written on her face.

"One of your rats just passed me in the hall." She closes the door behind her and turns to face me. "He looked like he was going to pass out when he saw me . . ." Registering the tension in my body and the flat expression on my face, she trails off and frowns. "Crux? Is everything alright?" she asks carefully. She knows something is up. She thinks she knows but isn't going to give it away, in case she exposes herself.

That makes me mad.

"I don't know, Alyx. Why don't you tell me?" My voice is deceptively light as I cross my arms over my chest, trying to keep my cool. However, I'm not able to hold myself back and find myself speaking again before she has the chance to answer. "How was your meeting with the king?"

Cursing loudly, she shakes her head and glares at the door as if she can see through it to the man she passed. "Fucking rats," she growls, realising what must have happened before she got here. Huffing out a frustrated sigh, she pushes her mass of unruly hair back from her face so I can see her glimmering green eyes.

"I was coming here to tell you what happened."

Raising a single brow, I tilt my head to the side. "I know what happened. The king stumbled through the Lowers, telling everyone he passed that he was looking for you. Everyone is talking about it. Thankfully, they just think he's a noble and not the king."

I'm angry, really fucking angry. If it wasn't the king and his guard dog, I would have him killed for exposing Alyx like that. Talk about being conspicuous. He's probably never had to lie low a single day in his privileged life and thought he was being stealthy as he bustled around and caused a fuss.

"That was the guy you saved the other day? The fucking king, Alyx?"

Her face shuts down as I speak, and she mirrors my stance and crosses her arms. "I didn't know that at the time."

Hissing a breath through clenched teeth, I close my eyes for a second as I attempt to regain my composure.

"What did he want?"

My rat only caught the end of the conversation and couldn't hear everything from his position. While I know the king offered her a deal and wants her to work for him, I don't know the details. Who does he want killed, and why does he want Alyx to do it? Doesn't he have enough soldiers to do that for him?

Alyx takes a deep breath, her expression contemplative as she tries to decide what to tell me. That makes me nervous. She never picks and chooses what she tells me, and we tell each other everything, so why is she holding back now?

"He needs someone on the inside, and he asked me to be the one to do it."

Time seems to pause for a moment, and I feel like I'm in a dream —no, a nightmare as I watch the horror about to unfold, but I am unable to do anything to stop it. She can't mean what I think she does, and even if she did, she wouldn't be so foolish to accept.

"On the inside. As in, inside the palace?" I hiss.

I'm getting ready to laugh with her over the stupidity of it all, but her expression tells me everything I need to know, quickly souring my mood further.

"Fucking hell, Alyx. He wants you to sneak in and snoop around? For what, information?"

Her neutral expression cracks, and dread rises in me like an insidious tide, threatening to wash me away. "It's not quite that simple . . ." Sighing, she shakes her head. "Look, he asked me to pose as his fiancée, and as queen-to-be, I'll have access to every part of the palace, where I can get information. I have the training of the Lowers but the knowledge of the Uppers, which makes me one of the only people who could do it."

I wait for the punchline, my eyebrow raised expectantly. When it doesn't come, I laugh out loud, but there's no humour in it. She's speaking in present tense, like she's already thought this through and has made her decision. That must just be a slip of the tongue, though, because Alyx would never accept something like this. She hates the stumblers more than anyone else.

"Are you serious?" I shake my head. What has this kingdom come to when our useless king is trying to hire assassins to be his bride and help him run the country? "I hope you told him what to do with his offer."

She steels herself, her expression determined. "I'm going to say yes."

"No."

The word comes out before I've even finished thinking it. It's an order, a flat denial. There is no fucking way I'm letting her do this, and I'm sure it shows on my face. This isn't the way to speak to Alyx, as it will just make her want to do it all the more, but I can't stop myself. I won't let her leave us, leave me, to do this.

Shock crosses her beautiful, stubborn face. "What do you mean, no?" Indignation colours her words, and in any other situation, I'd apologise for speaking to her like this, but not now—not when she's trying to leave.

"He's going to pay me," she explains, forcing her tone to lighten. "Plus, think of all the things I'll learn about the castle. This will make us rich. That's what you want, right?"

I close the gap between us, and she looks up at me with confusion and hope glistening in her eyes.

"It's not about the money," I bite out. "This is the king, Alyx. He's asking you to pretend to be his fiancée. A Lower. Doesn't this sound ridiculous to you? Are your alarm bells not ringing?"

Fiancée. Fiancée. Fiancée.

The word circles repeatedly in my mind, getting louder and

louder, crowding out all other thoughts. Jealousy is like a living thing within me, tearing me up on the inside and crawling into my brain, whispering foul things.

"I don't understand, Crux. This is what we do." Gesturing around us at the stolen art and luxury furnishings, she attempts to hide her hurt from the way I'm speaking to her. I see right through it though, hurting right with her. "We take jobs to kill and spy, and then we move on to the next. Why are you so against this?"

I want to explain and make her see why she can't do this.

Fiancée. The word whispers through my mind once more, and a flare of anger washes away my intended sentiments. "This isn't a normal job, Alyx. If you get caught, you'll put everyone here at risk. You'll destroy everything."

That's not what I meant to say. I wanted to tell her that I can't bear the thought of her spending time with the king. No matter if she's pretending to be his or not, the very knowledge of it causes physical pain within me. Would I care if my operation was exposed? Not as long as I know Alyx is safe, but in the palace, she won't be. I need her here, where I can protect her. I need her.

Why can't I tell her that?

My comment hits her like a blow, and I watch as she straightens, determination clear in her stance. "You know I've taken more dangerous jobs than this. Besides, last time I checked, I take whatever jobs I want. I'm telling you this as a courtesy to our friendship."

Friendship. That's what I'm left with, while the king gets a fiancée. It's not right, and it's not fair.

"You can't go. I won't let you," I command.

Laughing with disbelief, she takes a step back and looks me over, as if seeing me for the first time. "Let me? What the fuck has gotten into you, Crux? I thought we were friends."

I'm fucking this up. I can feel her pulling away from me, but I can't stop myself. I want to tell her so much and confess how I feel. I want to beg her not to go. The world is so much darker when she's not around. I need her. Why can't I just tell her all of this?

Because I am a fool who isn't eloquent, like the king.

Taking a deep breath, I push down my anger and jealousy and try again. "We are friends, which is why I'm telling you not to do this. I can't protect you inside the palace. I need you to be safe."

She huffs in annoyance. "I can protect myself."

My softer words come too late because her walls are already being built up against me, her decision made.

"I know, but—"

She cuts me off, anger flaring in her eyes as she jabs an accusing finger at me. "Fuck you for suggesting I can't look after—"

"I can't lose you!" I bellow, my heart bleeding in my chest as I open myself to her. I can't say everything I want to, but it's a crack in my barriers. I only hope that it's enough to convince her to stay.

We both fall silent as the words hang between us. Her eyes are wide, and for a moment, I think I see her softening as she reaches a hand towards me. Stumbling forward, I make the most of the moment and take that hand, pressing it against my chest so she can feel my pounding heart.

"I can't lose you, Alyx. Please don't do this," I beg.

She stares up at me, her expression a mix of sorrow, pain, and determination, and I know I failed.

"I can do this, Crux," she whispers. "I need to do this."

No. Please don't leave. Without you, life is pointless. All the riches in the world wouldn't make me happy if you weren't in my life. It's for you. All of this is for you.

Except I don't whisper those words. "If you go, I can't help you. You'll be on your own." It comes out harsher than I meant it to, my own pain causing me to lash out.

She stares at me, and it's clear she never expected me to say this, to give her an ultimatum. Dropping her hand from my chest, she takes a step back, and it feels like she's taking a piece of me with her.

"Then so be it." She pauses, taking one last look at me, sorrow lining her eyes. "Bye, Crux."

She turns away, and I watch the love of my life walk out the door and into the life of another man.

CHAPTER
ELEVEN

ALYX

As I stuff the clothing into my leather bag, my face twists in fury. Turning, I grab my leather satchel, filled with my lockpicks, and then slam them into the bag.

Crux and I fight all the time, our tempers are too similar, but we make up fairly quickly.

Not this time, though, because he went too far. I cannot believe he wouldn't only doubt me and my skills, but also try to forbid me from going like he owns me.

Snarling, I hurry around my room, shoving everything into the bag, and with an annoyed hiss, I attempt to buckle it up. It gets caught halfway. "Fucking bag," I growl, ripping up the buckles before I lay my hands on the bulging top and close my eyes.

I need to be calm, to be smart, and not let my anger get the best of me.

I'm heading to the palace, a place of perfection and games, so I must have my head on straight. I slow my breathing, focusing on my measured inhales and exhales to calm my racing heart. It's what I used to do before a hunt, a habit that comes in handy now. When I open my eyes once more, part of me expects Crux to be there, but he isn't, and I ignore the twinge of disappointment that moves through me.

Throwing the bag over my shoulder, I look around, not knowing if or when I will ever come back here. Even if I survive this mission, will my place still be here?

I blow the candle out, plunging the room and my past into darkness, and then I take a step outside, followed by another and another, until I find myself before the stairs that lead to a grate to the Lowers. Everyone else is asleep or hunting at this hour, our hideout empty, yet with my hand on the railing, I look back, expecting Crux to be there to make this right.

He isn't, so I turn away and force myself not to look back again. Despite the years we have spent together and our friendship, I will not ruin this chance at gaining revenge. If he cannot support me, then so be it.

I don't need him. I don't need anyone.

I pull the lever for the grate harder than I need to and watch it roll away before stepping out into the early morning darkness. I kick the outside hidden lever until the grate covers the hole again, unwilling to look back at the tunnels that have been my life and home since that fateful night.

Instead, I pull up my hood and face covering to conceal myself. Blending with the shadows, I hurry through the Lowers to the towering palace in the distance.

♪

THE WESTERN GATE they mentioned is easy to find. It's not often I come near the palace, even on this side of the Lowers. There are too many lights and soldiers, but at this early hour, it seems deserted. The huge stone wall separating poverty from riches is a constant reminder of where we stand—lower than the Crown.

Nestled between some rocks and trees is a deep brown wooden gate. Taking one last steadying breath, I rap my knuckles against it.

There is no going back now, not that I would even if I could.

I have made my choice, one that was set into motion many years before, when the very people I am about to investigate stole everything from me. Despite what Crux says, I know I can do this. I have to do this, and as I hear a bolt slide back and the creak of the gate opening, I step backwards.

My hand lingers over the sword at my hip, but when a familiar, shaved head peeks out, a small lantern held in his grasp, I relax and drop my hand away from my blade, allowing my cloak to fall back into place.

"Alyx?" the gravelly voice says, the sound moving through me as I pull down my face covering and smile.

"The one and only." When he just stares, I arch an eyebrow. "Going to let me in, big guy?"

"Come on then, shorty," he replies, opening the door wide.

For a moment, I glance back into the rundown Lowers, searching the darkness beyond for a familiar face. I know Crux wouldn't have let me come alone. He's out there somewhere, watching, and that gives me a little more confidence to turn forward.

"Well?" Orion prompts.

"I'm coming, I'm coming. Don't get your armour in a twist," I mutter as I move past him.

He hurries to shut the door, sliding the bolt into place before grabbing the lantern. "This way," he orders. "Keep your voice down and step lightly."

"Assassin, remember?" I reply distractedly, getting my first glimpse of the palace I will be living in.

It is huge, even from what I can see here in the dim light of the night. My booted feet sink into soft, perfectly trimmed grass. Beyond is a paved path that curves up and around, not a stone out of place. To the right is the large expanse of buildings, and I swear I hear the neighing of horses.

The moon illuminates enough to see structures but not to make out details. I glimpse lanterns hanging about, emitting low light, but not much back here.

More buildings are spread before us, but in the dark, it is hard to tell what they are. They remind me of the nobles' houses though. Although not tall, they are wide, with imposing, arched roofs that reach towards the Imperial Mountains that surround the palace.

It seems colder here, but far more ethereal.

"Come on," Orion murmurs, pulling my gaze away from the many buildings. I follow his surprisingly soft steps across the grass to a paved path. "You'll need to catch up and quickly, so let me give you a quick rundown. The palace is separated into many buildings, with the throne room being the centre. From the main gate on your left, there is the guards' barracks and training area, as well as the stables. Farther back are the servants quarters." He points to our right, past the western gate we just entered through. "If you keep going this way, you'll reach the concubines' palace, which is where we are headed since it's sealed up. Joha has not chosen any and it's empty. Beyond that is the lake from Lanide River and the Imperial Mountains. If you follow that around, we have the royal hunting ground, the king's palace, the queen's palace, Windfall Hall, forests, waterfalls, the Queen Mother's palace, the temple, Frey Hall, kitchens, gardens, and the greenhouse. There are also the scholars' buildings and school. It's basically a city within these walls, so try not to get lost. You must learn your way quickly."

"Understood." Luckily, I'm quick at picking up locations and adapting—part of the trade.

I hurry after Orion silently as we move down the path towards the concubines' palace. I find it interesting that Joha hasn't picked any yet. Usually, concubines are chosen shortly after a king is enthroned, but that's typically after marriage, so I guess that explains it. Will Joha pick concubines after our fake marriage?

It would make it easier to sneak around because I could use them as distractions or my own little spies. I remind myself to speak with them about that later.

The walk from the western gate to the looming concubine palace only takes us ten or so minutes, but it's clear Orion is afraid we will be exposed. The palace itself is a huge one-story building with lots of windows that are currently covered, and stone steps lead up to the main entrance.

"This way," Orion mumbles as we cross from the path and head around the back. We avoid any patrolling soldiers as Orion gracefully climbs up and swings over a low wooden balcony leading to sliding doors at the back of the palace.

He turns and reaches out to help me, but I gracefully leap and land on silent feet at his side, and he retracts his hand.

Putting the lantern down, he grabs one of the sliding doors and opens it, gesturing for me to enter the darkness beyond. It would be a good way to trap an assassin, but I walk past him with a shrug. He glances around before he picks up his lantern and steps in, shutting the door.

Leaving him with it, I tread deeper inside.

The flooring here is made from a hardwood only found in the Lunaris Empire, lined with fur rugs, and from the dim light, I can see opulent decorations in the hall we stand in. Sliding doors take up the entire long passageway.

A small light in one farther down catches my eye, so I pull my blade before I head that way. I move through the darkness, leaving Orion behind, and I hear him hiss my name, but I open the door and roll inside, coming up with my blade at the person's throat.

Joha blinks at me, wearing nothing but a grand purple robe. A small candle is set on the low table before him where he's crouched. "We have to stop meeting like this." He grins.

Rolling my eyes, I put the blade away. I drop my bag and sit opposite him, reclining in the cushions as Orion hurries in. He glares at me as he shuts the door. Orion leaves the lantern there, and it's clear they don't want to light too many candles or lanterns to give away our position from the windows.

I glance around the room as Orion huffs in annoyance. It's elegantly done and clearly awaiting its new mistress.

A small seating area surrounds us, with tapestries and paintings hanging on every wall. A huge candle chandelier hangs above, and to the right through a separator, I see a wooden octagonal tub and dressing area. On my left, through another separator, is a wooden bed, all done in purples and greys.

Joha's colours, I'm guessing.

"I'm glad you came," he says, and my eyes move back to him. He's sitting upright with his hands on his knees—a habit, I am sure.

"I wouldn't go that far," Orion mutters under his breath.

"So mean, big guy." I wink at him and focus on Joha. "I'm here, so tell me what I need to know."

"It's late, and we must be up early to execute our plan, so I will get straight to the point," Joha replies. "You need to discover who is trying to murder me. I will present you as my queen-to-be tomorrow, since it will not give Queen Mother or any other enemies time to deny the request or kill you. After that, you will be placed in the queen's palace and free to roam. You will be assigned teachers and ladies-in-waiting to accompany you and help your transition while they prepare for a royal wedding. It will no doubt make the scholars and council members wary, so be careful. You will also need a background, a story that is both believable and untraceable, otherwise we will not be able to go any further."

"Leave that to me," I tell him, my voice sure. His eyebrows rise as I lean back, not bothering to explain my confidence.

After all, I'm not just any assassin from the Lowers. I have an advantage no one else does.

I was born in a noble province.

CHAPTER
TWELVE

ALYX

"So, whom do you suspect?" I ask, getting right down to business.

Orion heads our way, dropping to his knees. He immediately pulls out his sword and starts to clean it as Joha focuses on me. It's a threat, but I ignore it and focus on the king. After all, I'm here to do a job, and I wouldn't be here if Orion could do his better.

"Honestly? Everyone." He gives me a bitter smile. "No one wanted me to be king. They were all hoping Queen Mother would have a boy child with the king, who would then inherit the throne, but she did not before his death. Therefore, the throne and the duty fell to me. When I was younger, I was foolish. I was not easily manipulated or turned. I fought back and rallied, and I'm paying for that now. No matter how dumb or malleable I appear, they know I am someone willing to fight for his beliefs, so that leaves the scholars, council members, noble families, and even Queen Mother. Take your pick. They all want me gone."

"Well shit." I chuckle. "Tell me about the attempts. The ways in which a person kills tells you a lot about them."

Joha leans forward, his handsome face and bright eyes lit by candlelight as he smiles. "What does your method say about you, I wonder?"

"That I hate everyone and I enjoy killing." I flutter my lashes as he barks out a laugh and leans back once more. I feel Orion's eyes on me, but I ignore him until he speaks, cutting through the tension.

"Two poisonings, three failed blade assassinations, and a suspected carriage accident." He lists them off without a hint of emotion, but when I glance at him, I see fury in his gaze.

"Poisoning is a woman's method. It's personal and filled with hatred. They want you to suffer but not be found. It's smart and often successful. The others came after the poisonings?" I muse out loud.

"Yes." Orion nods, stilling his hand on his blade.

"Then it's likely one person who changed their tactics after the poisoning failed. The longer you survive, the more desperate they will be to kill you. That's good."

"How is that good?" Joha asks, but he doesn't seem overly bothered by the fact that we are discussing his death.

"Desperation means sloppy work. Sloppy work means they are easier to catch."

"I see," Joha murmurs. "I knew there was a reason I hired you."

"What about your guards and servants," I begin.

"I do not trust anyone," Joha admits softly, eyeing me before looking at the candle. "I feel like everyone is against me. I never know whom I can trust here, except Orion. That is why you are here. Right now, I would lose an outright war against those feeding on our city. We must play their game."

"I am good at games." I sit up and nod. "Then it's settled. We will find whoever is trying to kill you, kill them—"

"Or arrest them," Joha interrupts, eyeing me sternly.

"Fine, fine, or arrest them." I lower my voice then add, "Probably kill them." I grin. "And then I get everything you promised, and you get a happy kingdom and palace." I hold my hand out. "Deal, Joha?"

"You should address him as Your Majesty," Orion grumbles.

I don't take my eyes from Joha, though, and with a matching grin, he takes my hand, but rather than shake it, he lifts it to his mouth and places a gentle, promising kiss on my knuckles. "Deal, Alyx."

"We must get you back, Your Majesty, before someone finds you missing." Orion stands, putting his blade away.

"Of course," Joha tells Orion before turning to me. "You can rest here tonight. Do not make too much noise or light. Soldiers patrol the grounds, and if you are caught, I will not help you. I do not have the power to do so," he warns, and I see a flash of anger in his eyes before he rises gracefully. "Until tomorrow, Alyx."

"Until tomorrow, Your Majesty," I tease.

He shoots me a smile before moving to the door and leaving. Orion gives me another searching look as he leaves the lantern.

"If you put him in danger, I will kill you myself."

"I'd love to see you try," I retort. "Oh, Orion?"

He stills, shooting me a concerned look. "There are some things I will need." Grabbing a piece of parchment, I quickly scribble out a list and throw it towards him.

He catches it midair, snatching it with lightning-fast reflexes despite his size. "Not bad," I tell him.

He sighs. "Behave, shorty."

"Me? Never." I wink.

Shaking his head, he follows his king, leaving me in the dimly lit room. I almost laugh at the idea that he expects me to stay put.

There is so much more to do, and while the king is away, the assassin will play.

I MEAN REALLY, did they truly expect me to sit tight until dawn like a good little girl?

Idiots.

I give them enough time to get their stumbler asses back to the king's palace and then I get to my feet. Tugging up my hood and face covering, I lean over and extinguish the candle before sliding the door open and heading back the way we came. I hurry to the side to peek around the concubines' palace.

It's dark in the palace at night, and I make sure to avoid the sporadically placed lanterns as I hurry across the paths. I map it out in my head, using the information Orion gave me to find my way. If I am to survive this game and emerge as the victor, then I need to know every inch of this place—exits, entrances, tunnels, and hideaways.

I need to become the master of the palace, so I move through the sprawling estate using the cloak of nightfall. I check out the lake and buildings, noting the soldiers and watching their patrol routes and schedules. I can't make out a lot of details or visuals in the dim light, but I can make out enough to give me a starting point. I make my way around it in a circular manner until I find myself near the western gate after passing the main gate. The stables are close, and as I watch, a small man scurries out from inside, stilling when he sees me.

He dips his head, holding his fist over his chest in a familiar gesture.

Daggers, this man is a rat.

I spot another sliding through the darkness, and another.

Crux sent his little rats in here. Turning away with a smile, I can't help but feel protected and cared for. I begin to head back to the concubines' palace to rest and think about what I've seen, but then I still when I hear the whisper of voices moving this way.

Cocking my head, I listen harder, staring into the shadows of the building ahead when a flame catches my attention. Shit, I can't get caught. I search for somewhere to conceal myself, but the only places that are close are a well or the concubines' palace.

I burst into a sprint towards the palace as the voices get louder.

I rush across the grass and look around, but I know I won't make it inside in time.

Stepping back, I dig my heels in and then run towards the wall of the concubines' palace. I leap at the last moment and grip the edge of the tiled roof. Using my arm strength, I yank myself up and roll onto the roof before the voices draw closer.

Lying on the edge of the roof, I flip over and blend into the darkness as I watch and wait.

It doesn't take long for two figures to appear below me. They look around, lit by the torch they carry, which washes over their white robes and hats. When they are happy there is no one around, their voices get louder and more confident, and I listen in.

They are clearly hiding what they are saying for a reason, which is more of a reason to listen.

"Are you sure?" the one on the left says. I try to memorise their faces, but the darkness makes it somewhat hard. However, I can remember their voices for the future.

"If we can get it past the king." They both chuckle. "We can increase the taxes within those provinces, and the extra money would go to us."

Ah, the rich getting richer, how surprising.

"They have already been taxed hard," the other responds. "Will they pay it?"

"We will not give them a choice. We can make it seem important, say it's for crops for the Lowers. Everybody likes to seem selfless and giving."

They turn slightly when the horses make noise, and it gives me a chance to scan their faces and implant them in my memory. They might not be killers, but they are clearly crooks who have no love for the king and use their positions to get what they want.

They are threats, and I'm here to dispose of threats.

"I will propose it tomorrow then," the other responds. "We should return before the guards come."

I watch them hurry away, happy with their dirty, rotten plans.

Now, don't get me wrong, I'm all for stealing from the rich, but only as long as it's me doing the stealing.

Waiting to ensure they have left completely, I stand and move across the roof to the back of the concubines' palace, where I throw myself off the edge. I flip in the air and land on my knees with a slight thud before climbing quickly to my feet. I hurry back into the palace, ready to get some rest and prepare for the big day tomorrow.

CHAPTER
THIRTEEN

JOHA

The whispered comments and worried titters from the councilmen and advisors follow me through the palace grounds as I make my way to the throne room. Ignoring them all, I force myself to look around obliviously, smiling as we pass those who live in the palace compound like I do not have a care in the world.

I called an emergency meeting as soon as I awoke, not giving them time to try and change my plans. I did not manage to get any sleep last night. My mind continued to turn over all my concerns and fears about what we are doing. Have I made a mistake in trusting the assassin? No. My instincts tell me that I'm right about her and that this is going to work. The most dangerous thing about this whole plan is the tiny spark of hope that blooms in my heart.

It has been a long time since I allowed myself to feel hope or anything akin to it.

Thanks to the last-minute nature of this mandatory meeting, I only have a handful of my normal entourage of advisors and scholars. My guards are all present as usual, with the ever-faithful Orion leading us all.

Wearing my formal, highly decorated purple cloak, I cannot help but feel amused by my councilmen's confusion. Usually, the king's cloak is only worn for ceremonial purposes, which has everyone even more confused about the reason for this meeting, yet no one has questioned me directly about what is happening. That will not last for long, I am sure, but in the meantime, I am going to enjoy this moment of peace before the interrogation begins.

"Do you know anything about why this meeting has been called?" one of my scholars asks quietly behind me, concern making his voice warble more than usual.

"There's nothing to worry about," Advisor Ruik chimes in snidely. He is one of my most vocal advisors and is coincidentally from the Queen Mother's family. If there was a way for me to dismiss him, I would, but unfortunately, that is out of my hands.

"This is the king, after all," Ruik continues, chuckling slightly. "He probably just wants to tell us he's decided to ban porridge from the kitchen or something equally ridiculous and mundane."

The others chuckle in agreement, placated for the time being.

With how often I hear them speak about me this way, you would think that I would be used to it by now. However, shame and anger burn inside me. Once upon a time, they used to at least do it behind closed doors, but now they barely even bother to lower their voices. I am their king, yet they treat me like a clown.

The only thing that's keeping me from simply rampaging at their obvious disdain is Alyx. She's going to change everything around here. My smile turns genuine as I imagine the horror and shock of my council when I announce my betrothal.

It's my turn to make decisions.

It's my move, and I just pressed my advantage.

I just made a queen.

"Your Majesty, I really do feel it's imperative that you tell us what you plan to announce to your people," my advisor scolds, once again treating me like a disobedient child rather than his king. "We cannot help you if we do not know what's happening."

Settling myself in my throne, I sit back and let my lords-in-waiting run forward to adjust my cloak as I peer out at the bustling building that houses the throne room. The throne room, placed right in the centre of the palace grounds, is massive in an effort to intimidate and remind everyone of my station, even if it has become a laughingstock as of late, but the kings who sat before me used it to their advantage, just as I will today. Like most of the rest of the palace, it's a one-story building with a high, decorative roof. My throne, whilst terribly uncomfortable, is carved from marble and has intricate patterns that must have taken the artist months to create, and it sits atop a raised dais, allowing me to look down at my people —another reminder they are below me, or should be.

The room itself is relatively devoid of furniture, allowing for many to stand before the king. Windows line the walls, spaced evenly throughout the halls like arched sentinels providing light. Lanterns hang from the walls where the light from the windows doesn't reach, their golden casings gleaming thanks to the huge team of cleaners who keep the place spotless. Tapestries of my family's long history are draped upon the walls as well. Two of the largest are fixed to the back wall behind my throne, the image depicting the triumphant win of the first king of this land. It's as beautiful as it is brutal and completely impossible to ignore.

My people are filing into the room, both the nobles who live within the palace compound and those who are from the upper part of the city who could make it in time. Scanning the room, I notice how almost everyone is wearing the same confused expression, splitting into small groups as they discuss their theories on why they have all been called together.

They are not permitted to kneel on the pillows to rest unless I allow it, so they mingle as they stand before the throne.

I do not reply immediately, needing time to cool my temper so I do not shout at the weaselly man beside me and ruin everything. Orion is standing on my other side and slightly behind the throne. He's silent, but I can feel his anger radiating from him. There is another reason I do not speak, though that has nothing to do with my frustration. Staring off into the distance, I pretend that I do not feel his eyes boring into me, even as I grow more and more annoyed with each passing second.

When it becomes apparent that I am not about to answer anytime soon, my advisor eventually loses patience and clears his throat. Blinking and whipping my head around as though snapped out of a daydream, I laugh, but it is devoid of any true mirth as I meet his stare boldly.

"Oh, sorry, Advisor Ruik, I forgot you were there for a moment." Smiling, I roll my eyes at myself and chuckle once more. "Thank you for your concern, Advisor Ruik, but you will know about the nature of the meeting soon enough. I have this all in hand."

Outrage flashes across his face before he quickly masks it, and I turn back to watch everyone file through the doors. The hall is packed, and almost everyone must be here now. Most of those waiting are males, with only a handful of females attending, and I would hazard a guess that is only because they live in the palace grounds.

We have had queens for generations, yet rules and restrictions on women still apply. It's foolish, if you ask me. My smile turns genuine then as I remember my future queen. Alyx will not conform to them.

I almost delight in the chaos she will cause amongst those gathered. It's enough to lift my spirits despite the whispered insults that reach my ears.

"Sir," the advisor squawks beside me, outraged at my dismissal.

He's cut off by the presence of another making their way to my side, and I've never been more grateful for the interruption—that is, until I realise exactly who it is. Ruik would only back down to one person.

Queen Mother.

I am sure the weather darkened with her arrival, or maybe that is just my mood.

"Your Majesty," Queen Mother greets demurely, her voice grating on me. However, when I turn in my throne to look at her, I smile widely.

I wait for her to finish her curtsy, making sure to drag it out to almost a disrespectful amount of time before I finally address her, something I know infuriates her, but with so many witnesses, she cannot make a scene. Above all else, she protects her image of a doting Queen Mother and widow of the former king.

"Oh, Queen Mother, good, you are here. I was worried that you might not get the message about today's meeting in time." Keeping the wide smile on my face, I run my eyes over her discreetly. Despite the last-minute invitation to the meeting, she looks impeccable as usual. Her deep purple dress is just a couple of shades off my colour, more blue than purple, in her own silent protest that no one else would notice. I see it though, along with her barely restrained contempt for me. Four ladies-in-waiting stand behind her—two holding the train of her dress, one carrying a folded parasol, and another cooling her with a white lace fan.

As she dips her head in acknowledgement, her smile is poisonous. "It was certainly a surprise," she replies carefully. Glancing around, she takes in the huge gathering of noblemen before returning her gaze to me, her brow raised in question. "What is this all about? Is all well?"

She could not care less if something was amiss. If something was truly wrong, she would have been notified by one of my guards or advisors. Her little spies would whisper it to her, yet she knows *nothing* about this, and it's clearly driving her mad. She's suspicious, and I will admit that this is out of character for the person they believe me to be. To organise something of this scale is above what many of them think I am capable of, and I can practically see her thoughts spinning around her cunning mind. She is smarter than most, but she also wants to believe this act so she can continue to rule the kingdom with me as her puppet.

"He will not tell us, Your Majesty," Advisor Ruik cuts in snidely, standing just to her side.

Pinning me with a look of disappointment, she tilts her head to one side. "What is this, Joha? Your advisors are here to help you. They cannot do that if you do not allow them to." Her eyes gleam with annoyance. "Think of your people."

"That is exactly what I am doing, Queen Mother, but I thank you for your concern."

The comment on its own is innocent enough, but this time, I do not hide my anger, so it's more of a snap than anything I have dared to say to her in years. I let it burn in my eyes for precisely two seconds, plenty long enough for her to see. I should not have done it, and I know that I play up to their assumptions of me, but to imply that I am not doing the best for my people when I do everything to keep them safe is an insult I cannot let slide.

Her eyes widen and then quickly narrow, seeing right through my now neutral mask. She's about to argue with me and possibly even make a scene in front of everyone. She might even attempt to provoke me into revealing myself by making an announcement to those gathered that the meeting has been cancelled.

I feel Orion stiffen beside me before clearing his throat, ready to step in and protect me from any and all threats, including the Queen Mother.

That never happens though. As if the old gods know we need something to break the tense atmosphere between us, the doors at the back of the throne room suddenly swing open. I am not even sure when they closed, but I certainly noticed the moment they opened once more, and I am not the only one.

Shock ripples through the crowd like a wave, slowly reaching me on my throne. Several gasps reach my ears, but I pay them no heed, my eyes locked straight ahead.

Light filters into the room, and there, standing in the doorway with the sun shining behind her like an angel, *she* is.

Alyx.

Thanks to the way the light shines behind her, I can only see her silhouette, yet I still know it is her. Like a kick in my chest, the surety of it rings through my entire body.

Taking a few silent, dainty steps into the hall, she pauses as the doors slowly shut behind her, and I can finally make her out.

Everyone falls silent, and I do not blame them.

Her auburn hair has been brushed and oiled to perfection, the locks gleaming in the updo it's been tamed and pinned into. Tiny pearls are nestled into her hair, catching the light as she turns her head. Two curls hang around her face, framing her flawless skin as she tilts her head demurely.

The dress is a work of art in its own right, and I do not have the faintest clue where she got it from, as it certainly was not one of those provided in the concubines' palace. My mouth goes dry at the sight. Although Alyx looks formidable and attractive beyond reason in her black assassin gear, Alyx in a dress is almost enough to send me tumbling from my throne. Cream in colour, the dress has a fitted bodice and modest, scooping neckline. Loose, floaty sleeves end at her elbow, the fabric slightly sheer so I am able to see the skin of her arms. The skirt cascades down to the floor in gentle folds of fabric, making it easy to move around in but still beautiful and elegant. What really sets off the dress, however, are the tiny purple flowers that are embroidered into the fabric. They are scattered evenly throughout the bodice, but the flowers increase at her waist and seem to flow down the skirt, lessening until there are only a few around the hem.

It's a beautiful dress, but there are several things about it that make it so perfect. Firstly, she looks like a lady, someone who could fit in amongst the crowd of staring nobles. Secondly, the flowers are purple, *my* purple. It gives a statement, especially once everyone knows the real reason she's here. Thirdly, the dress creates a youthful, girly appearance, the perfect ruse for my spy. She looks nothing like the hardened assassin I met the other night. In fact, I feel like I am seeing her properly for the first time.

Her eyes are lined like that of the ladies that flock to me, her lashes dipped in a substance and extended. Her cheeks are flushed, and her plush lips are stained a deep purple to match the dress, which fades to a pale pink at her cupid's bow. She seems softer, or maybe that is just the lack of weapons on her body, though I have no doubt she has some concealed somewhere.

After all, you can put an assassin in a dress, but you cannot change who they are.

I like that I am the one behind the secret for once and that when her gaze meets mine, we'll both know the truth, even if no one else will. Her eyes flash for a moment, making me smirk. It is the same Alyx, even if she looks nothing like the feral assassin I met in a muddy alley.

After giving everyone a chance to see her, she starts to walk towards me, practically floating through the hall with a gentle, almost timid smile gracing her rosy lips. The watching nobles clear a path for her, filling in behind her once she's passed. It's becoming clear to everyone that she has something to do with the reason they have all been called here, and Queen Mother seems to have realised that too.

"Who is she, Your Majesty?" Queen Mother demands, quickly tacking on my honorific as she watches Alyx glide towards us.

I ignore her, my eyes locked on Alyx. I could not speak even if I wanted to. She consumes my entire focus as she glides towards me. Is it possible that this isn't actually her? Does she have a twin sister I do not know about? Somehow, in those short hours, she's completely changed. Something about her demeanour and the way she holds herself catches my attention, and I realise that she's even walking differently. She looks like one of us. How did she learn the correct mannerisms so quickly? I was expecting to have to brush over slip-ups and teach her how to navigate the court, but it looks like I might not need to.

I'm getting ahead of myself. Just because she made herself look pretty and she's walking differently does not mean that she actually knows how to survive life in the palace.

Someone clears their throat beside me, their anger at my distraction pretty clear. I would love to say that I was ignoring Queen Mother on purpose and that it all played into my plan, but that would be a lie. I am completely captivated by Alyx, and I'm struggling to think of anything other than her. At least I will not have to pretend to be enamoured with her.

Continuing to ignore Queen Mother, I turn my head slightly and glance up at Orion. I expect to see his standard frown, since he has made his disapproval of Alyx pretty clear, but I am blown away by the surprise and hint of admiration in his eyes as he watches her too.

I don't blame him.

Every man in this room watches Alyx like she is an angel they want to corrupt. If only they knew the devil that hid behind those fluttering eyelashes.

"Joha, answer me." Pain flashes through my arm as a hand grips me tightly. Jerking my head around, I meet Queen Mother's fuming eyes.

"Queen Mother," Orion snaps in warning, glancing pointedly at her nails digging into my skin, his body seeming to grow even larger as he begins to move towards her.

I hold my hand up, and he instantly stops moving despite me not having said a word. I'm sure she's cut into my skin, but the pain helps remind me why we're here.

"You wanted to know why this meeting was being held," I comment quietly, making it seem as though I'm attempting to keep this from being overheard.

She seems suspicious at my sudden cooperation, her eyes narrowing. "Yes."

Nodding, I flash her a smile. "Well, you are getting your wish."

Using my free hand, I pry each of her fingers from my arm and slowly get to my feet. "She is to be my betrothed."

Horror flashes across her perfect face, and I overhear several of my advisors squawking with outrage, but there is nothing they can do to stop me now. I am already on my feet and addressing my people.

They seem to be caught between looking at me, their king, while also trying to watch the mysterious woman moving through their ranks. However, she has now reached the base of the dais my throne sits on. Smiling widely, I clap my hands together before gesturing towards Alyx as I offer her my hand to help her up the steps. She lays her palm in mine, and the rough skin makes me smile, reminding me she is just as lethal at wielding a sword as she is wearing a dress. She stands tall at my side, her hand in mine, as I smile at the now gawking crowd. When my voice comes, it rings out clear and proud . . . and maybe a little smug.

After all, I have a queen at my side.

One of the most lethal women in all our kingdom.

"Lords and ladies, I invite you to welcome my betrothed, Lady Alyx."

CHAPTER

FOURTEEN

ALYX

T'll hand it to the king—he knows how to get the room's attention.

I don't just mean the elaborate robe and headdress he wears, nor the throne he was perched on.

My entrance worked just as I planned it, my timing impeccable. The throne room is in the centre of the palace and has a large stretch of open space on either side. Thanks to the early hour, I was able to time the opening of the doors just as the sun rose over the top of the palace walls, gleaming down on me. I am here to play the game, after all, and nobody plays as well as I do.

Angelic. Mysterious. Beautiful.

Those were the words I heard whispered as I slowly made my way through the hall, and it makes me smile. Do I flourish under their praise? Yes. Am I vain? Also yes, but I own it, knowing my pride is one of my downfalls.

Keeping my head up, I ensure my steps are small and measured.

Don't slouch, head up, glide like a butterfly—the words chime through my mind, triggering a feeling in my chest that is familiar. A frown tries to mar my brow, so I focus on keeping my face smooth with a small, almost shy smile on my lips. *Keep them guessing, keep them wondering*, the same voice reminds me. All that training is coming in handy now, even though I despised it at the time. Every now and again, I flick my eyes up and look at the king demurely through my lashes. The expression on his face fills me with a feeling that surprises me. He's either a very good actor or he can't believe my transformation. When I look up at the brute of a guard dog who hovers around him, I'm also struck by his shock.

Typical. I wear a pretty dress and put my hair up and the males lose their senses. All men are the same.

Except, that doesn't ring true, not anymore. Shoving those thoughts deep down, I focus on why I'm here. I don't have time to get caught up in thoughts like that because it will only get me killed. No, I'm here for my revenge and to get paid.

It took me hours to get ready, and I had to sacrifice sleep to make sure everything was perfect. There's a dressmaker in the city who owes me a life debt after I saved her from some rogue bandits. She couldn't pay me in coins, so she creates clothes for me when I need them. I knew she would be awake, and she has several gowns in stock that are my size for emergencies such as this. When my eyes locked on the floaty cream dress, I knew that was the one I needed. It was regal yet slightly different from the stiff style the court ladies currently wear and fitted the image I want to portray perfectly. The only thing it needed was something to link it to Joha while still keeping it feminine. Embroidered flowers were already part of the dress; we just added the purple to the petals. It took her and three of her assistants to finish in time.

I kept out of sight, the lower part of my face covered and my hood up so if they did spot me, they wouldn't recognise me. Thankfully, they were too busy working, and I had to pop out to pick up several other items to make my grand entrance perfect. Once I returned to the shop and had the dress, I raced back to the palace and made it to the concubine's room in record time. Long ago, I'd been taught how to care for and present my hair properly, and as I sat in front of the mirror and wove pearls amongst the ginger strands, I could almost feel the soft touch of the one who instructed me.

I creamed, painted, tucked, pinned, and slicked, so I drink in their looks, knowing it was all worth it.

The lords quickly move out of my path, seeming to know that I'm walking to the front, their expressions confused yet appreciative. I doubt that will last for long. Does it make me a bad person that I can't wait for their outrage once they hear why I'm here? Probably, but I'm an assassin, the villain of most peoples' stories.

I'm almost at the dais where the king and his advisors stand when my eyes lock on an elegant older woman. She can't be that much older than Joha, but the way she carries herself gives away her position. She watches me with horror, her gaze shifting between Joha and me.

Her formal gown almost matches Joha's, and I have no doubt that was on purpose. She is beautiful, if ageing despite the ways she tries to hide it. From the gossip mill, I know she married young, and it is clear from the jealousy in her eyes that she is used to being the centre of attention, wielding her beauty like a weapon—one I have now stolen.

The Queen Mother is the one behind all the assassination attempts and wants to rule. I just do not know how far the rot spreads. Someone in the Lowers once told me that when a house's wood begins to rot and break, the only thing you can do is tear the whole structure down. That is exactly what I will do. I will burn the palace to the ground, and Joha can remake it in his image. The archaic rule about women not taking the throne is absurd, but in this case, I believe it's a blessing. Having someone as power hungry as her in command would only end in disaster. We all noticed the difference in the state of the city when the old king died, and it wasn't changed for the better. If Joha was telling the truth and this is all Queen Mother's doing, then we would be better off without her.

I could kill her, I think idly.

No. That's not what I'm here for, and if she has everyone wrapped around her fingers like I think she does, then it would only start a rebellion within the palace.

However, I plaster a smile on my face, beaming as though my every wish is coming true. There's a heavy beat of silence as I climb up the dais steps with the help of the king's proffered hand. Usually, I would slap it away, offended that he would even offer because it implies that I need help, but here, it's expected, so I take his hand and use my free one to hold my skirts as I step onto the dais. Smiling up at him prettily, I make sure to keep my eyes only on him, since we're supposed to be madly in love.

"Lords and ladies, please welcome my betrothed, Lady Alyx."

Hearing the king's voice echo through the throne room causes nerves to twinge inside me. Nervousness isn't an emotion I feel often anymore, so it reminds me of the risks I face by surrounding myself with these people.

Lady Alyx. That's something I'm not used to hearing.

The lords seem to realise that this isn't a joke, and pandemonium ensues. Shouts and calls of outrage all blur together, and Joha blinks slowly, as though realising that his people aren't as happy for him as he expected. The lords crowd around the base of the dais, all shouting to have their voices heard. Orion seems to take this as a threat and moves forward, stepping in front of us. His silent warning seems to remind them whom they are shouting at, the noise lowering slightly and their anger stuttering.

Shaking his head, the king faces his people, his fingers still threaded with mine. "As a king, I am expected to take a wife and to have a family and heirs," he explains, and although I know he's putting on an act, I don't believe that all of this confusion is faked. He genuinely seems shocked by the reaction to this announcement. I want to shake my head at his privileged and sheltered life showing through. He must know that every single person in this room is here because they want something. Daughters in high society are only useful to their families if they are traded to the highest bidder. There is no one with higher status than the king, so of course they wanted him to pick their daughters as his bride. If he's betrothed to me, then that option is gone.

He glances at Queen Mother. "I thought you would be pleased, Queen Mother. You've been trying to find me a wife for years."

Her lips are pinched, giving her the appearance of having just sucked on a lemon. She is not happy with this news or finding out in front of everyone else, where her hands are tied. "Yes, Your Majesty. A wife who has been approved by us, not some stranger you've plucked out of the woodwork."

I've been called much worse things in my life, so this barely registers on my radar. Lady Alyx would feel differently though. Pressing a hand against my breast, I gasp quietly, widening my eyes as though I'm offended at Queen Mother's comment.

Orion must hear it because he glances over his shoulder with a concerned frown. He doesn't want to care, but he can't seem to stop himself from checking, something that I know is annoying him based on the tick in his jaw.

"If you're going to take anyone as a wife, it should be from one of the founding families!" someone shouts from below, and several other male voices chime in their agreement.

"Screw the founding families! Anyone from the noble families would do," another voice calls out from the other side of the room. There is much more support for this comment, the room echoing with the sound.

I almost chuckle at them walking right into my plan. Joha might not have expected this, but I did.

Stumblers and Lowers might divide our society, but even within the nobility, there seems to be a hierarchy. Apparently, even money and privilege can't take that away.

"Who is this stranger?"

"The council needs to agree on this! Why is this the first we're hearing of this?"

The voices keep coming, each sounding angrier than the last, and I'm starting to realise that this is going to be much harder than I expected. This is going to take every scrap of my training and knowledge to make it seem like I belong here. Keeping my eyes wide, I pull a fan from a small pocket in my dress and begin to move it near my face, needing the movement of air to keep me calm. It fits with the role I'm playing, but also, this damn dress is hot. I have no idea how the ladies wear these every day.

My breasts have also never been pushed so high either. They nearly hit my fucking chin. Curse the bastard who invented corsets.

One of the men on the stage steps forward, an advisor I'm guessing from his uniform, and the crowd falls silent, all turning to listen to him. "The council will convene on this matter. Please wait here, and we shall return once this has been sorted." He speaks as though he believes this will be quickly resolved, clapping his hands together and gesturing for everyone to leave the stage before offering his arm to Queen Mother.

Who is that man? He just made an announcement without checking with the king and dismissed him like a child before flouncing off without waiting for his ruler to go ahead of him, as is protocol. It's clear where his loyalties lie, and if all of Joha's council is the same, then it's no wonder he asked for my help. Things are worse here than I thought.

Orion sighs gruffly and barks orders at the king's guards, and we start moving to the back of the hall and out a small doorway I hadn't noticed previously. The sound of many voices starts up as soon as we leave the dais, everyone speculating about who I am and what's about to happen. Stepping through the doorway, I blink at the sudden darkness that surrounds us, but my eyes quickly adjust as a large set of curtains are pulled back, exposing massive glass windows overlooking the palace grounds.

This room has another exit, as I expected, but the rest of the space is taken up with a large table and walls full of books, indicating this space is used as a meeting room of some sort. The Queen Mother is standing up by the head of the table, resting her hand on the back of the chair that is obviously meant for the king, with Joha's advisors gathered behind her. I guess that answers my earlier question about their loyalties.

"Joha," she announces as the door shuts behind Orion, "the court will not accept your choice of bride. You owe it to your people." The condescending tone makes me want to grit my teeth, and I don't even know the king well, but I can feel his anger and embarrassment at how she treats him.

Part of me wants to slap her for him, while another part wants to see him do it. I have a feeling seeing Joha unleashed would be a sight to behold.

"But she is one of my people!" Releasing my hand, he walks over to the table and braces his palms against it, staring at his stepmother. "They were just surprised. Once they have time to mull over the news, they will accept it. There are families in our land other than those here who would make perfect allies." He actually makes sense, surprising me, but I keep my face the blank, pretty mask it's expected to be.

Snorting, the older woman looks offended at the suggestion of other noble families being welcomed in the palace. Raising a well-sculpted brow, she looks me over and returns her gaze to Joha. "She is very pretty, and I'm sure she's lovely, but you should return her to where you found her. We won't have harlots here."

Honestly, the insult makes me want to laugh, and from the stifled laughter coming from behind Queen Mother, the advisors obviously think she's hilarious. However, in high society, I'm pretty sure I've just been gravely insulted. I move my fan a little faster, hoping I give off the impression that I'm offended and not that I'm trying to hide a smile.

Joha seems to take it to heart, though, and instantly jumps to my defence, raising my estimation of him—I still think he's an idiot, but a polite one.

"How dare you—"

Before he can dig us into a deeper hole than we're already in, I clear my throat and step forward, gently resting my hand on the small of his back.

"Your Majesty, may I speak?" I ask demurely. Several of the advisors look over at me in approval, and I know I can win them over.

Joha turns his head to glance at me, surprise in his eyes. He's questioning if this is a good idea, but I told him to trust me, and for some reason, he does. "Of course, Alyx."

Smiling at him sweetly in thanks, I turn to face the rest of the room. "Queen Mother," I greet, dropping into a shallow curtsy, offering respect even though I wish to carve that knowing smirk from her face and wear it as a hat. "It's an honour to meet you." Standing upright, I lift my head and clasp my hands in front of myself. "My name is Princess Alyx of Jade Empire."

The whole room seems to hold its breath at my declaration. Jade Empire is one of the closest neighbouring bodies of land that we do not own or rule over. While we're not actively at war with the empire nor hold any ill will towards it, we certainly don't have a friendly relationship with the country. Trade routes have always been argued over, and they have stood firmly as our kingdom has grown, refusing to give land to us.

By choosing to act as a royal from Jade Empire, not only am I giving myself a status that they have to respect, but I am also of high enough rank for the king that no one could argue against me. Not to mention, the council would be terrified of upsetting my "father" and starting a war.

My choice seems to have worked, as both surprise and understanding flash across their faces, but they still wait for more information, unconvinced.

"I am the youngest of two daughters. My sister will one day rule our kingdom. This means that I have more freedom and have been able to travel my land and see all the sights it has to offer. Being able to spend time with my people has been such a blessing." I chuckle lightly, letting excitement shine on my face as I glance back at the king. To anyone else watching, we're just a happy, young couple, and that's what I need them to believe about us.

"How did you two even meet?" the advisor from before asks curtly. He looks at me with a little more respect now, but it's clear he doesn't trust me. "The king doesn't leave the palace, and I've never heard of a Princess Alyx before."

Joha's smile seems tense. He's probably worried that he's not thought this far ahead. I have though. I never would have accepted a job without fully preparing first.

"My father is very protective of me, and I have a different mother than my sister. My father truly loved my mother. Apparently, I look just like her, so when she died, he clung onto me, terrified of losing me too. Because of that, my existence wasn't common knowledge," I explain with a muted smile, dulling my eyes as I speak of my fictional mother. Another benefit of my story is the fact that they can't easily check to discover if I'm telling the truth.

Blinking rapidly as if to hold back tears, I clear my throat and continue. "The king and I started writing to one another. He sent a letter to a friend, and it was accidentally delivered to me. I replied, explaining the mishap, not realising he was the king. He certainly didn't know I was a princess. We continued to write to each other, and we fell in love. We met in person for the first time last night when my carriage arrived. I had to see him before I went to my accommodations for the night."

It sounds ridiculous, like something out of a fairy tale, but if they believe the king is just a puppet and don't see his true strength, then they are going to think even less of me. Playing to this stereotype is what's going to make this work for us. Can two idiots fall in love after accidentally writing to each other? It seems his advisors think so.

I notice how several of them roll their eyes, while the one standing closest to Queen Mother actually sighs aloud and shakes his head. "Your Majesty, you can't marry someone you just met, especially one from a land we have no control over. You don't know her. If you really want to wed, we will find you a suitable bride." He seems to have made up his mind and is already turning to the other advisors, pleased with himself.

I'll hand it to the little man. He has balls for talking about a princess like that, especially right in front of her. In fact, he's talking as though I'm not even in the room. Oh boy, this guy is going to get what's coming to him, and I'm going to be the one to deliver it.

"No."

The king's voice seems very loud in the room, and everyone else falls silent and stares in surprise, clearly not used to hearing him disagree.

"I do know her, and she is my choice. This will be good for our lands. Besides, I get to choose whom I marry." He looks at me and takes my hand in his once more, threading our fingers together, a tiny smile pulling at his lips. "I choose whom I love."

My stomach flips, and I have to remind myself who this is and exactly what I'm doing here. Nothing he says is true—it's all part of our ruse. Thankfully, I don't have long to dwell on this, as several of the advisors start talking over each other, and I can sense that things are about to kick off again, so I clear my throat to get their attention.

"I know it seems strange and sudden, but his letter came to me by fate. It was meant to be. We love each other. Even my father could see it, and he gave his blessing for me to come here. Do you really think he would have done that if this wasn't serious?" I plead. "Please don't stop something that's so perfect."

I mould myself into the young, naïve, gullible woman they want me to be, and I see calculation in their eyes. Queen Mother has been silent for a while now, watching our performance with a narrow-eyed stare, and I know she's the one I have to convince.

"Joha, why don't you go and tell your people the good news about you and your betrothed?" she announces, smiling in a way that isn't all that friendly. "The princess and I are going to take a walk and get to know one another a little better."

Fantastic. Being alone with this woman is the very last thing I want to do right now, but Princess Alyx would love an opportunity to spend time with her future mother-in-law—not to mention, she just gave us the go-ahead. I'm not quite sure what changed her mind, and I'm going to need to tread lightly with her and not overdo it.

Letting my breath catch in my throat, I turn to Joha with an excited expression, squeezing his hand tightly.

"I'm not sure." He looks at me, sees my expression, and realises I can take care of myself. Besides, it would look strange for him to stop me from speaking with the Queen Mother. "Okay. Take one of my guards," he relents, gesturing towards Orion.

He's quickly waved off by Queen Mother though, her smile condescending. "Oh, she doesn't need one of your guards. Who is going to hurt her? Me?" She laughs as though this is the most ridiculous thing she's ever heard. "We shall have my guards and will not be going out of sight of the building. We will return soon, Your Majesty." Without waiting for his approval, she walks over to me and gestures for me to follow her, waving off her ladies-in-waiting.

Joha and I share a look, and I dip my head slightly, letting him know I can handle this. I momentarily allow my eyes to flick up to Orion, and his frowning face almost looks concerned. Is the big guy starting to care for me? That thought almost makes me laugh. No, he doesn't care about me, only that I might mess this up for his precious king.

Turning with a swish of skirts, I follow Queen Mother from the room and step out into the open courtyard. Four guards surround us, but they are all at respectable distances, so if we speak in low voices, they won't be able to overhear us. Queen Mother says nothing for a while as we walk a little way from the throne room. Clasping my hands behind my back, I stay silent, waiting for her to speak first as is protocol. I'm not kept waiting long.

"So, *Princess Alyx*"—she puts emphasis on my name so it sounds more like a slur than an honorific—"you want to be my son's betrothed."

Letting it slide off my back, I pretend to be oblivious and smile at her brightly. "Oh yes, I can't imagine being without him any longer." I almost allow a little skip into my step but stop myself at the last moment, deciding that would probably be overdoing it.

Slowing her pace, she frowns and looks me over once more, attempting to find fault or proof of me belonging to another empire. However, I know I look flawless today, and my posture is immaculate. One of the good things about the amount of training I do is that it helps keep my posture rigid and my body healthy, everything a princess would have.

Seeming to find nothing to complain about, she clicks her tongue and purses her lips. "What do you have to gain from this? Did your family put you up to it?"

I frown prettily and tilt my head to one side. "I'm sorry?" I play dumb, as though her question makes no sense to me at all. In all honesty, I am a little surprised by her bluntness.

A frustrated sigh leaves her lips, and as she speaks again, I can tell she's losing patience with me. "There has been silence from Jade Empire for years, and now all of a sudden, you turn up to marry our king. You don't think that's a bit strange?"

After letting several seconds tick by, I brighten my expression as I pretend to understand whom she's asking about. "My family? Oh, they didn't want me to come, since they think you are all murderers, but I told my father that wasn't true. A kingdom with a king as good as Joha is worth giving a chance," I explain, glancing down at the hem of my skirt and allowing a hint of sadness to enter my voice. "My papa didn't want me to leave, but he understood and reluctantly allowed it."

I keep my gaze down as I feel Queen Mother's penetrating stare on me, trying to pick me apart like I'm a puzzle she's dying to demolish. "Hmm, I see." Looking straight ahead, she admires a beautiful tree we happen to pass, pausing to reach up and touch its blooming flowers. "You know of the responsibilities that will come with being his queen?"

I've been so busy watching her that the change in topic almost throws me off. As she stares up at the blossoms on the tree, she smiles slightly, genuinely, and her whole face lightens. I doubt many people get to see that smile. Clearing my throat, I remind myself why I'm here and frown slightly again as I make it look as though I'm thinking deeply.

"Well, I've watched my sister prepare for the throne, and I know it will be hard work."

She laughs, looking away from the tree and shaking her head as she pins me with her stare again. "You don't have a clue, do you?"

I see the exact moment when she decides I'm clueless and that she can make this work for her—a perfect blank slate for her to mould into another puppet and leverage to use against the king if he ever decides to go against what she wants him to do. Her calculating expression is only there for a second, and most wouldn't notice it, but I'm an assassin who is trained to notice these things. Her face smooths into a smile as she offers me her arm.

"Luckily for you, Princess, I am going to take you under my wing. You shall attend court with me, and I'll teach you everything you need to know, and in return, you can tell me how the king is. I worry about him, you see."

Taking her offered arm, I link mine with hers and sound breathless as I smile up at her, not quite believing the kindness she's offering me. "Oh, of course. Thank you, Queen Mother."

In reality, I can see right through her honeyed words. She wants me to be her spy. What she doesn't know is that I'm already employed to do that very job, but with her as the target.

95

She just made my job a whole lot easier. I was worried I would have to beg and scrape to be near her.

Idiot.

Laughing, she squeezes my arm just a little too hard, digging her nails into my skin. "Oh, I think you and I will become good friends."

"Oh yes," I chirp, hiding the smug satisfaction I feel as we walk arm in arm for everyone to see. "The very best of friends."

It's almost too easy.

CHAPTER
FIFTEEN

CRUX

T he word fury doesn't hold enough weight to describe my feelings, but it's what I settle on, especially last night when I watched her walk into the palace. She knew I was there, yet she didn't call out or change her mind like I hoped she would.

She turned away and went inside.

I spent all night switching between feeling angry and proud and finally settled on infuriated, but despite how upset I am at her, I can't leave her alone in there. Regardless of what Alyx thinks, she is the reason I have done and built everything, and I will not let this argument be our downfall.

If she is determined to do this, then I know there is no changing her mind—it is one of the many qualities that both exhaust and humour me about her—so as the darkness changes to the bright colours of dawn, I put my plan into motion.

After greasing hands, forging papers and lineages, and breaking into official offices to plant information, I am ready.

All the while, I can't help but wonder why she is doing this. It can't just be for money. She has more than she could ever need, and even if she didn't and doesn't know it, she has half of everything I own. It leads me to question if it's the king.

That sour thought puts me in a bad mood all morning as I am shown to my new lodgings within the palace walls. They are much too open for me and shared with many other men all in the same position as I am. My back feels exposed, the light is too bright, and the creaking floor is too loud, but it's what I have to put up with as I change into the supplied gear. It is worth it to ensure she is safe.

Frowning down at the form-fitting bright colours of the palace guard uniform, I almost laugh at myself. Who would have thought I would end up here?

The fabric is itchy and tight and not easy to move or fight in, which is not a good thing for a profession such as this. It offers hardly any protection from the elements or blades and has nowhere to hide hidden weapons. The fools, it is clear the guards are mainly for show. When I find a hidden corner and make sure I'm alone, I cut away some of the material, hide daggers and wire within the uniform, and give myself more room for movement.

Despite being new, my forged lineage and papers afford me a higher rank, leaving them unsure what to do with me. It's perfect and means I am able to wander around the palace as they figure out my position. I don't see Alyx or the king, so I make a map in my head of every exit, entrance, hiding spot, and darkened corner or secluded area while wandering around, trying to force my expression into one of awe and neutrality when all I feel is rage.

I was never good at lying with my expressions, but I didn't need to be, not in my role as king of the thieves, but it's a skill I try to utilise now. I'll need it if this is going to work.

Does she even know I would put myself in this position to keep her safe?

I guess she will soon. Once more, my mind circles back to her reasons, unable to stop thinking about the decision that brought us both here.

Alyx has always had a mind of her own. I had no hopes of taming or breaking it, nor did I ever want to. It's one of the reasons I care so much for her. She challenges me, thinks for herself, and utilises her brain as another weapon in her arsenal, but for a moment, I can't help but wish she were a little less ambitious and calmer.

I almost snort. Alyx? Calm? The thought is comical, and I find myself smiling.

She would gut me for thinking so.

Unlike the night I first met her, Alyx has grown into a formidable woman, but even then, on that dark, rainy night when I followed the sounds of sobs into that darkened alley in the province and found the small, red-haired girl covered in blood, there was already a flame in her eyes. When they lifted to mine, an emerald hue brighter and rarer than any gem I'd ever stolen in my short thieving career, they glittered with glassy tears and pain, but under it all was a flame, a will to live, and a determination to right wrongs.

That flame grew into an inferno until I was left breathless when I peered into them.

It doesn't stop the protectiveness that rises within me, though, one that began that stormy night. Alyx has grown, but part of me always sees that blood-covered rich girl who was lost and alone, looking at me like she waited for me to end her life.

She was so small back then, so defenceless, but as she peered into my eyes, waiting for the blow to land, there was something there.

Before my mother passed of Cregin's disease, she'd often told me stories of the old gods, and one has always stuck with me—a person created in their guise with their blessing, possessing knowledge beyond their years and a destiny, a soul to rival even the gods themselves.

A blessed soul.

As I stared into those bright orbs, I knew instantly that what my mother had spoken of was true, even if I hadn't understood until that night.

Alyx changed my entire life, even if she didn't know it. I had been alone since my mother passed when I barely reached my tenth name day, but that night, I had a new purpose, a new person to protect, and that's exactly what I did.

I just never expected that person to become the sword behind my shield or come to mean as much to me as she does.

A platoon of soldiers passes me by, saluting me since the stripes on the shoulders of my uniform mark me as a higher rank. I keep my eye roll to myself and nod at them, and when the sounds of their heavy, booted feet no longer fill my ears, one of my little rats pops up in front of me.

I flooded the palace with them. If she is determined to do this, then she is going to need intel to keep her safe.

Hence the flickering eyes and nervous twist of the lips of the man before me as he lowers his gaze out of respect.

"Sir," the rat hisses as he glances around anxiously. It seems I'm not the only one unused to working within the bright light and open green areas of the palace versus the darkened alleys of the Lowers. "I have found her."

"Where?" I demand.

"Behind the throne room." I dismiss him with a flick of my hand and head back that way. I only get lost once, the internal map I created helping in the sprawling palace. Unlike the Lowers or provinces, I never had reason to learn this area. I never needed the intel, but I kind of regret that now as I slow my steps.

I walk out of a sheltered building, facing the back of the throne room, only to freeze.

For a moment, Alyx is all I see.

I have seen Alyx in many costumes to complete her jobs, but this might be my favourite. I love her leathers, since they remind me of home, but seeing her glide in a long, sheer cream gown dotted with flowers, I realise just how truly beautiful she is.

The old gods definitely created her in their image because

standing in the sun is a goddess wearing the face of my oldest friend, my family . . . my love.

She turns for a moment, and I swear our eyes meet. My heart stops, restarting only at her grace. I want to drop to my knees and beg her to run away with me back to our home so no other can ever see the beauty that is my Alyx. When she frees me from her gaze, however, I stagger back and suck in a harsh, uncertain breath.

The possessiveness inside me is not letting up, just as it hasn't since that night.

I wonder what she would think if she knew everything I did for her. She would probably kick my ass, and I can't help but smile at that.

When I force my eyes away, I realise there is someone else with her—Queen Mother and her guards.

I watch as Queen Mother pats Alyx's arm. Her smile is more akin to the venomous snakes one would find in the Lowers than anything sweet, but Alyx flutters her lashes and smiles stupidly at the woman as she turns and wanders away, taking her guard with her and leaving Alyx completely alone.

For a newly betrothed queen, it's an insult, but for me, it's perfect.

When Alyx turns, she rolls her eyes, her true expression showing as she picks up her skirts in annoyance and stomps past me on her way back to the king. "Fucking bodices. Why do they want to make it so hard to breathe?" she mutters, and I have to swallow my laugh, even as I step forward.

My arm slips around her throat and drags her into the shadows with me. She struggles, her dress getting in the way and slowing her down, which is the only reason I manage to pin her to the wall, my mouth going to her ear. "Hello, little assassin," I purr.

She softens at my voice but recovers quickly, and her elbow meets my gut with such force, it actually pushes me back a step, and within seconds, she spins and produces a blade from gods knows where, pressing it to my neck as she glares at me.

"Crux."

CHAPTER
SIXTEEN

ALYX

He stares at me like I'm a stranger, and I very nearly shrink under his dark, watchful gaze until I force myself to stand taller. I refuse to be ashamed, my hand holding the blade straight and true.

His eyes dart to it, and he steps into its path, pressing the tip just above his heart, though I have no idea why. I frown as he watches me. Crux is dressed in a guard's uniform, a major if I'm not mistaken from the marks on his shoulder.

Did he steal it or kill for it?

He looks good in it, I'll admit, since it's more form-fitting than his usual leathers, displaying his thick thighs and meaty arms. I can almost see his abs through the material before I drag my eyes back to his, seeing something burn in his gaze as he stares at me.

If anyone came upon us, they would see a newly appointed queen-to-be with a blade to a major's heart, but it's so much more than that. Despite the disguises we wear, we are the assassin and the thief king.

We are Crux and Alyx, just like we always have been, despite everything that was said.

He's here.

Despite it all, he's here, leaving his kingdom in the Lowers like he vowed he would never do. Why? How? I want to ask, but his mouth opens first.

"You fucking left," he accuses.

Sighing, I drop the blade and lean back. "I told you I was."

"I didn't think you actually would," he grumbles, his eyes flashing with an anger so strong, most would cut out their own hearts and hand it to him to make it stop. Mine beats faster, as if wanting to break free and fly to him. I wonder if he knows he already owns the traitorous organ in my chest. "Why are you doing this, Alyx?"

"I'm not going over this again," I argue, ready to slip away. He slams his hand into the building, making my eyes snap back to him. I watch his nostrils flare as he slams his other hand next to me, trapping me.

We both know I could get free if I wanted, but I relax, giving Crux the benefit of the doubt. "Talk to me." His voice changes, almost pleading, and I frown. "We don't keep secrets, Alyx. Please, tell me why." He swallows hard, searching my eyes.

I realise he's trying to understand.

His anger is gone, and mine melts away in the face of his pain. Wouldn't I be here doing the same if I were him? Taking a deep breath, I meet his eyes and decide what to say. It's never been this hard between us before, and I hate how much we are already changing, but I know better than anyone that change comes for everyone, and what's left after that is what's worth fighting for.

Is Crux? Are we?

I hope so.

Leaving him behind nearly cut my soul apart.

"It's a good job," I start, and he snarls.

"Cut the shit, Alyx. I know you too well for you to lie to me. If you don't want to tell me, fine, but don't fucking insult me," he snaps, slamming his fist next to me, but I don't flinch like most would. I know, even in his deepest anger, Crux would never hurt me. He would rather cut himself to pieces. "Is it because of him?"

I blink. "The king?" I ask, confused.

He jerks his head in a nod, and I stifle a laugh, but he stiffens at the sound.

"That idiot? Not in the least," I admit honestly, and he relaxes. He was truly worried about that. I don't know how that makes me feel, so I ignore it. I know at any moment, that Joha, Orion, or someone could find us. They will look for me, so I need to get back, play this part well, and complete this job.

A lot hangs in the balance, and I know the only way I'm getting rid of him is by giving him the truth.

"If I'm here, I can finally get my revenge." He frowns, and his brows furrow as a bird takes flight above us. For a moment, I track its path before glancing back at him, knowing he will be waiting. He would wait forever if I asked him to. That's how Crux is. Once you have his loyalty, you have it for life. "The people who killed my family are within these walls. I finally have a chance to find the truth and get revenge for what they did."

My heart races, and a pain that never goes away fills my chest.

I've not been able to draw in a full breath since that night. Crux made it better, but my chest is always tight and filled with a ball of agony. I'm close to the people who could have lifted the blade to end my family, so I can't back down now.

He's quiet for a moment before he pulls his hands away. "Okay."

"Okay?" I frown. "What does that mean?"

"It means okay. If you are doing this, then we are doing this." I blink, and he grins. "You didn't think I was wearing this uniform just for you, did you?" He winks.

"Crux," I begin, but he steps back.

"You better get going. Don't worry, I'll see you around." He gestures to his eyes. "I have eyes and ears everywhere, Alyx. You know that. You're not alone here. I'm here with you. You will get your revenge, and then we will go home."

Home . . . But what will be left when we are finished?

I truly don't know, but I nod anyway.

"Good. I have some things to do if we are going to do this right. I will find you later." He waves me on, and I give him another searching look.

"I'm glad you're here," I admit before turning and slipping away. I needed him to know because I am. Knowing he has my back when the blades are coming for it settles something within me.

Crux has always been my protector, fighting at my side, and I didn't want to do this without him, but I was prepared to.

"Alyx?" His voice is laced with humour as I glance over my shoulder at him.

He's leaning into the wooden wall as he runs his eyes down my body, and for a moment, that usual surge of desire rushes through me, almost making me shudder as my breath catches. When his eyes meet mine again, they burn with want before he covers it with humour, and I wonder if I'm seeing things.

Crux doesn't want me, not like that.

I would know.

"What?" I ask.

"You look good in a dress." He chuckles, dragging his tongue along his lower lip.

Narrowing my eyes, I flip my finger at him. "Shut the fuck up."

CHAPTER
SEVENTEEN

ORION

Everyone moves out of my way as I storm through the palace, nobility and servants alike. Most of the staff here are afraid of me, but today, my bad mood must be reflected on my face because everyone is staying out of my way. They usually avoid me purely due to my large size and constant frown. Joha says I look intimidating and I should smile more, but he makes keeping him safe so difficult that smiling isn't something I do often.

I march through the hallways and out into the palace grounds, wincing against the brightness of the sun. I've been in countless meetings for too long, listening for hours as the council and Queen Mother went around in circles about Alyx and how they can use her against Jade Empire. I'm not surprised by any means, but they haven't even waited for the dust to settle and they are already planning ways to use her.

Although I hate to admit it, Alyx played the role of betrothed princess perfectly. She has an air of expectancy about her that royalty tends to carry. They are so used to having everyone run to do their bidding that they automatically just expect someone to cater to all their whims. It seems like she might fit in despite my fears. Everyone appears to believe her story, and it's been announced to everyone that the princess is officially betrothed to the king.

It's all anyone is talking about, which partially adds to my sour mood.

Joha was excused from meetings after the announcement, which meant he disappeared as soon as he had the opportunity. Queen Mother and the advisors continued with these meetings, which I was allowed to attend. They didn't use to let me, but I argued that if the king wasn't in attendance, then I needed to be so I knew of anything that might affect his safety. They agreed reluctantly, but I'm not allowed to speak unless specifically addressed.

I hate meetings. Although they try to hide it behind veiled words, all they speak of is ways to run the country without checking with the king. Today was no different, except they have a new target to talk badly about—Alyx.

My bad mood has only worsened thanks to a comment Queen Mother made during the meeting. It was more of a passing remark, but I picked it up and filed the information away for later, registering it as a potential problem.

"One of my ladies-in-waiting told me that the princess enjoys frequenting the ale houses back in her empire. We shall have to make sure she is aware that will not be accepted here."

Her prim, tight voice plays through my mind, only making my scowl deeper. Who started that rumour? I don't know, but I'm determined to find the culprit. Rumours were always going to start about the mysterious princess that materialised out of nowhere, especially because she's essentially taken the king off the market. Jealousy, hurt pride, and ego all lead to catty behaviour like this. However, this can be a dangerous combination and cause those rumours to spread and twist, growing into something different altogether. I've already overheard one of the young lords joking to his friends that he heard the princess is a partier. Rumours spread quickly here, since many of the nobles excel in gossip, not having enough to keep them busy. However, in this situation, it could quickly get out of hand. This type of gossip can ruin lives.

Rounding the throne room, I step out into the main courtyard, passing two young female courtiers. Attempting to remember some of my manners, I dip my head in acknowledgement, but neither of the ladies seem to notice me in the slightest.

Snorting, I shake my head, once again disparaging the nobilities' entitlement, and continue my task of finding the king.

"Did you hear about the new princess?" one of the ladies asks the other, their heads close together as they gossip. Usually, I wouldn't even dream of listening in, but the mention of Alyx has me straining my ears—not that they are even bothering to keep their voices down, probably assuming no one will overhear them in the courtyard.

Slowing my march to a casual walk, I try not to make it look like I'm blatantly listening into their conversation, even though I don't believe they would care. I may come from a noble family, but at the end of the day, I'm a guard who's barely better than a servant in their eyes.

"Apparently, her father cut her off to try and stop her from drinking," she tells her friend, her voice becoming shrill. "So instead she sells herself to earn money!"

Her companion shrieks, her eyes widening as the two of them clutch each other, revelling in the juicy new gossip they can spread around the palace.

Fuck.

They are speaking of Alyx. Even if they weren't, they can't tell lies like that about a *princess* from another land. I doubt they even believe it themselves, but that doesn't matter. They have their ammunition, and they are prepared to use it. Heat spreads through my entire body as I try to contain myself.

"How dare you speak about your future queen that way," I snap, freezing in place and glaring at the two ladies like they are my new recruits. My muscles tense and bunch up around my shoulders, making me seem larger and more intimidating. It's not something I mean to do, simply my body's reaction to stress, but it doesn't help with my rough reputation. All of my fury is aimed at the young ladies, and I know it's probably not fair when they are just sharing what they heard, but I can't seem to rein myself in. "You realise that you could be hung for treason spewing venom like that, yes?"

I don't know why I'm so angry. Sure, I don't want any of this coming back on Joha, but the idea of them speaking about Alyx that way has me seeing red.

It's to protect the king.

Yes, it's to protect Joha, I tell myself, feeling a little better about my overreaction.

The courtiers look afraid, their eyes wide and faces frozen with fear. They hold onto each other for comfort now rather than for companionship as before—not that I particularly blame them. I just appeared around a corner and started threatening them with death. I think I would be afraid too. Well, perhaps not, but I'm not a young lady who has little to no defensive skills.

Fantastic, now I'm scaring ladies who are barely into adulthood. Is that really what I want to become? They stutter and stumble over their words as they try to come up with excuses, but I just wave them off, my anger slipping away.

"Just go. Don't let me hear you saying anything like that again."

They don't bother to stick around to see if I change my mind, spinning on their heels and hurrying away, darting scared looks over their shoulders as if they are worried I might follow them. Letting out a long, weary sigh, I rub my hands over my face. Today has been a long day, and it is only just past noon.

Grumbling to myself, I turn my back to the retreating ladies and start walking once more. I know exactly where the king will be, making my job easy as I stride across the grounds until I come to one of the tranquil gardens. The grassy area surrounding a large lake is hardly a garden, but who am I to quibble with the scholars who made it? Separate from the palace buildings but still within the protection of the walls, it's one of the few places Joha can escape to without the constant presence of the lords and ladies who want the king's attention. Most of them won't come out this far in case they soil their outfits, making it the perfect escape. Sometimes when you're here, you can forget that you are still on palace grounds.

Everything is so quiet and peaceful.

Cresting a small hill, I frown at the scene before me. Yes, the king is here as expected, but that's not the problem. The cause of my frown is that the four guards who should be within arm's reach of the king at all times are sitting on a grassy knoll several metres away from him. From there, it is impossible to protect him properly, something I demonstrate as none of them notice my approach. This only angers me more. Each one of them will be reprimanded and removed from this sought-after position.

Joha is sprawled against a tree trunk at the lakeside, book in hand. He looks peaceful, and for a moment, he could be any young lord enjoying a sunny afternoon, except he's not.

He's the king, and he needs to start acting like it.

"Your Majesty." I know I sound more like I'm scolding him rather than greeting him, but I can't help myself. Besides, Joha is used to me constantly being frustrated with him, so this is a fairly usual greeting for us.

The guards crap themselves, jumping up to try and get into position before I notice they broke formation, but it's too late, I've already seen them. "You four will be dealt with." Expression dark, I look them over with disappointment and shake my head. "Return to the barracks. I'll find you when I'm ready to deal with your incompetence."

Their faces show how disappointed they are, knowing this will cause them to lose the roles as king's guards. The benefits of this position reflect the responsibility and trust they are granted, and they just broke that trust. The guards say nothing to try and convince me to let them keep their jobs. They know better than to try and reason with me. The king's safety is their whole job and something I won't compromise on. I taught them better than that.

Dismissed, the four of them begin their walk back to the barracks, leaving me alone with Joha. I'm breaking my own rules by leaving the king without four guards, but we all know I can protect Joha better than those four put together.

"You're too harsh on them." His voice is threaded with amusement.

Raising my brow, I turn to look down at Joha, who doesn't glance up from his book. I swear he does this on purpose to mess with me. It's either that or he genuinely doesn't care about his own safety. The risks he takes are making me go prematurely grey, one of the reasons I keep my head shaved.

"They are your guards, Joha. You're too easy on them! They didn't even know I was here. If I was an assassin, you would be dead by now."

Being alone, I don't bother to hold back my frustrations. Right now, he's my pain in the ass friend, and I'll speak to him as such. He will always be my king, but there are occasions when he needs to hear the truth without it being brushed over with courtly, flowery language.

Lowering the book to his lap, he looks up at me with a grin, his eyes sparkling. "I guess it's a good thing you're not an assassin then." He smiles and sits upright, leaning forward and resting his elbows on his knees. Taking in my frazzled state, he raises a brow and tilts his head to one side. "I take it this isn't about my guards."

Perceptive as always.

"Yes," I snap back, crossing my arms over my chest. "Your *betrothed* . . . ," I seethe, the words tasting acidic on my tongue. "There are rumours going around about her, and they are only getting worse. Queen Mother has already heard them. You need to sort it."

Waving off my concern, he stands and smiles at me in a way I'm sure is supposed to reassure me. "Oh, they are only rumours. Don't worry about it, old friend. Everyone will soon forget it, and I'm sure they will welcome her."

Something about what he says suddenly triggers something in my mind, and a memory rushes to the surface. I'm in a similar position, except the male standing opposite me was the old king, Joha's father.

He looks like an older version of Joha, the familial resemblance between the two uncanny. He squeezes my shoulder in a comforting gesture, his smile filled with kindness.

"I'm honoured that you think I deserve your protection, Orion, but I have my own guards."

I had yet to join the guards, and Joha and I were practically joined at the hip. Due to this, I spent a lot of time around the king, and honestly, he acted more like a father figure to me rather than a ruler.

The previous night, I'd overheard a rumour about one of the king's guards. After sleeping on the information, I'd immediately gone to see him the next day.

"I don't trust them, Your Majesty. I heard that one of them is a thief from the city." My young face is pulled into my signature frown, my body tense and full of nervous energy.

Realisation fills the king's eyes, and some of the good humour leaves his expression. "I know the rumour you speak of, but I'm choosing to trust the guard in question. He's worked for me for a while now."

Startled by his response, I shake my head. "But—"

He stops me before I can get started, squeezing my shoulder again and giving me a kind but firm smile. "Orion, you will make a brilliant guard one day, but you must learn to trust others."

The memory fades away, and Joha's face replaces that of his father's. The old king was too trusting, and I had been right about the guard. Many priceless treasures were stolen, but thankfully no one was hurt in the process.

Joha seems to be following in his footsteps. It means that he's a fair ruler, but he is also manipulated by others. He immediately trusted Alyx, an *assassin* nobody trusts. Then there's me, who is at the complete opposite end of the spectrum.

Shaking my head, I cluck my tongue. "You're just like your father. Too trusting."

Joha's eyes flash at the mention of his father, and I immediately feel bad for bringing him up, but he smiles, hiding his sadness. "Is that a bad thing, old friend?"

No. The old king was a great man and kind in a way that nobility doesn't tend to be. He always saw beyond his own needs and genuinely tried to help his people—not just the lords and ladies in his court, but the workers in the city too. However, that's not the point I'm trying to make right now, so I simply raise a brow.

"It is if you want to survive long enough to have this grand wedding of yours," I point out.

Rolling his eyes, Joha turns and takes up his spot against the tree trunk once more, facing towards the lake. "Stop moaning and come sit down with me for a bit."

Grumbling, I do as he says, mumbling my complaints under my breath as I sit beside him. This is exactly what I disciplined the guards for, but I'm constantly aware of my surroundings and who is close by. I may make it seem like a chore to be here with Joha, but I love spending time with him like this. It reminds me of a simpler time, when it was just the two of us.

I suppose with Alyx around, things will never be simple again.

Why does that thought send a thrill through me?

CHAPTER
EIGHTEEN

JOHA

Aimlessly wandering around the palace, I attempt to make it look like I have a purpose. In fact, I *do* have a reason to walk the palace halls and grounds. I'm on a rumour hunt.

Despite how it looked to Orion, I was more upset by the talk of rumours than I let on. It did not help that he wouldn't tell me anything about them, causing my mind to spiral with all sorts of questions, which is what led me to this ridiculous mission I am now on.

From what I've learned, everyone essentially believes that the princess was banished from her empire because of various addictions and unsavoury vices. Of course, I know who she really is, but it has me wondering about these vices. Is what they say true? There have been several variations of the rumour now, and I was hoping that the more I heard, the easier it would be to piece together what the original story was. Currently, each version seems to be getting more and more vulgar.

No one will say anything around me, so I've taken to hiding

around corners and listening into conversations. This isn't easy with my four newly appointed guards hovering around me. If one of my advisors or council members sees me, they would think I've lost my mind. Because of this, I ordered the guards to warn me if anyone is approaching so I can listen in confidence.

What has my life become?

Thankfully, Orion is currently off duty, probably scaring some children somewhere or scowling at anyone who gets near him. My secret rumour mission would be impossible if he were here.

As I wander through one of the large hallways looking for my next target, my eyes light up as a figure steps through an open doorway and into my line of sight.

Alyx. My betrothed.

Of course she notices me immediately, a smile gracing her lips as she turns towards me. My steps suddenly feel like they have more power behind them, and I find myself in front of her within seconds.

"Your Majesty," she greets demurely, dipping in a curtsy. She is all poise and grace, but I can see the ironic smile on her lips as she dips her head.

"Princess, it is lovely to see you." I do not have to lie because she is gorgeous and a sight to behold. My mood is already lighter. When she glances over her shoulder, I realise she is alone—something a future queen should not be. "I am surprised to see you here alone. Have you not been assigned ladies-in-waiting or guards?"

Her eyes flick to my entourage behind me, then she glances over her shoulder and does a slow spin. When she returns her gaze to me, I see amusement in her eyes.

"Oh! I seem to have lost them."

Her performance is impressive. Most would believe she is just an airhead princess who lost her way and is stumbling around. Of course, I can see the mischief she tries to hide in her expression and know this is not the case. She probably managed to escape them within minutes.

I have to hold back my laughter.

I cannot say any of this though, not with my guards listening in, so I simply smile and nod my head. "Do not worry, my future queen. Will you walk with me? I can return you to your palace."

"I would love that, my king." Looking up at me with adoration, she flutters her eyelashes, and I have to hold back my snort. Alyx does not strike me as the type who has ever preened for a man, not unless it was for a job that is.

With a gesture to my guards, I order them to step back, giving Alyx and me as much privacy as a king in his own palace can receive. Offering her my arm, I stifle the thrill in my chest as she takes it, her side brushing up against mine.

We resume walking and step through the doors she just came through, exiting the building and moving out into the palace courtyard.

"I have heard some interesting things about you today, Princess," I say conversationally.

"Oh? I have been here for less than a day. What could they possibly be saying?" Her voice is light, but there is an edge to it. She does not like this new development.

"Rumours," I begin, flashing her a quick look before staring ahead once more. Unable to stop my curiosity, I veer to the right as we come up to another building, using the wall to shield us. I know we can still be seen, but I find that I suddenly have this burning need to know if the rumours are true.

"Is it true that you frequent brothels to earn coin? Or that you are addicted to ale?" As soon as the words leave my mouth, I know I have made a mistake, but it is too late.

Her look of confusion at my abrupt detour quickly shifts into one of outrage and anger.

"How dare you!" she says loud enough for the guards to overhear, and then she steps closer, lowering her voice so only I can hear. "*That* is what you want to ask me?" I see the real Alyx under the illusion of the princess, and it is a shock to see the sudden difference.

"You think I became the finest assassin in the realm by sleeping around?"

Ah, shit. I have offended her pride, a dangerous thing to do to a woman like her who could easily kill me in seconds. I have made a colossal mistake, and I believe I am about to pay for it.

"I cannot believe that is the first thing you ask me. Not if I have any information on who is trying to *kill* you, but about my nocturnal habits," she hisses low enough for only me to hear. Fury ripples across her face. "Do you remember why you hired me? I am *not* Princess Alyx of the Jade Empire. That person doesn't exist, meaning neither do the rumours." She looks at me with disgust, making me feel about one foot tall. "Get yourself together, or maybe you really are a puppet king after all."

I was going to apologise until she said that.

Maybe you really are a puppet king after all.

Anger and mortification surges through me, and I know if I do not get away from her soon, I am going to lash out and say something I should not. Gritting my teeth, I turn to my guards and gesture for one of them to approach me.

"Take Princess Alyx back to her palace, and make sure that she is reunited with her guards."

Seeing the understanding in the guard's eyes, I turn and begin walking away without another look at Alyx, my remaining guards hurrying to catch up. The second I step out of the shelter of the building, I feel eyes on me. There are too many people around for me to feel this way. I need to retreat and find somewhere to calm down.

Stalking towards my palace, I leave Alyx behind.

IT'S BEEN hours since I saw Alyx, the sun long since having set, yet I am still furious. I should be sleeping, or at least preparing for bed, but that is impossible while I feel this way. Pacing the length of my bed chamber, I attempt to think of anything but her, yet it is impossible. Her words continue to ring through my mind.

Yes, it was stupid of me to get stuck on whether those rumours were true or not. She created the persona, and therefore the rumours were never going to be real. I was foolish, and upsetting her was the last thing I wanted to do, but her reaction was also unexpected.

How dare she speak to me like that? I am her king. Even if she were a princess, she would not be allowed to get away with speaking to me like that. My ego has been bruised, and I want to lash out. Hiring her and concocting this plan was *my* idea. This is my attempt to take back control, to make a stand with as little bloodshed as possible, yet somehow, I am still being manipulated by a woman.

Is it fair of me to think of her that way? Probably not, and I do not want her punished in any way for speaking to me like that. She was right. My head was not in the game. I got caught up in the ruse and being around a beautiful woman such as her.

I must remember we are different.

The king and the assassin.

My insides are churning, and my mind is a mess. I barely ate anything at supper, something Orion noticed with a frown, but he didn't comment on it.

Alyx did not attend the meal, claiming a headache.

For some reason, this only made me angrier. At this point, I do not know if I'm angry at her or myself. Probably a bit of both, yet her final parting line haunts me.

Maybe you are a puppet king after all.

Of all the things she could have said, she went straight for the jugular, choosing the one thing that was bound to cripple me.

The thing is, this is not the first time I have heard those words—maybe never to my face, but they have not ever affected me in this way. When she said them, it made me question everything and want to tear the world apart in the same breath.

Taking a deep breath, I walk into my bathing chamber and turn on the cold tap, filling the sink basin. I splash my face with the frigid water, gasping as it touches my skin. I stand to my full height, my reflection catching my attention. Usually, I use the mirror to admire myself, yet tonight, I do not recognise the person staring back at me. My fingers brush the mirror as if to check it is real. The cool glass confirms that it is, and I'm forced to admit that the wide-eyed, angry-looking male is me.

Am I a puppet? Am I ridiculous for believing that I could ever stop being controlled by others? I thought Alyx could help me with this, but perhaps I am just a fool.

A call from outside alerts me to the changing of the guard, meaning that it is much later than I thought. Sighing, I rub my hands across my face before reaching for a towel to dry it.

I should go to bed, yet I know I will just be tossing and turning for hours, my mind too active to shut off right now. Glancing over to my closet where I keep my sword, I stride towards it.

I am too angry to rest, and I need to get some of this out of my system before I see Alyx again. Now is the perfect time for me to slip from my rooms: while the guard is changing over and they are distracted. Orion will be cross with me for leaving in the middle of the night on my own, but I *need* to do this for my sanity and to prove to myself I am not a useless puppet king.

CHAPTER
NINETEEN

ALYX

Nighttime is my favourite time. The darkness shields us assassins like a cloak. It's when we do our best work, moving between shadows and eavesdropping on whispered private conversations, and here, in the palace, it is no different.

To everyone else, I am Princess Alyx, the new, perfect queen-to-be, and that restricts me slightly. They all think I'm dumb and easy to manipulate, but they don't want to speak outright treason in front of me. A coup would change everything, and even an airhead would recognise conversations of that as a threat to her husband-to-be. As soon as the sun set, Princess Alyx went to bed and assassin Alyx came out to play.

I'm still annoyed about what Joha said. He practically accused me of being a whore, which I have no problem with. Many of my friends are whores and it's honest work. They have to work harder than most to survive, but it was the way he said it, like I was dirty and I had used my body to get where I am, not trained for years to make my way to the top. Yes, it infuriated me. I don't even know why. I never usually care about others' opinions of me, especially not a spoiled puppet prince. However, Joha has looked at me with nothing but awe and a healthy dose of fear since the moment he met me . . . but today, he looked at me differently.

I don't like that, which annoys me even more.

Hence, I'm stalking around in the dark, hoping to kill someone to let off some tension. Feelings are confusing and downright annoying, but killing is much easier, so I'll stick to that. His Majesty can go fuck himself. I'll complete this job and get everything I want.

It doesn't matter what he thinks of me as I do it. I have been called worse, much worse.

Words wash away, as does blood.

I focus on my work, sneaking around the palace, hoping someone is foolish enough to show their head so I can cut it off and throw it in that smug king's face and watch that disgust transform back into fear. Petty? Maybe.

However, I don't seem to be in luck. Everyone is being good little citizens tucked into their beds, bar the guards. I do find two fucking in the stables, others playing a game of yu-long, and some drinking when they should be guarding, but that just makes my job easier.

I'm running across a roof, my annoyance pounding in my head to the beat of my heart, as I head back to my new quarters that are attached to the king's by a small bridge when I hear it.

I cock my head, watching a figure dance smoothly across the packed dirt floor, followed by the sounds of grunts and a sword hitting a target.

The king's palace and the adjoining queen's are at the very back of Moonshadow Palace, tucked away from everything else, so there is no excuse for anyone to be here, especially not so deep. The stone gives way to dirt and then to trees beyond. Carved into that dirt is a rough practise arena I had barely noticed until now.

It's not one for the guards. No, this one is much bigger.

Targets line the arena's edge near the trees, with arrows shot perfectly at their centres. More hang from their branches, with gauges cut into the wood. Some are scattered on the dirt ground, forgotten and chopped to pieces, but it is the man in the centre who is captivating, and I do not look away from him as I crouch on the roof. The moon shines down on him, bathing him in its light like a lover's caress. Gone are the royal robes, and in their place are leather trousers and an untucked, loose black shirt. His hair is wound on the top of his head, his feet are bare and filthy from the dirt, and his muscles bulge as he swings the giant longsword in a practised, perfect arc.

Crouching lower, I remain enthralled. I cannot stop watching him.

The king is practising with a sword, and as I eye him, I realise two things.

One, he is very good with it, fast and precise. It is clear he knows exactly what he's doing.

Two, he is angry and wants to be alone.

I called him the puppet king and practically told him he was dumb and useless, but as I watch, his expression transforms into one of fury as he swings the sword above his head and then down in a slash before bringing it back up in a horizontal line across his face to protect from an imaginary blow. My lips tilt in a smile as his back leg slides backward and he leaps into the air, spinning in an impressive display as he spars alone, thrusting and cutting with his sword. If he had an opponent, I have no doubt they would be on the ground, yelling or dead.

Flinging his sword into the air, he catches it with his other hand, twisting it around his body as he spins, and with a roar wild enough to shake the mountains, he brings it down into the dirt with a clank. He kneels there, panting and covered in a sheen of sweat, his impressive muscles tightening under his clothing.

I thought him weak and useless, but hiding under his royal façade is a smart, calculating swordsman.

I was wrong, which never happens, and I cannot stop myself from silently dropping to a crouch behind the palace. When I straighten, he spins, his eyes widening as he holds the sword loosely at his side. We stare at each other, both shocked and wary.

I should have known better than to underestimate anyone.

If he can fight this well, then why didn't he the day he was attacked in the Lowers? It's what circles through my thoughts as I watch him, his strong jawline clenching as he waits for me to speak. He lifts his sword slightly, as if anticipating an attack and ready to protect himself.

Smart man. An assassin only comes to you in the dark for one thing—death.

"You look angry, Your Majesty," I remark, tilting my head as I run my eyes over him brazenly. He jerks, not expecting that. As far as decorum and rules go, he is practically undressed. His loose blouse gapes open almost down to his navel, showing his impressive pecs and abs. His trousers are tight enough that I can see a bulge running down one leg, and I purposely bite my lip before meeting his eyes. "Very, very . . . angry."

"Go away, Alyx." It's a command, and it almost sounds cruel. He is trying to brush me off, but I won't allow that. I like this brazen king. I like him rough and real. There are no robes, perfect façade, or dumb smile.

This is the true Joha, I realise.

"What? Don't want your new whore queen seeing you like this? Don't you know whores like our men sweaty and feral? It makes it that much more fun when we break them," I taunt.

His face tightens. Gone is the young, clean-faced boy pretending to be king. In his place is a stern, dark-eyed man, bristling with anger and unleashed fury. His body vibrates with it, making him a weapon down to the one he is holding.

The part of me that craves danger screams for more, for me to taste his blade and find out just how well he can fight.

"You really do not know when to stop, do you?" he growls.

"I have never been accused of being shy." I smirk as I pull my sword and twirl it effortlessly in the air, stepping around him. He follows me, moving to keep me in his line of sight.

Good.

"This might even be fun," I murmur, "though I don't expect you'll be much of a challenge. You're such a pretty spoiled king. I bet you practiced on servants who were not allowed to fight back. That sword"—I nod at it—"has not even tasted blood." Lifting mine into the air, I look boldly into his eyes before running my tongue along the edge of my blade, smearing it with my blood as it cuts my tongue. "Mine? It's tasted blood more times than I can count."

"You are trying to make me angry." He frowns, calculation flashing in his eyes. "You want me to attack first, but it will not work." His eyebrows lift. "I will not spar with you."

"Why not?" I flip my sword, holding it to my shoulder so the point is facing behind me. "We both know you need to burn off steam, and my hunt is unsuccessful tonight, so let's have some fun. No rules. You're not the king, and I'm not an assassin. We are just two people ready to push their bodies to the limit. Unless, of course, you're scared?"

It does the trick. No matter how smart a man is, he can't take a blow to his ego like that. Instead of rushing me like I expected, though, he plays it smart, and my estimation of this man's restraint and talent goes up.

He does, however, bring his sword up and slide his back foot backwards in a defensive position. "Fine. If you wish to fight, Alyx, then let us fight."

"Thank fuck, I thought we were going to talk all day." I take the initiative and race at him, darting left and right as his eyes track me, trying to figure out where I will attack. Just as I reach him, I move left, and he brings his sword up, but I spin to the right, slashing across his arm and stopping behind him. I see his blouse gape from the sharp edge of my weapon as I whisper in his ear, feeling him stiffen.

"Is that all you have, Your Majesty? I'm disappointed." He spins, and I step back in time to deflect his attack.

Laughing, I deflect his blows, and using my speed and strength, I slam my sword into him and push him back. He stumbles, his chest heaving as he watches me. He spins his blade, bringing it up.

"Enough talking," he mutters.

"Fine with me." I grin, and this time, I wait for him to attack.

He doesn't disappoint. He feints left and then right before hitting me head-on, and then there is no time for talking or teasing. We dance across the arena, our swords singing as they come together. He's stronger, but I'm faster and practically feral. He's still clinging to the way sword fighting should be won and using the rules, but I don't. I kick dirt at him, blinding him as I parry until he stumbles back, and I finally land another hit on his side.

Rules are made to be broken, and playing by them does not keep you alive. It just means you are a righteous fool when you die.

I would rather be alive and playing dirty.

Laughing, I smack his ass with the flat of my sword, not wanting to cut that perfect, round muscle. "Stop holding back. You won't hurt me, so give in to your anger," I taunt as I circle him. He pants angrily, watching me, but he's still restrained. "Let it fuel you, fill you. Think of everything they call you. Fool. Spoiled. Useless. Puppet. Take it and use it. Here, there are no rules, and no one is watching. It's just us, so fight!"

I slash at his side again, and he snarls, slamming the pommel of his sword at me.

I dodge it with a laugh. "What are you so afraid of, Your Majesty? That you'll like drawing blood? That you won't be able to go back to that perfect, little box you put yourself in? Don't be so naïve and weak. In this world, it is kill or be killed, something you know well. They are coming for you, and here you are, still holding back. Why should I bother helping a fool onto a throne?"

His eyes darken, and he bares his teeth in a feral smile. "No assassin can hand me my throne."

"Yet that is what I am doing, is it not? What, did Daddy not give his spoiled boy everything on a platter, so now he's angry?" I pout as I taunt him.

Mentioning his father gets the reaction I wanted, and I have to duck the sword I did not even see coming. He flung it at me like a dagger.

I jerk my head up, my eyes wide. "That was rude," I say, but he's sprinting at me.

I fling myself forward, rolling under his attack before getting to my feet. I see him slide across the dirt and grab his sword before he comes to a stop. His head snaps up, his eyes locked on me.

Oh, this just got good. It's about time.

I do not even have time to think as he comes at me, his sword a blur. His movements are fast and precise, if slightly feral. Good. I let go as well. I shed the cloak I always wear, a civilized façade, and we become animals, grunting and clashing swords, dirt smearing across us as we fight. My heart hammers with joy and adrenaline, and my need for bloodlust controls me. I don't hold back, even when I slash at the back of his knee. Luckily, he moves fast to avoid his tendon being cut, but it does slice his pants. It seems to infuriate him more, and he hammers at my sword as I hold it up to block his blows. He hits it over and over before his knee comes up and smashes into my chest, sending me flying back.

The air leaves my lungs in an audible woosh, but I ignore the slight twinge in my ribs and go low, sliding between his legs and slamming my elbow into the back of his knee. He goes down hard, and I press my sword to his neck.

I expect him to yield, to relax, but his hands come up and grip the blade, cutting his palms as he yanks. He uses my blade like a pole to pull me up and over his head. I hit the dirt hard, my back smacking into it, and for a moment, I'm disoriented. It gives him the opportunity he needs. He presses his sword to my throat, his lower body trapping mine. His head blocks out the moon, and all I see is him.

Both of us are panting and dripping with sweat and his blood, and our hearts race so loudly I can hear them.

Anger and bloodlust morph into desire for a moment as I stare into his dark eyes. He blinks, his gaze dipping to my lips as he lowers his head. I freeze, sure he's about to kiss me.

Need blooms between us, born from anger and adrenaline, but I know kissing the king would be a mistake, so I do the only thing I can think of to stop it—I slam my head into his.

He falls back with a yell, clutching his nose as I spin to my knees and lift my sword. "Cheap trick. You didn't really think I would fall for that, did you?"

My voice is tight, though, because I almost did.

I nearly let the king kiss me, and part of me is angry that I didn't. Fool. I squish that down with anger as he watches me. "Had enough?" I taunt, needing to push him, needing to fight off these feelings that I don't like. I roll across the ground, meeting his sword, and he gets the picture.

Luckily, he doesn't call me out on what happened. Instead, he fights back.

He meets me blow for blow as we once more dance across the clearing, our swords ringing true. My movements are quick but emotional, and he sees it. His gaze is observant and calculating.

That's the only reason he manages to do what he does next.

He swipes under my angry strike, hitting my arm with his sword.

Both of us freeze, and my eyes track down his outstretched sword to see my blood dripping from the tip. Panting, I drag my eyes higher, across my arm, and see the small, shallow cut there.

He landed a blow.

He cut me when no one else ever has, not even Crux.

"You cut me," I murmur, my fingers coming up to touch my blood in disbelief.

"You cut me first," he snarls.

"Then I will again," I growl.

I go to attack, but he grabs my sword, pressing the tip to his neck. "You win."

"No, don't you dare just let me win," I hiss.

"I'm not letting you win." He smirks. "You've landed five hits and cut me five times. I cut you once, so you win, and now I'm exhausted. I need to dress my wounds before my people have questions, and you need to get back before they see us. We have not exactly been quiet."

"Fuck that. Let's go again," I demand.

"No, we are done." He pushes my sword away and bows. "That was the best fight I have had in a long time." He puts his sword away and walks past me, giving me his back, trusting I won't attack.

"This isn't over!" I call.

He glances over his shoulder, his eyes twinkling as he meets my gaze. "Good, I hope not. Sleep well, Princess Alyx."

CHAPTER
TWENTY

CRUX

She doesn't know I'm watching her.

I know she's capable, and I know she can look after herself, but I can't resist trailing her as she prowls around the palace, searching for information and her target. I have my little rats working overtime, so I know we will gather some information we need, but she is a target, especially now that they all know her face.

I cannot resist protecting her, even now.

When I see her meet the king, however, fury and jealousy twine inside me. I hide in the shadows and watch them, a vice around my heart as they spar. It's something she used to do with me. I do not think she even realises she is smiling and enjoying herself with him.

I hate it. I hate the way she looks at him.

I hate the way he looks at her as well, and when he pins her down, both of them getting far too close, I swear I feel my heart break. I cannot look away, even as he drops his head to kiss her.

How many times have I had the same thought while we were sparring? Far too many, and now this man, this stranger, this . . . this fucking king is going to steal her kiss. For all her bravado and assurances, I see her hesitate. I see her giving into him. Her eyelids slide shut to kiss him.

My soul splinters, and the agony is hard to breathe through. It feels like I'm shattering into a million pieces right here in the shadows where I belong, where I cannot reach her in the light.

She smiled at another man, a man worthy of her and who is also level with her station, a man that can give her everything she deserves and more.

Did she lie to me about all her reasons for being here? Is she lying to herself? Does she want the king? The thought nearly causes me to sprint from the darkness, but I don't. I stay here and watch as they break apart, as he cuts her and then walks away.

I stay in the shadows where she left me.

My heart is trapped in my throat, a fluttering, broken thing as I watch her right up until the moment she heads inside, and then I turn away, trailing the king. My heartbreak and pain turn to anger, which is directed at him for seducing her away from me and being a man she could love.

She cannot if he's not here.

It's an irrational thought, a foolish one, but my hand goes to my blade. I am not even thinking as I stomp after him, uncaring who sees as I chase the king, ready to end his life for daring to look at my Alyx.

She is mine!

I move on instinct, my hands fisting the dagger, ready to drive it into his back and end his pitiful life. She might mourn him and hate me for it, but she will be mine again. He is oblivious, playing with the tattered edges of his cut shirt as he walks between the shadows of his palace and the one she is staying in.

No guard, no protection.

A vulnerable king.

My assassin's blade gleams as I draw it and move closer. I am about to strike when I see it, and I blame my own consuming emotions for not seeing it before—a figure. It darts out of the shadows of the small bridge separating the palaces and heads right for the king as he passes. I see a blade gleam and blink.

He's stealing my idea, but I react before I can think.

I throw my blade, and it soars through the air with a whistle before sinking deep into the man's shoulder. His hand twitches, causing him to drop the blade with a gasp, and the king whirls. I am a blur as I head to the cloaked, wannabe assassin. Plucking my blade free, I grip the cloak's edge and slice the man's throat, letting the blood spray over the king as he looks wide-eyed from the fallen dagger that was aimed at his back and the man dying in my hold.

He struggles before giving in, and I drop his lifeless body to the ground. My need to kill the king disappears as quickly as it came. "You should be more careful," I warn, my voice deep.

I know all he sees is my silhouette before I fade back into the shadows as he searches for me, leaving him with the body and the blade.

If this is what she wants, then so be it. I will help her. I will kill them and free her of her revenge and her job. I will end this entire world before I lose her, even to a king.

Alyx is mine. She always has been and always will be. She just doesn't know it yet.

I won't wait a moment longer. I will make her aware. I was so worried about ruining us before and losing what we had, but I did not realise until it was almost too late that I was already losing her.

Not now.

My eyes go to her palace, where I see a lantern on inside, and my hand drifts to the carving below my belly button, above my trousers.

I made it the night I met her, when I realised what she would mean to me.

My fingers trace over the familiar, scarred letters as a new deter-mination fills me.

ALYX.

She will be mine.

CHAPTER

TWENTY-ONE

JOHA

My whole body aches in a good way, and I know I am going to be covered in bruises come morning. Despite this, I have never felt more alive. Adrenaline courses through my body, and although it is the middle of the night, all my fatigue has vanished, dispelled by our little sparring match.

I was so lost in my own world that I did not even know what I needed. She found me when I least wanted to be found, especially by her. This should not have been a surprise to me, as the woman is like a bloodhound, sniffing out any display of weakness.

The very last thing I wanted to do was to spar with her, needing solitude to clear my mind, but Alyx is not the type of woman who can be denied, and she goaded me into a fight.

I knew what she was up to then, but looking back now, I recognise that she was trying to give me what I needed—an outlet for my anger. While I could have sucked it up and refused to fight with her, which would have been the sensible option and what I would have done with anyone else, with her it is . . . different. There's something about her that does something to me. She awakens me from this façade.

I let everyone believe I'm placid and easily manipulated while silently trying to keep my power. However, over time, my mind has begun to slow from having all decisions made for me. I didn't realise it until now, though, when she literally smacked it out of me, but I've let Queen Mother and the advisors get to me.

If I'm honest with myself, hiring Alyx was my last-ditch attempt at doing something, *anything* to try and regain control, and if this doesn't work, then I fear I will either be killed by an assassination attempt or I'll truly become what they whisper about behind my back—the puppet king.

If anyone found us, there would have been serious repercussions. Not only is it heavily frowned upon for women to wield a sword, but Alyx was not holding back. She's easily one of the best swordspeople I have ever fought against, and it would have raised suspicions if she had been seen fighting like that. A princess from another land who can fight better than most of the guards in the palace would cause major concern, and questions would be asked that could destroy our whole plan.

Was this a stupid, risky idea? Yes, and for far greater reasons than being discovered. I was out here without a guard, fighting against the self-proclaimed deadliest assassin in the land. No one knew that I had left my palace, and as a consequence, they would not know where to begin looking should anything have happened to me.

I may have landed a blow on Alyx, one I only feel the smallest twinge of guilt for, but I have no doubt that in a fight to the death, she could beat me. She would have to work for the kill—I have made sure to keep my sword skills up, training with Orion in secret—but I am not arrogant enough to think I could beat an assassin. My trust in her may make me gullible. She's even told me herself that I am stupid to put my trust in her, and if anyone else had devised this plan, I would agree with her. Still, I cannot seem to push away this instinct deep in my gut that tells me she is the key. The key to what, I'm not sure. The throne? A thriving kingdom under my rule? Happiness? Am I naïve to hope for all those things?

Probably.

Sighing, I shake my head at myself as I hurry across the palace grounds, sticking to the shadows as I make the short journey back to my quarters. Glancing up at the sky, I take in the position of the moon and realise it is far later than I thought. Orion is probably about to check on me, so I need to be quick and get back before he finds me missing.

A high-pitched whistle, one that a blade makes as it flies through the air, instantly puts me on alert. It is a sound that I know well, thanks to Orion's insistence on training in throwing daggers. It's knowledge that could very well be about to save my life.

Dropping into a defensive stance, I spin on the balls of my feet as the dagger makes contact. However, it seems that I wasn't the target after all. Eyes wide, I stare at the stranger who was steps behind me as I process what just happened.

The man's face is covered, and the light of the moon glints off his dagger. His blade falls to the ground as he grunts and presses his hands to the blooming wound in his shoulder, where he had just been hit by the whistling dagger. The weapon in question protruding from his skin is not one I recognise, and it certainly doesn't belong to my guards.

Cursing under his breath, the male glances around for the owner of the dagger. His eyes snap to me, and I watch as he makes his decision to carry through with his mission before he begins to move towards me.

That's when it hits me—this man is here to assassinate me.

All of this happens within a fraction of a second, my brain trying to process everything as my hand moves automatically to my waist, reaching for the sword I'm no longer carrying.

I'm not going to be able to stop him before he reaches me, and although he doesn't have a weapon, I have no doubt that he is skilled in hand-to-hand combat. Blood pounds in my ears, each thump of my frantic heartbeat reverberating through my head as I try to focus. My chest is tight with tension and adrenaline, as I've been caught completely off guard.

However, the mystery owner of the dagger magically appears behind my would-be assassin, materialising from the shadows like a wraith. Before I can blink, he reclaims his dagger and uses it to slit the assassin's throat.

I watch in mute horror as the male's blood pours like a fountain, splattering me in the process. The warm liquid rolls down my skin, and I know I should be disgusted by this, but I am too busy focusing on my saviour. He drops the assassin's body, letting him fall to the ground and lie in a heap, clearly having no care for the person he just killed.

My eyes stay on him. His body is no longer obscured by his kill, but all I see is a cloaked figure stepping back into the shadows.

"You should be more careful." His voice is deep, and although it is said as a word of advice, it feels more like a threat.

Before I can say anything, the male is gone. Stumbling forward, I try to follow him, but he seems to have disappeared completely, as though he were made up of shadows and dissipated now that his task was complete.

I press my hand against the wall and lean forward, squeezing my eyes shut as I take several deep breaths. What in the underworld just happened? I'm alone and still in danger, so I need to pull myself together and get back to my chambers before any more assailants jump out from the shadows.

You are the king, I remind myself. *You have dealt with worse things than this, and with Alyx's help, you will reclaim your power.* Those words become a mantra in my mind.

You will reclaim your power.

Perhaps if I manifest it, it will happen. No, I *will* have what is mine. Once Queen Mother has been dealt with, the assassination attempts should stop. Alyx is my secret weapon in all this.

For some reason, just thinking of her gives me strength. Letting out a long breath, I push away from the building as I turn to face the body that has been left behind. Groaning at the mess he made with his blood, I shake my head and close the distance between us.

I crouch down and remove his face covering. I am not sure what I was expecting, but I feel a flash of disappointment when I see the unrecognisable face. Of course Queen Mother would choose someone who could not be traced back to her. She is smart, which is how she has managed to keep power for so long.

Huffing out a breath, I stare at the face of the dead man at my feet. The assassin has been assassinated, how ironic.

What I really want to know is how the fuck he managed to get so close to me without me knowing. If I had been alert, I would have heard him, but my mind was elsewhere. I know better than to let myself get distracted. There are threats everywhere. If anyone were to ask me, I would tell them that this was a skilled assassin, which would explain how he managed to slip past all the defences and get so close. Really, I let myself get caught up in my thoughts of Alyx and our sparring match—not that I will ever admit this aloud.

Now, I have the corpse of an assassin at my feet and his blood covering me like a macabre painting. Although I have the training to defend myself, no one in the palace will believe that I took down the assassin. However, I can hardly admit that a mysterious cloaked figure killed the man because that would raise too many questions, including why I was outside of my rooms in the first place.

Not to mention the stranger who came to my rescue. The voice was that of a male, so I know it was not Alyx in disguise. She would have been my first guess, especially seeing as this is one of the reasons I hired her in the first place, which begs the question as to who would risk sneaking into the palace grounds and saving me from an attack. Did they know in advance about the attempt on my life, or were they here for other nefarious reasons?

Now that is a thought that causes a shiver to run down my spine.

I have so many questions swirling around in my head, the most pressing of which is lying at my feet.

How in the underworld am I going to get rid of this body?

CHAPTER
TWENTY-TWO

ORION

There is something different about tonight. I can't place why exactly, but I have this feeling in my gut that I have learned to trust over the years. Something is wrong.

The hairs on my arms stand on end, and no matter how much I try to push the ominous feeling away, it grows until it is impossible to ignore. Growling under my breath, I push up from my bed in the barracks and quickly tug on my uniform. I'm technically off duty, but there is no way I can sleep with this nagging feeling in my stomach.

Stalking from the building, I head straight towards Joha's palace, walking around the perimeter and checking for signs that anything is amiss. Nothing. Everything is suspiciously quiet. With a tightness in my chest, I enter the palace and head straight towards the king's bedchambers.

All of the guards are stationed where they should be, every one of them alert and greeting me with a respectful nod of their heads. None of them dare to question why I'm here when I'm off duty and not in bed. This isn't the first time that I've been to check on the king in the middle of the night, and it won't be the last. I don't stop until I reach my destination—the door to Joha's bedroom.

"Anything to report?" I ask roughly, looking between the two guards stationed in the doorway. No one should be able to enter the room without passing these two, so if anyone has come or gone or anything untoward happened, they would know.

The guard on the left shakes his head slightly but otherwise doesn't move, as per protocol. "No, sir. All is quiet."

Turning to focus on the other guard, I tilt my head to one side as I scan his face. He must feel pressure under my scrutiny, something that is shown by his Adam's apple bobbing in his throat, but otherwise, he doesn't move.

"The king retired to bed several hours ago and has not left his room since, sir."

Glancing between them, I weigh their words and slowly nod my head. The king's guards, who are stationed by Joha's bedroom, are chosen due to their diligence and hard work and are rewarded by being closer to the king. Although Joha hates having his every move watched, he agreed to the guards being outside the door if he could have complete privacy in his bedchamber. It was also agreed that the guards were to be as unobtrusive to the king as possible. As such, these guards are like statues, silent and unmoving unless needed.

I believe them, yet I am still unable to shake this feeling of something not being right.

"I'm going to check on the king. As you were," I tell them and reach past them to open the doors.

Entering Joha's chambers as quietly as possible, I make sure the doors are closed behind me before passing through into his bedroom. However, I'm almost immediately brought up short when I see the king's empty bed.

A combination of panic and dread holds me captive for a moment as I stare at the space where I should have found the king sleeping. It only takes me a second to break out of it, and I curse as I race forward, touching the sheets, only to find them cold. Wherever the king is, he's not been in bed for a while. With my heart in my throat, I force myself to calm down so I can focus on what needs to be done.

If I thought he was in danger, then I would immediately call the guards to help me find him. Gods, I would wake the whole cursed palace if it meant I could find him safely. However, this is not the first time he's wandered from his room during the night to get some air, and if that's what this is, then it would cause more problems than it's worth to get everyone involved in a search party.

Taking a deep breath, I consider my options. There's a known assassin staying in the palace and playing princess, and that should give me the answer I need right there, but for some unfathomable reason, I trust her not to hurt him—even if that's only because it suits her own purposes to have him alive and on her side.

If I hold off and delay getting help, resulting in Joha getting hurt because of how long it takes to find him, then I would never forgive myself. The very reason I'm here is to keep him safe. However, his physical safety is not my only priority, but his mental state too. If Queen Mother found out that Joha goes for midnight strolls, it would have severe consequences and take away the little freedom he currently has.

That would destroy him.

Gritting my teeth, I do one final sweep of his rooms, confirming that he's not here, and then I make a decision that I could live to regret. Cursing, I storm from the king's room, shut the doors behind me, and ignore the guards there. They'll probably be wondering about my foul mood and the fact that I was in Joha's room for less than a minute, but they don't dare say anything. They are too professional to do that. Besides, I don't exactly have a reputation for being warm and fuzzy.

Joha better be alive because when I find him, I'm going to give him a piece of my mind. He's been so reckless recently. People are trying to kill him, but he seems to think he's safe when he's here because of his guards—guards that he currently *doesn't* have with him.

Anger fuels me as I storm through the grounds, not caring about the cool night air against my skin. Thankfully, I don't have to search too hard for him as I'm pretty sure I know exactly where he will be.

There's one place on the palace grounds that he finds the most peaceful, and I would bet a year's salary on him being there—the lake. It's quiet, and for a while, you can almost forget the rest of the palace exists. None of the staff or residents of the palace go there, either too busy with their work or worried about staining their exorbitant clothing. Nature isn't something that seems to attract the lords and ladies. That's probably another reason why the king likes to disappear to the lake, knowing he'll get some peace. I've found him there on several occasions without his guards when he needs to escape, and with everything that's happened today, I can't say I blame him.

Winding my way through the maze of palace buildings, I head towards the lake when I hear a strange noise. Frowning, I slow my pace and listen for it. I hear the sound again and freeze, trying to make it out. It's almost like a cross between a drag and shuffle, but I don't know what would cause it. There aren't any guard patrols around this part of the palace, and no one should be wandering around at this time of night. Tilting my head, I attempt to work out where it is coming from.

There.

There is a small clearing between two unused back buildings. It's almost completely closed in by the structures, and the space is only really used as a cut through to reach other parts of the grounds more quickly. However, I'm sure that's where the noise is coming from, and despite my burning need to hurry and find Joha, my gut is telling me I should check it out.

As quickly as I can manage while trying to stay silent, I hurry over and walk along the side of the building until the wall opens up into the clearing. I peer around the corner, and my eyes widen and my chest goes tight at what I see.

Joha, the king, is covered in blood and attempting to drag a body across the clearing.

Moving faster than I have in a long time, I race across the space until I'm at the king's side, pulling him away from the body and looking for the source of his injury. Content that he's not going to die on me immediately, I glance around for any threats, scanning the dark corners of the clearing and the rooftops in case the attacker is still around. There's a dead body at the king's feet, and I doubt very much that Joha was the one to kill him. While I know the king has the skill, he's not the type to unless he has no other option.

Assured that we're alone, I turn my attention back to the king, scanning his body once more. My heart pounds so loudly that it almost drowns out all other sounds, but I force myself to focus. The king needs me. "Your Majesty, you're hurt. Tell me where the injury is. We need to stop the bleeding," I order, my voice even and smooth, not showing even the slightest hint of fear. "I need to go raise the alarm."

Joha has just been staring at me in a state of shock since I appeared at his side, resembling a fish as his mouth opens and closes without any sound. However, this seems to snap him out of his daze, and he grabs onto my arms and pulls me to a stop.

"Orion, no! I'm not injured. You can't tell anyone about this. You have to help me hide the body." He's pale, all the blood having drained from his face, and his eyes are wide, but his grip on me is strong. Relief floods me knowing that he's not injured, but it quickly vanishes as I absorb the rest of his comments. *Hide* the body?

Feeling exasperated, I frown and shake my head, gesturing to the large patch of blood on his clothing. "Joha, you're covered in blood and you're dragging the body off." I trail off as I notice the dagger lying on the ground beside the body. My heart sinks as I make the connection. The wolf symbol carved into the hilt of the blade is unmistakable.

That dagger belongs to a guard.

Leaning down, I gently roll the body over and sigh when I recognise the face of one of the palace guards. My head hangs heavily for a moment as I process this. I'll have to discover his name and find a way to contact his family to let them know of his passing.

"A guard is dead, Joha." Sighing again, I push up from my crouch and meet the king's gaze, knowing I'm about to say something he won't agree with. "Someone needs to know."

His expression shifts into one I've seen many times before, his stubborn streak showing as he moves past me and grabs the dead guard's arm. "No. I am sorry, friend, but I cannot allow that."

He only gets half a step before I grab the back of his shirt and haul him to a stop. If anyone else tried a move like that, they would be tried for treason with me at the head of the trial, but there are some perks to being the king's best friend and head of the guard.

"Have you lost your mind?" I bark out between clenched teeth, anger burning hot in my stomach. I firmly believe in respecting the dead, especially a guard who has given his life to protect his king, so seeing said king dragging his body around is infuriating. "What in the underworld are you doing?"

Finally losing his composure, Joha shakes me off and jerks his hand towards the body. "This man tried to kill me, and now I need to hide his body!" Anger laces his tone, but I hear the undercurrent of shock that he's trying to hide. Now that I look more closely, I see his hand trembling slightly.

As a soldier, my mind processes things differently and I'm able to compartmentalise, removing the fear from a situation so I can focus on what needs to be done. That skill can make me appear like I don't have feelings or that I'm cold-hearted. In most cases, I don't care, as that is what helps me survive. Occasionally, like right now, I have to remind myself to switch that off so I can understand how others might be feeling.

Joha was almost assassinated tonight. He could have died.

A flare of panic bursts in my chest so hard it almost takes my breath away, followed quickly by fury that threatens to overtake all. I want to rage at him that this is exactly what we've been trying to avoid by forcing him to have guards with him at all times, but I know now isn't the time. I might be his protector, but I will always be his friend.

Huffing out a sigh, I step forward and place a hand on his shoulder again, but unlike last time, this is a gesture of support. "You're okay, Joha. You're alive. Tell me what happened," I coax, needing to get through to him. The longer we're out here, the more at risk we are of being found.

Joha meets my steady gaze with a wide one of his own. He's lost in his own mind right now, and I watch as his Adam's apple bobs in his throat.

"You are sure he was a guard?" he finally croaks out, looking down at the body again.

Releasing his shoulder, I cross my arms over my chest and grunt in answer. "Yeah, he's new, but I recognise his face." I try not to be impatient or shake him and hope answers fall out, but we really can't risk being out here much longer. "What's going on here, Joha?"

Sighing, the king puts his hands in his pockets, his expression reluctant. "I was unable to sleep, so I snuck out and went to the old training ground to let off some steam."

My blood pressure shoots through the roof at his comment and my whole body tenses, but I don't interrupt him as he continues his story. He tells me about how Alyx found him and goaded him into sparring with her and how he was followed when he was returning to his room. When he tells me of his cloaked rescuer, I think I'm going to have a heart attack. Someone tried to kill the king, but before they could, someone else killed the would-be assassin. If this person was friendly or of honest intent, then they would have stayed around to make sure the king was safe, not hidden their identity and threatened him.

There are some serious lapses in security that allowed all of this to happen, and I *will* get to the bottom of it. However, what worries me the most about this whole story is the sparkle in his eyes when he speaks of Alyx. This is an assassin, someone who is only here to help him because he is the highest bidder and it suits her, and he's talking about her as though she's a shiny new toy. This is only going to get Joha hurt or killed.

By the time Joha finishes his story, I'm pacing, and he's watching me with a resigned expression. He knows he's in big trouble. He's been at the end of my dressing downs on more than one occasion before, so he knows it's useless to protest.

There is so much I want to say, and my mind is a twisted mess as I try to understand the absolute stupidity that caused him to leave his chambers in the first place.

"What if someone saw the two of you sparring?" I say through gritted teeth. "That was beyond careless. She's an assassin, Joha!" Seeing the stubborn set of his jaw, I know I'm not getting through to him, so I take a deep breath and try to focus on what's important. "I'm assuming that the guard's attack was another assassination attempt courtesy of Queen Mother. Do you have any idea who the cloaked male who saved you was?"

Shaking his head, Joha raises a hand and brushes back his usually pristine hair. "I didn't recognise his voice, and I had no idea he was there. I think it's safe to assume that he wasn't from within the palace."

Wonderful. We have a dead guard turned assassin and strangers with deadly skill from the outside wandering in and out of the palace grounds as they please. I need to speak to the guards and increase security around here as soon as possible. We've obviously become too lax.

Sighing, I rub my hand over my face. "Go back to your rooms, and for the love of all that's holy, don't leave until I come for you in the morning. I'll sort this out." We both know I'm referring to the body.

A look of profound relief floods his face. He trusts me to handle this with discretion and doesn't question me further. The less he knows about what I'm going to do next, the better.

Uncharacteristically quiet, he nods slowly in agreement and turns to leave.

"Joha," I call before he gets far. "This isn't the end of this. We will be talking about this." My no-nonsense expression tells him how serious I am. His safety is one thing I won't compromise on, and I'm not afraid to shout at the king if it means he won't do something this stupid again.

Looking sheepish, Joha nods, turns, and jogs towards his rooms. Waiting until he's out of sight, I roll my shoulders and neck, wishing I could escort him back. However, I have a job to do.

Growling down at the body, I prepare for a long couple of days. I need to discover if there are any more traitors in the guard, in *my* guard, and I need to make sure the palace is properly protected. An assassin was killed by an assassin.

Shaking my head in disbelief, I bend and lift the dead guard, throwing him over my shoulder. Usually, I'd have more respect for the dead, but this man attempted to commit treason, and I have zero respect for people who try to hurt my king.

Where was Alyx during all of this anyway? It seems convenient that she disappeared during the attack. I'll deal with that in the morning, but for now, I have a body to bury.

Checking that the coast is clear, I cross the clearing and head to the place that I'd been heading to anyway, and the only place where you can hide a body without anyone finding it—the lake.

CHAPTER
TWENTY-THREE

ALYX

My hand drifts to the small cut on my arm. It's not even bleeding anymore, but the skin is torn. I sweep my hand over it, smiling as I remember my shock at Joha landing that blow. Shaking my head at the foolishness of what we just did, I drop my hand and turn away, leaving my torn, bloody clothing on the floor of my rooms. I will need to move them before my ladies-in-waiting attend me in the morning, but for now, I'm alone and allowed to be just Alyx, not the queen-to-be.

I hurried back after Joha left, not wanting to be caught slinking around. Something about our encounter unsettled me anyway, so I wanted to get away so I could clear my head.

The candles flicker brightly, casting my sprawling rooms in warm white light and shadows. I've been assured these are very good rooms, and my ladies-in-waiting seemed overjoyed, but to me, it is just another place to lay my head.

I have not had a home since that night, not even my room in Crux's kingdom.

My bed is set back in a rectangular addition to the suite with windows above it, which is currently shaded and covered. Before it is a sitting room with a formal table as well as all the knickknacks expected of a queen-to-be. To the left is a separate dressing chamber filled with more clothes than anyone could ever need, a mirror, and a vanity table. To my right is a private bathing chamber with a huge, clawfoot, metal tub and indoor toilet.

There are gilded decorations everywhere, along with ancient pottery and tapestries. It's like they took all the opulence they could think of and threw it into one room. Take the ceiling for example— they hid the wooden beams by draping red, gauzy fabric around it, creating a soft, cosy interior.

It works, settling the nerves inside me, which isn't necessarily a good thing. There are, however, lots of places to hide my weapons without snooping guards or ladies-in-waiting finding them. It was the first thing I did when I came in here.

Sighing, I slide a dagger back into the holster on my thigh, unable to sleep without one or two on my body. Wearing nothing but a blue sleep gown they provided, which I must admit is the comfiest thing I've ever felt, I begin the task of darkening the room from the many candles.

My mind drifts as I do.

I remember the look on Joha's face as he left me there. I remember the way it felt to spar with him. It felt good. He wasn't the king, and I wasn't an assassin. It was just Joha and Alyx.

Snap out of it, I tell myself. Annoyed at my own feelings, I lean over and blow out a candle, extinguishing some of the light leading to my bed.

I stiffen, bent over as the air behind me changes.

It's a slight shift, but one an assassin would recognise anywhere.

I'm not alone.

Dragging my blade from my thigh, I turn with a whirl and bring it up to gut whoever dares attack me, but I hit the bedding hard as a body clashes with mine, their hands capturing my wrist as if knowing my movements. My blade is flicked away, embedding in the wall to my left with a thud. I kick and twist, adrenaline fuelling my actions as I act on instinct. Freeing my hands, I roll us until the person is below me. I hold another dagger in my hand, having pulled it from my bedding, and press it to his neck before I truly look at who it is.

"Crux?" I frown in confusion, not understanding.

Using my hesitation, he flips us again, slamming my hands to the bed repeatedly until my fingers spasm and the blade drops. Gripping my hands in one of his, he presses mine above me, stretching me out below him. He sits on my thighs to stop me from bucking and freeing myself, and I freeze below him.

Annoyance and confusion swirl through me, as does a spark of desire as I stare into his tanned, scarred face. The candles flicker behind him, caressing his skin and lighting up his almost black eyes as he peers down at me silently.

I glare up at him as he grins down at me, a cocky, smug smile curving his lips. I jerk my eyes up and away from them, letting my irritation fuel me and ignoring the spark of desire that ignites inside me at being so close—pesky fucking thing. "What the fuck do you think—"

He cuts off my words with his movement, his head tilting down. His intention is clear in his eyes.

My whole heart freezes, my eyes widening, but I do not have time to figure out how to react because his lips are on mine. He nips, licks, and kisses my unmoving lips.

Crux is kissing me, tasting every inch of my mouth as I lie shocked beneath him. Of all the times I have imagined this, I never thought it would happen, and now he's here, in my rooms, kissing me . . . .

It's like the spell pops. My hands grip his back, my lips part, and he rumbles a satisfied groan, deepening the kiss. His tongue sweeps inside my mouth and tangles with mine as we duel for dominance and submission.

I've been kissed before—I am not a virginal maiden, after all—but I have never been kissed like this.

It's as if I am the air Crux breathes, as if he could not bear to part with me even for a second. We melt into one.

His hair hangs down around his face, shielding us, and his hard body pins me down more securely as he deepens the kiss. It's brutal and hard, just like him.

Perfect.

It's is better than I could have ever imagined, but annoyance fills me—annoyance because he waited so long and that he dared to kiss me right now, while my mind is on another man.

Unable to let him be in full control, I wrap my legs around his waist and flip us once more. My hands pin his above his head and my thighs bracket his waist, pressing my core to his rapidly hardening length. The feel of the huge organ makes my eyes widen as I perch atop it. He arches up, chasing me and kissing me harder.

"Are you happy to see me, or is that a blade?" I ask between kisses.

His lips tilt in a smirk. Sliding one hand down his body, I find a dagger in his pocket and tug it out, throwing it away. "Happy to see me it is," I murmur as his hands snap up, breaking my grip. His meaty fingers grip the back of my hair and pull me solidly down across him, holding me hard and fast as he bites and sucks my tongue until all I can do is moan and relent.

His knee suddenly wedges up and flings me back.

I tumble to the mattress as he crawls up the bed, stopping to kiss my chest over my rapidly racing heart, and then his lips are on mine again. Groaning, I fist his messy hair, tugging him harder against me until our teeth clash.

Desire so strong I choke on it races through my blood, heating me until I cannot take it. I roll my hips, needing more of his brutal, punishing touch.

Needing to be lost in him.

All the years of repressed desire, wondering, and wanting from afar erupts between us until we fight to get closer and gain the upper hand.

We fall from the bed with our momentum, and I grunt as my back hits the wooden floor. When I hit a post, I jerk away and slap his face in warning. His head jerks to the side, his brown hair still gripped in my fist, and when he slowly turns back to face me, my heart stutters at the gleam in his black eyes—pure hunger.

I gasp when he lifts me to my feet with just one arm, throwing me back against the post as he forces himself between my thighs and kisses me. The power of our bodies rocks the table behind me until I hear something smash as it hits the floor, but I don't care.

I reach up and tear away some of the gauze attached to the wooden ceiling, wrapping it around his throat and yanking him back. My feet hit the floor as I step away, touching my raw, bruised lips as we both pant.

We stare at each other, shock and desire reflected back at me in his eyes.

The very things I am feeling.

"Run, little assassin," he growls.

I turn to race to the closest weapon, but he hits my back, knocking me to the floor and flipping me. More decorative items fall around us as we hit them, and his mouth finds mine once more.

I dig my teeth into his plump lower lip, making him growl like an animal as he jerks above me. "Alyx," he warns.

"Crux," I retort, licking the sting as I stare into his black eyes.

Snarling, he cuffs my throat and kisses me again. What was hard and feral turns drugging and loving as we kiss leisurely, like we are making up for lost time, until we break away.

Our foreheads press together as we pant.

As I come to, blinking away my desire as much as I can, panic winds through me, and he must see it in my eyes.

We crossed a line we never should have crossed.

I'm going to lose him, lose everything—

"Shh, don't. Don't think right now. For one moment, let's just be.

Tomorrow doesn't exist; neither does yesterday. It's just now, just us and how much we want each other. No other worries."

I nod my head slowly, relaxing at his words, and he kisses my forehead. "Just us," I whisper.

I do not know why Crux kissed me or why he came here tonight, but I cannot be sorry or even regret it. I have wanted to kiss Crux since I was a girl, and it was better than I could have ever imagined.

It felt right, like we were made for each other, but it does not stop my shock or secret delight.

No, I don't know why Crux kissed me, but I can't seem to care right now—not with his taste on my lips and him looking at me like he is debating eating me alive.

CHAPTER
TWENTY-FOUR

CRUX

I can feel Alyx spiralling. She wasn't thinking when I kissed her, just acting, and I don't want her second-guessing or, worse, regretting what we did. Instead, I carry her to bed, holding her in my arms like I have so many nights before, and kiss her softly until she relaxes once more.

"Sleep, Alyx," I command.

"Crux," she starts, fisting my shirt, our legs entwined together. Something has shifted between us now. I crossed the line I said I never would. She kissed me back though.

She wanted me.

My years of worry disappear into triumph and desire so strong, I'm almost unable to contain it.

"Tomorrow," I promise as I kiss her head. She's stiff at first, and I can almost hear her spiralling thoughts, but I stroke her back, not letting her go, and she finally relaxes until she falls asleep where she belongs.

In my arms.

My lips curve in a smile, and I know I just won a battle. My other hand drifts up, stroking my bruised, throbbing lips. My bottom one is bleeding from her teeth, and I hiss in pleasure and pain as I trace it.

Kissing her was better than I could have ever imagined. I don't know why I waited so long. Oh, right, I didn't want to lose her, but I already was. I could feel it. Panic consumed me until I ended up here without realising it. It wasn't a logical thought. It was instinct.

I saw her here, surrounded by wealth where she belonged, and I imagined my life without her.

I needed her to understand that everything I have done is for her, so I kissed her. I crossed that line, and I don't regret it one bit.

How can I with her taste on my tongue and her body in my arms? Maybe it was selfish to kiss her after seeing her with him, or maybe I've been a fool for waiting this long, but I will not lose my Alyx.

My entire existence, my entire life was built for her, and now she will never escape me.

I have a piece of her, and she owns all of me.

I close my eyes, soaking in her softness and warmth, and remember where it started all those years ago . . .

Rain blurs my vision, and the stolen coins jangle in my pocket as my hands are finally cleansed of the blood I spilled. I feel sick at what I did just to be able to eat, but it was him or me. I need this money to survive, to eat, and to live at least another day.

The stone walls of the nobles' houses line each side of me. Their lights are off in the early hours of the morning as darkness threads through the streets, so it's just me and the rain as I tip my head back, letting it wash me clean even though I feel like I never will be again.

I darkened my soul tonight, and I will do it again.

That's when a noise reaches me above the pelting rain. Cocking my head, I drop my eyes to the street with a frown. My lanky, skinny frame shivers in the cold despite spending most of my life outside. I have survived it all, yet that sound cuts me to my core like nothing ever has before.

Someone is crying.

I track the sound. Years of having to watch my own back have made my senses sharp, even over the pattering rain. Heading to the side of a noble's house, I find the source.

It's a young girl, but it's hard to tell her exact age. She is cowering in a white sleep dress stained with blood. The bottom is ripped and coated in mud, sticking to her soft, pale skin. Her hair hangs in wet, bright orange waves, and her arms shake as she wraps them tighter around herself. She lifts her head when she hears me, squeezing her eyes shut in fear.

She's a few years younger than I am and absolutely terrified.

"Hey, it's okay. I won't hurt you."

She whimpers, tightening her arms around herself protectively.

"I'm Crux. What's your name?"

She doesn't answer for a while, so I crouch and wait, and when she realises I'm not going to pounce and hurt her, she sniffles. "Alyx," she whispers, her voice soft and small.

I smile reassuringly as she glances at me. I know what she sees— tattered, holey clothes I managed to steal and long, unkempt hair.

I am the total opposite of her. Even covered in blood and rain, it is obvious she comes from money.

"Are you okay, Alyx?" I ask as softly as I can, blinking away the rain.

She hesitates before shaking her head.

"Okay." I press my knees to the hard stone, ignoring the way it hurts. "Do you want me to take you back to your family?" The second the word is out of my mouth, she begins to sob harder. "Okay, okay, I won't. Hey, it's okay. Don't worry, I won't let anyone hurt you. I promise." She lifts her head. "I promise, Alyx. How about you come with me and we find some shelter from the rain? Get you warmed up and fed?"

It will cost me all my coin, but I don't care. I can earn more, despite my earlier misgivings about what I did to get it.

I hold out my hand, covered in dirt and dried blood. She swallows, looking from me to it. "Promise?"

"I promise," I vow. Staring into her bright, glassy eyes, I realise some very important things.

This girl will be everything to me, and I will do anything, give her anything so I never have to see her cry again.

I am nothing but a street rat, a homeless boy, and I know what I have to do.

She lost her home, so I will build her another.

I blink the memory away and look at the sleeping woman beside me. I don't want to go, I want to spend eternity with her in my arms, but I know she will need space to think through what happened. I know my Alyx better than I know myself, and I don't want her to be upset.

I place a lingering kiss on her forehead. "I love you, Alyx. I have since you placed your trust in me that night, and one day, you will be ready to hear that," I promise softly, and then I slip from her bed.

I set my gift down with a note and slip out of her room and into the dawn, a smile I cannot get rid of branded across my face.

CHAPTER
TWENTY-FIVE

ALYX

My dressing room is packed full of women I don't know, all poking and prodding me with critical eyes and making my sour mood even worse than it already is. Standing in a room full of people while only wearing a see-through top is certainly not how I wanted to spend my morning.

I have no qualms about being naked in front of others and feel no shame about my body, so this isn't an issue. However, my skin is covered with scars, an occupational hazard and something you wouldn't expect to see on a princess's body. The last thing I want to do is blow my cover before I've even properly started.

Today is my first true day at court, and apparently that means having a dozen assistants and maids attending me. While perfectly capable of bathing and dressing myself, I know this is expected of someone of my status. What I didn't expect was so many of them fluttering around me like hummingbirds, their voices high-pitched and blurring into one as they bustle around me.

Two are working on my hair, and another is covering my face

with a light dusting of powder. There is a young woman who is working on my fingers, cutting, buffing, and painting my nails a pale, feminine pink. The other four or five maids are rushing around the room, exclaiming over dress choices and colour combinations.

To be honest, I zoned out a long time ago, lost in my own thoughts. My head is already pounding, and I'm dreading the day ahead. Despite sleeping like a baby last night, I'm exhausted, and if someone snags my hair one more time, I'm going to lose my patience and throw a dagger at somebody.

The fact that I woke up alone in my bed probably isn't helping with my mood. Realistically, I know that it's too big of a risk for him to be in my rooms. He shouldn't be in the palace, let alone my bed. I can only imagine the pandemonium that would ensue if was found.

All of this is true, and from my years as an assassin, I knew better than to expect him to be there when I woke. Feelings are dangerous; they cause you to make mistakes and get you killed. All of the lessons I've learned in my life have taught me this over and over again.

However, my head and heart have very opposite opinions. While I *know* all of this, I can't help but feel disappointed that he didn't stick around. Last night felt like a monumental moment, and he just . . . *left.*

We had a moment . . . more than a moment.

He kissed me.

He surprised me, but I quickly kissed him back without thinking. Things could have gone a lot further, and I *wanted* them to go further at the time, yet I'm glad he stopped us when he did. Sex will just complicate things, and I want to keep things as uncomplicated as possible, at least until I figure out what in the underworld is going on.

Fantasies of the two of us together have passed through my mind in the privacy of my rooms on dark, lonely nights, but I never thought that anything would ever actually happen. He's Crux, king of the underworld. Besides, a kiss doesn't mean anything, not in our world, but why does it feel like it means everything?

Crux has always had my back, and I trust him more than anyone else in this world. He's been the only constant in my life for as long as I can remember. Last night alone proves how much I trust him.

I fell asleep in his arms.

I've never fallen asleep with anyone else in my bed, always kicking my bed partner out before then. A person is at their most vulnerable when they are asleep, and I don't allow myself to be vulnerable.

Ever.

When I woke, I found he had left me a letter promising that he would be back and we would talk, but instead of calming me, it only put me on edge. I destroyed the letter as soon as I finished reading it, not wanting to risk it being found.

It doesn't help that I'm being prodded, poked, and changed into the image expected of me. Tired, frustrated, and grouchy are just the beginning of my turbulent emotions this morning, and being pushed around is only making my mood worse. I've played many roles in my life, and while a princess was never one of them, I've acted as a maid to noble ladies enough that I know what happens.

One of the young women tries to pry the cami from my hand, holding it tightly to my body, and I bare my teeth at her in a snarl, momentarily forgetting the role I'm playing. The maid jumps back as though I actually bit her, clutching her hand to her chest. Good. That will teach her to ask before grabbing a stranger's clothes.

Madame Kane, the strict, matronly woman who arrived this morning with the troupe of maids and ladies-in-waiting, walks over to me with a heavy frown, her arms crossed over her ample bosom.

"Princess, you must release the camisole if we are to get you dressed."

The chatter in the room quietens as all attention turns to me and the madame. It's clear that she takes no nonsense and isn't used to people refusing her staff's help. She might be below me in hierarchy, but that doesn't stop her from staring me down.

My first reaction is to lash out and tell her to back the fuck off, but I force myself to remember why I'm here. Racking my brain, I search for a reason that would make sense.

I raise a delicate brow as I fall back into character. "Where I am from," I begin, my voice soft, "it is an offence to see the undressed body of a royal."

The madame's eye twitches as she realises I'm not going to back down on this matter. Swallowing back whatever retort she was going to bite out, she smiles tightly and dips her head.

"Then perhaps you will allow the two who bathed you to get you into your undergarments?" Her expression is so rigid, it looks as though her face is about to crack. "They have already seen you undressed. The others and I will wait in the other room until you are covered."

Getting me to agree to being bathed by others had been a battle in itself. I had insisted that I was able to bathe myself repeatedly, but that was a fight I wasn't going to win. Madame Kane explained that they would be remiss not to bathe me and would be punished if they did not complete their duty. After a long discussion, the madame and I came to an agreement that only two ladies would assist me in bathing.

They have already seen my scars, so it makes sense that if anyone is to see me naked again, it would be them. While it's more of an order than a suggestion, I reluctantly grit my teeth and nod my head. For the briefest of moments, a smile flickers on her lips, becoming real as I agree. However, it's gone in a flash, and before I know it, she's clapping her hands and ordering everyone else into the other room.

Finally alone with the two ladies from earlier, I drop my cami to the ground, exposing myself so they can begin their job. Neither of them bat an eye at my sudden nudity nor the scars on my body. However, I know they saw them when they were bathing me earlier from the hesitation I felt as they washed the largest of the marks.

As they quietly get me into the hellish undergarments those in higher society wear, I allow my mind to wander. Attending court is one of the main responsibilities expected of me as the future wife of the king, and although I'm dreading it, it will be a good opportunity for me to get the lay of the land. Women of high society are treated like pretty little objects to be seen and not heard, but really, they know everything that's going on. It's the perfect place to pick up on the newest gossip, and I might learn something about the plans to kill Joha.

Underwear, camisole, bloomers, petticoats, and a corset later, I'm ready for the rest of my outfit. Staring at myself in the mirror, I hardly recognise the woman in the reflection. My skin has been scrubbed and buffed and is glowing slightly from the bronzing powder they brushed over me once I'd bathed. The corset and skirts enhance my figure, giving me a curvier appearance, and my hair has been braided and twisted up on my head like a crown.

While I hate all the layers that restrict my movement, there is plenty of room to strap weapons to my body without anyone knowing. The corset is a hindrance, but thankfully I've trained while wearing a corset after almost losing my life due to one, so I know I can manage if necessary. Once the madame leaves, I'll see if I can convince one of the maids to select dresses that don't require corsets.

The ladies-in-waiting begin fluttering around once more, and I have to keep still as they drape me in fabrics. I hate this more than I can say, and my hands start to become twitchy with my wish that I had my daggers on me. Madame Kane watches on with stern approval, occasionally commenting.

Eventually, after what feels like hours, I'm ready.

Even I have to admit that the dress is stunning.

The deep forest-green dress has a high neckline that almost reaches my chin, hugging my collarbone and winging out over my shoulders in an armour effect. The rest of the bodice is just as form-fitting and would seem fairly modest if not for the peephole on the neckline, revealing most of my chest, only stopping just above my breasts where the bodice begins once more. There is golden detailing on the edge of the bodice, and light gold chains crisscross over my exposed skin.

Long, gauzy sleeves flow down my sides, giving the look an ethereal effect. The skirt itself is plain, the fabric layered artfully over my petticoats.

I may not be wearing a crown, but I look like a queen.

When they were dressing me, I thought they were going over the top for a session in court. This is the nicest dress I've ever worn, and to waste it on court seems like a crime. However, now that I'm looking at myself, I feel like I'm ready to tackle the day.

"I think you're ready, Princess." Madame Kane appears in the mirror behind me, and I slowly turn to face her. Running her gaze over me, she steps forward and brushes an invisible piece of lint from the dress, then she nods her head once. "Men wear their armour into battle, and it's just as fitting that you wear yours as you head into your own battlefield."

I'm surprised at her words, and it must show on my face because she gives me a rueful smile and steps back.

"My job is to keep you presentable and alive, Princess," she explains, gesturing towards the dress that hugs me like a second skin. "The ladies of court can be vicious. This way, they might think twice before attempting to sink their teeth into you."

Her words are a warning as well as an explanation, and it's one I'm going to heed. Meeting her gaze, I keep my own expression solemn and genuine as I speak. "Thank you, Madame Kane."

Surprise flashes in her eyes, and it makes me wonder how many entitled women she's worked with don't bother to thank her and the ladies-in-waiting for their work.

Shaking herself out of her stupor, she starts gesturing towards the door, pushing on my shoulders to get me moving.

"Come now, you're going to be late."

CHAPTER
TWENTY-SIX

ALYX

Downing the rest of my sparkling wine, I can't help but wish it were something stronger. I scowl at the bottom of the empty glass when it doesn't magically refill, huffing a frustrated sigh.

When I agreed to act as Joha's queen, hiding behind a pillar from courtiers was not how I imagined it. The one I am currently seeking shelter behind is only just wide enough to hide me, my voluminous skirts nearly giving me away, and I know that it's only a matter of time before I'm found.

Joha always refused a wife before now, and with my backstory bringing me from another land, I'm new and shiny, something everyone wants a piece of. Some are merely curious, while others are downright scavengers, trying to pick me apart for information about the king and our relationship.

The ballroom is large and grand, much like the rest of the palace. At the far end of the hall is a row of thrones, the largest of which is Joha's. Beside his is a slightly smaller throne, but it's no less grand, carved with crowns and roses, designed for his queen. Smaller thrones sit on either side of those. Men and women dressed in their finest court clothes fill the space, some dancing to the light music being played by a string quartet in the corner. However, most of the courtiers are doing what they do best—gossiping.

Standing in groups of three or four and clutching their wine glasses, they speak in low voices as they trade stories before moving onto other groups, and so the cycle starts again.

When I arrived, my ladies-in-waiting directed me through the crowd to the back of the hall where all the thrones were empty. Any thoughts that I may have had about taking a seat and watching from afar were quickly wiped away. There seemed to be a near constant line of people who wanted to speak with me. When I did have a moment of peace, my ladies-in-waiting were faffing around with my dress or brushing stray hair back from my face. All of the touching was becoming a little too much, so the moment I could, I snuck away.

Hence why I'm currently hiding behind a pillar.

Peering around the pillar, I spot Queen Mother sitting in one of the thrones, talking to several courtiers. I'm not sure when she arrived, but it's clear she's leading the court. My blood boils as I note which throne she's sitting in—the one for the queen. It's a challenge if ever I've seen one. She's testing me to see if I'll stand up to her or if I'll bend to her will. Madame Kane was right. Court is just as vicious as battle. We just use words instead of blades.

Challenge accepted.

Taking a deep breath, I brush down my skirts and force my face into a bright smile, then I slowly integrate myself into the crowd as though I was never gone. Ridding myself of my empty glass to a passing server, I smile and acknowledge those who notice me or call out as I pass. It doesn't take long for my ladies-in-waiting to reappear at my sides, looking relieved that they didn't lose me completely.

Locking my gaze on my target, I ensure my steps are smooth and graceful rather than the prowl of a predator, which is my usual walk.

"Queen Mother," I greet with a sweet smile, dipping my head slightly in greeting—I refuse to bow to this woman. "I believe you're in my seat."

Someone gasps quietly behind me, but I don't waver in my stance. From what I've gathered, no one messes with Queen Mother, and here I am, ruffling feathers on my first day.

I'm walking a fine line between oblivious, airhead princess and outright challenging her. If I want to keep this façade going, then I have to convince the watching courtiers that it's the former. With my smile still firmly fixed in place, I shrug my shoulders lightly as though this is a classic mistake and I'm gently reminding Queen Mother. Really, I'm putting her in her place, and from her narrow-eyed look, she knows it. The glare only lasts a matter of moments and is quickly replaced.

"Oh, my dear." Pressing her hand to her bosom, she slowly gets to her feet, her smile apologetic. "I do apologise. I'm so used to sitting here from when my husband was alive and I was queen."

Her excuse is about as believable as a crocodile in a dress masquerading as a woman, but the small gathering of courtiers around us coos and nods their heads as though it explains everything. Their disappointment hangs in the air, though, as they watch the two of us with predatory eyes, looking for any sign of drama they can share amongst themselves.

I clutch my hands together in front of me, tilting my head to one side. "It must have been difficult losing him and your title at the same time." Placing myself in the now vacant throne, I smooth down my skirts and reach over to squeeze her hand as she sits on the smaller throne to my left. "Even so, don't worry. I always get confused too."

"You're too kind." With acting skills that would rival that of the professionals in the royal theatre, she smiles in return, hiding her obvious disdain for me.

166

She returns to talking to the lady she'd been in discussion with before I forced her from the throne, and I'm saved from having to say anything more as my ladies-in-waiting bring over several of their friends to meet me. Everyone comments on my dress and how beautiful I look, and discussion mostly turns to who I know in the city— no one other than the king—and the weather, which is unseasonably warm for the time of year. The conversations repeat as one lord or lady is replaced with another, and I have to pinch myself discreetly to stay awake.

Queen Mother and I mostly ignore each other as courtiers come up to speak to us, and I'm starting to regret challenging her because now I'm stuck here. Boredom is driving me crazy, and I start playing a little game with myself on how many different ways I could escape the ballroom when I feel cool fingers on top of mine.

Glancing up, I see Queen Mother is the one whose hand is on mine, her smile polite but her eyes assessing. The courtiers around us seem to realise that we need some space and take a step back, giving us the pretence of privacy.

"It was a bit of a shock to hear that you and Joha are to be married. He never mentioned you before, nor any desire to take a wife."

Oh, I bet it was. While this may look like a casual conversation between two royals, I know that she's really trying to get information from me. Either that or she's attempting to sow doubts in my mind about my relationship. A future husband hiding the existence of his fiancée would usually signal a red flag. Of course I'm not worried about any of that, what with this being a fake relationship, but I still have to sell this. Queen Mother is already suspicious of me, so I can't risk blowing my cover.

"Yes, we kept the whole arrangement very quiet, but I couldn't be happier." I flash her a wide smile as I gush, pressing a hand to my chest as though I can't contain my excitement.

"Yes, I can imagine," she replies dryly, her eyes following the movement and flicking over my dress. "This will be a big change for you, I am sure." She pats my hand, her expression shifting into what I am sure she thinks is motherly, only it comes off as stiff. "If you ever need anything, please know that you can come to me."

That is never going to happen, but I nod solemnly, looking as though I'm taking her advice to heart.

Before I can say anything, she quickly clears her throat and changes the subject. "How is Joha anyway? Did he seem well this morning?"

She seems genuinely interested in my answer, which takes me aback. I've seen no fond emotions towards Joha from his stepmother, and this sudden change of heart makes me think there's more to her question than would appear. Not knowing what else to say, I allow my bright smile to dim a little and shrug lightly.

"I've not had a chance to see him this morning."

Nodding in reply to my comment, she smiles, but there is a twinkle in her eyes that puts me on edge. Something about my response pleases her, yet I can't seem to place my finger on it. My instincts are telling me that something is going on, and my hands itch to hold the daggers I managed to strap to my thighs before we left my rooms earlier.

A large figure appears in the corner of my vision, saving Queen Mother from being interrogated by me. Tilting my head, I look up at the handsome, hulking figure and take in his scowling expression. For once, he actually seems to be making an effort in hiding his blatant dislike of everyone. In fact, I swear I see shock pass over his face as his eyes land on me. It's gone within the blink of an eye, but I know I saw it.

"Your Majesties." Orion bows to us in greeting.

"Sir Orion, to what do we owe the pleasure?" Queen Mother asks loudly, drawing the attention of those around us. "I do hope that everything is alright with the king."

That's the second time she's mentioned Joha and whether he's well or not, and it's raising all of my internal alarm bells. Has something happened to him? No, I would have heard about it already if he was hurt. Perhaps she really does care about him . . . No, my instincts are telling me that I'm right. She knows *something*. I just need to figure out what that is.

"Yes, Queen Mother, the king is well. Thank you for your concern," Orion replies, dipping his head once more. "There is a matter I wish to discuss with the princess." His words are aimed at her, but he looks at me as he speaks, and I get the feeling that whatever he needs to speak to me about is related to whatever Queen Mother has been hinting at.

"Anything you need to share with her, you can share with me. Isn't that right, Alyx?" Saccharine sweet, she pins me with a look that would make most shrivel in their seats.

Thankfully for me, I'm not like most.

Smiling in apology, I get up from my throne before she can stop me. "If you'll excuse me, Queen Mother, this might be news regarding my family." Gesturing towards the large doors to the ballroom, I smile at Orion. "Please, sir, lead the way."

Sir. I want to snort.

The two of us leave the ballroom with calm, unhurried steps, and I'm acutely aware of the eyes on me as I go. My dress makes a soft swishing noise as I walk, and as soon as we leave the ballroom, Orion glances around before placing his hand on the small of my back and guiding me through a set of corridors until we reach a small, secluded room. He practically shoves me into the room, then he looks around once more and shuts the door behind him as he steps inside. Anger grew inside him as we made our way here, but he managed to keep it contained while someone might see us. Now that we're alone, though, I'm fully expecting him to rage at me.

Raising my eyebrows, I gesture widely as apprehension builds within me. "What's going on? Is Joha okay?"

"That's His Majesty to you, and don't play dumb with me." Jabbing a finger in my direction, he begins pacing the length of the room. "I'm sure you know everything going on in this palace, sneaking around after dark. You probably even know who the attacker was."

He's not even looking at me at this point, lost in his anger. I've never seen him like this before, and I'm so taken aback that it takes me a moment to digest what he just told me.

"Wait, attacker?" Standing up straighter, I go on alert, my voice sharp as I try to assess the danger. "Are you telling me that Joha was attacked?"

"Yes, last night after your little sparring match." Scowling, he shoots me a glare but continues pacing, his hands now flexing at his sides. "You couldn't hang around and make sure the king was safe? You just killed and ran, doing what you do best."

Oh, we're going for personal attacks now. Thankfully, I don't give a shit what he thinks of me, and I have thick skin. Stepping into his path, I hold up a hand to stop him.

"Hold on a second." Surprisingly, he does, glaring at me the whole time. Placing my hands on my hips, I give him attitude right back. "One, I have no idea what you're talking about, and two, I'm offended that you think I'd just leave Joha after he was attacked."

It's true. I might be an assassin, and my morals are pretty low, but Joha is my client and fake fiancé. He might be a dreamer in a world of naysayers, but he genuinely wants the best for his people. Despite myself, I kind of respect that.

Orion looks at me properly now, some of his anger draining away, and his eyes scan my face, truly taking me in. "You really didn't know?"

"No! Tell me what happened," I demand, and for once, he doesn't fight me.

Sighing, he scrubs his hands over his face. "After you and the king trained together, which we will be having words about, someone attempted to murder him. Before they could, a dagger flew out of nowhere and killed the assassin. Until now, I thought that the person who killed the attacker was you."

Queen Mother is still the top suspect for wanting Joha dead, but she wouldn't get her hands dirty by hiring an assassin. The fact that he was then killed by someone who didn't raise the alarm causes more questions. It can't have been a guard, as the whole palace would be talking about it if that were the case. My head is spinning with possibilities, but one thing keeps swirling in my mind—Crux was here last night. There's only one person in the kingdom who's better at knife throwing than I am and that's him. However, if it was him, then why didn't he say anything when he came to my suite? He hates the king, so I don't understand why he would save him.

"Where's the body? I might be able to identify who it was," I force out, breaking the thoughtful silence between us.

"Already disposed of. I couldn't allow a body to lie around and have it linked back to Joha in any way."

Damn. That's going to make things more difficult, although I understand why Orion did what he did. There are several groups of assassins in the city, and if I recognised him, then I would know who their master was. Once I knew that, it would only take a small amount of digging to find out who ordered the hit. Pursing my lips, I nod slowly as I think through my options.

"I'll take a look around and see what I can find out."

I expect him to snap at me about keeping my cover, but he surprises me by reaching out and brushing his fingers over one of the pointed shoulders of my dress.

"You might want to take off that ridiculous dress while you're at it. You are not exactly inconspicuous." He's looking at me like . . . I'm not sure how to describe it, but as though he doesn't quite hate me anymore. It's an expression I'm not used to seeing on his face, and it takes the sting from his words.

Snorting, I roll back my shoulders to show off the full effect of my outfit. "I rock this dress and you know it. I saw your expression when you first saw me in it."

Any softness that graced his face quickly vanishes, and he shakes his head with his signature frown firmly back in place. "You're so vain." Walking over to the door, he pauses and looks over his shoulder at me.

For a moment, I think he's going to say something encouraging about us working together, and I wait expectantly.

"Don't mess things up."

With those final words, he turns and leaves, shutting the door behind him and leaving me with the task of finding my way back to the ballroom.

"Bastard," I mutter under my breath, but my lips quirk up at one corner. I'll get him to like me before the end of this job, whether he wants to or not. Now I have the mammoth task of figuring out what the hell Crux might have been doing lurking in the shadows of the palace.

CHAPTER
TWENTY-SEVEN

ALYX

Do I use this as a reason to ditch the gathering? Absolutely. Do I make excuses? No.

I am to be queen, so I can do whatever I want, and if they have a problem with it, then I'll just play dumb and pretend I got lost. Luckily, Orion gave me a perfect exit. My maids are nowhere to be seen, and no other partygoers are hiding down this hallway. Picking up my skirts, I turn and hurry farther down the corridor, knowing there must be a door somewhere.

It doesn't take me long to find it, and I burst out into the cool afternoon air just as some guards pass. They frown and slow to look at me, so I drop my skirts and give them my sharpest cutting look until they hurry on. Shaking my head, I walk quickly down the stone steps before someone realises I'm gone. I have an idea where Joha might be, but I need to speak to him right now.

I need to know if I'm right or not.

Luckily, I have already mapped out the palace, and I find the meeting chambers, or Windfall Hall as they call it. Ignoring the guards, I hasten up the steps to the closed wooden doors, but I come to a stop when they press their arms across it.

"Princess, they are in a meeting. Please return to your rooms, and we will let the king know—"

"Move. Now," I order.

They share a look, but then they shake their heads. "It is improper—"

I move closer, pressing the soft soles of my slippers to his boots, narrowing my eyes. "I am to be queen. Do you really wish to annoy me?" He blanches at the implication. "Didn't think so. Now, I need to see the king, so either move or I will move you."

"Princess, please," the other implores, clearly realising they are backed into a corner. They will probably get in trouble for this, but I cannot find it in me to feel sorry for what I am about to do.

Knowing this won't work, I step back with a new plan in mind. "You're right. I apologize—oh my gosh! What is that? Is it an assassin?" I point to the side with a fake gasp.

They snap to attention, pulling their swords from their sides as they turn and hurry to face the threat.

Morons.

Nobody can resist a damsel in distress. Sniggering to myself, I hurry past them since they are distracted and open the wooden door, striding into a long room where men sit around a table. All turn to me with wide eyes, a mixture of shock and anger greeting me. They wear an array of coloured robes, which swish as they surge to their feet. I ignore them all, my eyes focused on a bored-looking Joha, who quickly blinks and stands, frowning at me.

"Alyx?" he queries, his gaze dropping to my body. His eyes widen as he takes in my dress.

I'll admit that it feels good to see him checking me out, but we have more important things to deal with.

"My king, this is improper," one of the scholars protests.

"Very." I nod in agreement. "You will have to excuse me. I just had to see my king." I bow my head respectfully, demurely, and look up through my lashes. "This is all so new to me, and I am very lost. Please excuse my ignorance, my lords. I know how very busy and important you are, but may I steal a moment of your king's time?"

It works—flattery always does with men like this.

"Well, we can understand it's a lot to learn. Things may be different here than in your land, Princess," one of the men replies.

"You are too kind, sir." I bow deeply, laying it on thick.

"You are all dismissed," Joha booms out, eyeing me worriedly.

"My king—"

"I said, you are dismissed," he warns, turning his eyes to the table, giving them a dark look. I have to hide my smirk as I watch. It's a very sexy look on his usually emotionless face. Ignoring their grumbles, we wait for them to file out of the room, and only when the doors shut do I straighten. Ignoring him watching me, I head over and hop onto the table, swinging my legs as I watch him.

I expect him to be angry at me barging in, especially after last night, but what I don't expect is for him to slump in his seat, his chin perched on the palm of one hand as he rubs his head with his other hand. "Thank you, that meeting was so tiresome. I mean, how many times must we discuss taxes?" he complains.

Laughter tumbles out before I can control it. "You're welcome. I'm not here to rescue you though." I wink as I slide off the table and lower my voice, all traces of laughter gone. "I need to know the description of the person who saved you last night."

His eyes cut to me. "Orion?" he queries, knowing he was the only person who would tell me this. I smirk, and he rolls his eyes at my lack of an answer. "Why?"

"I have a theory. Indulge me, my king," I reply.

"I have a feeling indulging you wouldn't be wise," he mutters but straightens and quickly lists what he remembers of the person who rescued him last night.

Just like I thought.

Cruz saved the king, but why? He hates him, and he would take any opportunity to get me back home, so surely letting the king be killed would accomplish that?

"Well?" Joha prompts, interrupting my thoughts, and I blink and bring him back into my vision. "Alyx?"

JOHA

Her eyes flash as she stares at me, lighting up with recognition. She knows who saved me. I wait impatiently, my eyes sweeping down her body once more before I jerk them back to her face. She looks different today. The juxtaposition of the leather-clad assassin last night with this perfect princess is throwing me off. The deep emerald dress only enhances her tanned skin, and the way it drapes across her body protectively reminds me of armour, yet the cut-out across her chest has me swallowing hard.

I remind myself that Alyx is an assassin and her body is an extension of that, a weapon that she wields effortlessly. Even now, as she slides from the table, each movement is lithe, graceful, and purposeful. She exposes some of her tanned leg, drawing my eye there to seduce and distract me.

Does she even know she's doing it?

Does she even know that I have to fist the wood of the chair to stop myself from reaching for her? She is beautiful, and that is just as much of a weapon as any blade. She is deadly, and I can't afford to forget that. She is no mere woman, she is death itself, and falling into that trap might bring pleasure but also my end.

Would it be worth it?

Would death be worth it for one taste?

Her words snap me from my dangerous thoughts, and I ignore the heating of my cheeks as I force my eyes to meet hers. "I know. I'll be going now."

"Who was it?" I demand as I stand.

She stills, eyeing me. "Death. If you see him again, run, Joha. Run and do not look back."

"I am not afraid. I have faced you, and you are like the Grim Reaper," I joke, but it falls flat as she steps closer with a swish of her skirts, almost touching me, and my breath catches at her proximity. She peers up at me through her lashes, her painted lips curving in a wicked smile. She is enough to tempt any man, never mind a king.

"And even the reaper answers to death. Who do you think taught me?" She lets those words drop into my stomach like lead as I swallow. "If he saved your life, it was not a kindness, Joha. Do not mistake it for one. Run if it is not too late." She steps back, freeing me from her spell, and I inhale deeply as she turns to leave.

"Where are you going?" I ask.

"They are stepping up their schedule. We need to make a move," she calls casually.

"And do what?" I ask, feeling like I am playing catch-up. Even though I am king, she's pulling my strings, I answer to her and she knows it.

She glances over her shoulder, her eyes sparkling with mischief as they meet mine, and grins.

"Alyx, what are you going to do?" I call as she starts to move towards the door once more. "Alyx."

With her hand on the doorknob, her words reach me. "You'll see, my king. You'll all see." She disappears as quickly as she came, leaving two bewildered guards looking at me before they drop to their knees.

"Your Majesty, forgive us, we could not stop her."

"Nobody can," I reply, but when they give me concerned looks, I realise I am smiling. Clearing my throat, I give them a stern look. "Back to your positions."

CHAPTER
TWENTY-EIGHT

ALYX

I wait impatiently for the sun to set, and as soon as the last rays disappear over the horizon, I am out of the window of my rooms and racing through the dusk. My body is concealed in an all-black outfit, and my weapons are strapped to my body. All the jewels that hold me down are left behind. I shed them all like a cloak, and I let the real me out to play. What I told Joha was true, we must make a move, but first, I have an assassin to deal with.

I may have kissed Crux, slept in his arms, and known him all my life, but I cannot let this slide. I was not joking when I told Joha that Crux is death, and just like death, he does not have the same morals most do. Even I have more than he does. To Crux, Joha is just in his way. He would kill him as easily as he would take his next breath and not feel a thing. I admire it even though it scares me.

Joha could be facing certain death right this moment, so even though I have been at Crux's side for years, I leave the palace to warn him to leave the king alone.

I tell myself it's because I need him alive for my plan. I tell myself lots of things, lots of lies, but my racing heart betrays me. Each second I waste is another Crux could be stalking the king. His little rats in the palace told me, however, that he is in the Lowers tonight, so that is where I head.

Usually, you do not find an assassin, we find you, but not tonight because I'm hunting him.

I should have known, though, that when we do not want to be found, we will not be. I spend hours searching the Lowers and all our safe houses, but he is nowhere in sight. Either he is in hiding or he does not want to be found, and despite my skills, Crux taught me everything I know, so he knows exactly how to avoid me if he wishes.

Snarling in annoyance, I leave the abandoned house behind, my last hopeful spot to find him. I could spend days searching and never find him unless he allows it.

I have wasted too much of the night as it is, and I still need to make my move before the sun rises or the king will be in even more danger.

Who knew keeping a spoiled, rich man alive would be so tiring?

He was right. He has enemies everywhere.

Deciding to switch up our game, I snag one of Crux's little rats from the next street. Pinning him to the wall, I raise my eyebrow at him. "Send a message to your master for me."

"Mistress." He nods, his eyes eager and wide, face streaked with dirt.

"Stay away from the king. Find me or I will find you." I release him and watch him scuttle away to deliver the message.

Turning, I pull my hood higher and leave the Lowers behind, using the tunnels under the bridge to cross to the other side.

I have other things to attend to, and most might have thought I spent my afternoon aimlessly wandering the palace or painting near the lake, but I was waiting, watching, and learning, and tonight I put the information I gleaned into action.

Crux's little rats are good for some things, and I might have been stuck acting as the perfect princess, but they were not, and they got me exactly what I wanted.

I stand before a noble's house within Cairn Province. This family deals with shipments of jewels, which is not surprising since everyone in Cairn is in the shipping business. This noble family, Beaumont, is one of the wealthiest, and after some digging, it was obvious they have been smuggling other things in their shipments. One of their cargo ships sank just last moon, however, leaving them in debt and in desperate need of money.

Desperate people do desperate things—like try to kill the king.

As I stare at the grand stone house, I let my anger consume me. It's the darkness I use when I hunt, and I let it wrap around me like a lover. The lights are bright inside, and the flowers shine even in the moonlight, yet in their midst is an assassin and they have no clue. For all their power and advantages, nothing can protect them from the dark or the likes of me.

I will make my move to secure the king. It will help further my plan for my own revenge. That is what I tell myself anyway, and it does not stem from worry about Joha.

Not at all.

I am just about to make my way over the wall when the door opens and the very man I am looking for leaves. Dressed in a deep red robe with his hat pulled low, he hurries from the house. Since it is so late, it wouldn't do him well to be seen leaving suspiciously during the night.

The little rats were right.

The man who tried to kill the king might be dead, but the ones behind it are not, and like most noble families, they stick together.

Smirking, I stalk my prey through the cobblestone streets. He stops every now and again, searching the area to make sure he isn't being seen, yet he never once spots me.

Is the hair on the back of his neck rising?

Is his skin filled with goosebumps?

Can he taste death in the air?

I hope so.

We eventually stop at a tavern near the water, and I grin when I realise exactly why he's been acting so shady. I watch him slip inside, and I follow.

I have been here a few times before. It is a good place for information, and a convenient area near the water to dispose of bodies—not to mention those who work here are all ours as well. Some see them as desperate for money, but nothing could be further from the truth. They earn more in one night than their patrons. They are assassins in their own way—of information. They keep this kingdom running, especially for us Daggers.

Music flows through the tavern, men cheer rowdily in their expensive robes, and money is thrown onto wooden tables as women make their way through, serving their beer and dancing. They steal and listen as they go, but it is the rooms upstairs where my man goes.

The bar is in the back, and I nod at Antlia, who is working alongside Willian. The tables down here serve food and alcohol while good music plays. Dancers move lithely through the crowd in gauzy material, their bodies art themselves. Doors separate more on the back wall where you can have private meetings or meals, but I turn away and head to the wooden stairs on the left. Satisfied men and cunning women come down the stairs, and I nod at those I know, and the women part for me, knowing all too well who I am.

When I get upstairs, however, I cannot see my target.

The walls here are made from sheer cloth until farther down the corridor, where sliding wooden doors lead to private rooms where, for enough coin, you pay for the entertainment of a lifetime.

"Mistress." One of the entertainers nods as she watches me, no doubt waiting for her next patron. Wearing a sheer pink number that wraps around her body, she looks like the beautiful temptress they want. Her makeup is heavy, and unlike the proper ladies of the noble land, she screams of seduction and happiness.

I grin behind my mask. "I am looking for a man who just came in. Red robe, Beaumont."

"Room four, I am due in there." I pull a pouch from my waist and throw it at her. She snatches it from the air, pocketing it, and blinks her long lashes at me with a wicked grin. "Enjoy your evening, mistress." She turns and heads back downstairs to look for her next target.

Heading to room four, I chuckle at the singing coming from one of the others and the moans from the next. Here, you can buy whatever you want if your pockets are deep enough, and it seems that despite Beaumont's worries, these ones are.

Sliding the door open softly, I step into room four, eyeing the back of the robed man I have been hunting. He is sitting at the wooden table with his back to the door. His hat is off, and his long black hair hangs in a plait down his back. It's another symbol of his status. To the left is a small stage with some instruments ready for the entertainers, and sofas and a bed are to the right.

"I do not like to be kept waiting," he barks sharply, all high and mighty as he throws back a shot of his drink and lifts it into the air. "Pour me another quickly."

I head over and grab the glass before grabbing the bottle, and then I pour him a drink. As he lifts it to his mouth, I round the table and sit in the other chair.

His eyes widen, and he spits his drink across the room as he pales. "Who are you?" He goes to stand, panicking. I don't blame him.

"Sit," I demand, and he sinks into his seat, confused but knowing this isn't good.

"Your brother was a fool," I tell him casually as I pour myself a drink. Pulling my mask down, I shoot it back and slam the glass onto the table. "Are you a fool?"

He hesitates. "My brother?"

"Hmm, the news probably hasn't reached you yet. He failed and is dead." He freezes.

"I do not know what you mean," he replies carefully. He's good at hiding his disappointment and grief—if he actually feels any. It's not enough though.

"Oh, let us not play games, Mr. Beaumont. Your family was selected because of your recent struggles with money after your ship sank. They knew you were desperate and used that against you. You took the payment, and your older brother, a captain of the guard within the palace, tried to assassinate the king last night. He failed. Now, shall I carry on with everything I know? Like the fact that you are here proves your money troubles are over or that your wife has no idea you have three bastard children?" He gasps, his composure broken, and I grin. "Good, you understand me now. I know everything. I see everything. You can't fool me."

"What do you want?" he whispers.

At least he is no longer trying to act stupid. That makes it easier.

"I do not care about you or your other secrets. You are inconsequential and not deep enough to be part of it. They used you knowing it could be traced back, but I want the one behind it. I want the one who approached you. I want the one with the money who gave the order," I admit as I pour him another drink.

He doesn't touch it. He just watches me. He might be foolish enough to accept the money, but he's not foolish enough to give them away, knowing it means death.

He just doesn't know he's screwed either way.

"I truly do not know who it was. They wore a mask and approached us on the docks a few nights ago. They knew everything, that we were ruined and desperate. They offered us more gold than we could make in ten lifetimes if we did one simple task."

"Kill the king." I nod and shoot my drink as I wait.

He swallows and nods. "He spoke with a lilt, but I do not know what kind. He was not from here, that is for sure. He was neither short nor tall. That is all I can tell you."

"I need more than that," I warn him. His description is useless. "You fear that man, I can see it, but you should fear me right now, boy. He cannot and will not protect you. You are a dead end to him, but to me, you are the key. You know what I am, yes?" He nods, and I grin. "Then you know what I am willing to do to get the information I need. It is your choice how. You booked this room for an hour. I will have you broken within half that time, or you can tell me what I want to know now and make it easier on yourself."

He pales even further, slumping into his chair as he realises just how fucked he is. Suddenly, he reaches into his side, and I stiffen, my hand drifting to a blade on my hip, but he pulls out a silken coin pouch and roots around inside it.

He tosses me a coin, and I catch it midair, my gaze on him for a moment before I turn it to the gold coin. I flip it in my fingers, noticing the difference. "I do not know their names, truly, but that coin can only belong to those within the palace who have access to the treasury."

"Why?" I ask, needing to know his reasoning. I will not be led on a wild-goose chase.

"Why? Because that is the new currency being rolled out this year. The only ones who would have access to it yet are the ones closest to the king and the treasury. There are only certain people who could have it. Find that list and you will find the one who hired me. That is all I know. I was a fool, I know that, but we had no choice."

"There is always a choice," I inform him as I stand. I press the coin into the pocket over my chest as I watch him. "You chose wrong." He stiffens, but then I walk past him, and he slumps, thinking he is safe.

"I am going to use you to send a message," I murmur in his ear from behind.

"What message? I will convey it eagerly." He straightens with purpose.

Placing my hands on his shoulders, I straighten. "I know you will." In one quick move, I snap his neck, watching his head hit the table as he crumples. I grab his glass and down his shot before pulling the rest of his coins, leaving them as a tip for the entertainers who will find him.

After all, he knows too much.

He saw me, and he saw them.

I cannot let them know I am coming for them, not yet, but this is a warning to them. Next time, they will second-guess their moves, and it will buy us time to trace this coin and find out who is behind it.

This is a game. They move, we move, and it goes like that until one of us wins . . . and I never lose.

That will not change now, not with my revenge and Joha's life on the line.

CHAPTER
TWENTY-NINE

ORION

Alyx is up to something.

I know she's here to find out who is ordering the hits on Joha's life and that requires her to sneak around, but something deep in my gut is telling me that she's up to something else. If she were truly just working to keep him safe, then she would share her plans with me and we could work together. While the thought of that makes me wince, I would do it for my king.

I would do anything for him.

This is the reason I am sneaking around the palace in the early hours of the morning. I went to see Alyx after our argument earlier in the day and she wasn't there. I had it in my mind that perhaps I had been a little harsh, yet finding her missing from her rooms only aroused my suspicions again.

Why did I go to her private chambers late in the night in the first place? I could have waited until morning when I saw her next. There is no justifiable reason for seeking her out at this unsociable hour.

A sickening thought comes to mind. Do I just want to see her again? Her dress had been ridiculously over the top, but it suited her personality, not to mention the way it hugged her body . . . .

The stirrings of something I refuse to acknowledge start up again, and desire shoots through my nervous system. Taking a deep breath, I shake my head and focus on the task at hand. Yes, I do want to see her again, but for information. That is all.

I have searched all around the palace grounds and am unable to find her, which brings me to the conclusion that she is *not* on the palace grounds.

She is an assassin, which only worries me more.

My thoughts turn inward as I become frustrated with myself. What good am I to Joha if I cannot keep track of an assassin who may or may not be a threat to his life?

Sheltered in the shadows of one of the palace buildings, I lean against the wall and drop my head, rubbing my temples in an attempt to ease the tension there. It's useless. I have had a constant headache since she arrived.

A flicker of movement catches my eye. It is barely anything, more like a blur of shadows, and most would not have even seen it. In other circumstances, I might brush it off as my exhausted mind, but I know it is her.

With as much stealth as I can manage, I push away from the building and follow the shadow across the grounds. I don't know why I'm so certain that this is her and not another assassin, but I can feel it in my gut.

It doesn't take me long to figure out that she is heading back to the queen's palace. She must be done sneaking around for the night. I hold back as she slips into her rooms and attempt to calmly formulate what I want to say to her. For some reason, when I am around her, I cannot seem to make sense of my words and end up replying in anger instead. It makes me seem like a jerk.

Not that I care what she thinks.

After five minutes or so, I sneak into the queen's palace and move through the corridors to her rooms. It is far too easy to get into. I will have to have a conversation with the guards in the morning.

In the privacy of her rooms, where no one else is around to overhear, I stride straight over to her bedroom, a dim light shining under the door. I slam the doors open and barge in, only to come to a sudden halt.

She's standing in just a thin vest, her underwear visible for me to see. Where she hid her dark clothing from earlier, I have no idea. I am sure she is an expert at hiding things. All my thoughts become foggy as my eyes trail down the length of her body.

I need to focus . . . focus . . .

"Just come in, why don't you?" She rolls her eyes, stripping off her vest so she's only in her chest wrappings and underwear. "You finally decided to step out of the darkness and confront me then?"

Her words snap me from the delirious spell her body put me under. It is only now that I realise what I am feeling is arousal. No, this is not happening. I know it is just a physical response, my body reacting as it is supposed to, and I have no control over it. However, I do not want to feel anything for someone like her, not even physical attraction.

She is toying with me, casually wandering around in her underwear, and clearly trying to get a reaction out of me. I want to look away, to give her privacy, but from the smirk on her lips, I know that is exactly what she expects me to do.

Taking a deep breath, I continue to look at her, and her last comment finally registers with me. She knew I was following her all along. Damn, she's good. Embarrassment, frustration, and anger all flare within me. Balling my hands into fists at my sides to keep myself from shaking her, I glare.

"Where did you go?" I ask, trying to keep my mind on the reason I am here.

"Why? Did you miss me?" She flutters her lashes, her voice seductive as she teases me.

I grit my teeth against a sudden urge to silence that sassy mouth. "Answer the damn question."

"So grumpy," she chides as she pulls on a dressing gown, tying it closed. I'm suddenly able to think clearer now that she's covered, even if the image of her nearly naked body will be ingrained in my mind forever.

"I was looking for information," she answers, perching on the edge of her dressing table, her eyes locked on me as she removes the braids from her hair.

This is fucking painful. She is determined to make this difficult.

"And?" I grind out. "What did you discover?"

She raises a brow, and I can see how much she's enjoying this. "Why would I tell you that? All you need to know is that I'm dealing with it."

That does nothing to reassure me. In fact, it does the exact opposite. I have a pretty good idea what she means by "dealing with it," and it makes my teeth clamp together tightly. "You can't just go around killing people when you feel like it."

The look she gives me is pointed, and she slowly gestures to herself. "You know what I do, right?"

I realised as soon as the words came out of my mouth that she was going to turn them back on me, making me feel like an idiot. I meant it though. Working for the Crown, she cannot just murder whoever she likes. This should be done properly.

"I am well aware of your profession." Disgust colours my voice on the last word, making it acutely obvious what I think of her life choices.

She finally loses her temper, jumping up from the dressing table and stalking up to me, her arms crossed over her chest as she glares up at me. "What the fuck is your problem?"

"My problem is that it's my job to protect Joha from people like *you*, and here you are, parading around the palace as though you own it." I'm close to losing control, raising my voice. There's no one around, but the guards will come running if they hear a male shouting in the queen's rooms. "People like you don't listen to reason or things like the laws of the land. You create your own rules, and that disgusts me."

Her eyes narrow. "Disgust, is that what I saw in your eyes just a moment ago? Or earlier when you saw me in my dress?" Ripping the tie from her dressing gown, she pulls it open and slides it off her shoulders so she's standing before me in just her underwear. "What do you think, Orion? Repulsive, right?"

She steps closer, each word pointed and harsh.

Despite myself, I can't help but run my eyes over her. She is anything but disgusting. Her body is perfect, even with the scars that mar her skin. Every inch of her is perfection, yet she drives me crazy. When I first met her, I barely noticed how beautiful she was, but seeing this other side of her made me take a better look.

I *should* be disgusted at her vulgar display, especially knowing what she's been doing tonight, but then why the fuck do I want to pin her down and feel her skin against mine?

"Just tell me what you know." My voice is tight, betraying my internal struggle.

Her expression turns livid. "Why in the underworld would I tell you anything? You're constantly snarling and snapping at me."

She is right. I am. I'm pretty sure I have valid reasons though. She has only ever had to look out for herself. In the long run, if Joha dies on her watch, all she is going to lose is the reward money. Can she really care for a king she has no attachment to? I am not about to have that conversation with her though.

Taking a deep breath, I remind myself why I am here. "I'm trying to keep Joha safe."

"Funnily enough, so am I!" she retorts, throwing her arms up in the air. It draws my attention back to her body, her breasts almost close enough for me to touch.

Focus, Orion.

"I don't trust you."

"I know." She jabs me in the chest with her finger. "Which is one of the reasons I'm not going to share my plans with you."

My jaw is clenched so tightly, I am surprised I have not broken a tooth. "You might be used to working alone, but we both have the same goal here. We need to be a team." The words sound strange leaving my mouth, my voice deeper.

She stares up at me with a scowl that I am used to seeing when she is around me. With Joha, she manages to hide it, playing it off as though there is nothing that could disturb her unflappable nature. When it is just her and me though . . .

She can't hide it.

"What if I don't want to have anything to do with you?" Each word is pointed, sharp enough to wound.

The tension in the room is electric, the two of us glaring at each other. She aggravates me so much. Everything she does goes against my principles, against who I am.

Why do I find her so damn attractive?

Leaning down so we are almost nose to nose, I lower my voice to a whisper. "I would say you're a liar."

Something shifts in her eyes. I don't understand why calling her a liar has that effect on her, but the tension shifts. She cocks out a hip and places her hand there, drawing attention to her body.

"Disgusting. Assassin. Betrayer. You can just add it to the list of names you've given me," she whispers like she's telling me a secret.

I have no idea what to say to that. Honestly, staring down at her, our bodies almost brushing, I don't remember what we were even arguing about.

I don't know who moves first, but we suddenly collide in a rush. Our lips crash together in a flurry of kisses, tongues, and teeth. It is not gentle, it is anything but, yet her kisses are addictive. We kiss like we are fighting, roughly grabbing onto each other.

It's a battle, only there are no weapons, just desire, and whoever gives in first loses.

Her sharp moan of pleasure against my rough lips only spurs me on, and my hands cover the final distance between us, tracing the sides of her body before gripping her tight ass and pulling her closer. The plump cheeks fit perfectly in my hands, and I can't help but groan as I drag her up onto her toes to deepen the kiss. Never one to be outdone, she bites my lower lip so hard it makes me grunt, and I swear I taste the coppery tang of my blood.

I can't stop. Backing her into one of the posts, I devour her mouth.

More. I need more.

A sudden sound from outside the room causes us to jump apart in shock. We gawk at each other, our faces flushed. Her lips are raw, and her hair is a mess from my hands. I know I do not look any better. Luckily, she has more sense than I do. Her lashes flutter, shuttering the fire in her gaze, as she takes a deep breath and whips her gaping dressing gown back into place, tying it before brushing her hair back. I take the moment to slow my rapid breathing. There is nothing I can do about my pounding heart, but I do my best to act unaffected as I put some distance between us, walking to the other side of the room, needing space from the addictive assassin.

The door slides open swiftly, drawing our gazes, and we find Joha framed in the threshold. I do not know what he is doing here in the early hours of the morning, but I would be a hypocrite if I said anything—not that he can know that. What the fuck do I think I am doing? Messing around with the assassin will only end in disaster.

I have to get myself together.

Joha seems confused to find me here, slowly looking between us with a raised brow.

I am so fucked.

CHAPTER
THIRTY

JOHA

The tension in the room is electric, and as I look between my best friend and fake fiancée, I know I just interrupted something. The question is, what?

If it were anyone else, I would say I intruded on a personal moment, especially since the two of them cannot seem to look at each other. However, this is Orion and Alyx. They despise each other and can barely tolerate being in the same room. The idea of them having a secret rendezvous is laughable.

Why would my guard be in her rooms at this time of the night though? Finding anyone in a person's private chambers at night is going to raise some eyebrows. Their rumpled appearances do not help convince me otherwise either.

"Did I interrupt something?" My lips curl into a teasing smile, like I do not have a care in the world, but jealousy twists my insides. I was not going to ask them about my suspicions, yet I cannot seem to stop myself, even if I am making it seem like a joke.

Orion jerks like I hit him, a scowl morphing his features. "Absolutely not." He sounds offended that I would even suggest he would have an affair with the assassin, as though I were personally attacking his character.

"No," Alyx replies at the same time with a shrug of her shoulders, her voice smoother. "You are always welcome in my rooms, Your Majesty." Her lips mimic my playful smile, but there is something dark in her eyes that has my eyebrow rising.

Orion stiffens, as though he's outraged by the implication of her words, and although this is how he would usually react to the assassin's blatant teasing towards me, I cannot help but wonder if there is another reason behind his response.

Jealousy perhaps?

No, I need to stop looking into his actions. I hate that I am starting to question what he does. He is my closest friend, one of the only people who believes in me. If anything like that was going on between them, he would say something to me. Honestly, I don't think his sense of duty and morality would even allow him to get into any sort of relationship with anyone, never mind an assassin.

"You need to be careful. If anyone sees you, you will start rumours." Smirking, I nod towards Alyx's state of undress. I can't seem to refrain from digging myself further into this conversation.

"The same could be said about you, Your Majesty." Orion narrows his eyes, and I know that when we are alone, he will have some stern words about this. "It's dangerous to be out alone at night, wandering the palace grounds, especially coming to see *her*."

He sounds more like the disapproving guard I know and love like a brother. Even so, I do not like to be lectured, and for some reason, his comment strikes something within me. "She is my betrothed, and I am king. I can go wherever I please."

Orion straightens, looking taken aback at my tone. I immediately feel bad. This is not who I am. Exhaustion and stress must be making me delirious. I open my mouth to apologise, but I'm interrupted by a lithe form coming between us.

Alyx.

My gaze goes straight to her, tracking her movements. Her flimsy dressing gown does little to hide her body, and it does not take much for me to imagine what is beneath. In fact, I will spend the rest of the night imagining. I might be a king who is supposed to be virtuous, but Alyx makes that very, very hard.

"Boys, let's not fight." She sighs and rubs her temples. "I've had a long day, and all I want to do is fall into bed."

Right. Yes, I came here for a reason, not just to think about her naked. I am perfectly capable of doing that during my own time. Wiping those images from my mind, I clear my throat. "I'm here to get an update from you and see if you have made any progress."

Nodding, she runs her hands through her fiery hair. "That is what Orion was here for as well. I have already updated him, so he can leave now and get some rest."

It is a clear dismissal, and I raise a brow as I turn to take in Orion. There is an intense stare happening between them, and the tension rises as neither of them look away. They are both strong-willed, never being the first to back down, and for a moment, I think Orion is going to argue that his place is here with me. However, I am knocked back with surprise when he drops his gaze, scowling.

Out of everything I have seen here, that is what makes me pause the most. What is going on with Orion? Something is happening. I just cannot figure out what it is.

Shaking his head, he finally looks up and meets my gaze, his expression stern. "I will be keeping guard outside. It will look strange if we are both seen leaving at separate times."

He is right. If anyone were to spot me without a guard, that would raise questions, especially at this time of night. While what I said is true, I am king and can go where I please, if I am spotted alone, assumptions will be made. It will make it harder for Alyx if everyone believes she is not a virgin. While it is fine for a king to be promiscuous—not that I ever have been—if the future queen were to be found having premarital sex, then she would be viewed differently. At least if I am spotted and I have Orion with me, then we can say we had a chaperone and nothing happened.

Nodding my agreement, I watch as Orion turns as if to say goodbye to Alyx. There is a heavy, awkward moment as he scowls at the assassin, at a loss for words. Eventually, she arches an eyebrow, and that seems to kick him into motion. Grunting, he shakes his head and leaves the room.

I wait until I can no longer hear his footsteps, then I turn to my betrothed and smirk, crossing my arms over my chest. "That was strange."

She climbs up onto the bed, leaning against a mountain of cushions, and pats the foot of the bed, inviting me to sit. "It has been a strange day," she agrees, exhaustion lacing her voice. "What do you need, Joha?"

Perching where she patted, I turn so I'm facing her. Now that I'm closer, I can see the fatigue lining her features. It is selfish of me to keep her up when I should be allowing her to rest, but I want an update.

At least, that is what I meant to say.

"I wanted to see you."

She smiles and bats her eyelashes. "I bet you say that to all the ladies." Her expression becomes more serious. "I have a couple of leads I am following, but I don't want to say anything about them until I am more certain. You are better off not knowing, so when all of this comes out, you are blameless. Plus, your reactions will be genuine."

Everything she says makes sense, and from an outside perspective, I would agree with her. This is about *me*, though, my safety, and traitors in my court who are plotting against me. I want to know every little detail, even the parts she thinks are irrelevant. Curbing my frustration, I ball my hands in the blankets beneath me.

"I hate not knowing, especially when my life is at risk," I admit, showing some weakness.

"I won't let anything happen to you," she promises swiftly, her voice hard.

A thump in my chest makes me pause, her words echoing in my mind. I am pretty sure she means it too. I hired her to keep me safe, but something has changed since that first day. I've gone from being a job to someone she would protect.

"I know," I reply, suddenly feeling weary, the weight of my responsibilities weighing on me. "Between you and Orion, I am safe. I just hate feeling so useless."

"You are not useless."

Her response comes instantly, and I turn my head to look at her to see if she's being genuine. Deep down in my soul, even since I became king, I've felt inadequate. My advisors and stepmother have never believed in me, and they treat me like a fool. I have no real say in what happens, and my ideas to help my kingdom prosper are just laughed away. I'm just a figurehead, a puppet for them to use.

Alyx doesn't make me feel that way. She listens to my ideas, and while she thinks most of them are ridiculous, she helps me despite it, so hearing this from her makes me feel more confident.

I don't know what to say in return. Thanking her doesn't seem right, and I don't have the words to express what it means to me. She's curled up against her cushions, the blanket wrapped around her knees, looking just like a young lady and not the deadly assassin she truly is. I should leave her to rest, yet I cannot seem to make myself go.

"Can I stay just a little longer? I hate sleeping alone," I say, but as soon as the words leave my mouth, I regret them. I sound like a needy little boy who needs comfort.

She snorts and rolls her eyes. "I'm sure you have a list of bedmates a mile long, Joha."

"No, I don't mean in *that* way." Leaning back, I spread out at the bottom of the bed, my legs hanging over the side as I rest my arm over my face. "I just hate the silence of the night. It makes me feel so alone." She says nothing, yet I can feel her surprise. I know I seem easy-going and like nothing bothers me, but actually, there is a lot about me that I have been forced to hide over the years.

"I've never told anyone that before," I whisper, fearful of her reaction.

"Your secret is safe with me." Her response is just as quiet.

Lowering my arm, I look over and watch as she smiles softly and pats the other side of the bed, inviting me to lie down properly.

Pausing, I wait to see if she is serious or will take the offer back. I really should not be climbing into bed with her, but I am not here to sleep, just spend time in her company.

Thirty minutes or so will not hurt anyone.

After kicking off my boots and removing my jacket, I crawl across the bed as she watches me with sleepy eyes. In any other situation, this would go very differently. When I crawl across most ladies' beds, as infrequently as it happens, they do not look like they are about to nod off. Reaching the pillow beside hers, I lie down and roll onto my back, staring up at the ceiling. She snuggles beneath the covers, her breathing becoming deep and even.

We don't speak, and I stay above the sheets, letting my mind wander as I listen to the gentle sounds in the room. She falls asleep after only a few minutes, and I tuck her in, making sure she's warm.

My eyelids grow heavy, and I know it is time for me to leave. However, as the sun starts to rise and I know the palace will begin to awaken with the dawn, I finally climb from her bed and sneak out of the room, loneliness nowhere to be found.

CHAPTER

THIRTY-ONE

ALYX

J oha is gone when I wake up. I didn't hear him leave, but I imagine he snuck out not long after I nodded off. He is all about presenting an image, and being caught in my bed would not look good for the king. What I said was true though. I will keep my promise about the loneliness he feels. After all, I feel the same.

How many nights have I lain awake, staring into the dark, wishing someone were next to me? Just the warmth of their body reminds me I am not alone in this world. Maybe that weakness is why I let him stay, but I cannot believe I fell asleep so easily.

It's just another worry to add to my list, like the fact that I kissed Orion last night. Well, technically, *we* kissed, since he is not innocent when it comes to blame, but we did kiss, and the night before I kissed Crux. What is happening to me?

There is also my promise to keep Joha safe. No doubt news has spread about Beaumont's death. I do not want to give the people behind this too much warning, which means I need to move fast. The list of who has access to the new treasury coins cannot be too long, and once I find the man or woman behind it . . . well, we are going to have some words.

First, though, I must dress the part. As soon as I think this, my ladies-in-waiting bustle into the room, ready to prepare me for another day as a princess.

Joy.

I am scrubbed, pinned, and primped again. It is something I am becoming used to, though it never gets any less uncomfortable. Today, I am allowed to negotiate my outfit, and I settle on the least restrictive option—a flowing, long, simple purple gown. It's cinched at the waist but has plenty of room to hide weapons. After I'm dressed, they circle me with critical eyes, pinning my hair and adding jewels as I stand still under their inspection.

"Your schedule is very open today, my lady," one says as they slide on my cloth slippers that offer little to no protection from the environment, but they are queenly.

"It is?" I ask with surprise. It seems like I'm supposed to attend a million unimportant events and rites of passage every day, so why would today be any different?

The giggle the lady lets out has my eyebrow rising. "Queen Mother requested a tea later as well as a banquet tonight, but the king has cleared your schedule, stating you are tired and in need of rest. He must be very taken with you to stand up to her like that."

Or more likely, he's impatient for me to find his would-be killer.

I simply smile as I stand and look into the mirror, nodding in approval at my outfit.

"So, my lady, what would you like to do today?" another asks nervously.

"I have some ideas." I grin, and no doubt it's a wicked one if their expressions are anything to go by.

🖋

I SPEND an hour walking around the palace to at least show my face, and then I put my plan into action. I have sent my ladies on a wild-goose chase, claiming a stomach ache that can only be fixed by a certain flower—which, to be clear, does not exist. The only reason they left me in my rooms was due to my insistence.

It's far too easy to sneak past the bored guards, and then I am out and alone in the palace, ready to track down the person the coin belongs to.

I start at the most obvious place—the treasury. It is hidden within Frey Hall and has barely any protection, which is foolish. It is far too easy to sneak inside the dimly lit building, and once there, I quickly navigate to the records room, hiding in a closed passage as some robed workers pass by. Once they are gone, I quickly scan the shelves. There are rows upon rows of them, detailing every currency, exchange, and intricacy of the crown's wealth, but what I need is somewhat close to the door. It is a list of the new coins which will be rolled out soon, and at the bottom are the signatures of those who witnessed and agreed to it. There is Joha, of course, Queen Mother, and then below that are two advisors' names. One is the head of the treasury, and I have a hard time believing he would be stupid enough to bribe someone with coins only he seems to know about. The other is a name I do not recognise.

A'lan Wrynn, witness.

Hmm, witness, so he isn't someone important? A noise has me shoving the scroll away, and I duck into the alcove as two whisper-ing, robed men pass, and then I sneak back out.

Once outside on the palace grounds, I casually walk behind a building and wait. It doesn't take long for a little rat to scurry to me, no doubt following my every move. "Find out what you can about an A'lan Wrynn. Fast," I demand.

"Yes, mistress." He hurries away, and I watch him go with nothing to do but kill time.

I'M IMPATIENT. It has been two hours of hiding in the palace so no one questions why a princess is wandering around alone. The little rat finally returns, red-faced and anxious. "Sorry, mistress, the records were hard to locate. A'lan Wrynn is a noble from Stormhallow Province. He's lowly but managed to find a job here in the palace due to his father's connections. They say he is desperate to cut his teeth, and he has quickly climbed the ranks and now sits upon the council as an advisor. Many say he is dirty, stealing from the crown to fund his life, which has seemingly improved."

Bingo, that's our man.

I just know it. I also know he's working for someone. A desperate noble suddenly coming into money and achieving a rank? Yes, someone helped him because they needed his assistance—like bribing other nobles to try and kill the king. No doubt they thought if this got back to them, then A'lan would take the fall and nothing else would come out.

We are getting closer, but the only way to find out the master behind all this is to question A'lan.

"Where is he now?" I ask.

"I thought you would want to know that. He's over in the baths. His company was just leaving as I hurried here."

"Company, huh?" I smirk, tossing some coins at the rat. "See that no guards disturb us for a while."

"Yes, mistress." He scurries away once more, and I can't help but grin. A'lan and I are going to have a nice little chat, and I might get some of this impatient anger out while I'm there.

Two birds, one stone, or better yet, one bath, two motives.

I make my way over to the baths, avoiding the guards, and once behind the stout, one-story building set next to the wall, I let the change come over me. Gone is the smiling princess, and in her place is the assassin. Heading to the slightly open window at the back, I peer inside and almost snort at what I find.

Low, wooden baths are set into a deep floor and spread out across the room, steam wafting throughout. Luckily, all are empty

202

bar a larger one at the back, where a nobleman, whom I am assuming is A'lan, rests. His arms are spread across the back, leaving his scrawny chest on display, and his head is tipped back, his black hair slicked with water and sweat. He wears a happy grin on his lips as he floats in the flower-filled water.

Lifting the window, I keep my eyes on him as I slide inside and land on silent feet. He still does not move, so I head up the ramp to the main entrance, where I slide the wooden bolt through the double door.

"Is someone there?" he calls, not worried in the slightest.

The fool.

I giggle. "Just an attendant, Lord Wrynn."

"Oh, attend away." The smirk is evident in his voice, and the dumbass just confirmed everything I need to know. Grabbing a robe from the side, I wrap it around my body and steal a water jug, keeping my head down as if in respect as I hurry through the baths. I kneel slightly to the side and behind him. "Would you like some water, my lord?"

"Yes." He picks up a goblet and holds it out without even looking at me. "I have been waiting far too long."

"I am very sorry, my lord. I was busy." I make my voice smaller as I pour the water, and when it starts to overflow, he turns with a glare.

"Do your job properly," he begins.

"Okay." I shrug as I smash the jug into his head.

He yells and falls into the water with a splash, sputtering as he nearly drowns. He gets to his feet, his hand on his head. "You dare attack me? Me? I will have your head for this!"

"I'd be worried about your other head right now." I smirk, still crouched as my eyes drop down his very unimpressive naked body to where his cock bobs in the water.

Gasping, he covers himself, looking around as his cheeks redden. "You . . . You . . ."

"Me . . . Me . . . ," I mock as I tilt my head, watching him. "Relax, you don't have anything I want to see, trust me." I laugh as he swings his head to me, obviously realising we are the only ones here and no one is coming to help him.

"Who are you?" he asks, his haughty noble attitude in full effect despite the fact that I just hit him and he's naked. Truly, their audacity never ceases to amaze me.

Tugging the coin from my pocket, I hold it up to the light. "Does this look familiar?"

"No, now get out!" he roars.

Tossing it to him, I watch him catch it more out of reflex than anything else—thank fuck because I don't want to root around in his body soup water. "Take a closer look, my lord," I mock. "You left this behind. Now, you have two options. Either tell me who you are working with to assassinate the king"—I watch his face pale in realisation, his mouth opening and closing on denials and excuses I do not let him speak—"and I'll let you die with dignity or don't tell me, and I'll spend my time making you and then you'll die without dignity, left to float in your own filthy water, naked, to be found in all your glory." I grin widely. "Oh, and then I'll destroy your entire family."

He looks from the coin to me, his eyes wide and scared.

"Do not think I won't," I warn, sliding a dagger from my thigh and letting it catch the light. "I grow tired of waiting."

"I cannot tell you." His shoulders slump, and tears glisten in his eyes. For all his bravado, he's afraid. "I fear them more than I could ever fear you, so kill me because it won't stop them. Nothing will. They are everywhere, and they are more powerful than you could ever imagine. They are untouchable. You've chosen the losing side."

"And you chose their side, yet you're going to die here alone. Isn't that losing?" I murmur softly. Annoyance flares within me at the resolve I see in his gaze. Despite his attitude, he's stronger than I imagined. He won't speak. I've tortured and killed enough people to know that. He might break eventually, but he would never tell me what I want, and I would waste too much time. It seems like every lead I track down is another dead end.

If he knows who is behind this, however, then there will be someone else who does as well.

I will find out who and, powerful or not, I will destroy them. They think they are untouchable, but they have no idea who they are playing with.

"I guess you're right." He smiles sadly. "I didn't do it just for the money. I don't know why I'm telling you this, but I am. I suppose someone should know if I'm going to die. It wasn't just the money."

"Then what was it?" I ask curiously, despite my anger.

"Love," he admits. "Love makes us do foolish things, don't you think? Whether it be family love, romantic, or friendship. We do things we never thought we would in the name of those we care for."

"And the one you did this for . . . were they worth it?" I murmur.

He blinks, his smile dropping. "I thought so at the time, but time changes everything, even those you thought you knew. I'm ready." He nods, wading through the water until he stands before me with more courage than I thought him capable of. "Try not to make it too messy. I don't want my family to suffer."

"I am the best, so it will be clean," I tell him despite everything I told him I would do. I soften my voice, ignoring my own frustration. "Close your eyes so you won't know it's coming and think of something happy."

He might have accepted this out of greed, but he's just a man trapped by his choice, one that leads him to death, and part of me feels sorry for him.

His eyes close, and although I strike out of frustration at another dead end, I also make the slice clean. The knife slips through his neck like butter, the cut so deep he won't feel it over the shock. He falls back with a gasp, reflexively reaching for his neck as he chokes. I watch. I refuse to look away. I took his life, so it is my duty.

When he stops fighting, his lifeless body floats in the red bathwater. It's a warning and a promise to those behind it.

I see you. I'm coming for you.

Reaching over, I pluck the bloodied coin from the water and pocket it as I stand.

With one last look at the man who chose to die rather than betray those behind this, a new sort of determination fills me.

I will end this once and for all.

CHAPTER
THIRTY-TWO

CRUX

I watch as Alyx sneaks outside, slipping out of the window as quickly as she climbed in. The bottom of her purple dress is wet—with blood or water, I don't know, but knowing her, it's probably blood.

It seems my girl has been busy, but so have I.

I know she has been looking for me. No doubt by now, my Alyx knows I saved her precious little king. She's smart, and she knows I don't do anything without cause, so she is probably worried about what I want from him. She should, however, be more worried about what I want from her, and I usually wouldn't avoid her, but I had important matters to take care of, and one day, she will understand why.

Everything I do is for her.

Besides, a little longing won't harm her. It's good she looked for me. It proves she still cares and that after our kiss, she still wants me.

I wait for her, leaning against the wood building where it faces the wall, offering us some privacy. I can't help but grin when she spots me, her eyes flashing with that fire that drives me crazy. Her back straightens as she marches straight up to me, poking my chest.

"You! Where have you been? I searched for you all night," she hisses.

My hand drifts out, capturing some stray strands of her fiery hair. She smacks me away, and I sigh. "Missed me, did you?" I ask, not necessarily to avoid the conversation, but because I'm genuinely curious.

"You wish. I mean it, Crux. Where were you?" Her arms fold over her chest, pushing her breasts up until they almost spill from her dress. My mouth goes dry at the sight, and the same desire I always feel when she is near, or even mentioned, pumps through my veins.

I wonder if she would be scared if she knew how much I craved her and all the dirty, depraved things I imagine doing to her even now, when she is standing here in her princess dress, looking divine and untouchable.

I like the leathers, but there is something about dresses that drives me equally crazy. I want to rip them, stain them, hike them up, and feel the skirts wrapped around me as I pound into her tight body. It's the image that keeps flashing through my brain, even as her lips twist in anger.

"I mean it though. Did you miss me?" I ask seriously.

I watch her throat bob as she swallows, something in her softening as she searches my gaze. "Crux," she murmurs. It's just my name, but I am lost. I would give her anything.

"Hunting," I growl, offering some truth. I don't tell her who or what. She doesn't need to know yet, but Alyx should understand that everything I do is for her.

I push from the wall, and our positions change quickly as her back hits the building and I lean closer.

Despite it, she doesn't back down, tilting her head up in defiance. "Leave the king alone, Crux."

"Hmm." I just continue to stare, unable to do anything else.

She's just so fucking magnificent. Her anger drives me wild, and I wish she would unleash it across me.

"I mean it, Crux. Do not make me your enemy," she warns, her eyes flashing with a fury so beautiful, it renders me speechless for a moment.

Stepping closer, I tip her chin up so her gaze stays on mine. "You could never be."

For a moment, we just stare until I can't take it anymore. I've missed her. It's been a day, but I've missed her so fucking much, and after finally kissing the woman I've been in love with for years, I can't seem to stop thinking about it, so I take a chance. She might kill me, but it would be worth it.

Her anger morphs to desire as I slam her back into the wall, placing one hand near her head and the other on her side, and then I crush my lips to hers. My tongue tangles with hers in a battle of wills, both of us fighting for the upper hand.

Alyx is and always has been my weakness, and I let that show as I devour her. Her sweet taste drives me crazy, and my cock is so hard beneath my trousers it hurts, jerking with the need to be buried in my girl until she forgets why she's mad at me.

I feel her muscles bunch and almost grin against her lips, knowing what she is planning.

Groaning, I block the hand that comes up to stab me, sending the dagger spiralling away. Her frustration is evident, and she changes her plan of attack from stabbing me to making me surrender. Her lips harden, feasting on mine, and her hands grip my body.

If only she knew I had already surrendered everything to her all those years ago.

My mind, body, and soul are all hers.

She could force me to my knees and have me wait there for years just for another taste of her and I would, but here she is, kissing me back, and the fire I've tried to tame overtakes me. I cannot hold back. I need her to know how much I want her. I need to know she wants me too.

It's selfish and greedy, but it doesn't stop me from hiking her dress up and slipping my hand into her underwear. I swallow her gasp, feeling her body shudder against mine. We are crossing a line, but I don't care. I want her too much to stop. I need her too much. She might always win the war against me, but I will win this battle.

"Crux," she whispers, trying to pull away. She turns her head, my lips sliding across her cheek to her neck. She moans in my ear, and I feel the hot flesh of her clit throb in my palm. She's so hot and wet for me as I keep my hand pressed against her centre, letting her decide. Her legs part, and it's all the permission I need.

That last shred of control leaves me as I push them wider, lifting her skirts as I kiss her once more. She's so soft, so hot, that I can't help parting her pussy lips and stroking my fingers across her to trace every inch. I know I should move slowly and be soft, but I can't with her—not when she bites down on my lower lip, urging me on.

Alyx doesn't need my protection, not right now.

Sucking on her lower lip in retaliation, I press my thumb to her throbbing bundle of nerves, feeling her jerk as she moans. Satisfaction and pride fill me as I watch her, playing her body and wanting every drop of her pleasure.

I need it more than I need my next breath.

Rubbing her clit in slow circles, I work out what she likes, and when she cries out, I know she's lost. Leaving her pretty clit, I slide my fingers lower, circling her tight, little hole as her eyes open, clashing with mine, burning bright with desire.

"Crux." She pants my name, and it goes straight to my pounding heart and leaking cock.

Locking my eyes on hers, I slip two fingers inside her, forcing them deep. She lifts up, trying to escape me, but I press my other hand against her hip, pulling her close and slamming her down onto them.

There will be no escape from me. She needs to know that.

Whimpering, she grips my shoulders as I curl my fingers inside her, stroking those nerves that have her eyes sliding shut again, whimpers falling from her lips. When I add a third, stretching her channel around my scarred digits, she cries out so loudly, I wouldn't be surprised if someone heard, and that thought only makes me wilder.

I grind my hand into her clit as I pull my fingers free and thrust them back in, showing her exactly how I plan to fuck her, and I will. Alyx will be mine.

The sound of footsteps reaches us, and she panics, trying to push me away, but I push her back, pinning her as I fuck her with my fingers. The footsteps stop in front of the building, and there's a mumble of voices and then rattling doors.

"Crux," she warns, breathing heavily, her chest heaving. Leaning down, I lick across her breasts before rolling my eyes up to hers.

"Don't tell me to stop. I couldn't even if I wanted to. I need to feel you come so I can survive the rest of the day while I am not at your side," I admit, my voice rough, and she clenches around my fingers, making me groan. "Fuck, you feel so good, so hot, so wet . . . It's all I'll think about today. Someone could sneak up on us right now and sink a blade into my heart and I still wouldn't stop. They would have to pry my dead body from yours."

Her breath hiccups, and she pulls me closer, her lips meeting mine again as I grind my palm into her clit. Her channel flutters around me, letting me know she's close, but I want to drag this out for eternity. I want to be locked in her body forever.

We hear the guards breaking in the doors of the bathhouse we're behind, but we don't care. The splitting of wood and confusion in their voices reach us. Still, I don't stop, and she doesn't ask me to. She rolls her hips, grinding her cunt into my palm, all while letting out little mewls that drive me crazy.

"Shh or they'll find us," I warn as she whimpers, her channel clenching on my fingers. "Alyx, if they come back here, I'm going to kill them for interrupting something I have dreamed about for years."

My threat does nothing but spur her on, so I grab a blade and force the flat edge between her teeth.

"Bite down and stay silent." I demand. "Because I have no plans to stop until I feel you come around my fingers."

She nods, biting into the blade as she muffles her moans. We hear splashing and yells, but neither of us stop. My fingers are buried deep inside her, stroking that tight, wet heat until her eyes roll back in her head and a muffled scream emerges from her throat as she finds her pleasure.

I feel her tight channel clamp around my fingers as her cream drips from her, her legs shaking as she comes.

I drink in every inch of her release, memorizing it. I've never seen anything more beautiful, and I know I could die a happy man right now.

She finally slumps back into the wood building, and I slide my fingers free of her channel as she watches me with a bewildered look.

I have to force myself to step back, leaving her there. She looks more beautiful than I've ever seen her, and it makes it difficult to breathe. For a moment, I allow myself to be weak and throw down the flag in a truce.

Licking my fingers, I groan at the taste of her cream. It's so sweet, my teeth ache, and I know I'll never taste anything as incredible ever again. Her eyes flash with want as she watches me, and it takes every inch of my strength not to throw her to the ground and have my wicked way with her.

"I do like fighting with you, Alyx, even if you're not my enemy," I admit, and her mouth parts slightly. "It's so . . . sweet," I murmur as I suck my fingers before grinning. "Your king is safe . . . for now."

I disappear before I make her mine for all to see, just as yells emerge from the building about a body being found.

I cannot help but chuckle. Busy indeed.

THIRTY-THREE

JOHA

I don't have to feign my surprise as I stare at my advisors and the captain of the city guard in wide-eyed shock. My meeting room is full of people, all of them looking as horrified as I am at the news he just relayed to us. The fact that he came all this way to inform me personally should have warned me that something serious had occurred. Usually, any information from the city guards would be passed through my guards and advisors, not given as an in-person report.

Perhaps I misheard the captain, as there is no way anything on this scale would happen. Things like this don't just transpire in the Uppers, and certainly not the palace. My mind is spinning, my thoughts tripping over each other as I try to formulate an acceptable response. The advisors are all looking at me. For once, they have lost their haughty attitudes and seem to be frozen in horror. After all, it was one of them who was murdered.

"What?" The question slips out of my mouth, making me sound

as dumb as they believe me to be. I heard him the first time. I just can't comprehend it.

Even so, the captain clears his throat and repeats himself. "Lord Beaumont was found murdered, and his house was set aflame. We believe his family and staff were burned alive in the fire and that it was started on purpose."

My throat constricts painfully, and I reach for my glass of water. The cool liquid does nothing to take away the feeling, and I am no closer to knowing how to respond to this.

Leaning forward in her chair on my left, Alyx clears her throat delicately, placing her hands lightly on the table's edge. "Are you sure they are all dead? There is no way they could have escaped?" she asks quietly, her words strained and face pained at the very thought of innocents dying.

She's a good actress.

The captain looks awkward, not wanting to talk of death and murder in front of both Queen Mother and my betrothed, but I give a sharp nod of my head, indicating for him to go ahead.

"We have found bodies, Your Majesty. All of which fit the descriptions we were given of the victims."

Unlike most of my meetings, Alyx's presence was requested due to the seriousness of the situation. I'm surprised they came to this decision by themselves. I assumed I would have to force the issue to have her attend. Perhaps they are realising they cannot shut both of us out.

However, the situation is unprecedented. Not only was Lord Beaumont and his family killed, but A'lan Wrynn was found dead in the bathing house in the palace. Here, on guarded palace grounds. All of us feel on edge and vulnerable. The palace is supposed to be the safest and most guarded area in the land, yet several attempts on my life have occurred, and now this.

"The house was set alight in the early hours yesterday morning." The captain glances around the room as he speaks. "I would have come to inform you then," he continues. "However, it took us an entire day to get the fire under control. It required all of us as we tried to stop it from spreading to other properties. Because of this, I was unable to spare even a guard to tell you. As soon as I felt it was safe, I came straight here."

He clearly knows how to handle disgruntled nobles, as well as preempting the questions I could feel bubbling up around me. He's a good captain of the city guard. My advisors like to be the first to know what's happening in the city, so the fact that the house was burned and they are only just learning of it a day later is not acceptable to them. However, when he explained the situation as he did, it is impossible to be mad at him.

Orion told me that this captain was good when he was promoted, and I see now that he was right. He put the welfare of others before bowing and scraping to the Crown.

There is still quiet grumbling in the room, although as I glance around, it is impossible to tell who is making the noise. If anyone tries to berate the captain for his actions, then I'm going to snap. I'm too exhausted for that sort of nonsense.

First thing this morning, I was disturbed by Orion barging his way into my rooms. I didn't sleep much thanks to my midnight rendezvous with Alyx. While it had been my intention to get a little rest beside her, as soon as she fell asleep, I found myself watching her. When she sleeps, her guard is down and her face is beautiful. She looks younger, less fierce, and it made me wonder what she would have been like if her life had turned out differently.

When the sun started to rise, I snuck back to my palace and into my rooms, Orion dutifully guarding me. I hoped to get a few hours of sleep before I was disturbed, but it seems that the gods had other plans for me. My head of the guard strode into my room and told me something terrible happened, which is how I ended up here, at the head of the meeting table with Alyx at my side and all of my advisors staring at me.

Firstly, they told me about A'lan Wrynn. All of the advisors already seemed to know, but Queen Mother looked surprised. It was only as we were discussing how someone had snuck past the guards and into the palace to kill him in the first instance when there was a knock at the door.

It was the captain of the city guard.

All of the guards in the land ultimately answer to me, but the divisions outside of the palace generally run themselves, with appointed captains.

One stands before us now, telling us of Beaumont. We had been so focused on A'lan's death and the safety *inside* the palace that we hadn't even thought about the safety of those on the other side of our walls.

A'lan Wrynn's death is more alarming than tragic. He was a young, fairly new noble who had been rising in the ranks recently. I never paid him much attention, but I saw him around. I am now wondering if I should have been keeping an eye on him. Was he involved in any of the assassination attempts? Is that how he ended up dead? His neck was sliced, so it's clear it was murder and not an accident.

Beaumont, however, is a major shock. Is it worse because we already heard of Wrynn's murder? It is not often that two lords are killed a day apart. The lords do not know about this, but there was also the fake guard who was murdered on palace grounds when he tried to assassinate me. So much death and destruction.

If it was just Beaumont who was killed, then that is one thing. He was a greedy bastard, and I suspected he was involved in some shady business for a while, so it was only a matter of time before he annoyed someone enough to die. It wasn't just him though. His entire family and staff are dead. It is such a waste of life that I am barely able to comprehend it. Setting fire to his property and killing innocents is sick and unnecessary. The murderer went through the trouble of doing this, and it sends a message.

Alyx looks shocked and innocent at my side, her hand pressed against her chest as if needing to physically hold back her emotions.

Did she have something to do with this? Looking at her, no one would ever expect her, but I know what she's capable of. For a moment, her eyes meet mine, and I see a burning happiness in her gaze before it shutters and goes back to looking shocked. A'lan's death is the way I would expect her to act, quick and clean, but why him? I find it difficult to believe that he had anything to do with the attempts on my life, so why kill him? He has next to no power, seeing as he comes from a lowly family and has only just started to gain a good reputation, so why would he ruin that?

Once again, Beaumont's death is something I can imagine Alyx orchestrating, and his dodgy dealings make him a candidate for working against me. However, if this was her doing, then her trail of destruction is making me see her in a different light. If she did kill A'lan, then I was cuddled up with a murderer last night. How could she do that and then just return and fall asleep as though nothing happened? She slept like a baby, clearly unbothered by her actions.

It is the death of the family and staff that I keep getting stuck on. If it was her, killing the rest of those people was sick. Would she really do that? During the time we've been working together, I have started to get to know her and see past some of those barriers she wears so well. I thought that perhaps she'd become an assassin because she had no other choice, and I had romantic visions of rescuing her from that life. However, I'm starting to realise now how much of a fool I have been. Do I even really know her at all?

I need to get out of here and talk to her.

There is still more I need to learn, but I know Orion will stay behind and get as much information from the captain as possible, filling me in later. I don't even have to order him to do it, simply sharing a look with my friend and king's guard. He nods, understanding what I'm silently asking for.

I sigh loudly and rub a hand over my face, aware of the advisors and guards all looking at me exactly as I wanted.

"Excuse me. My betrothed is looking quite unwell with all this talk of death. I am going to escort her back to her rooms." Pushing my chair out, I get to my feet, and the rest of those in the room do the same, dipping their heads as per protocol.

No one bothers to stop me as I place a hand on Alyx's back and guide her from the hall. We stay silent as we walk across the palace grounds towards the queen's palace, our guards following closely. It doesn't take long to get there, since the grounds are quiet thanks to the early hour, and with only a look, I order the guards to stay by the doors and continue until we get to her bed chamber.

As soon as the door shuts behind me, she sprawls across the bed, resting her arm over her face as a wide yawn splits her lips. She's not the least bit troubled.

Frustration and anger bubble in my gut as I watch her relax on the bed as if the last hour's meeting was nothing more than an inconvenience. Does she care in the slightest about all the innocent lives lost here? I stew in silence, getting more and more worked up.

I can't hold myself back any longer.

"Did you have anything to do with that?"

There is a long pause, and when she lowers her arm, she stares at me incredulously. "Is that what has you in such a twist?" She sits up, still pinning me with her gaze. "Is that why you have barely been able to look me in the eye? Or is it because you let yourself be vulnerable the other night?"

Jerking back like she smacked me, I scowl and shake my head, not understanding the relevance of what she's saying. Why bring that up now?

"That has nothing to do with this." I try to keep control of my voice as I speak, making sure it's low and even. "Did you kill those people?"

She arches her brow, giving me a look that tells me she thinks I'm being stupid. After a moment, she snorts, but there is no amusement behind it as she pushes herself off the bed and stands at her full height.

"What is it with you men? You know why you hired me, right? I'm an assassin. This is what I do."

I can't allow her to talk her way out of this or speak in riddles. This is important, and I need to hear it from her. "Did you do it?" I ask, my voice deadly calm.

"Yes, I did. Both men were involved in trying to kill you." She looks exasperated, not understanding why I would be upset about this. "You wanted me to work out who is behind the attacks and keep you safe, and that is what I'm doing."

My stomach sinks. Does she truly have no conscience? She killed so easily and then pretended to be shocked by their deaths when surrounded by others. I have no idea how to deal with this. All I know is that I have made a huge mistake.

"You're a monster." I meant for it to come out as an accusation, yet my voice is weak and full of shock. "How could I have ever thought having you around was a good idea?"

For a second, I see hurt flash across her face and I feel guilty, but it's gone in a second and is replaced with a smirk that I'm used to seeing. She saunters over to where I stand, the tension in the room high. "I don't know. I told you it was a bad idea to hire an assassin." Her voice is a purr as she speaks, sounding as though she's enjoying my anger and horror. "If you didn't want anybody to die, you should have hired a guard or some noble warrior. That is not who I am." Despite her tone, I can tell that she's angry at me, although I can't fathom why *she* would be the one hurting right now.

"I didn't expect you to kill innocents, Alyx!" I take a step towards her until we're toe to toe, and I stare down at her. "What kind of a twisted demon do you have to be to kill a child?"

There's a pause, and her face suddenly clears as she absorbs my words. "You really think I killed all of those people?" She laughs, shaking her head. "Beaumont and the baby lord, yes. I killed them and feel no regret. What I can't believe is that you'd really think I would kill staff and children just for being at the house. They can't help who their boss is."

Confused, I stare down at her, no longer sure of anything.

"There were bodies found." I trail off, suddenly feeling a cold chill as I realise I might have made a mistake. Burnt bodies that would be almost impossible to identify.

Alyx nods slowly as she watches me put everything together, her arms crossed over her chest. "Yes, bodies I stole from the morgue. I faked their deaths and gave them money to start a new life, then I put the bodies in the house and set it alight. Why do you think I chose fire? It sends a message and erases all traces of who they were, leaving only their bones."

"You didn't kill innocents." It's not a question. I feel stupid for not speaking with her about this and assuming that she did it. My heart lifts a little, knowing that she does have some sort of moral compass.

"No, but you have to realise something," she starts as though she's able to read my mind and see where my thoughts are heading. "I am an assassin. I'm not a good person, and I can be ruthless. I have killed innocents in the past when I had no other options, and I will do it again if I have to."

My feelings are so mixed. She killed two men under my rule, and I wasn't bothered about it other than when I thought she killed the children and staff. I should be disgusted by all death. When did it start to become acceptable?

"You hired an assassin, and now you don't like how I work. You can't have it both ways, Your Majesty."

She stalks from her room without another word, and I feel like I'm just as stupid as everyone thinks I am.

CHAPTER
THIRTY-FOUR

ALYX

Perched on the roof of a one-story home in the Lowers, I quietly seethe.

I tell myself that it's because of the male I've been stalking for the last hour and the atrocities he's about to commit, but all I can think about is how disgusted Joha looked when he hurled his accusations at me this morning.

Of course, that only made me madder—both at him and myself. It has consumed my thoughts. I hoped that a little hunting would help distract me, clearing my mind and letting me sink into the quiet stillness that's required when taking out a target—one of which is striding through the streets below like he owns it.

This part of the Lowers is one of the nicer areas. Most of the houses have roofs and doors that close properly. However, it is still part of the Lowers, and as such, poverty and crime run rampant. I could sit in wait anywhere in this part of the city and witness some sort of crime happen.

In the Uppers, they have well-lit, clean streets, windows, and doors that lock, as well as guards on every street corner to keep the peace. The difference between the two is sickening, and after having stayed in the exquisite opulence of the palace, the city I grew up in seems more derelict than ever.

After my argument with Joha this morning, I feigned a headache and told my ladies-in-waiting that I needed to be alone, and then I promptly headed into the city. I needed space to clear my head before I did something stupid. I spent the rest of the day exploring the city, trying to pick up any information that would be helpful in my hunt for more answers.

Most of the talk on the streets is about Beaumont's death and what happened to his family. No one seems to realise that only the man himself is dead, all believing that everyone perished. Everything went exactly as I planned, and no one suspects that I spared the innocent.

Why am I so mad that Joha instantly believed that about me? It is what I wanted the world to see, yet I suppose there is a part of me that thought Joha had started to get to know me in a way only one other person ever has.

This makes me irritated with myself though. I don't let people close for a reason. I am everything he accused me of being—a murderer, an assassin, and a thief—and putting me in a pretty dress and calling me a princess was never going to change that. It is in my blood. He needs to realise that, taking the good with the bad.

If he thinks I'm evil, then I'm going to show him exactly how ruthless I can be. Many might go in the opposite direction and try to prove that they are not as bad as they were accused of being, but I am not like most. I am not a good person, and the quicker he realises that, the better for both of us.

My trail of bodies started a couple of hours ago. I've been watching the guards who prey on the weak and go out of their way to be cruel. The first death was quick and silent. Since then, though, I've been making it more interesting for myself, playing with my prey before killing them. They are all males who would have been hung had they not been in the guard, so really, I'm doing the king a favour.

This makes my other job difficult though. It has been quiet on the streets and the gossip front. The news of Beaumont has spread, and people are afraid. They know my patterns, and with the trail of bodies I've left behind, they know I'm back on the streets, so they are being more careful because of it. More guards are patrolling the area now, looking for the killer who took out five of their men. It makes things a little more challenging, and I have to be more careful, but that has never stopped me before.

I need to stop playing and try to get more information. First, though, I need to deal with the guard who just cornered a young woman in a dark, secluded alley below me.

I noticed the way he was watching young women and girls in the market when he was on patrol and have been following him for the last hour, my instincts telling me he's going to act on whatever sick thoughts are twisting his mind. It seems my patience has paid off.

"Please, I have no money," the woman tells the guard, her voice shaking as he backs her farther into the darkness, but she brandishes a small knife, trying to scare off her stalker. Good for her. I mean, the blade will be like a toothpick against a guy like him, but she's brave.

She'll need to be to survive the Lowers.

"It is not your money that I want." The guard grins cruelly, his face lighting up with the prospect of what he's about to do.

Having seen enough, I walk to the edge of the roof and drop down just behind him. My descent is nearly silent, and he doesn't even know I'm there, the idiot. The girl does, though, and something flashes in her eyes as she calculates if I'm here to help or harm her.

Clucking my tongue, I shake my head slowly when the guard spins around in surprise. "Where do they find you guys?" I'm wearing a cloak and a covering over the bottom half of my face, but I make sure I'm standing in enough light so he can see the loathing in my eyes. "They really scraped the bottom of the barrel for you."

Anger flashes across his face, and he balls his hands into fists, but he holds himself back. "You're the one who's been killing the guards."

Brows raising, I tilt my head to one side. "Huh, you have more brains than I gave you credit for."

"Now, now, don't play with the street vermin," a mocking voice sings out of the darkness. Crux's familiar lilt washes over me like a wave.

His presence is comforting, but just like any ocean, he can turn deadly in a second. I knew he would find me eventually, considering I've not been subtle with my kills. Cocking my hip out, I glance over my shoulder at him and grin at the approval I see in his eyes.

"Oh, but they are so fun to chase." I pout, pulling my scarf down so he can see my expression. It doesn't matter if the guard sees me, as he's already solidified his fate. Crux smiles, playing along, and shakes his head. Sighing as if I'm disappointed, I palm one of my daggers, making sure the guard is unable to see it. "Fine . . ." I extend the word.

Without looking away from Crux, I flick my hand out with a snap of my wrist, and the guard makes a gurgling noise that tells me I've hit my mark. The girl gasps at the sight of the knife now sticking from his neck, but she doesn't scream. Good.

"Go, and don't tell anyone about this." I don't need to threaten her because she knows I could track her down if I wanted to. She nods and runs past us without a word, escaping into the streets.

Pushing away from the wall, Crux slowly walks towards me, looking every inch a predator, and I'm his prey.

"You've had a busy evening."

Of course he knows what I've been up to. He has spies everywhere. In fact, I am surprised that it took him until now to track me down. He'll have his reasons for it, I am sure. I boldly meet his gaze. Just looking at him has my core clenching, remembering what happened the last time we were alone together. From the glimmer in his eyes, I know he's also thinking about it. It would be so easy for me to push him against the wall and finish what we started the other night.

No. I'm on a mission, and I've wasted enough time today.

"I need more information on who is behind the attacks on the king."

He looks at me in that way of his that tells me he's able to see right into my soul, past my masks. All he would have to do is kiss me and my resolve would disappear, and he knows that. However, he also knows me better than I know myself and understands that I need to do this right now.

"Okay." He gestures for me to follow him. "I know somewhere we can start, but you need to change."

⚘

STUMBLING ALONG THE STREET, I laugh drunkenly as I bump into someone walking in the opposite direction.

"Whoops. Sorry, sir," I slur, pocketing several of his coins in the process. It's as easy as breathing to me, and I know Crux is doing the same to the man's companion. Old habits die hard.

I'm not just stealing to pay for my next drink, although that is a bonus, but to see if the king's advisor, whom I just walked into, is carrying the newly minted coins. I don't think we're going to find any more. After all, only a fool would carry them around now that the main people involved have been killed. Even so, I'm looking for new leads, and this is something I can easily check.

Dressed as a man, I'm not given a second glance as we weave through the streets, nor does anyone notice as we turn around and follow the two men we just bumped into. Everyone ignores drunks. They are seen as a plague across the Lowers, getting in people's way and causing damage when they get into fights. Because of this, pretending to be drunk has become something that I'm very good at.

While my acting skills are pretty solid, my disguise seals the effect. I put on fake bushy eyebrows and a beard, as well as inserts in my mouth to change the shape of my cheeks and jawline. I've learned to disguise myself since I was a child, so it comes naturally to me now, as well as changing the pitch of my voice.

The two we're following are advisors to the king, and according to Crux, they enjoy frequenting the brothels in the Lowers. They weren't hard to find, since their disguises are poor. Their clothes might be plain and covered by cloaks, but they are far too clean and well made for an area like this. Even the way they walk around like they have all the time in the world makes them stick out like sore thumbs. I bet they think they are so stealthy.

Crux and I follow them to their favourite brothel. Apparently, they frequent this one a couple of times a week, which is good for us. If they come here often, then they will be more relaxed and their tongues will be looser, so perhaps they'll let something slip that will be useful.

We stay back, occasionally stopping to lean against a wall as though we're trying to catch our balance. Once the advisors have entered the brothel, we wait a couple of minutes before following. The guard lets us straight in without asking for payment, instantly recognising Crux.

Something uncomfortable twinges inside me that feels suspiciously like jealousy. I want to bury the feeling deep down and focus on the task at hand, but I can't help wondering why the guard recognises him. Is it because of his notoriety in the Lowers or because he frequents the brothel often?

I'm not sure I want to know the answer.

Once inside, it takes a moment for my eyes to adjust to the dim lighting, the red lamps giving the room a strange, mysterious feel. While I know of all the brothels in the city, I've not been to this one before. The room is surprisingly large. One wall is taken up by a long bar, where a barman makes drinks for his customers who are perched on stools. In the centre of the room are several lounge chairs and tables for customers to sit and enjoy the view with their drinks.

The remainder of the space is taken up with booths, over half of which are currently occupied. Most of the brothels in the city have setups like this. It's cheaper than having rooms out back and safer for the girls if someone gets rough. Each booth has a wide, semicircular couch with a low table in the middle, and they are surrounded by thick red-velvet curtains that can be closed to offer privacy should you choose a woman to entertain you.

I spot our targets settled in a booth, talking to a giggling girl, as Crux and I make our way to the bar. We have not even sat down on our stools before we're joined by a buxom woman with bright blonde, curly hair. The pink wisp of a dress she wears is sheer, showing that she's not wearing anything beneath it.

"Your Majesty," she coos, leaning against the bar in a seductive way that pushes her chest out. "We've not seen you here in a long time. May we please you and your friend?"

Clearly, she knows who he is from the title she gave him. He flashes her a quick glance before turning and ordering drinks for us. She doesn't give up though, sticking with us as we get our drinks, winking and wiggling her body in a way I'm sure is designed to attract men.

It's only after Crux has taken a long sip of his drink that he turns his full attention to her. "We want a booth close to those two." He nods in the direction of the advisors.

Her eyes brighten with curiosity, and I spot an opportunity. "What do you know about them?" I ask, sliding a coin towards her.

She pockets it as soon as my hand lifts, the coin disappearing in the blink of an eye, then she shrugs in answer to my question. "Not much, to be honest. They are from the palace, although I don't know what they do. They are into some kinky shit and always come here together, if you know what I mean."

Now that is new information. Raising a brow, I glance at Crux. His face gives away nothing, but I know him well enough to know he's cataloguing everything and probably already has a plan.

Returning my attention to her, I tilt my head to one side. "They are in a relationship?"

She shrugs again. "If you can call it that. They are poor tippers, so we only do the bare minimum with them, so we don't hear much." Pushing away from the bar, she takes my hand and pulls me from my stool. "Let me take you to a booth."

Diamond, our new whore friend, leads us over to the booth on the left of the advisors, their curtains now closed. We don't need to see them to get what we need, though, and curtains aren't good at blocking out sound.

"Come back in fifteen minutes," Crux orders, tossing a coin her way.

Once again, the coin disappears in a flash, and she leaves us in peace. Settling against the seats, we make ourselves look comfortable, sipping our drinks while listening to the conversation happening in the booth next to us.

We don't hear anything interesting because the advisors are too busy with each other and their whore. The noises make me wrinkle my nose, and I'm glad I'm not able to see into their booth. Crux and I make small talk about nothing so anyone watching us doesn't get suspicious. Diamond approaches our table once more, joining us to keep up appearances. You don't go to a brothel and not spend time with the whores.

Perching on the couch beside Crux, she shakes her hair back and pushes her chest out once more in an attempt to catch his attention.

"Are you sure I can't help you two?" she murmurs, placing her hand on Crux's thigh and slowly sliding it towards his crotch.

I stiffen and reach for my dagger as blinding jealousy ignites, pushing me into a rage I've never felt before. Before I can act on it, however, Crux's hand comes down on hers, stopping her in her tracks. Her face twists into an expression of pain as he squeezes it hard.

"You are dismissed."

His voice is cold and hard, not to be ignored. Several silver coins appear on the table between us, and she grabs them, leaving us in a flash, not needing to be told twice.

What in the underworld was that? I have never had a reaction like that before. We're not in a relationship, so why would I snap so fiercely over something like that? She's a whore, it is literally her job to seduce us, and I have never been mad at a whore for doing that before.

Crux has been watching me the whole time, his keen gaze not missing a thing, and I can see his curiosity and a hint of amusement in his eyes.

"You're jealous." His lips pull up into a grin as I simply arch my eyebrow, not giving him an answer, although annoyance and confusion still flow through me. Clucking his tongue, he slides closer to me. "You think I would want a whore over you?"

His voice is like velvet, and before I know it, he's in front of me, his hands pressed against the couch on either side of me. "Tell me, would you have killed her if she touched me there? If I hadn't stopped her?"

I could lie or make up an excuse, but alcohol has made me brave. Today has been shit, and I want to forget how Joha's accusation made me feel. Crux can take that away.

"Yes," I reply simply, not feeling a single ounce of regret for my answer. "One second longer and she would have been dead."

Instead of calling me a demon for my answer, his eyes flash with arousal and approval and his grin turns victorious. Reaching out, he drags a finger down my cheek and cups my chin, lifting my head so I'm unable to look away. Despite my disguise, all I see is pure lust and obsession in his gaze. "My vicious, little Alyx."

Giddiness flares through me at his new pet name for me, and the possession in his voice turns me on in a way I didn't think was possible.

"You love it," I counter.

His expression shifts, becoming more serious. "Yes, I do."

We surge forward, our lips crashing together. The noise of the brothel fades away until it's just Crux, me, and the burning need blazing between us. Our kisses are animalistic and rough, and we bite each other's lips and tongue. I don't know what this thing is between us, but I feel like I'm falling under his spell. This could end horribly, he's my best friend, but in this moment, I can't find it in myself to be bothered, simply needing him.

He reaches for my breasts, only to realise they are bound thanks to my male disguise. Cupping my crotch through my trousers instead, he starts to rub circles against me in time with our kisses. Sparks of pleasure shoot through me, and I'm desperate to touch him, to feel the evidence of his arousal for me.

Tugging the opening of his trousers, I struggle to get it unfastened while my mind is distracted by his lips and hypnotic touch. I just get them open when the curtains to the booth are jerked open.

We both whirl in an instant, our blades hidden but ready to go should we be attacked. However, a very drunk man looks at us with confusion, glancing at the other booths in the room. When he turns back to us, he looks us over. Holding his hands up in a gesture of peace, he takes a step back.

"Hey, man, whatever does it for you."

Stumbling away, he moves over to the booth on our other side as we watch him carefully.

I know the moment is gone now, so I start to straighten my clothes, but I cannot hide my smile at the longing I see in Crux's gaze. Reputation is everything to him. In our business, it's all we have, but he doesn't seem bothered that the drunk might blab about Crux's new proclivities. When our eyes meet, though, there is a promise of things to come in his expression, and I cannot help but shiver in want.

CHAPTER
THIRTY-FIVE

ORION

Alyx has left a trail of bodies behind over the last few days. I know it is her, and Joha knows it is her—hell, from the twinkling mirth in her eyes when she looks at us, she knows we know it was her.

It's put me on edge. Joha seemed angry during the meeting, but after, when I came for him to report my findings, he looked forlorn and even muttered strange ramblings about never judging an assassin by its blade. Ever since then, he has been down, and it doesn't seem to help that Alyx is avoiding him. I know she is busy doing whatever fake queens-to-be and assassins do, but his eyes linger on her when he sees her in the palace, and I see unspoken words in his gaze that don't bode well.

He cannot afford to be attached to the assassin, but it's growing clearer by the day that he is. He spent the night in her bed, he looks to her for guidance, and he trusts her.

Not only that, but I kissed her and let her in.

She's tricky, and she's a problem, and I need to understand anything that is a problem to my king. Alyx didn't come from nowhere. She must have a past, a weakness, something I can use if need be, just in case, because despite me wanting the assassin, my king comes first. It is my duty and my honour to protect him as his guard and his friend, if that be from blades or afflictions of the heart, which is exactly why I find myself squishing my lumbering frame into the small spaces of Scholars House, where all records of every being in the kingdom are kept. Each province in the Uppers holds more in-depth details. As for the Lowers, I am not sure, but every birth, family name, and information legally has to be kept here. It's as good a place as any to begin my search. After all, she is not the only one who can hunt. I do have to be discreet, though, because if anyone findsout who I am searching for and why, it could ruin everything Joha is working for, not to mention get us killed. This is why I bribe some of the scholars with time off of basic training, which every male is required to do, and they leave me in peace. Shelves of scrolls dating back before the years the kingdom began span before me, with tight, little walkways leading a merry path throughout.

I settle in for the long haul, but I do manage to narrow it down between certain years on a supposition of her age. It leaves me with leeway of around eight years' worth of scrolls to look through. I discard all males and all of those related to marriage—I cannot imagine Alyx has been married as of yet, not unless she did it to kill him. Slowly but surely, my pile dwindles, and I tug ones out in order, quickly scanning them before putting them back when I realise they are not her. Is Alyx her real name, or is it close to her real name? Was she born in the Lowers? What about her family? These thoughts plague me. Families are harder to track within the Lowers but not impossible. It will just take time.

I cannot be gone from my post all day, however, so I resign myself to having to come back and continue the search until I find what I'm looking for—the truth about the assassin.

I manage to search a good chunk of the scrolls before my eyes begin to blur from the dim lighting and dust and I give up for the day. I don't want Joha to remain unprotected for too long, especially not with his absent mind and the assassination attempts. I thank the scholars on the way out and emerge from the three-story building into the late afternoon sun. It blinds me for a moment, which is the only reason I don't see her straight away. When I do, I jerk back, my hand dropping to my sword on instinct.

She smirks. "Easy, big guy."

"Alyx," I snap.

Her grin only grows as she leans next to the door in another dramatic dress, this one blood red and showcasing her every curve. Her hair is artfully piled on top of her head, showing off her slender neck, and her hands are decorated with ornate rings. She twirls her fingers in the air like she wishes there were a dagger in her hand. It wouldn't surprise me if there was. I often wonder where she hides them in the dresses she wears, but that thought only leads to trouble, so I shake my head.

"What are you doing here?" I ask, glancing around for Joha or her maids, but none are to be found. She is far too wily.

"I could ask you the same thing," she retorts with a knowing look.

"I was looking up births for the year, you know, for celebration rituals and dates. I thought Joha could use a celebration to cheer him up, not that he's sad, but it was just an idea. He likes parties, but then I remembered that would be a prime opportunity for an assassin to strike—not you, or maybe you, I don't know. Either way, I was . . . looking." I cough to cover my embarrassment over my blundering attempt at a lie, which was more of a rambling concession of guilt.

Her eyebrow arches as she pushes away from the wall and moves closer. "Don't forget whose side we are on, Orion. Lying to each other does not form trust." Her hand lands on my breast plate, and with a wicked grin, she presses up on her toes and places a taunting kiss on my cheek. It burns me through like a brand or a promise.

There's a flurry of movement, and my eyes track it as it goes back behind the building, but not before I spy a palace maid's skirt.

Shit, that isn't good, not at all.

CHAPTER
THIRTY-SIX

JOHA

You would think in a palace the size of Moonshadow, there would be far too much for the staff to do other than gossip, but you would be wrong. One hushed sentence can develop into a flame that burns throughout the entire palace, passed from whispering lips to open ears, changing and evolving each time. These rumours are just as dangerous as the daggers my assassin hides in her skirts, sometimes even more so. They have the ability to change public opinion, destroy those who have been scorned, and ruin futures, and they have in the past. Marriages have been broken, jobs have been lost, and even lives have been taken from the evil little whisperings, and now they have started again. Those keen, hungry eyes look at Alyx and the rumours aren't good at all. They even reach me, which shows how quickly and widespread they have become.

It does not matter that Alyx and I have barely spoken a word since I accused her of murdering innocent people. She is still my wife-to-be and someone fighting on my side. I cannot let them tear her apart, which is exactly what they want. They want to rip someone who could be a problem from my side, and they are using everything they have to make that happen. It doesn't matter that, on the outside, she has been nothing but a perfect, naïve princess. She's an unexpected problem to whoever is behind this, and they don't like it. I knew they would strike sooner or later, and it seems now is the time.

Eyes follow me as I make my way through the palace grounds towards Queen Mother's palace, where she invited me for tea. Usually, I would decline, stating Crown business, but I accepted today. I need to defend my fiancée as most would expect, but I also need to silence these rumours once and for all. If Alyx's reputation is ruined before we are married, it could cause an outrage that would prevent me from marrying her, and then she would be torn from the palace. I need her here more than I would like to admit.

The doors to Queen Mother's palace are open upon my arrival, her staff bowing deeply to me as I enter. I show no emotion, no greeting. The role is so comfortable to me now, it's like a second skin.

"She is in the gardens, Your Majesty." A lady's maid quickly hurries forward, and I follow her through the living space to the open door leading to the back of the palace, which Queen Mother has turned into a private garden.

Rare flowers bloom in a variety of colours and sizes, perfectly placed around the grass and shaded under oak trees. In the centre lies a large table, and sitting in the chair under the shade is Queen Mother with a welcome smile on her face. The chair opposite is arranged to be in the sun to blind the occupant and leave them at a disadvantage. Pointing it out would be rude, but to endure it makes you weak. It's just a game she likes to play, and it indicates how this meeting will play out. She came to remind me of her power here.

This is all a perfect ruse, but I'm done playing her games. I don't move the chair or ask for a new one. I head straight to Queen Mother and bow. "Forgive my lateness, Queen Mother, but there is much to do as king. You must understand, as you saw my father in this role for many years. As important as our teas are, being king must come first." I throw the first barb, stronger than I would have before, but I follow it up with a kind smile. "I do not suppose I could trouble you to stand for a moment, could I?"

Her eyes tighten at my remarks and quick change of topic before she can retort, but she rises elegantly from the table, one hand holding a teacup. "My king?" she says, and with a mocking smile, I take her chair and pull it around so it sits next to the one in the sun.

Petty, but funny.

"This way we can both enjoy the view of your beautiful garden and let the sun cleanse us of this horrid week. It seemed a shame to be the only one to enjoy it," I tell her, my head tilted as I watch her.

She knows she cannot do anything, so with a flare of her nostrils, she rounds the table and sits, banging her cup down harder than necessary. "So thoughtful of you, Your Majesty." The smile she gives me is filled with poison, and her lashes flutter as she tries to block out the sun that burns our skin.

If I burn, then so will she.

I am done being their fool. If they come for me, then fine, but if they come for my wife, then they better start running.

"I'm afraid I do not have much time today. I won't bore you with the details." I wave it away as I accept the cup one of the maids pours, but I don't take a sip. I can never be too careful, after all, and it could be poisoned.

"Oh dear, I heard about the passings this week, a terrible shame. Please let me know if you need any help. I understand these matters might be challenging to deal with for someone so young." Her hand touches my arm in a comforting gesture but tightens to the point of pain—point made, she's calling me a young fool.

"You are the thoughtful one, Queen Mother," I reply. "You wished to see me?"

"Oh yes." Her hand flutters over her chest as if she's embarrassed, and her voice lowers as if to prevent anyone from overhearing her words. "I heard a troubling, terrible rumour recently and thought you should hear it from me. I, of course, do not believe it, and I have instructed my people to never speak of it again." She lowers her eyes, playing the perfect part.

"Please, do not keep me waiting." I feign sincerity, despite knowing what she'll say.

"Alyx was spotted by a member of the kitchen staff . . ." She looks up as she speaks, no doubt waiting for a reaction. ". . . kissing your guard. It is shocking and scandalous. It cannot be true, can it, my king? But of course, these rumours are dangerous, not just due to her reputation, but that of you and the Crown."

I hold up my hand to stop her tirade. "I have heard these as well, Queen Mother. Rest assured, they have been laid to rest. No false rumours about my future queen will be tolerated or accepted within the palace, and anyone caught whispering such vile gossip will find themselves facing punishment," I respond as if offering comfort, though it is a threat, and we both know it.

"Good, that is good. You truly are your father's son. You know best in these ways. I just worry for the reputation of your father and the kingdom. As an outsider, she will face more obstacles than most, but with this . . ." Queen Mother shakes her head sadly.

"She will handle it with grace and understanding. We must do the same and offer her our support." I stand, and with my eyes on her, I drain the now cool tea, showing her I am not afraid of her anymore. "Now, if you will excuse me, there is much to deal with. Do enjoy the sunshine, Queen Mother, while we are busy working." I bow, and without waiting for a reply, I leave her to her tea and her flowers, glaring daggers after me.

I do not let them see me hurry, nor show any signs of anger. I make my way through the grounds with purpose and calm until I reach my palace, and then I take the back route into Alyx's. She is in her rooms, lounging on her bed and throwing daggers into the ceiling. She heard me enter but didn't even move.

"Is it true?" I demand, once again finding myself aiming my anger and jealousy at her.

"Is what true? You will have to be more specific," she says without looking at me.

"That you were caught kissing Orion outside of the Scholars House." Pacing back and forth, I glare at her as her eyebrow arches. Without waiting for a response, I begin to rant to her. "Do you know what that will do? They can ruin your reputation, use it to say you are not fit to be queen, and have you taken care of!" I throw my hands in the air, and it's only when I stop that she slides softly from the bed, her dagger in hand as she twirls it effortlessly. She doesn't stop until she stands before me.

"Why do you care?" she asks slowly.

Taking a deep breath, I try to slow my racing heart and swallow the bitterness in my mouth. "It will ruin our plans—"

"I apologize. Why do you care so much to burst in here panting and shaking?" she questions, her eyes flashing with fire.

She wears an expression that both arouses and terrifies me, but I will not back down.

I clench my jaw, biting back retorts, and her hands press against my chest and shove. I stumble back, my eyes widening in astonishment, so she does it again. "Well, Your Majesty?" she says mockingly, pushing me once more. When she goes to do it again, I capture her wrists and squeeze them, reminding her I am not as weak as everyone assumes.

"Because I am jealous," I admit. "Jealous that it could be true. Jealous that you kissed him."

That fire in her eyes seems to grow as she watches me, the skirts of her dress swishing against my robes, but then it is as if she remembers she is mad at me and her gaze turns cold.

"I kissed his cheek. I am not sleeping with him," she says carefully, almost softly. "I am attracted to him. I will not lie about that. I will be more careful next time." She delivers it like a blow, and I thrust her hands away as I step back.

"Next time? You are going to ruin us."

"There is nothing to ruin. You forget this is a farce," she points out. "So what is there to be jealous of? You wouldn't want a child murderer as a wife, would you?" She throws my words back in my face as she strides to the mirror near her bed. "You can see yourself out the way you saw yourself in. I have engagements to get to as your future queen, and I better not be late. As you said, I need to be without fault."

I stare at her back, wanting to approach her and talk about this feeling between us, but I know now is not the right time. She is still angry, and I do not blame her. I have done nothing but berate and judge her for days now, and every time we speak, it is an argument. Instead, I turn and leave like the weak fool they call me, running away with my shame heating my cheeks.

CHAPTER
THIRTY-SEVEN

ORION

I'm burning up with guilt.

Although I had already been feeling guilty for the moments of lust and lack of control I've had around Alyx, now that there are rumours floating around the palace—rumours that I was seen kissing Alyx in the Scholars House—that feeling has only grown. Of course this is a lie, it was a peck on the cheek, but I *have* kissed her before and I want to again.

Something does need to be done, however, about the rumours before they destroy us, and then I need to lock these feelings away and make sure I never act on them again. Joha is my king, my best friend, and I never should have let that assassin worm her way between us.

At least, this is what I keep telling myself. I have a will of iron, and I have never let *anything* come between Joha or my duty before, so what is it about her that is so damn addictive? She is like a slow-acting poison that has infected my system and is taking over me a bit at a time. Poisons have antidotes, even if they are hard to find, so I just need to find my antidote to Alyx, and once this is over, I can return to my usual self.

Striding through the palace grounds, I make my way towards the meeting hall where Joha should be with his other guards when I hear hurried footsteps. Frowning, I look up, my gaze locking on the doors of the queen's palace.

Alyx, is she—

The doors burst open, and Joha practically runs from the building without a single guard to be seen.

Frustration and concern race through me as I hurry towards the king.

"Your Majesty, is everything okay?" My gaze sweeps over him, searching for any signs of injury, but luckily, he seems to be physically intact. Before he has a chance to answer, I'm already scolding him. "You cannot keep ditching your guards, Joha. Someone is trying to kill you."

"I am well aware, Orion," he snaps, his temper fraying in a rare display of anger.

He's never spoken to me like that before, and I recoil before I can recover. Schooling my features into a professional mask, I nod my head sharply. "Yes, Your Majesty."

Sighing, he seems to shrink as all the air leaves his body. "I'm sorry, Orion. I'm just . . . Everything is getting to me. I shouldn't take it out on you."

I want to comfort him, yet I am fully aware we're being watched. There are very few places in the palace that are safe from prying eyes, and the king's bedroom is one of them, thanks to the strict security I put in place.

"Let me escort you back to your rooms, Your Majesty." It might sound like an order or dismissal, but I know he can see it for what it is—an invitation.

Nodding, he gestures for me to lead the way. We walk in silence, but the source isn't anger, but companions who don't need words to communicate. When we make it back, I send his other guards outside of his suite and personally check his bedroom to make sure we're alone. Joha watches me the entire time and eventually clears his throat.

"Orion, I—"

"I kissed Alyx."

I hadn't meant to cut him off, and this was certainly not how I planned to tell him about my moment of weakness, but it seems my mind has different ideas. The guilt coursing through me is driving me wild, and I have to tell him, even if he hates me for it. It is a huge lapse of judgement on my part. I kissed the king's betrothed. While I am well aware that this is not a love match and is all part of our plan, I have seen the way he looks at her. If he wasn't my friend, I could be tried for treason.

Joha freezes at my blurted admission, his eyes travelling over my face, and I wonder what he's reading there. Taking a slow, deep breath, he nods his head.

"I heard the rumours. Alyx just reassured me about the kiss on the cheek in the Scholars House, but I get the feeling you're talking about something else."

There is no accusation in his tone, which takes me aback. I fully deserve his scorn. Finally able to think past my shock, I speak once more. "She told you?"

"Yes." He winces, rubbing the back of his neck sheepishly. "I stormed into her rooms and demanded to know if the rumours were true."

I can imagine exactly how that conversation went down, and it explains why I found him trudging from her quarters. Some might leave the conversation at that, since I have been given an out and at least this way I won't damage our friendship any further, but that just isn't who I am. Rolling my shoulders back, I prepare myself for the backlash of what I'm about to do.

"There was another occasion." I pace around the room, unable to look at Joha, fearful of what I might see on his face. "I don't know what happened. I was so mad at her. She infuriates me! One moment, I was shouting at her, and the next thing I knew, I was kissing her. It didn't last long, and I quickly came to my senses."

I don't tell Joha that his arrival was actually what stopped our kiss. While I'd like to think I would have stopped before we took anything further, I cannot say that for sure—not with how crazy she drives me.

"Well, they do say that love and hate are often confused." There's humour lacing his tone despite the conversation.

I snort, my nostrils flaring with agitation at the mere suggestion. "I do *not* love her." I put emphasis on the words, slashing my hand through the air between us. "It is purely physical attraction, nothing more. You are the most important person to me. I have dedicated my life to making sure you are safe, and that will not change now that she is here." My sense of duty burns in the back of my mind, and I take a deep breath for what I have to say next. "However, I understand if you no longer trust me and feel the need to demote me. I can recommend some trusted guards to take my position."

The words taste like acid, but I have to be honest. Our relationship is built on trust, and if I have shattered that, then I am no good as his guard.

"Orion, stop." Crossing the room, he places his hands on my shoulders and fixes his gaze on me. "You are the only person I want protecting me. Thank you for being honest with me." Sighing, he drops his arms and takes a step back, brushing some of his long hair from his face. "I have no idea what is between Alyx and me. I will not pretend as though I don't like her. She is a beautiful woman, and she intrigues me. Everything about her pulls me in, but I know how dangerous loving a woman like her would be."

His words are like a kick in the chest, but I force myself to ignore the feeling and slowly nod my head. "I strongly recommend not getting romantically involved with her. However, I will support you no matter what you decide."

Despite my twisted feelings over Alyx, I mean every word I say to my king. My recommendation doesn't come from selfish motivations, but as pure desire for him to be safe and happy.

"Thank you, friend." His eyes sparkle, and a smile pulls at his lips, lighting up his whole face. "We should do this more often."

"I do not know if you are talking about the heart-to-heart or getting involved with an assassin," I remark, my voice full of mirth. "Either way, my beard is going to be completely grey by the end of the year."

Joha laughs and slaps me on the shoulder. "Me too, Orion. Me too."

CHAPTER

THIRTY-EIGHT

ALYX

The gentle sound of string instruments and the warmth of the room attempt to lull me to sleep. My constant fatigue isn't helping with the situation. During the night, I have been searching the palace or sneaking into the city to get information. Every spare moment when I am not playing princess has been spent training to keep me in top shape, and it is starting to take its toll.

Sooner or later, I will have to have a full night's sleep to recover from all the snooping and spying. Despite the little rats Crux has scurrying around the palace for information, the trail of the king's attempted murderer has gone cold, which is why I am struggling to keep myself awake during yet another session in court.

What does not help is that I find these gatherings so boring. Each one is the same with the same people, sharing the same gossip and trying to one-up each other. These places are dangerous, though, and I can't risk falling asleep in front of these people.

"You look tired, my dear," Queen Mother coos from my side,

instinctively making me grit my teeth. "I do hope that my son's midnight visits aren't causing too much disruption to your sleep schedule."

Somehow, she knows that Joha has been visiting me in the night, which means someone is watching and feeding the information to her. We need to be more careful. All we need is another rumour and they might decide I am not suitable to be married to the king, whether the rumours are true or not. Her comment does confirm that she does not know *what* we have been doing. Oh, she assumes I am promiscuous, something that is better for her to believe than what is actually happening.

Smiling sweetly, I turn to look at her, batting my lashes several times. "I don't know about any late-night visits, Queen Mother, but I can assure you I am sleeping well."

She will not call me out in front of everyone, not without evidence, but I can practically hear the cogs turning in her mind as she attempts to work out the best way to cut me down. It is almost laughable, her jealousy as bright as the emerald-green dress she chose for today. We look like complete opposites, with my dress a seafoam so pale that it almost appears white, the layers of fabric much lighter and fluid than the stiff gowns I usually wear.

"Oh, what a surprise," Queen Mother says, her attention pulled to the other side of the room. "The king has decided to join us. How lovely."

The tightness in the way she speaks tells me exactly what she thinks of the king's attendance, and it's certainly not "lovely." However, I find that I am happy to see him. He looks particularly handsome today, his navy-blue jacket perfectly displaying his physique.

The guests seem to notice him at the same time we get to our feet to greet him. Their bows and curtsies are like a wave as he walks through the groups of courtiers until he gets to us on the dais. Both Queen Mother and I dip into welcoming curtsies as is expected of us.

I have not spoken to him since our argument last night, and until now, I thought I was still angry with him, but with him here in front of me, our fight seems pointless. All thoughts of last night flee my mind as I take in the tension in his shoulders and the tight expression on his face.

Something is wrong.

"We didn't expect to see you here today, Your Majesty." Queen Mother is either oblivious to the king's mood or she just does not care. Neither would surprise me about her.

Plastering on a tight, fake smile, he meets her gaze. "A last-minute decision, Queen Mother. Don't let me interrupt, though. I simply wanted a word with my betrothed."

"Of course, Your Majesty," I reply quickly before Queen Mother can object, and then I take his proffered hand.

He leads me away from the crowd and into one of the secluded alcoves of the hall close to the entrance. It is far quieter here, the only people even slightly close being the palace guards.

"What is wrong?" I ask quietly as soon as we are out of earshot.

He smiles at me, but it's off, not the usual wide smile I've come to expect from him. "Can't a man just want to see his betrothed?"

He's attempting to downplay whatever is bothering him, and that just tells me this is more serious than I first thought. I give him a look that portrays exactly what I think of his question and wait for him to explain himself properly.

It doesn't take long for the fake smile to drop as he rubs his hand across his face, letting me see his true feelings written on his features.

"Fine. You are going to think that I am mad, but . . ." He scans the room as though to find inspiration. "Something just feels off today."

"What do you mean?" I don't laugh at him like he expects me to, taking him seriously. I often get gut feelings about situations, and they have never been wrong. If Joha is getting a warning, then he should listen to it.

"I'm not sure." He huffs out a breath, looking more dishevelled than I have seen him in public before. "I am on edge. It feels as though something is going to happen." Laughing without humour, he attempts to brush it off. "I'm being paranoid."

I don't agree. Gut instincts should be taken seriously. Cursing internally, I glance around to see which guards are on duty today, searching for one male in particular. When I don't see him, alarm bells begin to sound in my mind.

"Have you told Orion?"

Joha nods, a concerned frown pulling at his brows. "Yes, I told him when I left my meeting to come here. He assigned me extra guards and is scouting the area for anything amiss. He will join us shortly."

I nod my head. That's good. If anyone is going to find anything, it will be Orion. Luckily, I am here with Joha, and I will make sure he is safe until his friend arrives, then I can start to investigate.

"Your Majesty!" The shout fills the air, impossibly loud considering there is no one close to us, but perhaps it only seems loud compared to the hushed conversation we were having.

Joha groans quietly as he glances over his shoulder to see who called out to him. My eyes narrow on the newcomer. He looks vaguely familiar, but I think it's just because he looks like all the other young lords I have seen over the last couple of days. There is nothing particularly spectacular about him, nothing that makes him stand out in any way, yet I automatically dislike him. He's tall and slim in build. His brown hair has a floppy element to it that annoys me, his every move making it jiggle. I want to cut it off and remove that stupid smile from his face.

Why I have taken an instant dislike to this young male, I don't know, but it is pretty strong. From the reluctance written all over Joha's face and his tight smile, I know I'm not the only one.

"I'm sorry to interrupt you, Your Majesty," the young male states, not looking the slightest bit apologetic as he bows in greeting. "Could I trouble you for a moment?"

Taking half a step back, Joha turns towards the newcomer. "I suppose so, Jules. My betrothed and I just finished our conversation."

The lord glances at me, dismissing me instantly.

"Fantastic," the young lord, Jules, caws with entirely too much sarcasm.

Placing a hand on the king's arm, he guides him away. Watching from the alcove, I lean against a pillar and keep an eye on the two males. I expect them to continue to the other side of the room, yet Jules stops them in the middle. *An odd place for a conversation*, I think to myself.

I should return to the dais, yet I cannot make myself move. I tell myself that it's because I don't want to return to the monotony of the conversations of the court. However, my gut is telling me that the king is right and something is wrong.

Staying in place for another ten minutes, I continue to watch them. The king looks bored. Six of his guards are placed strategically throughout the room, interspersed with regular guards who protect them all. He is in one of the most guarded areas within the palace grounds, so there is no way anyone could hurt him here. I am being paranoid.

With a sigh, I straighten my spine and brush my hair from my face, preparing to return to my throne.

As I turn, a strange glint catches my eye, momentarily blinding me. Shielding my eyes, I scowl and try to find the cause of the bright light. Two guards are standing by the door, the sunlight streaming in from the window above shining off the silver buttons on their uniforms. Normally, I would dismiss it as an accident and move on, yet something about it makes me pause. The guards seem to be standing strangely, as though one is hugging the other.

No, that's not right. It looks more like one guard is holding the other up.

What is going on here? Has one of the guards fallen ill? I recognise the one slumped over as one of Joha's personal guards, yet I can't place where I've seen the other male's face. I am pretty sure I have never seen him on palace grounds before, his startling blue eyes making him stand out, which would mean I know him from the city. Why would a guard from the city be here in a standard court session?

My instincts scream at me that something is wrong, and I search harder for whatever is setting off my internal alarms. Something gleams, once again catching my attention, and I see what looks like the tip of an arrow appearing from the male's cloak—an arrow that is aimed straight at Joha.

That's why the two guards look strange—one of them is clearly dead or unconscious, and the other is holding a crossbow under his cloak.

Joha was right, and he is about to be killed.

I hear the thud of the bolt being pulled, and I know I only have moments. There is no time to plan or even think about the risk to myself. All I know is that I *have* to save Joha.

Without a chance to think about it, I run towards the doors and the would-be attacker who is positioned by them, the perfect place for him to make a swift escape. Time seems to slow down as I move, my heart pounding in my chest as I try to do something before it is too late.

The attacker is so focused on his target that he only realises I am barrelling towards him when I appear right at his side. Leaping towards him, I knock into the male at the same moment he pulls the trigger.

Thankfully, the momentum of my hit sends us tumbling to the floor, knocking the arrow off course, burying itself in Jules's chest. Seeing that Joha is safe for the moment, I turn my attention to the attacker I just dragged to the floor. He's bucking beneath me, trying to throw me off, but I know a thing or two about keeping my seat on a man.

I want to use my blade to stop him and put an end to this, but if I do that, it will raise too many questions. The princess of another land and king's fiancée would not be carrying a dagger. Keeping my identity a secret is vital to keeping the king alive, something that is becoming much more difficult than I ever imagined.

Courtiers and guards hurry towards us, all trying to help me up, no one quite realising what just happened.

"Oh, I am so sorry," I call out loudly, as though I accidentally fell into him, making sure others hear me. "I just feel so sick. I need some air."

That's when the screaming begins, someone finally realising that Jules has been shot, his body falling to the floor with a loud thump.

Pandemonium ensues. No one seems to know what to do. Guards shout and run around, trying to make sure the king and other important people are safe. Screams, heavy footsteps, the slamming of doors, and the sound of more guards filling the room become constant in the background. It's utter chaos, and that's exactly how I want it. This is the perfect distraction. No one is going to remember me running across the room, focusing instead on the dead body.

Joha runs over to me, looking disturbed and shaken up, yet his first thought is to check on me. "Alyx, are you okay?"

"I bumped into this man and now there is blood . . ." Waving my hand in front of my face as though I'm trying to cool myself down, I sway on my feet, gasping as I look towards the middle of the room. "Did someone get shot?"

Guards surround us, separating Joha and me from the rest of the nobles in the room. They quickly realise that one of their guards is dead and the attacker was the one to fire the shot at Jules.

"He tried to kill the king! Take him to the cells!" one of the guards yells, taking charge of the situation.

I look around and gape at the chaos around us, fully aware that everyone is watching. Looking up at my betrothed, I blink vapidly and place my hand on his arm as though to steady myself. "Your Majesty, what just happened?"

CHAPTER
THIRTY-NINE

ALYX

J oha helps me stay on my feet, righting my rumpled dress for me, his hand pressing against the base of my spine as he pretends to comfort me. I look around in false shock and horror as the guards pin the attacker and surround us.

"Thank you," he murmurs softly. "Thank you for saving my life, Alyx." He speaks louder then. "It is okay, my love. You are safe. Everything is okay."

I turn my head as if to bury it in his shoulder, seeking comfort. He wraps his arms around me protectively, playing into it as my mouth brushes his ear.

"You're welcome, my king." He shivers, and I can't help but smirk. "That was a close one. You were right, Joha. You should trust your instincts."

More guards burst into the room led by a red-faced, furious Orion. I lean back from Joha, desire swirling in my chest at the sight of the huge man as he storms through the crowd with efficiency and power.

253

"Get the nobles and everyone else out of here. I only want guards, now!" he roars, and within seconds, the room is cleared of everyone but us, the guards, the attacker, and the body. It's then I notice Crux winding through the guards, dressed in his uniform. He sends a wink my way as he ambles close to the body and crouches, pretending to check for life.

"He's dead," he calls to Orion. "Shall I take the body for investigation?"

Orion looks at Crux, his eyes narrowing, clearly trying to figure out who dares to question him. "My king," I say, "are you okay? Did someone truly just try to kill you?" I cover my mouth in horror, drawing all attention to me.

"There, there, everything is okay. We are safe. Orion, I think we better take my betrothed back to her palace." Orion looks our way, and I narrow my eyes at him, trying to speak without words. We need our hands on that body, which means letting Crux take it. It's the closest thing we have had to a lead in days.

I glance at Crux and then Orion, and the slight tilt of my head makes him grind his teeth. "Yes, take the body away. I will escort the king and queen to their palaces for protection. The rest of you are with the assailant. I don't want him to even move in his cell!" Guards move quickly and with precision, dragging the struggling attacker away while Crux carefully lifts the body and strides from the room, shooting me one last look. I give him a slight nod before leaning into Joha like it's all too much for me.

My hand flutters over my chest. "Yes, yes, I think I had better lie down," I murmur for effect.

"Let us go, my love," Joha says, his arm around me as Orion follows. No one would dare attack again so close unless they were total fools. However, Orion escorts us to the king's palace, and once inside, he turns to us.

"You were right, my king. I should have been there—"

Rolling my eyes, I shove my hair up in a pin, out of my face, and interrupt his self-deprecating monologue. "I was there, and he's safe.

That's all that matters. Stay here. I don't think they will attack again so soon with the guards on alert, but I need to check that body for clues."

"I will come with you," Orion starts, no doubt wanting to be helpful.

"No, protect Joha. I cannot do both right now." I look at him. "You were right, Joha. I guess you're not the fool they all say you are." With a wink, I head to the window, sliding it open and glancing back at them. "Be back soon." I drop to the ground below and burst into a run, ready to intercept Crux and find out everything I can about Jules and why he was involved in getting the king into place, which he clearly was.

It was a trap, and I didn't see it until it was almost too late. My fury makes me run faster, using the rooftops to avoid the patrolling guards whose eyes are sharper than ever. There was an attack on the king, and it's something the whole palace feels. It failed, but it was close. They are getting bolder and more desperate, although that means they will make more mistakes. It also means more danger to Joha.

We need to find out who is behind this before it's too late.

CHAPTER
FORTY

CRUX

The noble's body isn't too heavy, so I manage to cover the distance quickly. I wait for the other guards to look away, and then I duck behind the building and into the trees. I want privacy for what I'm about to do. When I heard from my little rats that something was happening, it had been too late, and Alyx had almost paid the price.

I know she can look after herself, but there are so many enemies here that not even my assassin can take them all. The fact that I know she is okay is the only thing keeping me calm, that and she isn't their main target. However, to get to the king, they would gladly go through her. What was once just a game for me is now real. I can't let anything happen to her, which means helping her figure out who is trying to kill the king.

How many times will we have to save his life?

It baffles me that Alyx could like such a weak man. He might have power in name, but not in body. Tugging off the stupidly uncomfortable helmet, I kneel by the body as Alyx appears around the building, having escaped the guards protecting her at the palace. She's panting slightly as she kneels on the other side of the body.

"Well?" she prompts.

"I waited for you. Do you want to do the honours?" I ask, leaning back.

"So romantic, saving desecrating a corpse for me." She winks as she laughs.

I chuckle. "I have a feeling he would like it more than if I did it."

Her nose crinkles in disgust as she rips his robes open and shoves her hands into the pockets, searching quickly. Despite my words, I take off his boots and check inside, knowing that's one place where most people hide things. While we search, I look her over, double-checking she's okay.

"I'm fine, stop staring," she snaps, no doubt feeling my gaze. "Ah, what's this?" I lean closer to see her running her fingers along the front of the robe where it seems more padded. She flips it over to reveal a secret pocket within. Slipping her fingers inside the shallow pocket, she extracts a small square of parchment before leaning back from the body.

"Idiot, why hide it on his body?" I murmur.

"They thought they would succeed and not get caught. It's called being cocky, and it will be their downfall, but it's good for us." Opening the parchment, she scans the contents before showing me. "Orders with time and place. It seems they wanted him to know as little as possible, just a promise for a payment if he could lure the king there, and see that? That is a noble's family crest. If we can figure out whose and talk to them, then we might be able to connect it back to who is pulling the strings." Standing, she brushes off her dress. "Let's go."

Taking the parchment, I shove it into my pocket. "I'll go. Stay and protect the king. It will look odd if you suddenly disappear. We need to avoid suspicion." Her face clouds with anger as I smirk. "I know you hate sitting still, but I will handle all the boring stuff, and when the fun starts, I'll get you. I promise."

Sighing, she glances at the body and then me. "Fine, I know you're right. Princesses never get to have fun killing. What's the point of all this power if I can't get away with murder every now and again?"

Laughing, I cup the back of her neck and drag her closer as her eyes widen, her mouth parting on a moan as desire takes over her expression. I lean down and steal a quick kiss. The need to deepen it, to taste her moans fills me, but I pull back as her eyes flutter open. "You did good. Now go play with your king while I hunt for us, and when I come back with answers, I will tell you everything with my head buried between your thighs. After, this pretty princess can come play murder with me, okay?"

"Okay," she murmurs before blinking. "I'll hold you to that." With a flick of her hair, she starts to walk away before glancing back. "Oh, and you deal with the body. He smells like oils and ball sack."

I can't help but laugh as I watch her go, my eyes drifting to the body. "She's something, right? Consider yourself a lucky bastard. If anyone else had her hands on them like that, they would die a very slow and painful death."

CHAPTER
FORTY-ONE

ALYX

Sequestered away in my rooms, I make myself comfortable on the large bed, wrapped in a luxurious silk dressing gown that probably cost more than a year's salary for the average worker in the Lowers. Pulling the fabric closer, I notice the gazes of the two men in my room following my movements.

Orion stands near the door, leaning against it as though he's relaxed, but I know it is all an act. If anyone were to attack now, he would be ready to fulfil his duty at any moment. Joha sits on the end of the bed, making himself comfortable as he and his friend fill me in on what happened after the attack.

As soon as we parted ways earlier, the two of them were called to meetings, recapping what happened and trying to work out exactly how this had been able to occur in the first place. The fact that someone managed to infiltrate the guard a second time is worrying. Whoever is behind this is getting more desperate. They attacked during the day when there were witnesses. It's sloppy, but that makes them more dangerous. We need to discover who is truly behind this before it's too late, which is exactly why Crux is busy following the orders we found.

I can't be with Joha every hour of the day, and neither can Orion. Sooner or later, one of us will make a mistake that could cost the king his life.

My heart clenches painfully in my chest at the thought. This has gone beyond just a job now, despite what I might tell Crux. Not only would I feel guilty if Joha is killed when I'm supposed to protect him, but I think I would actually mourn him.

It's a strange feeling to know I would grieve for someone who isn't family. When I lost my own, I told myself I would never let myself feel so vulnerable and care for another like that ever again. Sure, over time, Crux has worked his way into my heart. He was there when no one else was and taught me how to survive. We are a different breed than the king though. We both know that each day could be our last, and that each new day we live is because of the life we have carved through death, deception, and blood. Joha is the complete opposite, and despite the multiple attempts on his life and the scheming of the court, he manages to stay positive and have hope for this cruel world.

Blinking, I bring the two males back into focus. Both of them are looking at me expectantly. Their meetings were mostly about strengthening our defences, and there was no news on who the attacker was or why it happened in the first place. The assassin in the cells killed himself before we could get any information out of him, meaning Orion is investigating how this was allowed to happen.

Apparently, the advisors are convinced that Jules was an innocent bystander in all of this, and that just confirms that the council is involved somehow. They even argued for his family to be taken care of and his funeral to be a big event. Jules's act was not convincing in the least, and the advisors are fully denying his involvement, which is suspicious, especially given what I know.

"Your advisors are liars," I counter, not bothering to hide my scorn as I address Joha directly. Even reclining back on the bed like this, I know he looks to me for advice and judgement. "Or at least some of them are. I found proof that Jules was involved in the plan to kill you." We already suspected this, but now we know for sure, so it gives us a direction to look in.

Joha looks troubled, and honestly, I don't blame him. This was someone he knew who was directly involved in trying to kill him, someone he trusted. When the attackers are unknown, it's easier to think of them as evil, yet when your assassin wears the face of someone you know, it is so much harder to accept. The betrayal stings much more. Orion, on the other hand, looks as though he's ready to start tearing heads from bodies.

"Jules was just a pawn. He was never pulling any of the strings," I continue before either of them can question me. "He just had to get the king into place and take the fall if it backfired. I doubt he even knew much about who ordered it anyway."

Any face-to-face contact was most likely done through a third party to stop any links from being made, leading back to the mastermind at the head of it all.

"What was the proof?" Orion asks, pushing away from the wall and taking a few steps towards the bed. Anger seems to hover around him like a cloud, and for once, it is not aimed at me. I don't let it faze me as I meet his troubled eyes.

"Parchment with a family crest. Someone from the Oakenstram line wants the king dead."

There is a heavy pause as both males process what I just said and who I just accused. They are clearly surprised, and while Joha looks concerned, Orion's expression is full of scepticism.

"Are you sure it was them and you didn't confuse them with another house?" he asks.

Crossing my arms over my chest, I arch a single brow. He really thinks I don't know the noble houses? I'm an assassin. No place in the city is off-limits to me, and it's my job to know who the power players are.

261

"Their crest is an oak tree with two swords crossed over the trunk. It's fairly unique, so there was no mistaking it." Clucking my tongue, I wait for his reply. Joha wisely stays out of the argument.

"The Oakenstram family has been loyal to the Crown for centuries. They practically run the Oaken Province in the city," Orion argues as though it changes everything, as though none of the noble families have ever rebelled against the royals.

It's true. Oakenstram is one of the most powerful families in the land, despite not living close to the palace.

While the city is split into the Uppers and Lowers, the Lanide River splits them like a great giant cleaved the land in two, and there is still a hierarchy within the upper-class part of the city. The provinces closer to the palace are where the upper nobles live. The farther away they get from there, the lower they are in status and power.

As the province bordering the palace, Stormhallow has the most influence. Oaken Province is almost at the same status level, even though they are farther from the palace, but the Grand Market is situated there, making it one of the busiest provinces in the land for fine clothing and foods. This brings money to the district, and wealth brings power.

Joha is pale as he contemplates what this means for him going forward. "If it truly is them, then we are in big trouble." Concern and confusion flickers across his face, an expression I'm not used to seeing on him. "They are one of our biggest supporters."

"I don't think it is them, Your Majesty," Orion reassures him, needing to comfort his friend, but I can see the caution in his eyes. He would never risk the king around them unless he was sure. "However, until we get proof to prove otherwise, we need to be careful around them."

Honestly, I thought that Orion was going to put up more of a fight, yet I misjudged how strong his protective instincts are around Joha. That's good. It means we at least agree on something, and that involves getting more information about the Oakenstram family.

Joha shifts his position on the end of the bed, looking distinctly uncomfortable but needing a plan. "How are we going to get proof?"

Yes, this is what we need to focus on, and between the three of us, we should be able to come up with a plan. Nodding, I glance between the two men. "Let's discuss what we already know."

"The Oakenstram family has lived in the city for centuries. When the city was divided into sections after it was destroyed in the great war, Oaken Province was named after them to reward them for their help in rebuilding," Joha says, sitting taller. This is textbook information, impersonal and factual, so it doesn't give us any direction to go in.

Humming in thought, Orion rubs his bearded chin as he thinks. "They own most of the market and are probably one of the wealthiest families in the city. They deal in exotic fabrics by trade, but also have a strong presence within the palace."

Why would a family that has so much wealth and power want to kill the king? They are not related in any way as far as I'm aware, so it isn't as though they would inherit the throne should the king die. I will have to check the records to be sure.

Blowing out a long breath, I lean back against the cushions and go through the mental checklist I use when I have a new target. They have a strong presence in the palace, but what are they like socially? Who are their friends? Their allies?

Clicking my tongue once more, I glance towards Joha. If anyone will know, it will be him. "We need to know who the power players are in the family so we know whom to focus on."

"They have a good relationship with most of the other noble families, but no particularly strong alliances with any of them. They mostly stick to themselves," Joha muses, shrugging his shoulders and writing off the information.

"After that scandal with Jessamine Oakenstram and the miner from the Flame Strand Province, I don't blame them. They need to rebuild their name and reputation." Snorting, I shake my head as I recount the incident. The affair between a lady and a miner had been all over the city. The rumours spread like wildfire, and Lady Jessamine had been sent away to a family in a distant town.

"Jessamine was always trouble, even as a young girl." Rolling my eyes, I pick at my nails, remembering the spoilt child she had been. "She caused mayhem at one of the harvest festivals one year when she insisted that no one but her was able to wear pink ribbons. All of the other noble girls refused to have anything to do with her after that. It's only over the last few years, as her father has become more powerful, that she has been seen socialising with the other ladies."

As I speak, the confusion on their faces morphs to suspicion, and then a slow realisation has me going cold all over. I've revealed too much information.

"How do you know all of that?" Orion asks quietly, scanning me as though he's seeing me for the first time.

There is no way a lowly Lower dweller would know any of that, even an assassin, but it's the only excuse I have. If they find out the truth, then they will never trust me again. I can kid myself and say that bothers me because I need them to trust me for this to work, but I know deep down it's because I have begun to care for them.

"I'm an assassin. It's my job to know what's happening in the city," I reply with a lazy shrug and quick smile, praying they don't see through it or hear the pounding of my heart as the lie slips from my tongue.

"The scandal, yes, that was public knowledge." Orion narrows his eyes. "Not that story about Jessamine and the ribbons though. That's personal information."

Joha's eyes flicker, and I feel the tension in the room rise.

"Those festivals are very selective, for nobles only, and you would have been too young to masquerade as anyone else. I remember the party and the ribbon incident," Joha tells me in a quiet but firm voice. "How did you know about that?"

I can see that he's piecing it together bit by bit, and it is only a matter of time before he fully works out who I am. That will change everything.

"The king is right. This is knowledge known only by the houses." Orion shifts his weight from foot to foot, his hand hovering over his sword at his hip. He doesn't trust me, and the sharp pang that sends through my heart almost has me doubling over. "Who are you really, Alyx?"

Maybe it's time for me to put my faith in them and explain my deepest secret. They might trust me more because of it and see me in a different light—or it could backfire and get me killed for treason—but it seems I don't have much choice anymore.

Looking between them, I bite my lip as I try to make up my mind. They have both worked out that there is more to me than just being an assassin. If I try to lie now, this thing between us will be broken. I need them as much as they need me, so I take a deep breath and meet Joha's gaze.

"I know because I was there." I am a mess of excitement and fear as I speak. Keeping my identity hidden is the only thing that has kept me alive this long, and getting out of the habit of hiding it is going to be hard, yet I can finally be myself around them. I have to trust in them the way they have trusted in me so far. Maybe letting someone in won't be too bad . . . . Maybe they can even help me.

"You want to know how I know so much about the nobles?" Taking another deep breath, I look from Orion to Joha, my expression solemn. "I used to be one."

CHAPTER
FORTY-TWO

JOHA

Staring up at the high beams that make up the ceiling of my bedroom, I gaze out of the small window built into the roof. I can see the moon, which is exactly why I had my bed placed here: for nights like this when I cannot sleep. The moon is almost at its fullest, but not quite. At first glance, you might believe it full, but when you look closer, you can see that's not the case.

That is exactly how I feel—on display to the world, looking to be in charge, but if you look closer, you can see the cracks. I know that I need to stop thinking of myself as a puppet and forge myself into the ruler that I want to be, but despite all of Alyx's and Orion's work, we still seem no closer to finding who is behind the attacks.

After the disaster of a day, it makes sense that I am unable to sleep. I very nearly lost my life and then found out that one of my biggest supporters within the nobles might be behind the plot to kill me. However, that's not what is keeping me awake.

I have always known that there is treachery and scheming within the houses, and while I suspect Queen Mother's involvement, she couldn't manage this alone, meaning one of the families is behind it.

No, the turbulent, twisting thoughts chasing me from sleep are of the revelation that Alyx was born into a household of nobility. After she dropped that bombshell, she refused to tell us anything more of her past and simply told us we would speak tomorrow when she had a plan for the family. She didn't disclose which family she was from, how she ended up training as an assassin, or why she broke off from her family in the first place. Nothing. No matter how many ways we asked, she stubbornly stayed silent.

Orion clearly wanted to grill her for more, but from the stubborn set of her jaw, I knew it was no good. There was never a single point where either of us didn't believe her though, and I think that is a sign in its own right. I know Orion suspected there was more to her than she let on, and it seems he was right.

Sighing, I roll over onto my side and close my eyes, attempting to sleep once more.

However, as soon as my eyes shut, images of *her* fill my mind—in her dark stealth clothing, her court dresses, that skimpy dressing gown that hardly covers anything. Always her. My mind is consumed by her. My favourite memory of her is the one of her sleeping peacefully, no masks to hide behind, just Alyx.

Groaning, I try to force the images from my mind, but they are replaced by more questions. What would she have been like if she had grown up in her family as she was supposed to? She would have been a force to be reckoned with as a noblewoman. Instead, she has hidden her true identity since she was a child.

It must have taken a lot of trust for her to tell us even that snippet of information. Knowledge like that could be dangerous, and if it got back to her family, it could have disastrous consequences. My heart warms a little at this. She is a difficult woman to get to know, but trusting us with that is a huge step forward. Towards what, I am not sure.

Her knowledge of the nobility makes sense now and has probably been a factor in helping her survive this far. I cannot even imagine how difficult it was to give up everything she has ever known and turn into a killing machine, especially surviving in the Lowers. She did not tell us how old she was when this happened, but we know she was young.

As I lie in my bed, alone and aching with the need to rest, I cannot help but wonder what she would have looked like as a child, or what she was like when she was safe and protected.

This is my last thought before I fall into a deep sleep.

TEARS RUN down the boy's face as he stares at the boats in the dock. His well-made clothes are muddy and torn, and he is clearly in distress, yet no one stops to help him.

He's had it with the constant scolding and reprimands from his father and tutors. There is so much to learn, and the pressure on his small shoulders is too much for him to handle. If only he could find the courage to run across the dock and climb onto one of the boats to be taken away. He does not care where he would go, only that he needs to get away.

Far away.

The only thing holding him back is his father. He will be so disappointed in him, and all he ever wanted was to make his father proud. A fresh wave of tears stings his eyes, and he feels as though the pressure is going to tear him apart.

Stay or go?

A whistle rings out, followed by shouts, and he can see one of the ships is about to leave. If he is going to go, now is the time. Taking a single step towards the dock, he prepares to make the run across the open space and hide aboard.

"Are you okay?" a soft voice calls out behind him.

Spinning around, the boy sees a young girl who is watching him intensely. Her hair is like a flame atop her head, and her eyes are wide with childlike concern. She must be a couple of years younger than he is, six or seven perhaps.

His chance to leave is about to disappear, but for some reason, he struggles to take his eyes off the girl in front of him.

"I cannot do it anymore," he blurts out, shame and pride warring within him. He shouldn't be speaking to her. He isn't allowed to speak to anyone who has not been approved by his tutors, yet there is something about her that makes him feel better, and admitting it aloud feels like a band of pressure has been released from his chest.

Unaware of the turmoil in his mind, the girl tilts her head to one side. "Do what?"

"They want me to be king one day. It is too much responsibility." Dropping his gaze to look at his shoes, he realises that he sounds selfish.

"Whoa. I would like to be king." The girl takes a step closer, and the boy looks up in surprise. "I would make sure that everyone is safe and that no one goes without food. Have you seen the market in the Lowers?"

She speaks fast, as though she only has limited time to talk, so it takes a couple of moments for him to absorb it all. There is no condemnation in her voice, only childish innocence. He cannot help but think she is right though. He was told about the Lowers and poverty that runs rampant there, although he has never visited it.

"No, I have never been allowed to go to the Lowers," he replies, internally questioning why he has not been allowed to visit when it will soon be part of his kingdom. "Besides, you can't be a king. You're a girl."

"Oh." She looks really sad at his comment, and he immediately wishes that he never said anything. "I think that being king must be hard, but an honour to dedicate yourself to the people. That must be great."

She looks off into the distance, her eyes full of knowledge that one wouldn't expect to see in a child. Something shifts inside the boy as he takes in her wistful expression. He knows that being king would be an honour, and the hard work he puts in now will contribute to how good of a ruler he will be in the future. He just needed this girl to help him put it into perspective.

"You are right." Taking a deep breath, he wipes his cheeks of any

residual tears and smiles at her with a cheeky wink. "Maybe one day you could marry a king, then you would be queen."

She laughs, high-pitched and full of glee. "I could marry you! I think we would be a great team."

The smile she gives him as she takes his hand causes his heart to flip in his chest.

This is it, he thinks to himself. She is the girl I will marry when I am king. I will see to it.

I WAKE WITH A START, the dream still fresh in my mind. No, not a dream, a memory.

I forgot my encounter with the little girl who stopped me from doing something stupid that day—the girl I have been looking for ever since, even if I didn't realise it. My father and Queen Mother tried to set me up with many suitable women over the years, but none of them was ever right. What I didn't realise was that it wasn't because they were missing anything, but because they weren't *her*.

It has to be her, right? The resemblance is uncanny, and now that I know she is of noble birth, there can be no mistaking it.

Alyx is the girl from my dream, the girl from my past, and she seems to have no idea. She was young at the time, so she probably forgot, much like I did. Will she remember and realise that boy was me?

Smiling up at the ceiling, I cannot quite believe my fortune. Fate has brought us back together and we didn't even realise it.

CHAPTER
FORTY-THREE

ALYX

Amidst all the drama with the recent assassination attempt and the death of the so-called criminal "behind it," we all seem to have forgotten about the impending holiday—Laurel's Day. It's an annual occurrence to welcome in the laurel crop, the flowers that are said to have saved many from the great wars after apothecaries and medics realised grinding them up produced a life-saving medicine. Ever since, they have become something to celebrate, and we use it as an excuse to get drunk, run rowdy, and basically do whatever we please for the day. Usually, I'm in the Lowers. Even assassins take Laurel's Day off, and I usually spend time with Crux drinking and playing games, but it seems this year will be very different. As Joha's future bride, I have duties and many stuffy celebrations and honours to attend.

I have been on edge, worried for Joha's life as well as for Crux, who still hasn't returned, and concerned about how Orion and Joha will treat me today after the bombshell I dropped last night.

They looked shocked, and then they demanded answers. They asked so many questions my head hurt, but I closed up, panic taking my voice at their insistent quizzing. I trust them or I wouldn't have told the truth about my birth, but I cannot bring myself to tell them everything because I know it will change things between us, especially Joha.

No, I'll keep it to myself, even if I know they will be eyeing me with those same questions.

However, once my maids have finished with my elaborate dress, since we are to be in the public eye, I sneak many blades onto my body just in case before checking myself over in the mirror to make sure none show. It's only then I truly take in what they have put me in. Although intricate, it is not over the top, and it's actually very beautiful.

The floor-length gown fans out at the back, creating a train. The deep V-neckline, although showing skin, is obscured by real laurel flowers spread across my chest, their pink petals contrasting with the cream colour of the fabric. More flowers are woven into the gown, draping over my sides and hips, looking like a waterfall. My hair is tied up under a headdress made of laurels. I almost look like a flower fairy from childhood stories. My makeup is soft and pink to match the flowers, and even I can admit that I look beautiful and very regal.

"My lady, are you ready?"

I nod as I turn away from the mirror and take their hands to help me through the threshold. Once outside of my palace, we are met with a congregation of scholars, council members, and staff. My eyes widen as I take in the parade of people. The council is spread across huge palanquins, boredom in their eyes as they wait. Queen Mother is at the back, and although I cannot see her, I assume she is not happy about that.

A palanquin awaits me at the bottom step, the side open with Joha standing before it and Orion at his side. I stop at the top of the steps as I look him over. He's not looking my way yet, and it gives me a chance to analyse him or, if I'm being honest, check him out. He is in a cream robe as well, decorated with laurels like my dress so we match, but unlike me, he has his crown on, and I know he did that to remind them who he is. He is regal and tall, his hair unbound. He looks perfect and untouchable. When his eyes find mine, though, I see worry and anger in his gaze. I nod slightly to let him know I am here and that he is safe, and my eyes find Orion as a reminder that he wouldn't let anything happen to the king as well. He's currently scanning the gathered crowd, no doubt hating that today must happen, especially after yesterday.

It is not often I see Orion in his full, decorative armour, and I gaze at him far longer than is appropriate. It glistens brightly in the sun, the silver catching the light, and the ornate royal crest is proudly displayed across his chest. His beard is trimmed and styled, and his shaved head shines like his armour.

"My lady?" Blushing slightly since I have just been caught staring, I descend the walkway. Joha takes my hand, kissing the back of it, his eyes twinkling as he plays the part.

"My love, you look more stunning than the first blossom of the year," he murmurs. "I cannot wait for the city to see your beauty."

"You are too kind, my king." I grin, fluttering my lashes and acting lovesick for anyone watching.

He releases my hand as he looks over the congregation. "I believe we are ready to go."

"One moment, Your Majesty, we are just waiting for more guards," Orion supplies, and Joha sighs but nods, shuffling at my side as we wait for the procession to begin.

With nothing else to do, I find myself looking at Orion once more. Unlike Joha and me, who match, Orion's ensemble sets him apart, and for some reason, I don't like that. I want them to know we are a united front—a threat to one is a threat to all—and maybe that's why I do what I do next.

Plucking a flower from the top of my shoulder, I lean into Orion, whose eyes widen. Ignoring his incredulous stare, I weave the flower into the top of his breastplate and smile as I step away. "Now we all match, like a team." I nod before turning back to Joha. I feel Orion still watching me, but I refuse to look, something akin to embarrassment filling me at what I just did without thinking.

When I find the courage to look back at him, he's smiling slightly, scanning the crowd once more. Seeing this big, scarred warrior with a tiny pink flower on his armour shouldn't be adorable, but it is, and I giggle as I take Joha's arm and let him help me into the palanquin. He sits elegantly next to me, our hands joined between us and on display for the entire city to see.

I was informed how we would be paraded throughout the provinces, giving hope and bringing in the first blooming of the laurels, then after that, we are to attend the docks to watch the ships sail away with the first medicine of the year, off to trade with our neighbouring kingdoms. Once that is done, we will go back to the palace for the banquet and the ball. It's a busy day with so many opportunities for an assassin to strike, and it has me on edge. Sitting stiffly, I force a smile as we leave Moonshadow Palace and head out into the city beyond.

"Just remember, Alyx, smile and wave. That's all they want. They don't want the truth. They want the pretty image we represent, nothing more," Joha murmurs as we make our way into Stormhallow Province. It makes my heart ache, since I have not been back here in many years.

I can feel Joha's eyes on me, but I keep looking forward, reminding myself this is part of the job.

I can do it.

The entire procession through what was once my home is painful, and at every corner, a memory pops into my head. When we make our way into the neighbouring province of Oaken, I finally relax.

I can do this. I can do this.

274

I have to do this.

⚜

PRETENDING to be wildly in love with Joha is easier than expected, and I cannot admit to myself I don't even hate it. I take liberties, like teasing him and flirting with him throughout the day, loving the way the blush stains his cheeks for everyone to see.

Once back at the palace, we are the centre of attention in our thrones as entertainment is conducted within the hall. No doubt the entertainers have spent months practicing. We have singers, dancers, and musicians, each act more elite and impressive than the last, but my focus is on Joha—not just keeping him safe, but seeing how much I can tease him before he loses it.

It's become my favourite game and the only thing keeping me sane through the longest day of my life.

Reaching over, I lay my hand on his robed thigh. His eyes widen even as he claps along with the drums filling the air. Smirking, I keep my eyes on the entertainment as I trail my fingers across his thigh, leaving random patterns. I feel him shudder under my touch, but he says nothing, nor does he stop me. The exposed tip of his left ear, the one closest to me, is turning bright red though.

Hmm, I can do better.

Leaning in, I blow my breath across his ear, feeling him jerk. "Having fun, my king?"

He clears his throat, glancing at me as I pull away slightly. "Are you?"

"Hmm, well, I've been playing a game with you and also guessing what others are saying." I nod at a burly man in a council robe. "He's saying, 'I know I slept with your mother, but it was a one-time thing. Why don't we forget it?' Or her, she's saying, 'You remind me of a badly bruised orange.'"

His laughter bursts from him, causing heads to turn, but he doesn't notice, his eyes on me. "Is that so?"

275

I grin. "Your turn."

His eyes rove over the crowd before landing on two females huddled together, whispering. "The one on the left is saying—" He clears his throat, and when his voice comes, it's higher, making me grin. "'I did see his muscles, but did you see his butt?' The other is now saying, 'His butt is so cute, but I saw his thighs in his armour.'"

I can't help but laugh, and he grins at me as I pick out another. "He's saying, 'This food tastes better than my wife's cooking, but don't tell her. She'll chase me from the house again, and I'll have to sleep with the pigs.'" I grin as I glance at Orion, who stands at Joha's side. "Your turn."

"I'm working," he comments without even looking at us, but his jaw tightens.

"So am I. Come on, big guy, just try one. It's fun," I promise.

"Come on, Orion," Joha cajoles.

Orion sighs, and I think he's going to ignore us until his deep voice comes out, sullen and sure. "She is saying that she loves her friend more than her husband." He glances at us as we both stare. "Did I do it wrong?"

Joha and I share a look before bursting into laughter, leaning into each other. "Good one." I nod. "Oh, him!"

We spend our time making up conversations and laughing with each other until we are all genuinely enjoying our time, but then a shadow falls over us, sobering us.

"My king." Queen Mother bows before us. "How nice it is to see you two connecting and so very obviously infatuated with one another during such a special occasion, especially after yesterday's festivities." She clutches her throat.

"Indeed," Joha replies, all traces of laughter gone as his eyes sweep over the crowd, not even glancing at her.

Her eyes narrow, her barbs not landing like she wants, so she turns to me. "That dress is very beautiful. I once wore something similar."

"I have no doubt you looked as beautiful in it as you do today." I smile sweetly. "I think I saw the dress you are wearing in the presentation of last season's must-haves, didn't I? How very forward of you, Queen Mother, to recycle and give back to the designers of the city."

That does the trick. Her cheeks heat, and with narrowed eyes, she turns and heads into the crowd, snubbing me, which is exactly what I wanted.

"Let's get out of here," Joha whispers as he leans in.

It's my turn to jerk back, eyeing him. "What?" I blurt.

"Just for a minute. I need some peace from prying eyes," he pleads, turning his wide eyes to me, and I'm helpless to say no. Nodding, I let him take my hand, and then he hurries from the hall with me in tow. I hear Orion's footsteps behind us, which is good, as Joha leads us through the winding halls and a double door into a room beyond, leaving Orion behind in the hall.

"Stay here," he commands Orion.

"Joha," he begins.

"I'll sweep the room," I promise as Joha shuts the door on him and slumps against it, looking far too tired.

"I just needed to get away. All I kept thinking was, which one of those smiling faces betrayed me? Even now, are they plotting my death?" he admits, rubbing his head as he pushes from the door, marching across the room and slumping onto the cushioned seat under the window that looks out onto the lake, giving us privacy and a beautiful shot of the scenery.

After checking the room, I head his way and carefully sit, arranging my skirts so I don't rip the dress. It means our knees are touching, but he stares out of the window, looking lost and confused. I don't like that. I want my smiling king back. I want happy Joha. The assassination attempt is taking a toll. He looks tired and so much older than he did when he first found me in the Lowers.

For one moment, I want to remind him that he can be happy. I want to see him smile. I don't overthink it nor question why it's important to me. I'm leaning in to do just that when he speaks.

"I used to enjoy these things when I was younger and my father was alive. He would make a game of it. We would laugh and joke all day. Now, they are simply duties I must do, but today . . ." He glances at me. "Today, you reminded me what it felt like to enjoy myself, even if I worried about the weapons trained on me. I enjoyed it. Thank you."

"You're welcome," I murmur. "We are a team, remember?"

He nods, looking out the window again, and he looks so forlorn and lost that my train of thought circles back to what I was going to do. Before I can second-guess myself or move away, I lean in and use my fingers to turn his face to me. His brown eyes widen at how close I am.

"Alyx?" he whispers, but I ignore it.

"You look better when you smile," I murmur before I press my lips to his. It's a soft, chaste kiss, but he gasps all the same, opening his lips, and I can't resist biting down on his lower one. He jerks, and I chuckle as I lean back.

His smile is slow, but it grows as I stare at him. "There it is, my king, the smile you deserve."

His laughter is low and soft, and when his hand comes up and cups my cheek, I lean into it. "I did not have a reason to smile until you," he admits, and before I can work out how I feel about his confession, his lips are on mine once more. When he pulls away, I'm wide-eyed and staring.

"Why did you kiss me?" I ask.

"To make you smile too." He grips the back of my headdress, tugging me closer, our lips clashing. It starts sweet and slow, but it isn't long before we are devouring each other. My hands are on the front of his robes, tugging him nearer as our tongues tangle, both of us unable to get close enough.

His other hand drops to my hip, urging me on, and I swing my leg across his lap, both of us laughing as our clothes get tangled, but it soon ends in a moan as I press down onto his crotch, kissing him and unable to stop.

I know we should, but as his hand slips under my dress,

caressing my thigh, I let myself live for a moment. I let myself enjoy this because I know once we stop his killer, I will lose Joha, and I can admit now I don't want to.

I don't want to lose him.

I want him.

CHAPTER
FORTY-FOUR

CRUX

My nostrils flare in anger as I perch on the beam near the ceiling. I came to track Alyx down after finding the thrones empty, but I didn't expect to walk in on this.

The window in the ceiling allowed me to gain access, and I was going to surprise her, maybe even let her attack me before she would give me a reward for all my hard work. Instead, I'm staring at her and Joha locked together, their moans filling the air. His hand sneaks under her dress as she pins him to the window.

I hate it.

I hate him.

She's mine. She has always belonged to me, and she will always belong to me. He doesn't get to take her away. He might be a king, but so am I. Forgetting why I'm here, I drop to my feet loudly. They break apart, both breathing heavily, their eyes wide.

"Crux?" Alyx asks, her cheeks heated with desire.

I lunge across the room, my anger taking over, and grab the king before he can say a word. I slam my fist into his stomach, and he bends over, gasping for air as I lift him by the neck and throw him across the room. I crouch above him as he lies on the floor, pressing my dagger to his neck.

"You think I won't kill you?" I growl, pressing it in until I see a drop of blood. "I spared you once, but I won't again."

"Enough." I hear the order as a blade presses against my own neck.

Alyx.

"You would kill me to save him?" I snap.

"No, but I'd maim you," she replies. "Let him go. He is not your enemy, Crux."

"Anyone who tries to take you from me is my enemy," I snarl, turning my head slowly and meeting her conflicted gaze.

"I am not yours to own. Don't forget that." She presses the blade deeper. "On your feet." I rise slowly, her dagger unwavering—I taught her well.

"You forget that I taught you everything you know." I bring my arm down, snapping it across hers so the dagger goes tumbling to the ground.

She turns, her leg coming up as she spins, hitting my chest, and I fly into the wall. "Not everything." She smirks, raising an eyebrow. "If you want to fight, Crux, then you'll be fighting me, not him."

The door bursts open just then, but neither of us spare it a look as Joha clambers to his feet. "My king," comes a worried shout.

"Get Joha out of here," she calls to the guard dog Orion. "I've got him."

"Alyx," Joha protests.

"Go," she demands, no doubt reading the intention in my eyes. If he stays, he's dead.

There's some shuffling, but neither of us looks away until we hear the door close, and then we move, hitting each other midair.

Her fist connects with my face as we land on the floor, both of us in a crouch. Lifting my hand, I prod at my split lip as she smiles, and then I move again. I sweep my leg out, but she jumps over it, her fists coming up once more. I block them, and my elbow hits her side, sending her stumbling back a step. She rights herself quickly, sliding a dagger free from her dress and chasing me with it. Every swipe is intended to wound, but I twist and turn to avoid each blow, and finally, I see my chance. Grabbing her wrist, I spin and pull her arm behind her, watching the dagger fall, and then I shove her away.

Her headdress tilts as she climbs to her feet. Blowing a few strands of loose hair from her face, she rips the headdress off, letting it hit the floor with a soft thump. She raises her fists again and gestures for me to come at her.

She flies at me, her anger taking hold, and I catch her midair, turning with her momentum. I fling her so she sails across the room, hitting a wooden table on the other side.

She rolls across the table from the force but lands on her feet on the other side, grabbing a decorative vase before throwing it at me. I lift my arm at the last second, blocking it, then I leap over the table, but she's already sliding under it and out the other side, her dress flowing behind her. I stomp down on the train, jerking her back.

"Crux," she snaps.

Smirking, I slide my foot backward, and I hear the telltale sound of her dress ripping.

She turns, her eyes narrowed. "You fucking prick, you ripped my dress."

"Sorry, Princess," I mock, but I have no time to carry on because she flips across the table, grabs the ruined fabric, and wraps it around my neck. My hands come up automatically to stop it from snapping my neck as she climbs up the bookcase behind me, yanking me until my feet kick inches above the floor.

My lungs scream as I struggle, my fingers fighting to get between my neck and the material before I give up. I lower my hands so I can grip a dagger, then I lift it and slide the blade across my neck, cutting myself in the process. I hit the floor with a gasp for air as I lift my watering eyes to see her wrapping the material around her fists, stretching it between them.

Surging to my feet, I slash out with the dagger, but she dances back as I try to hit her, only to wrap the stretched material around my hand and yank it to the side, sending the dagger spiralling away.

"You really want to do this?" I murmur, lowering my head.

"You started it, so I'm just finishing it," she snaps. "You jealous bastard."

"Oh yeah, Princess, I'm jealous as hell." This time when I hit her, I tackle her to the floor. Her fists come up, hitting my sides, but I ignore them, and instead I press my lips to hers. She pummels my sides, wrapping her legs around mine as she tries to flip us, but I pin her down and kiss her until I taste blood.

She continues to fight, her legs wrapping around my head before she rolls us, pressing me to the ground. "Seriously. You try to kill the king and then you fight me just to kiss me?" she says, pressing her arm across my throat. "You stupid, overgrown—"

Her words end in a yelp as I buck and twist, catching her as she falls and pinning her once more. I capture her fist when it heads towards my face, and then I slam it back into the ground, doing the same with her other. She writhes beneath me, her eyes flaming with anger and her lips tight.

"Finished?" I smirk.

"I'm going to beat you," she snaps, still fighting beneath me.

"I love fighting you. It gets me all hot." I press my hips to her so she can feel the proof. She freezes, fury dancing in her gaze along with desire. "I'm betting you like it too, right, Alyx? If I ripped up your pretty fucking dress, I'd find you wet underneath. Despite all these jewels and the act you put on, you want to be thrown around and pinned."

"No, I fucking don't. Get off me," she snaps, trying to shove me away.

"No? Let me prove you're a liar." Holding one of her hands in mine, I slide the other down and pull her dress up before I press it to her pussy, feeling how hot and wet she is. Her nostrils flare as she continues to fight. Stroking across her heat, I lift my fingers into the air to show her they are glistening. "Such a liar, Alyx."

"I hate you," she retorts, looking away.

"No, you don't," I murmur as I press my hand against her pussy again. "Shall I prove that wrong too?"

"Get off me," she snaps, turning her head to face me, but her eyes are filled with heat.

"We both know you don't want that." I pet her pussy until she groans, making me laugh.

"So stubborn," I comment, but she kicks me free, jumps to her feet, and storms to the door.

I can't let her leave.

I chase after her, smacking her into the wood as I lift her dress and thrust my fingers into her tight channel.

Her cry is muffled by the wood, but I hear it. I can't contain my smile as her pretty cunt clenches around my fingers. "Now stop being a brat, Alyx, and play with me." I lick the shell of her ear then bite down until she cries out, gushing around my fingers. "We both know you want to. We both know you love us fighting and love us making up even more. I'm tired of only tasting what's mine. I want all of it, and I'm going to have it right here in the palace with your jewels on. Are you going to try to keep running, or are you going to meet me head-on like you always do?" There's a moment of hesitation after my words, and I worry I pushed her too far. Suddenly, her elbow swings back, knocking me away, and she turns.

"You want to fuck me, Crux?" She tilts her head to the side, her eyes running down my body possessively. "Then come and get me."

I lunge towards her, gripping her hips and hoisting her up the door as she gasps, her eyes widening. "Hold the edge," I order.

She reaches up, gripping the edge of the doorframe as I drop to my knees.

"You think I'd just bend you over and fuck you like one of the whores, Princess? No, I've been dreaming about the day I'd get to be inside this sweet, wet cunt, so I'm not rushing it, not even if a thousand armies surround us. They would have to pry my dead body from yours. I'm going to take my time worshipping you, fucking you, and reminding you that you have always belonged to me."

"Crux, we don't have time—" She moans as I press my mouth to her cunt, silencing her for once. Despite her protests, she throws her legs over my shoulders and moves her hips, begging me for more.

Our fight turns into a different kind, and I can't resist sliding my tongue down her wet folds, tasting every inch of her. There might have been others before, but right now, she is mine, and I'm going to show her how good that can be. Slipping my tongue inside her channel, I taste her sweetness with a groan, my hands flexing on her hips to pull her closer.

My cock jerks with desire, leaking within my trousers, but I ignore my own hunger and focus on hers as I slide my tongue up and flick her little bundle of nerves. She cries out, her legs clenching around my head. Chuckling, I pin her with one hand, the other sliding down so I can thrust my fingers into her, filling her channel like I will with my cock. I stroke her as I attack her clit, and she gasps, riding my face and hand. Her legs shake around me, and I know she's close, so turned on by our foreplay.

"Crux," she begs, "please don't stop."

"Not even if a thousand men were attacking me," I reply, nipping her clit. She jerks with a cry, so I do it again as I add another finger and stretch her.

Her channel clenches, so tight and hot, and then she comes.

Her thighs constrict, choking me as she screams my name for everyone to hear. I could die a happy man right now, and even as my lungs beg for air and dots dance in my vision, I lash her clit. I'm on the verge of passing out when her thighs loosen, but I tug her closer again, needing more.

"Crux." She falls from my hands and kneels before me.

Her face is flushed as she reaches out and rubs her thumb across my lips. With her eyes on mine, she pulls back and sucks her pleasure from her finger. "My turn," she declares, and before I can react, she pushes me back to the floor and crawls up my body.

She tugs my shirt open, exposing my chest, and then her mouth moves across my abs, tasting my muscles as she slinks up my body, leaving me grunting and struggling beneath her.

"No wonder men give everything for one night with a woman like you. I haven't even had you and I'm ruined, Alyx. If you ask me for a kingdom right now, I'd give it to you. If you ask for a thousand warships, an army, I'd give them to you. I would give you anything to keep going."

"All I want is you," she promises, kissing up my chest before licking her cream off my chin. "Fuck me, Crux. Fuck me like you've always wanted to. Show me."

Not needing to be told twice, I hook my leg around hers and roll. She smacks into the floor as I slide a dagger free, then I cut up her dress, exposing her tight body to my gaze. I lay my dagger over her heart—a promise. It's my first dagger, the one I used to make my initial kill, and now it's hers.

My weapon is hers, just like I am.

"Scream for me," I tell her as I undo my trousers and free my aching cock, letting her look me over before I slide up her body. I lift her leg and wrap it around my waist as I press to her entrance. "Let them hear the assassin defiling their queen-to-be."

Her mouth opens to deliver a witty retort, but it dies on a silent scream as I slam into her tight, wet cunt. I force my length deep inside her, making her take every inch. "That's it, Princess." I fight her tightness. She's wet, but I'm big. "You were made for me, so take every inch of me. Don't you dare pull away. You're stronger than that."

Her back arches into the air as I bottom out and pull back. I thrust forward, sliding into her body. My eyes drop to where we are joined, and the sight of me finally claiming my girl makes me wild. My muscles bunch like I'm in battle, my emotions lashing at me. I hammer into her, slamming her into the floor with each thrust, and she cries for me, begging for more. Leaning down, I yank the remains of her dress away and seal my lips around one of her nipples.

She clenches around me so hard, I groan, fighting to keep up my brutal rhythm. I need to fuck her harder. I need her to remember this every time she looks at me.

I know I never pushed her hard enough before because she begs silently for more, lifting her hips to take me deeper as she tugs my hair. I wasted years of us being together because I was too worried about losing her. I won't ever again. I'm hers and she's mine, at least at this moment, and that is all that matters. Even if she never loves just me and wants others, I love her enough to hold onto her. I'll stay, even with a dagger in my gut, knowing I'll never be her only one.

"Mine, you're mine now, Alyx," I say against her nipple before leaning back on my knees to watch her while I fuck her.

"Only if you make me come." She smirks, tilting her hips to take me deeper. When I slide my fingers through her messy cunt and rub her clit, her eyes roll back in her head.

"What were you saying?" I ask.

They open and my girl, never one to be outdone, clenches around me, making me groan and my hips stutter. Her smirk tells me she did it on purpose, and I want to laugh. She can never give up the fight, even flat on her back while taking my cock. She's in control and she knows it.

"Fine." I bite down on her nipple, leaving a bloody ring of teeth marks behind. "I'm yours, and when I make you come again, you're mine. I'll go out there with your cream on my cock while you dance and play merry queen, all while knowing my cum is sliding from your pussy."

"Fuck. That's so hot."

"My dirty fucking queen." I drive into her harder until we practically slide across the floor. Leaning down, I grab her hands and pin them above her head, lacing my fingers with hers as I pummel into her cunt. Our breaths mix as we both groan, both of us chasing our release but also not wanting it to end.

Pleasure spirals down my spine like red-hot fire, drawing my balls up, and with each thrust into her wet cunt, I'm lost. Pressing my lips to hers, I whisper, "Come for me, Alyx. Let me feel your pleasure. Let me die a happy man."

As if my words are the catalyst, she groans and closes her eyes as her pussy tightens around my cock, fluttering as she comes. I watch her orgasm play across her face, memorising the sight, but when she wraps her legs around me, keeping me buried inside her and whispers, "Then fill me with your cum, let me feel it," I can't hold back.

I explode with a bellow, thrusting deeply as I fill her with my release. I let her feel every drop as our lips meet in a messy, loving kiss.

Pleasure rolls through me like a never-ending wave until it finally releases me, and I slump into her, panting heavily.

She laughs, her cunt still fluttering around my cock. "We should have done that years ago."

"Definitely," I agree, laying a kiss over her racing heart as I get to my knees and slip from her body. I nearly fall, my legs weak, but my eyes are locked on my cum dripping from her channel. I press my fingers inside her, pushing it back in, and she moans, clenching around me once more.

I hear the footsteps too late, but I turn as Alyx gets to her knees, no doubt hearing them too. The door opens, revealing Orion.

"What the hell is going on?"

We glance at each other, covered in blood and cum, the room destroyed around us.

"Oops?" my girl replies with a shy grin.

CHAPTER

FORTY-FIVE

ALYX

It's a dark, dreary night, the sky covered with a thick blanket of clouds blocking the moon. These are perfect conditions for sneaking around, and thanks to the light drizzle of rain, many have taken shelter for the night. The streets in the Uppers are usually fairly quiet, but many lords like to stay out past midnight.

Dressed in my dark tunic, trousers, and cape, I blend right in. My hair is tied back, I have a covering over the bottom part of my face to hide my identity, and my body is laden with weapons.

Checking my coverings are all still in place, I dart across the deserted street and meet Crux at the spot we arranged yesterday. He is exactly where he said he would be, hiding in the shadows between the tailor's and the baker's in Oaken Provence, near the market. He's using the uncanny ability he has to blend in with almost anything, and if I didn't know him so well, I never would have noticed him there.

"Are you sure you want to do this?" His voice is a whisper of smoke.

That wasn't exactly what I was expecting to hear from him after what happened yesterday. Sure, I wasn't thinking he was going to shower me with declarations of love, but he does not even acknowledge that we fucked. When Orion burst in on us, sweating and covered in cum, our moment was over.

Orion was furious and wanted to slaughter the assassin for the wounds he caused me. He doesn't understand our relationship or that there is a dark, twisted part of me that calls to Crux. As my best friend, saviour, and now lover, Crux gets me in a way no one else could. He has seen the darkness inside me, his own speaking to me in a way I've never experienced with anyone else. Orion might not want to admit it, but I'm an assassin, and violence is how I thrive. During my time working for Joha, I have discovered that I have several parts to me, but there is no denying that underneath it all, I have done some terrible things.

After giving me a hot, blistering kiss, Crux quickly dressed and whispered for me to meet him. He had a lead and we were going to investigate together, which is what brought me to the Uppers in the early morning hours.

The fact that he has not acknowledged yesterday's climatic meeting burns, but I try not to let it eat me up. I know how possessive he is of me, and he is simply focusing on the task at hand. Like most of our jobs, this could end badly, and if our concentration slips even for a second, we could lose our lives.

Taking a deep breath, I push those thoughts aside and close the remaining distance between us.

I glance over my shoulder, checking we are still alone. "We need to get proof, and they could give us that." My voice is low so I'm not overheard.

"You know what we are going to have to do to get information from them." His eyes are dark as he scans my face, his gaze intense.

Frowning, I pull my face covering down so my mouth is exposed. What the hell is he asking? He trained me himself, and now he's questioning if I'll be able to carry out my role as an assassin. How is this job any different from my previous ones? Puzzle pieces slowly start to shift, and suspicion builds in my mind.

It's almost like . . . like he knows the link between my family and the Oakenstram family. That would be impossible, though, as he does not know that part of my past.

"I'm perfectly capable of using pain during interrogation, Crux. You know this. Are you starting to doubt me?" Quiet outrage coats my tongue. That would possibly be one of the worst things he could do to me other than betrayal.

He adamantly shakes his head, taking a step closer until his chest brushes against mine. "No. Never," he promises, pulling down his own face covering so I can see his sincerity. He waits for my slow nod of understanding before he begins to turn. "Let's go." He pauses abruptly, and I almost walk into him. I'm looking around for threats, but he only has eyes for me. "Oh, one more thing."

He grabs my face and pulls me against him in a smouldering kiss. I push into him, forcing him to take a step back as we battle for dominance. The kiss is messy and fucking hot, and anyone could find us. Not wanting to tempt fate, though, I pull back and stare into his eyes.

He presses his forehead against mine. "Yesterday was the best day of my fucking life. Never forget it."

His words are an order, turning the sweet comment into a demand—one I'm happy to follow. He must see the agreement in my eyes because he grins at me and pulls his face covering up so only his eyes are on display. Doing the same, I follow him from the alley, and we make our way to the Oakenstram estate.

It doesn't take long and is easy to find, the gated property filling a large portion of the province. Their house is easily one of the largest in the Oaken Province, thanks to the wealth they make from running the market. Due to this, they have guards who patrol their grounds. This does not deter us, however, and we easily slip past the patrols and over the fence into the lush garden.

Crux seems to know where he is going, and it would not surprise me if he had already been here, scouting the area for ways in before we met.

We quickly make our way to the house, and he rounds the corner, leading me to a low, one-story building that looks as though it was a later addition to the house. Crux scales the building, standing on the roof of the squat structure. As I get closer, I get a waft of clean, fresh laundry, and I realise these are the servants quarters. I listen closely and hear the sounds of someone washing dishes, confirming my thoughts.

I think about what he said as we break into the Oakenstram house. I hate that he said it—not because of his doubt, but because now I have to acknowledge the small, niggling part of my brain that is trying to get my attention. A part of me is reluctant to hurt anyone who was so close to my family. My father and Lord Oakenstram were good friends, and he was loyal up until the very end.

Now he seems to be involved in trying to kill the king, and I want to know why. From what I remember, he was a family man and always kind to me as a child. I do not relish the fact that I am probably going to have to hurt or kill him, but I have to protect Joha.

Thanks to the aid of a drainpipe, I join Crux on the roof, glancing at him to find him pointing to an open window on the second floor of the main structure. Removing my daggers from my thigh sheath, I stab them into the brick and begin climbing, using them to gain purchase.

Getting into the house is easy. No one in the Uppers expects to be broken into, especially not a family as large and influential as Oakenstrams. The hired guards outside would be a deterrent to most too. The rich never learn, comfortable with their perceived sense of safety. What they never realise until too late is that money does not buy their safety. By leaving a window wide open, they are practically begging to have their house burgled.

We are not here to steal anything though, unless stealing secrets counts.

Inside the building, we start with the bedrooms. At this time of night, most people will be fast asleep. When we reach the master bedroom, however, we only find a sleeping woman, the other side of the bed still untouched. Wherever the lord is, he has not come to bed yet.

I tilt my head, recognising the quiet sounds of a crackling fire downstairs. Crux hears it at the same time I do and gestures for me to go down the large, grand staircase. He turns in the other direction, and I know he means for us to split up.

Light on my feet, I tiptoe down the steps, my dagger raised as I stalk the hallways. Light and warmth guide me until I find myself outside a study. It's a huge room lined with bookshelves and a large, mahogany desk facing the marble fireplace. There are many different ways I could enter the room, but stealth is not the aim right now, so I simply walk through the doorway as though I own it.

It takes Lord Oakenstram a few moments to realise he's not alone, and when he spots me, his face pales. Slowly, he reaches towards his sword, which is leaning against the desk, but it's too far.

"Take whatever you want, just leave my family and me in peace," he says quietly but firmly, as though that is going to deter me.

Clucking my tongue, I continue to walk towards the desk. "What I want is information."

He seems genuinely confused by the comment. "What information could I possibly have that someone like you would need?" Is he so sure of himself that he didn't think the assassination attempt would be linked to him?

I snort at the comment. Someone like me? If only he knew.

I don't bother to beat around the bush. "The attacks on the king. I know you are behind them."

His face pales as I speak. "I know nothing of that." His voice shakes, giving him away.

"Liar." Jumping over the desk, I knock him from his chair and press my blade against his throat. "I will hurt you to get what I need, but we can do this without bloodshed, your choice."

It's easy to kill and hurt bad people, but with good people, especially ones you are familiar with, it's harder. It doesn't mean I won't do it, especially for Joha, but it does cause me to twinge.

His hands come up as though he plans to grab the blade, but he thinks better of it at the last moment and drops them. "My family—"

"I will kill your family to get what she wants," Crux croons, standing in the doorway with the terrified, sobbing woman we found upstairs not long ago and a tall, young man who must be his son. He looks just like his father, and despite having just been dragged from bed, he holds himself like a lord, standing tall and proud, refusing to cower despite the threat.

"Please, let my father go," the boy asks, surely no older than seventeen. I have not seen him at court yet, so I'm guessing he has not yet reached adulthood.

"Why are you trying to kill the king?" I ask again, pressing my weight against him and making him lean forward. "Or are you just the dogsbody who organises the attacks?"

"If I speak, I'll put my whole family at risk." He shakes his head adamantly, and I have to admire his balls. His family is at knifepoint, yet he won't say anything because his family would be hurt? Find the logic in that one.

"Look," I coo, lowering my voice as though I'm sharing a secret. "My friend over there likes to play with knives, and if I don't get any information, then he's going to start cutting. Once he gets started, it is difficult to get him to stop."

"I think I'll start with the woman," Crux remarks, ignoring the shrill cry of Oakenstram's wife.

That woman once chased me through our back garden, playing hide-and-seek with me. She's older now, with more lines and grey hair, but it's her. The memories keep on coming, and I force them back. I cannot afford to be weak.

The lord's eyes widen, and I see genuine love and fear for his wife, but he presses his lips together and squeezes his eyes shut. From the corner of my eye, I see Crux examining his blades, letting the light gleam off the sharp metal before lowering it to the woman's skin.

"Wait!" the son blurts out.

Crux pauses, looking over expectantly.

"Son, no!" the lord exclaims, his fear palpable. I press my blade harder against his throat, and he stops talking but watches on, aghast, as the son starts singing like a canary.

"It was the only way we could get our revenge. We knew we would never be able to kill him on our own, so we needed support from inside the palace."

This is good information. I was right when I said they were just the dogsbody, following someone else's orders because it suits their agenda. I just need to prod them for more.

Tilting my head to one side, I ask, "Revenge? Why are you trying to get revenge? What has the king done to you?"

"We did it out of loyalty." Lord Oakenstram takes over, unable to hold himself back any longer and no doubt wanting to draw our lethal attention away from his son. He's just as I remember, so willing to die for his family—like my father. "We never would have agreed to work with her otherwise." Shame laces his words, and I get the feeling it is due to working with this mysterious "her" and not the fact that they organised the king's assassination.

They did it out of loyalty, but not to the woman they have partnered with. There seems to be some regret that they are working with her in the first place, but getting their revenge made it the lesser of two evils.

"Her?" I question lightly.

Both the lord and his son seem to realise they've said too much, sharing a look. They have reached their limit. Something is scaring them more than the threat of us killing them here and now.

"If I tell you anything else, then I'm as good as dead," he says, confirming my suspicion.

"Or you could be dead right now." Crux strides across the room to where I stand with an arrogance that suggests he knows the lord's family wouldn't dare try to run. Even if they did, he would enjoy chasing them down. Stepping behind the lord, he takes my place, pressing his own blade against his throat then gesturing for me to guard the witnesses.

His wife whimpers in the corner at the silent exchange, trembling and backing into the wall as I cross towards her, not realising that between Crux and me, I'm probably the least dangerous—at the moment, anyway.

A female within the palace asked them to work with her to kill the king. She would have to be in a position of power, someone who has something to gain if Joha were to die. An image appears in my mind.

"The woman whom you partnered with . . . was it the Queen Mother?" I ask carefully, needing to know.

"I won't tell you," the lord answers. "Kill me if you have to, but if I tell you, then my whole family will be slaughtered."

His eyes give him away, telling me the answer even if he doesn't speak it.

I knew it.

I can also see that the lord is serious about not giving away any further information. Crux glances at me, sensing the same thing and confirming I'm okay with what has to happen next. With a quick jerk of his hand, the blade slices across the male's neck. Blood gushes from the wound, splashing all over the floor, his eyes wide as he dies in front of his family. It's ruthless, but we couldn't risk him warning Queen Mother or anyone else. We got everything we needed from him. Besides, I owe him no loyalty, whereas I owe Crux and Joha everything. Maybe it makes me a bad person, but if it's to protect the ones I care about, then I'll be the villain in this tale.

When Crux turns his attention to the screaming wife in the corner of the room, I step into his line of sight, shaking my head slightly. There is no need to kill the wife nor the son. They seemed reluctant to work with the mysterious "she," so I think they will keep their mouths shut if we give them a way out. Maybe I am also honouring the man who stood at my father's side in the only way I can now.

"They will tell someone about this. They have to die." Crux doesn't bother to lower his voice, and the family whimpers behind me when they hear him.

"This is one of the biggest families in the kingdom. If we kill them all, it will make things difficult for us. The young one will become lord, and we can make sure he behaves."

His eyes are troubled, but he nods despite his concerns.

I turn to the wife and eldest son. The wife is still sobbing uncontrollably, but the son's eyes are dry. He's frightened and his face is pale, but he stands strong, shielding his mother with his body. He's brave. Good, he'll need to be to get through this.

"We are going to spare your lives, but if we hear one word about the conversation we had with your father, then we'll be back, and I'll let my friend here finish the job." They started to look relieved as I spoke, but fear sparks in their eyes again as I gesture to Crux, who flips his dagger for emphasis.

Striding forward, I step right up to the son, casually brushing the front of his nightshirt, reminding him how dangerous I can be. "Tell the guards you found him like this, that's all." My threat is clear. "You are the head of the family now, so rule them well. I will be watching."

He meets my gaze, and I see the acceptance in his eyes. "I understand."

Yes, I think he does. This is his chance to get his family out of the mess his father put them in—one that none of them wanted to be involved with anyway.

There is shouting outside the house, and I realise our time is up. I glance over at Crux. He's already moving, grabbing me as he passes and dragging me down the hall. Once again, he seems to know where he's going, and it does not surprise me that he has an escape plan or six.

It is ridiculously easy for us to climb out of a window at the back of the house and slip into the dark garden. From that point, we don't even have to worry about the guards thanks to Lady Oakenstram's screams echoing around the house.

The problems start when we reach the market, the area swarming with guards. Cursing, Crux and I spend the next hour dodging them on our journey back to the palace. This is not hard to do, since they are easy enough to evade, but it makes it a far longer journey than necessary, giving me plenty of time to process what I learned.

My number one suspect is Queen Mother. I've had my suspicions about her for a long time now, but I did not believe she had the power or ability to actually carry it out. However, with Oakenstram behind her and indirect access to their connections, she basically had control over the whole city. I suppose she is after the crown, wanting to rule, her current role not good enough.

If Oakenstram was working with Queen Mother, then their comment about not wanting to work with her is puzzling. It could be because they don't want any connections to the royal family. They were once completely loyal to my family before the betrayal, so I suppose this could make sense.

All I know for sure is that my gut is telling me Queen Mother is behind this. I just need to find proof before I tell Joha and Orion because this doesn't just affect the Crown. It also affects the whole kingdom.

One doesn't simply kill Queen Mother and live on.

CHAPTER
FORTY-SIX

ALYX

Much to the frustration of my guards and lady's maids, I managed to cancel all of my plans for the day and retire to my bedroom after breakfast, claiming I had a migraine. Once I was sure no one would bother me, I changed and went over my plan once more.

Today, I am Alyx the assassin, not Princess Alyx. Donning one of my many guises, I pulled on a servant's uniform, tucking my distinctive red hair up beneath a cap. Thankfully, many of the palace staff members wear their hair like this, so it will not make me stand out. The point of this disguise is to blend in, and my hair does the opposite. I also have to be conscious of my posture. Nobility walks around with an upright stance, their sense of self-importance giving them a lift. Assassins move fluidly, like a cat through the darkness. Servants, however, are always in a hurry and keep their gazes down to avoid offending any of the nobility.

Nobility never notices the servants, and the guards are so focused on making sure no one gains access to the palace that they don't bother to check that all of the servants are supposed to be here, which means I have full access to the palace and no one will question why I'm here. The staff turnover seems to be fairly high, so I shouldn't be called out by the rest of them, not to mention they are so busy they don't have the time to look for new faces.

With a huge mound of folded sheets, I hurry across the courtyard, keeping my steps even. If I run, that would catch attention, just as it would if I were to slowly cross the open space. With my gaze lowered and focused ahead, no one will know that I am actually tracking Queen Mother from the corner of my eye.

I am determined to find proof of Queen Mother's betrayal. I have been watching her since the moment she awoke. The news about Oakenstram was broken to her this morning and discussed over breakfast. She seemed shocked at the loss of the lord, but I detected no sign of fear that it would lead back to her. Joha was more distressed, his gaze darting to me in what would look like concern for his betrothed, yet really, I know he's wondering if I was the one who killed the lord.

Once I excused myself with the tale of a migraine, I donned my maid's uniform and continued stalking her. So far, I haven't seen or heard anything incriminating. I am a patient woman, however, and do not give up that easily.

Joha and Queen Mother don't get on, but she is the only family he really has left, so I won't accuse her of this until I have proof. Crux would call me weak and soft-hearted for this, delaying our plan to protect the king, but he doesn't understand the situation like I do.

Perhaps I am going soft, but I will not destroy the king in the process of trying to save him.

Once I reach the outbuilding that I was heading to, I dump the sheets in a cupboard and glance through a gap in the wooden walls to check if the coast is clear. While I am least likely to be discovered while disguised as a servant, that doesn't mean I should let my guard down. That is when mistakes happen, and I haven't gotten to where I am today by making sloppy mistakes.

When I cannot be with Queen Mother, I know Crux's little rats will direct me to her. Just as the thought crosses my mind, I see one scurry past, flashing me a signal with his hands, telling me that all is clear.

Standing up straight, I brush down the front of my dress and hurry across the courtyard once more. Queen Mother was heading towards the hall for a day at court, her entourage around her as she slowly moved through the palace grounds. She has no idea she's being stalked by a predator.

I remember the first time I was ever brought to the palace, the memory ingrained in my mind. I must have been around five years old and viewed everything with a child's eye.

With my father holding my left hand and my mother on the right, we walked together as a united family. My mother explained that most children of nobility had nannies who looked after them all the time to allow their parents to work and attend court. We did things a little differently. While my father worked a lot, he always made sure to spend the evenings with us, telling me fantastical stories and kissing my forehead before bed. Mother spent as much time as possible with me, teaching me to make bread and cakes as well as read and write, which was unheard of back then, and when she did have to attend court, our housekeeper would care for me.

Over time, my memories have faded, partially because I pushed them away, too painful to remember. Because of this, I don't remember what my parents looked like, but I know my mother was beautiful and that my father had a beard that used to tickle my face.

Even now, as I glance around and remember that very first visit to the palace, my heart swells with fondness and aches with grief. I will not push those memories away any longer. I will embrace them and hold them close to me like I should have done all these years.

The palace seemed so much bigger when I was a child, and all the lords and ladies were arriving in coaches, wearing glittering gowns and tailored jackets. I don't recall what event was being cele-brated, but I know my mother was anxious about the whole thing.

She and my father had argued about it the night before, not wanting to attend. My father must have won the argument, though, since we did go.

Reaching the main palace building, I blink several times to shift from the memory to the present day. I have the strangest feeling as I weave through the corridors, as though I am seeing two versions of what's before me—the present and my memory of the hallways as a child.

I shake my head. If I get caught disguised as a maid, then everything we have done so far will be for nothing.

Slipping into the servants corridors to avoid the arriving nobility, I head straight to the hatch that separates the kitchens from the hall. The palace is much busier here, bustling with servants and cooks all getting ready to serve the gathered lords, ladies, and royalty. Thankfully, the memories don't plague me here, perhaps because I never visited this part of the palace as a child.

Servants gather to take trays of food into the room, each being checked over by one of the advisors before getting approval. I bustle over and head straight to the overflowing tray I know to be for the Queen Mother.

"Stop," one of the cooks calls out, stepping up to the hatch and looking me over with a critical eye. "That is the royal tray. Where is Elle? This is her assignment."

"I was sent as her replacement. Elle is sick."

Poor Elle, coming down with food poisoning or something just as terrible. It must have been that cake she ate first thing this morning—the one I laced with a purging potion. She will be fine after a day or so, but in the meantime, she will be curled around a toilet bowl.

The cook doesn't look convinced, his hands curling around the edge of the tray to stop me from taking it, but one of the other servants behind me steps up to the hatch.

"She's right. I share a room with Elle, and she was vomiting her guts up all morning," the maid comments, not even looking at my face to see if she knows me or not, just grabbing her tray and scurrying out of the room.

I hadn't planned for that little interaction, but it came at the perfect time. Not bothering to say anything further, I patiently wait for the cook to make up his mind.

"Fine," he grumbles, heading back over to a bubbling pot, but not before pointing a wooden spoon at me in warning. "Do not mess this up."

Nodding, I take the tray and slip through the servants door and into the hall where everyone is gathered before anyone else tries to stop me. I have been unfortunate enough to attend court many times now, and I have been paying attention to where the servants stand. Thanks to this, I know exactly where I need to be, and I silently take up my position by the throne on Queen Mother's left side.

There is a little part of me that is anxious the Queen Mother might recognise me, but she doesn't even glance in my direction, and after an hour passes, that part of me relaxes, embracing my disguise fully.

Court is boring.

Nothing Queen Mother or any of the nobility say is of any use. At first, I got excited any time Oakenstram was mentioned, but it is all the same gossip repeated over and over.

I'm not quite sure what has gotten into me today, but my mind wanders into my memories once more. Perhaps admitting my heritage to Orion and Joha unlocked that part of me. I cannot decide if that is a good thing or not.

A memory materialises in front of my very eyes—the nobility coming to greet my parents and marvel over me, and the jokes my father would tell me when we were sitting at our table, just the three of us. My fondest part of the memory, though, is when the three of us danced together. None of the other children did, but my mother and father pulled me up and onto the ballroom floor.

My mind and body are split. While I am aware of what's going on around me and can react in a second, mindlessly scanning for words that might incriminate Queen Mother, my memories fill my mind. For the first time in years, I feel like crying over the loss of my parents. Of course, I would never do that now, especially not here.

Instead, I allow myself to cherish the memory of five-year-old Alyx enjoying herself before her world shattered and her life was changed forever.

CHAPTER
FORTY-SEVEN

JOHA

I wish I could say I know exactly what is going on in my court, but I would be wrong. Alyx has disappeared, Orion looks troubled, and there are more deaths. The bodies are practically piling up around me, and I have no idea who is friend or foe. I am living with a target on my back, and the worst part is, I do not know who I can trust.

It leaves me exhausted, and that night, I find myself sneaking into Alyx's rooms again, needing her reassurance. She is the only one who understands. We might have different opinions on how she handles things, but I know she's doing everything to keep me alive and safe. Plus, there is something almost comforting about her presence, which is ironic since she is an assassin.

She's lying on her bed and doesn't even look over as I enter. Heading her way, I gracefully flop down next to her, my eyes on the ceiling. "Where have you been all day?" I ask. The last time I saw her, she kissed me, changing my entire world, and then she protected me from Crux and I left. I feel confused and slightly irate. I thought we had something special, I thought there was a bond between us, but maybe I am just overthinking things.

There is no way a person like Alyx could want a person like me, not to mention all the troubles that come along with my station.

Her head turns, her eyes tired and sad. That one look breaks my heart, and I want to vow to tear down the entire kingdom to see her smile again. "What happened? Tell me who upset you and I will have their heads."

Her small, crooked smirk makes my heart pound. "Would you?"

"I am king. I might not always act like it, but to defend you, yes, I would have their heads," I admit shamelessly. No, Alyx might not need or want me the way I want her, but it doesn't matter. I am in too deep to care, especially when she reaches for my hand. That one innocent touch consumes my entire being.

"Sweet, but I can take my own heads if I need to." Sighing, she moves closer, looking back to the ceiling. "I was with Crux. We had a lead."

"Oakenstram?" I ask, needing to know.

"Yes," she says without a hint of reproach or sadness. Taking a life is easy for her, and it always surprises me, but it shouldn't. When her head turns, however, her eyes betray her cool words. They look haunted. "He had to die. The lord was working with her to kill you. I let his family live, and hopefully, they will choose better in the future, but it was one of the single hardest deaths I have ever faced. I knew him, Joha, from my past. I knew the lord. He was kind to me, but I did what I had to."

Swallowing hard, I search her eyes, seeing the truth there.

How could I ever doubt her feelings for me? This might have started as a bargain, but Alyx has made it clear she would kill and die for me. We both might not be willing to admit why, but I was wrong. This thing between us is real, and despite our differences, I want it to work.

I want Alyx to be my queen, but I will settle for anything as long as it keeps her at my side.

"I am sorry," I tell her, squeezing her hand. "Thank you for protecting me."

She just hums, her eyes roving over my face as if searching for something. I feel almost shy under her gaze before the rest of her words click into place.

"Wait . . . her?" I ask. "You have found out who is behind it?"

She doesn't deny it. Instead, she turns her head, another soft, tired sigh escaping her.

"Alyx, please tell me. I am losing it here. Everywhere I turn, I'm looking for threats. I cannot even bear to let those I trusted close. I feel like I am going insane. I need to know."

"Knowing will not help. I wanted to wait until I was sure." She glances back at me. "Despite everything, it will hurt you, and I'm reluctant to hurt you."

"Please, I will beg if I have to." It isn't something I have ever done as king, but I will for her.

"Are you sure you can handle the truth, Joha? There is no going back once I speak it," she asks carefully.

"It will not change just because I know it. I want to know. I need to know," I plead.

"Queen Mother." She lets that sink in, and something inside me shatters slightly. "I know you don't like it, but I also know how that must sting. I cannot offer proof. I spent all day tailing her, but she is good. She plays too well, but I know it's her, trust me. She is the one behind all the attacks on you. Your stepmother is trying to kill you and take your throne."

It doesn't surprise me, which is the worst bit. I let my eyes shut for a moment before opening them and looking into the eyes of a person I do trust. "I trust you." I nod. "Even without proof. I guess, deep down, I always wondered . . ." Grinding my jaw, I laugh bitterly. "I even once suspected her of killing my father, though we could never prove it, and everyone convinced me I was simply grieving over his sudden death. I chose to believe them for the kingdom, for the throne, and for the last remaining shred of my family, but she was never my family. She was always a snake." It hurts that she hates me so much, but if what Alyx said is true, then she definitely killed my father and did it all for the power.

I cannot let naivety or emotions stop me this time. If she killed him, then she would kill me, and I will not be a fool like my father. I will not be blinded by love and obligation.

"She always wanted power. So now that we know who's behind it, what do we do?" I ask her, needing her to guide me.

She watches me before leaning over and kissing me softly. "I am sorry, Joha. I truly am."

I nod and lean into her hand as she cups my cheek, letting the warmth remind me that I might have been betrayed, but she is here with me.

"We cannot outright kill Queen Mother, no matter what proof we have, and I suspect she has hidden her trail well. If what you said about your father is true, then she is good at getting away with it. No, we cannot best her that way. Instead, we need to beat her at her own game. We have the advantage now because she has nothing to hide behind. We know who she is."

Nodding, I let her comfort me. "Then we'll do this together. We'll stop Queen Mother for everyone she has killed on her way to the throne."

Power corrupts, and sometimes I worry it will change me, but as I stare into Alyx's eyes, I know she would never let that happen. She will ground me, but when this is all over and she's gone . . .

How will I go on without the woman who is quickly becoming my entire world?

CHAPTER

FORTY-EIGHT

ALYX

I know I should not enjoy playing these games with Queen Mother, but I do. Maybe that makes me wicked, but when Joha and I share a smirk over our teacups, I know he is enjoying it too.

We can be wicked together.

She peers at her cup worriedly, making every excuse not to drink it while we brazenly drink ours. She suspects they are filled with poison since she had them laced this morning, but before she even had poured the poison into the tea, I'd sneaked into her rooms and changed it. It's a simple herbal liquor for stomach aches instead, and it smells and looks the same. She's getting bold, the deaths of her accomplices making her act out.

"Queen Mother, you offend me by not drinking with us. Is there something wrong with your tea?" Joha murmurs, watching her as he downs his cup and pours another before pointedly looking at hers.

She smiles tightly and grips the china. She expected us to drink it and die before she had to sip it. The fool. I stare into her narrowed eyes and wonder if her beauty really blinded so many to the evil in her gaze.

It fooled us for a little while.

"Of course, my king," she murmurs. Her sudden invite for tea last night was expected. She is desperate to kill Joha, and now, it seems, me as well. She knows we are getting close, and from the tightness of her shoulders, I can tell she's worried.

She takes a sip, holding it in her mouth, and I stand. "It's such a pleasant day. How about a walk, my king?"

"Sounds wonderful." He stands, and both of us tip back our cups, swallowing the contents.

"Such a lovely blend of tea, Queen Mother. You will have to share it with me." I smile widely as she nods, refusing to talk. I almost burst into laughter at her puffy cheeks filled with what she thinks is poison. "Are you quite okay? Oh no, are you choking?" I hurry to her side, hitting her back harder than necessary. "Oh gosh."

She coughs, swallowing and spluttering, and hits the table, making the china jump. "Thank you, you are so kind," she sneers.

I smile. "Of course," I reply demurely. "I am glad you are okay now."

"My love, you are too sweet." Joha sighs and smiles at Queen Mother. "We will allow you your peace once more." Joha offers me his arm, and I take it, letting him lead me from her garden which we were summoned to.

As we wander away, our arms linked, I hear her coughing up the liquid, and we share a wicked grin. No, we won't kill her this way, but we are playing her games and pushing her as far as we can so we can catch her in the act.

This time, we are one step ahead.

⚘

THERE IS A PREARRANGED trip into the kingdom today to show our faces. It has been scheduled all week, and I know Queen Mother has planned something. She is getting more desperate by the moment, and each day, there is a new threat. Yesterday, she tried to have us killed by arrows. Little did she know, I invited all her greatest supporters to walk with us. The panic as one arrow flew before they realised it was hilarious, and I pretended to fall and pull Joha with me, so it went overhead.

Today, I smile brightly as we climb into the palanquin—the palanquin she ordered to be damaged last night. I simply swapped ours with hers with Crux's and Orion's help, and we observe with glee as she eagerly heads towards hers, thinking today will be the day.

Pulling out a bag of roasted nuts, I offer it to Joha, and we both eat as we watch with anticipation. "I'm enjoying this way too much," he admits.

"Me too," I agree as she climbs in. A few moments later, just as we pass the gate into the kingdom, her damaged palanquin shatters and breaks. I have to hide my head against Joha's shoulder as I burst into laughter at her surprised yelp as she tumbles out of it, over the short wall, and into the river below.

After I school my expression, we hop from ours and turn to the guards. "Oh no, Queen Mother has fallen into the river! Help her!" Joha commands, his lips trembling with laughter as she screams. Peering over the wall, I see her struggling and spluttering in the water, her dress holding her down but not drowning her.

I chew a nut as I watch the guards leap in and wade after her. "Are you okay, Queen Mother?" I call.

She's pulled from the water and set on the ground, breathing heavily. Her dress and makeup are ruined.

"Don't worry," I call to her. "You still look wonderful as always." Her eyes narrow on me as I grin innocently. "Doesn't she, my king?"

"Of course, Queen Mother, do not worry. I will ensure the palanquins are checked thoroughly from now on." Turning to the guards, he orders sternly, "Escort Queen Mother back. We will continue on alone. My love." He offers me his hand, and we get back into ours and set off, leaving her staring after us as we giggle to ourselves.

SHE REALLY IS DESPERATE, I think as I stare at the food sent to our palaces that night. The kitchen staff was ordered to tell us it's an apology for ruining the parade. Apparently, she feels horrible. In return, I order medicines to be sent in case she gets sick. She will not take them, but the threat is there, hidden behind innocent gestures.

"It looks delicious," Crux remarks. "So much food, what a waste."

"What a waste indeed." A vicious smirk curves my lips, and Orion groans.

"I know what that look means."

"So do I," Joha and Crux say at the same time before sharing a narrow-eyed look.

"Please take the food to her personal guards. Tell them we are full and send our apologies. We do not want it to go to waste," I tell Orion.

"They are my men. They could die," he protests.

"Nah, I spoke to a rat in the kitchen. This was simply supposed to make us indisposed, no doubt to later slaughter us when we were weak. He said the kitchen staff wouldn't dare kill us. They'll simply be . . . very uncomfortable for a few days, leaving her weak and anxious."

Orion sighs but gets up to do as ordered.

Sitting back, I sip my wine. "I wonder what her next move will be."

"I guess we'll see," Crux replies, staring sadly at the food.

WE DON'T HAVE to wait long. She is furious about her guards, and her anger and desperation makes her quick to act without thinking.

312

Honestly, it is almost too easy. After all, she is not used to being beaten or outsmarted.

She called a hunt to welcome in the spring, undoubtedly planning a fatal hunting accident for both Joha and me. Little does she know, I am an excellent hunter.

When we successfully avoid all the assassins within the woods and return with the biggest haul of all, the nobles cheer for us.

She, however, sits on her chair, her face tight and eyes narrowed.

Holding up a bleeding animal to her, I grin triumphantly at the arrow through its eye, perfectly placed—a warning, even if she doesn't know it.

CHAPTER
FORTY-NINE

CRUX

As I watch the woman I love between the chimneys of the closest building, I feel my heart break for her. The open space behind the palace is the perfect place to get lost when you need some time alone, which is exactly why she came here. A lake takes up a large portion of the wild garden, and near its centre is a small island, which is connected to the mainland by a bridge. A large tree and small metal structure are all that fit on the tiny island, and that's exactly where I find Alyx.

She stares out over the water, her knees pulled up to her chest and her arms wrapped tightly around her legs as though she can keep herself together if she holds on firmly enough.

Alyx is the strongest woman I know, and she rarely lets anyone know what she's thinking. I can count on one hand how many times I've seen her cry. Even then, that has only ever been on one specific day each year, and that day is today.

Today would have been her brother's birthday. From what she told me, she was his world. He was older than her by several years and absolutely doted on her. While the death of her parents ripped her life apart, losing her brother destroyed her.

We never speak about it and have a mutual understanding that on this day, she will disappear to be by herself. I've never pushed the matter, knowing it won't help anything, but there is no way I'm going to let her out of my sight when she's grieving, so I always follow her. Usually, I let her roam wherever she wishes, but today, I need to know she's okay. Whether she's aware that she has a tail, I'm not sure. What I do know, though, is that she has never called me out on it.

Soft footsteps from behind me have me freezing, and I slowly shift my position to see who's walking this way in the middle of the night. This part of the palace is rarely ever used—one of the reasons Alyx chose to escape here in the first place.

"This is the only place we haven't checked yet."

The king's voice reaches me, and I have to hold back my snarl of annoyance. Can they not give her even a modicum of peace? Where the king goes, so does his guard dog, and sure enough, the brute's gruff voice floats up to me.

"She's an assassin. We will not find her if she does not want to be found, my king." He sounds pissed off, as though tracking down an assassin in the middle of the night is not what he planned for his evening.

The two of them round one of the outbuildings, their voices hushed and footsteps light, but they are not quiet enough to get past me. I sit and watch as they sneak through the grounds, using the buildings to hide their movements.

"Something is not right, Orion. She was so quiet today," the king comments, his observations far better than I would have thought from someone of his status. "She's not in her rooms, so I need to find her." The urgency in his voice tells me it's time to take action.

Swinging my legs around, I leap from the roof of the one-story building and land on the ground with a barely audible thump.

"Alyx is safe, and I will make sure she stays that way," I promise, my voice dark. "You can return to your rooms."

It gives me great pleasure to see that my entrance caught them by surprise, the men spinning with their weapons raised, ready to attack. Well, at least the guard is ready to attack. The king just looks wary, trying to decide if I'm friend or foe today. I don't blame him after the last few times we saw each other.

"Crux. What are you doing here?" Orion growls. His sword is drawn, and I know he's ready to use it if I so much as twitch in their direction. I suppose his reaction is legitimate, since I tried to kill him not that long ago. *Oops.*

Orion is so fucking tall, he makes me feel small, so in the shadows of the building, I stand taller, rolling my shoulders back. "I'm making sure she's protected."

The king hurries over, moving into the shade of the building I was using to watch Alyx. His expression is open, his voice giving away exactly how he feels about her. "Is she okay? I need to see her."

It must be nice to have the freedom to love so openly, but it is a risky move for a king to be so obvious with his emotions.

"She's not okay, but she will be," I answer. "By tomorrow, you will have your usual Alyx back. Tonight, though, you need to leave her alone."

The clear order in my voice causes Orion to bristle, his whole body seeming to grow with outrage. "You cannot tell the king what to do, assassin." He begins to step forward with a hiss, but then he seems to think better of it and stays at his king's side.

They are clearly not going to listen to me without more information, so with a growling sigh, I relent. "Look, the only reason I have not killed you for touching her is because for some unknown reason, she cares for you both, so I am telling you this because of that. Do not push me on this. Leave her alone tonight or I will be forced to stop you."

There's silence as both of them watch me, various emotions

flashing across their faces. I did not think they would heed my warning, yet they seem to be taking me seriously.

Suddenly, the king gasps, his eyes widening. "You love her."

It sounds more like an accusation than a question, and I have to give him credit for working it out. He's right, and I don't bother to deny it.

Orion's eyes narrow as he watches me, obviously waiting for me to tell the king he's mad, but that never comes, and his entire body stiffens at the realisation. He already knew this, he had to after our fight in the barn, but he seems to have pushed that to the back of his mind. Wishful thinking perhaps?

"Yes, I do. I have since I met her. Now I just need her to realise it," I say without a modicum of shame.

We slept together, and I told her I will burn this world for her, yet I don't think she truly understands the depths of my feelings for her. I am obsessed. Every thought, breath, and fibre of my being belongs to her.

My entire life was built for her.

"Can someone like you truly love?" Orion snaps, his jealousy obvious, yet when I look at him, I realise he doesn't see it that way. His emotions are even more tangled than mine are, and I am not about to help him work through them.

I snort instead, shaking my head. "I'm not even going to answer that question." I shift my gaze to the king, ignoring Orion. "Ever since I met Alyx, I knew she was destined to hold a piece of my heart, and she has, even all these years later."

I don't expect any guards or interruptions, since my rats would warn me, but the longer we stand around here chatting, the greater the chances are of us being spotted. The fact that my rats let the king and Orion through makes me pause though. Why didn't they warn me about them?

"How did the two of you meet?" Joha asks quietly. Unlike his guard, he does not seem to be as jealous, wearing an understanding expression on his face. He knows the feelings I have for Alyx because he has them too. It is impossible to deny them. How could he deny me loving her when he so clearly does as well?

I consider not answering his question, but perhaps they will understand my attachment to her if I explain it. It might finally get Orion off my back.

"Alyx's story isn't mine to tell, so you will have to ask her about the details, but after her family was killed, I found her hiding in the Uppers, her hiding place doing nothing to protect her from the rain." My voice lowers both in volume and pitch as I remember that day so many years ago. "She was soaking wet, filthy, and shaking from the cold. I'm not sure exactly how old she was at the time, perhaps six or seven? She was a little thing." I shake my head at the images that fill my mind. When I saw the state she was in, I made myself a promise that she would never have to look at anyone with such fear again. It makes me sick to think of what could have happened to her if I had not been there that day.

"She didn't stand a chance on her own, but there was a spark in her that made me pause, an inner strength that shone back at me. When our eyes met, I knew she was mine."

Silence settles over us as they absorb what I just told them. Joha looks troubled, but Orion is watching me with an expression that I have never seen on him before, as though he is reassessing me and realising that perhaps he judged me too harshly.

He hasn't. He is exactly right to judge me by my crimes. I have committed atrocities, but for her, I will do anything.

"You saved her," Orion finally remarks.

I nod slowly. We all know what happens to young women and girls who have nowhere to go. While she might have lasted a day or two on her own, there is no hiding the fact that she would have ended up dead without my intervention.

"I was a thief at the time and working for one of the gang leaders, but I wanted to give her safety so she would never have to be afraid ever again. I took her in and started teaching her the ropes, working my way up in the gang until I had enough followers to kill the boss and create my own. I created an empire for her, but she's never seen it for what it is."

Orion looks confused again as I mention my crimes and the deadly underworld that I run, attempting to weigh that against the fact that I saved the woman he has feelings for.

"Is today the anniversary of her parents' deaths?" the king asks quietly, dragging my attention back to him.

It's a sensible assumption given what we have been speaking about. I won't give away her truths, though, because it is up to her if she wants to share.

"No, but she is mourning all the same," I explain, giving away as little information as possible. I can see they want more, but they will have to wait. "Give her today and then ask her about it tomorrow."

The king frowns in consideration, clearly struggling with the idea of leaving her when she's grieving. However, he knows she wants space and that I won't let anybody disturb her.

"You'll watch her?" he asks, yet there is an edge to his voice that tells me this is no request—this is an order. "To make sure she's safe?"

Thankfully for him, it is an order that I am happy to follow.

"Always."

That single word holds so much meaning, the atmosphere heavy as they make their decision to leave her with me. The king is not used to being denied, but having seen his reactions tonight, I am reconsidering my opinion of him. He is not as entitled as I thought, giving Alyx what she needs even when it goes against what he wants.

Joha finally nods, accepting that he will learn nothing further tonight. He shares a look with Orion, and the two of them turn and begin walking to the main palace, skirting the buildings to give them cover. Just before they disappear from sight, I notice Orion throwing a narrow-eyed look at me over his shoulder. He doesn't like me, that much is clear, yet he seems to trust me with Alyx's safety.

Climbing back up the side of the building, I take my place between the chimney stacks, something settling inside me when I see Alyx in the same place. Releasing a deep breath, I watch over the girl who owns my soul as she grieves—like I always have and always will.

CHAPTER
FIFTY

ALYX

A knock on my door has me turning in surprise. I don't usually have visitors before breakfast, so I have no idea who it could be this time of the morning. One of my maids goes to answer it, returning a moment later to tell me that it's the king with a shy smile and sparkling eyes.

My stomach does a strange little flip, and I nod, gesturing for her to let him in. The rest of the royals will still be eating their morning meal in the hall, so I'm curious why Joha is here and not there. I'm dressed and requested breakfast in my own chambers this morning, still feeling a little delicate from yesterday.

My brother's birthday is the one day I allow myself to remember my family and the life I should have had. While I do miss my parents, I cannot fully remember what they looked like, time making those memories fuzzy. My brother's face, though, is vivid in my mind. He was my idol, protector, and best friend. I would give up everything I have, everything I have worked for if it meant I could have him back.

Pity and grief are emotions that have no place in the world I grew up in and would quickly get you killed—this is something all children in the Lowers learn early on—but no matter what I do and how I try to distract myself, my brother's birthday always hits me hard. They say grief dulls over time, but they lie because his death still hangs over me like a ghost, haunting my every move.

Yesterday, I simply went out to the lake behind the palace and enjoyed the peace around me. Atticus would have loved it there.

Joha enters the room like a breath of fresh air, his presence lighting something up inside me. There is just something about him, as even my lady's maids turn into giggly maidens when he's around. Despite the nobility thinking he has no power, he has a presence that lifts the moods of the people around him.

"Good morning, Your Majesty," I greet, dropping into a curtsy as I wait for my maids to leave the room.

He smiles at me—not just a shallow twitch of his lips, but a full smile that reaches his eyes, telling me he's genuinely happy to see me. It's a rare sight and so beautiful, it leaves me flustered for a moment. "Betrothed." His voice is warm as he returns my greeting. "How are you feeling today?"

Aware that my maids are still milling around and leaving the building, I mind my words. "Well, Your Majesty. To what do I owe the pleasure?"

His eyes scan me, taking in my simple purple dress and gently curled tresses. He looks at me as though I'm wearing the most beautiful outfit he's ever seen. Raising my brow, I wait for him to speak, smirking as I watch him shake himself out of his stupor.

He clears his throat. "I thought that we might take a stroll around the lake. The morning air might be good for us."

That actually sounds like a wonderful idea. The last thing I want to do is sit through court and the nobles' posturing when my heart is still aching from yesterday. I skipped out on my duties yesterday, though, so I cannot miss another day or rumours will start to flow.

"I would love to, Your Majesty, but what about court—"

Cutting me off with a wave of his hand, he steps forward, closing the gap between us. "I cancelled court and all of my commitments for today. I thought that with everything going on recently, we could all use a break. Besides, I'm king, and if I cannot take some liberties, then what is the point?"

With the almost constant attempts on his life, I can understand the need to get away, even if it is the lake on palace grounds. We will have guards with us, not to mention I will be there so I can protect him against anyone who is stupid enough to attack him.

"In that case, a walk sounds perfect."

Smiling at him, I take his proffered arm, and we leave the queen's palace, picking up guards as we go. By the time we wander across the grounds, we are surrounded by them. Orion has doubled the guards' presence around the king in the hopes it will turn away any would-be attackers. Joha hates it, but he understands it is necessary.

We're silent as we walk, and I begin to wonder if he knows about yesterday, his behaviour so different from usual. He's quiet and thoughtful, and when we reach the wild gardens behind the palace, my suspicions are confirmed. Somehow, he figured it out. He might have seen me out by the tree on the little island on the lake. I know Crux was out there somewhere last night, keeping an eye on me like he always does on that day every year. I suspect he knows that I'm aware of his presence, but neither of us have ever mentioned it. That is a part of my life I have only ever spoken about to him, and even then it was only once.

With Joha walking quietly beside me, I glance at him from the corner of my eye, his expression so much more relaxed now that we are away from the hustle and bustle of the palace. For once, I find myself wanting to talk about it.

"Yesterday was my brother's birthday. He died in the fire with my parents when I was a girl." I feel Joha startle beside me as I speak, surprise lining his features. I don't acknowledge his shock, simply continuing with my explanation. I do it out of necessity, my voice tight. If I stop, I might not be able to speak about this again. It's something that still has the ability to hurt me, even after all these years.

"I looked up to him, and he was my best friend. He was filled with so much joy and life, and when he was taken away, it was like the sun fell from the sky. Most of the year I'm fine, but on that one day every year, I like to spend time alone with my thoughts." Sighing, I shake my head. "Everyone says grief fades with time, but if anything, I only miss him more. He was extraordinary and would have been an amazing lord. It saddens me that he isn't in this world."

A gentle squeeze on my arm has me turning to look at the king. His expression is solemn as he clears his throat. "Thank you for telling me."

At this point, I am fairly certain he already knew about my brother, or at least some of what I was going through yesterday, but he doesn't comment on it, and from the look in his eyes, I know he means what he said.

My lips quirk up in a small smile, and I dip my head in acknowledgement, having no more words to say thanks to the lump in the back of my throat. We continue on in companionable silence, enjoying the fresh air and gentle breeze blowing my hair from my face.

The sun suddenly breaks through the layer of clouds above us, and glorious warm rays shine down on us. Joha makes a quiet humming noise, and as I glance at him, I see his head tipped back and a gentle smile on his face. I smile as I watch him enjoy the sunshine.

I cannot help but notice just how handsome he is. Without the weight of court and constantly being watched in the palace, he looks younger. It makes me view him in a different light, all of our interactions replaying in my mind.

A memory slowly works its way into my thoughts. It's old, from before my family was taken from me, and as such, parts of it are missing. I do not remember much from before then, the memories often too painful to recall. This one, however, flashes vividly in my mind as I look into Joha's face—a young boy, only a little older than me, who had run away from home.

He was a prince, and we spoke. I don't remember what we talked about, but I managed to convince him it was better to stay with his family and become the king he dreamed he could be.

"It's you." The words are out of my mouth before I can stop them, my heart in my throat. "You're the boy from my memories. You ran away . . . ."

Joha slows to a stop, pulling me around so we face each other. The guards position themselves around us, but I'm in such a state of shock that I hardly even register them being there.

Cupping my cheek with his hand, Joha stares into my eyes. "I remember."

His words hit me like a ton of bricks, my chest constricting. This is real. The memory was not just a dream, but something that actually happened, and Joha remembers it.

"What? How?" I exclaim, not really sure what I'm trying to ask him, my mind a mess of mixed thoughts and feelings.

"The memory hit me the other night." He smiles, and I see true happiness glimmering in his eyes. "You have been influencing my life for a long, long time now."

I don't know why my mind chose now to remember the time I stopped Joha from doing something stupid, since most of my other memories from that time are gone. However, I cannot quite believe how fate worked. My life was knocked off track with the fire, yet somehow, Joha and I were reunited despite the changes in our circumstances. The king and the assassin. We had no idea at the time, but now it feels like I was on the right path after all.

"The fates have brought us back together." My voice is little more than a whisper.

Joha closes the distance between us and rests his forehead against mine. "It seems our paths were destined to cross."

Having him this close does something to me, and in my mind's eye, I can see how it could have been if the fire never happened. I would have grown up as a lady, met with the prince again in court, and then perhaps we would have begun courting.

It is a fanciful dream, but just for today, I'm going to allow myself to pretend there are no attempts on his life or assassins and we are just two people falling in love.

CHAPTER
FIFTY-ONE

ALYX

I can do nothing but stare into those eyes that are becoming very important to me. This might have started with revenge and a deal, but it is turning into something much more . . . messy. I can't seem to care, though, especially when Joha smiles at me like that, and instead of me taking his arm once more, as is protocol, he laces our fingers together and tugs me into a walk.

"You are the reason I am here," he says softly as we walk towards the lake. "If I left that day on the boat, all this would already be in the Queen Mother's hands. You kept me here, Alyx. You have given me purpose and hope, and I have carried that with me, and now here you are, at my side, doing the same once more. It seems you are always here when I need you."

We stop at the shore, watching the way the sun reflects on the lake. The trees blow in the breeze, and the flowers grow around us. It's beautiful, and sometimes I get so lost in the darkness and death of the world I live in that I forget to appreciate it. "I guess I am. It's gorgeous here."

There's a slight pause that makes me lift my head to see Joha watching me, a wicked grin dancing across his lips as his eyes sparkle in the sun. "It is," he agrees as he runs his eyes over me, letting me know he doesn't mean the place like I do.

I feel a slight blush tinge my cheeks, and I'm about to taunt him for his cheesy flirting when my eyes catch on something shiny—something that does not belong. If I had not been facing him this way, I would have missed it.

There, upon the peaked roof of the closest building, is a black shadow. My eyes narrow, trying to focus through the sunlight to figure out what it is. My brain catches up before my eyes do. The shine is an arrowhead, and it's pointed this way. The black shadow is an assassin.

My eyes widen, and my heart freezes as more shadows appear on either side of him until a whole band of assassins are aiming right at us.

Our guards have stepped back, giving us privacy, so they are too far away.

We are exposed.

"Sorry, was that too corny?" Joha laughs self-consciously as I spin to his guards.

"We are under attack!" I scream as I grab Joha's arm, ready to pull him back to the safety of the buildings, but I hear the bows let loose. The sound of the arrows screaming as they cut through the air reaches us, and the guards do not stand a chance. They turn, ready to defend us from an assault, but as they do, the arrows hit their marks.

I watch in horror as their bodies jerk, and then they fall. Orion ducks behind a tree, his dark, angry eyes turning to us, and we both realise the truth at the same time—the arrows cleared the path, exposing us to their next batch.

Just as I think that, I hear more cutting through the air, and I meet Joha's scared eyes, but despite his fear, he grabs me and shoves me behind him, hunching his back to protect me.

No, this is not how this will end.

Joha will not die today.

The king will not die protecting me.

In a split second, I make a decision. I grab his arms and meet his eyes as I spin us, giving my back to the arrows heading right to us, and before he can protest, I throw myself into him, knocking him back. He stumbles, grabbing hold of me, and then he falls right into the water, splashing into the deep lake. I dive in after him.

I meet him under the darkness, his eyes wide as he struggles and tries to swim to the surface. Three arrows hit where we were in the water, and I grab him, dragging him deeper into the depths. We need to obscure their view of us, and the only way to do that is to go down.

Turning his face to mine, I cup his cheeks and drag him closer, blowing air into his mouth as we start to sink, our robes weighing us down. My hair comes unbound and floats around us as we stay like that. Amazingly, he does not fight me, trusting that I know how to keep us alive.

I pull away, keeping his body pressed to mine. He swallows, bubbles escaping from his nose, and jerks his head up. Looking at the top of the water, he starts to struggle. He can't hold his breath for long periods like I can, and the panic of running out of air is a difficult one to overcome. I know I have to take a risk. I swim to the top, peeking my head above the water for a blink of an eye, only to see more arrows heading our way. Sucking in air, I dive back down to give Joha what he needs.

I hear the arrows hit the water around me as I swim hard to get away when one sinks through my shoulder.

I jerk, the sudden agony making me want to scream, but if I do, I'll choke. Instead, I grit my teeth and narrow my eyes. Ignoring the arrow in my body, I grab Joha and give him my air once more, and then I start to swim towards a murky structure in the distance. He nods in understanding and follows, both of us swimming hard towards the lake house. We can't stay here, it's too open, and if they come after us in the water, then we are at a disadvantage.

It's a hard swim. Each time I move my arms, it pulls on the arrow, sending a fresh, hot wave of agony pulsing through my body. I ignore it as best as I can, knowing I don't have time to be weak. My heart thrums with adrenaline, keeping me going.

My lungs begin to scream since I gave Joha so much of my air, but I push forward, ignoring it and the pain in my body. I need to get him to safety.

Once there, I surface with a gasp, sucking in air as we cling to the wooden legs of the structure just above the water. The floor of the house protects us from above, and out here, their arrows cannot reach us. My eyes rapidly rush over Joha. He is wet and worried, but unhurt. I look back to the shore to see Orion is gone.

That has to be good, right? He's not dead. He can't be.

"Alyx!" Joha gasps, grabbing my injured shoulder, and a pained moan leaves my lips. He freezes and turns me. "You're hurt!"

The water around us turns red, and I shudder from the chill and shock as I gently tug my shoulder away. "Don't pull the arrow out. It's keeping me from bleeding too badly at the moment," I tell him, fighting against my chattering teeth as the adrenaline starts to wear off. Kicking to keep myself afloat, I rip off a segment of my robe and hand it to him. "Tie it around my shoulder to keep the arrow from moving and block most of the bleeding."

"We need to get you help—"

"Joha, now!" I demand. "If they come here, we will be in trouble. I need to protect you, so do as I say."

I cannot worry about infection or lasting damage, not right now. That will be something we can deal with later if we survive this. Doing as I say with a pale face, he binds the wounds as best as he can as I press my face to the wooden leg and breathe through the pain. When he's done, he turns me, running his eyes across me worriedly. "We need to get you help. Can we go up?"

"Not yet," I murmur as I run my gaze over the part of the shore I can see. My eyes catch on the bodies of the guards before I move on.

"We need to be sure first. We can stay here for a little bit. It's a good hiding spot."

"Orion," Joha whispers.

"Can take care of himself. That man is un-fucking-killable," I mutter. "Focus on yourself. You're all that matters, my king. You need to be kept safe. Do you understand? Do as I say."

"Okay." He nods, blowing out a breath as we tread water, but his eyes worriedly glance from my shoulder to the shore once more.

"Don't worry, I can still protect you like this. I could kill them with one arm tied behind my back, so this is no different," I joke, and it works, making him smile slightly.

I press my finger to my lips when I hear footsteps, and he stills, nodding in understanding. I slide my hand under the water to my hip and I pull my dagger as the footsteps grow louder.

I count three sets. I show him my fingers, and he nods. I push him deeper under the structure, using the wooden poles to move slowly to the edge where I peer up and over to see if it's friend or foe.

Suddenly, a hand reaches down, gripping my hair, and I'm yanked up and out of the water with a grunt. I'm thrown over the wood railing, and before they can pin me to the floor, I flip out of their grip, landing in a crouch with my knife held out.

There are three of them in black robes, their faces and heads covered. They are assassins, and not local ones either since they don't dress like ours. "Guess she's going wide," I mutter as I lick my lips. Queen Mother must be running out of options.

"You're hurt," one comments, his voice thick with an accent.

"I can still kill you. Come and see." I wave my hand to urge them on. I need to end this quickly before I lose too much blood and become useless to the king.

I hope Joha stays hidden. I cannot fight them and keep him safe at the same time.

They rush me in practiced formation. It's clear they are well trained and used to working together. This is no measly assassination attempt, this is a very real one, and if I'm not careful, I could die today. I need to play this smart.

I trust my instincts as they attack, my body knowing what to do before my mind does, and all of my training kicks in. They are worthy opponents, and maybe it's wrong to think so, but it's almost exciting to face someone who could actually kill me for once. I have always loved a challenge.

I hold nothing back. I meet them in the middle, ducking under one of their blades and slicing up across another with mine as I twist from their midst. We clash, and I feel cuts opening on my skin as I battle against all three. I kick out at one rushing me, sending him back, all while blocking the blade of another and turning to slice at the third. They stumble back, and I run at one of the posts holding up the ceiling. I feel them chasing me. I get two feet up it and then use it to flip over them, landing behind one. I kick his knees out and drag my blade across his throat. He gurgles as I slice through his neck, choking on his blood as he stumbles forward, hitting the railing and falling over it. He drops into the water, but I know he's dead.

Something hard hits my hand, making me hiss, and my blade spins out of my grasp and across the room. I dive for it, and my hands have just hit the pommel when I'm yanked back, the force sending my dagger over the edge of the railing and into the water below.

Snarling, I flip and kick the assassin away from me as he brings down his own blade to end me. I roll to avoid it and climb to my feet, facing the two assassins as I pant.

I have no weapon and they do. I'm outnumbered, or so they think.

They should have learned not to underestimate me by now. I reach back to my shoulder, and with a snarl, I yank the arrow out. The agony is excruciating, but I ignore it as I twirl the bloodied arrow, the sharp tip a weapon.

They hesitate and share a look, knowing I'm willing to do what it takes to survive.

"Well?" I spit. "Or are you scared?"

The taunt works, and they lunge at me again, desperate now.

I cannot even go on the offensive. All I can do is defend, ducking and weaving under their blows to stop them from gutting me as we dance across the floor. I manage to avoid any serious blows, but I'm slowing from blood loss. I need to end them quickly. My eyes narrow in irritation as I analyse their movements like Crux taught me. Everyone has a pattern, and as I force them through the motions, I pick up on them quickly.

Smirking, I purposely drop my shoulder for the next blow, leaving my stomach exposed.

As expected, the one on the left kicks out, hitting my stomach and sending me flying back. I hit the railing hard once more, the air leaving my lungs in a whoosh as they come at me. I roll forward to avoid the blade heading for me and come up behind them, stabbing the arrow into the back of one of their thighs. He yells, and I yank it out, spinning and crouching on the floor, but not even that wound can stop them.

I flip backwards to avoid the next blow and sweep my leg out, knocking him down to my level, and then I kick him. He tumbles over the railing but grabs it. It gives me the opening I need.

Using the arrow like a dagger, I grip the slippery wooden shaft and leap at the assassin not dangling from the railing. He ducks under my wild swing like I was expecting, then I turn so my back is to him and stab backwards. There's a scream, and when I whirl, he's falling back, holding the shaft as it sticks from his eye socket. Smirking, I leap once more, kicking as I go. My foot hits the end of the arrow and drives it into his skull, and he falls backwards, dead.

I duck under a grabbing hand and spin, sliding between the last assassin's legs and ripping his robe as I go. Jumping to my feet, I wind the material between my hands and tug it taut as I face him.

"Last one, and here I thought you would be worthy opponents. I was wrong."

This time, I make the first move. I feint forward, as if I'm aiming for his injured leg, and like I anticipated, he dives to protect it. I roll over his back, wrapping the material around his throat before yanking him up and back, choking him.

A dagger skims off my leg as he fights, but I lower to my knees, using all of my body weight to choke him. He slows, still struggling, and a dagger comes at me. I have no choice but to roll away, taking the material with me.

He coughs, but I don't give him a chance to recover, heading his way again. I block his wild swing and wrap the fabric around his dagger, sending it spinning away. He falls back into the railing, and with a yell, I wrap the cloth around his neck and throw myself over the railing. I dangle there, my feet almost touching the water as I cling onto the material around his neck. Looking up, I see him fighting to get it off, smacking the wood with a snarl, so I use all my weight to drop lower until I hear a snap.

Breathing heavily, I spin midair and grab the railing, then I haul myself up. After ensuring he's dead, I grab the dagger from the floor and glance around to make sure there are no other threats.

Water and blood steadily drip to the wooden floor from me. Adrenaline pumps through my veins, making my blood flow faster. I can't see any other assassins, but that doesn't mean there aren't any. We need to get Joha somewhere safe with guards before the blood loss takes its toll. Assassin or not, even I can't fight that.

I grab the edge of the railing with gritted teeth and peer down, but I don't see Joha. Good, he's hiding like I told him to. Holding my bleeding shoulder, I lean as far over as I can. My hand has started to go numb, my fingers tingling, and I know that's not good. I did some damage when I ripped the arrow out, but I had no choice. "Joha, it's safe."

He appears, looking worried. "Are you okay?" he hisses.

Reaching down with my good arm, I offer him my hand. His wet one slaps into it, and I jerk him up. He's heavy, and I have to haul him back. His feet hit the wooden railing, and he uses it to climb up, falling into me.

We both collapse to the wooden floor, wet and panting. He turns his head, his eyes widening. "Alyx."

"I'm fine." I climb to my feet, stumbling slightly. My head feels woozy and my knees give out. I land on them hard with a wince, but I keep the dagger as I kneel before him, facing the entrance to the lake house. I'm weaker than I thought. I lost too much blood.

Fuck! I underestimated the wound. I turn my head, almost throwing up as my vision wavers, to see my entire back soaked with blood. That isn't good, but I don't have much choice. I cannot move, I cannot get him somewhere safe, so I turn forward to protect him with my last breath.

"Oh gods, Alyx!" Joha presses against my back. Fighting the dizziness that seems to want to claim me, I narrow my eyes. I need to protect him. I cannot pass out, not now.

"Alyx!" he screams just as the sounds of rushing footsteps reach me.

Orion appears with Crux at his side, both bloody and panting, and I smile. "Thank the gods." I stop fighting it. My dagger hits the wood as I fall right into Joha's waiting arms, and the darkness claims me.

CHAPTER
FIFTY-TWO

JOHA

I stare down at Alyx's pale face. Her eyes are closed, and her jaw is slack. She's quiet and so small in my arms. Panic fills me as I cup her cool cheek. "Alyx?" I call, but she doesn't respond, and I lift my head to meet Crux's and Orion's worried eyes as they hurry over.

"My king, are you okay?" Orion asks.

I nod rapidly. "Alyx saved me. She got hurt," I explain, sounding weak before I shake it off. I'm king, and she's depending on me. She saved me, and now it's my turn to save her. I stand and lift her into my arms, uncaring about the blood covering me as I hold her tightly. One of her arms hangs low, and Crux places it over her chest as he runs his eyes over her face. I see fear there I have never seen in anyone before, and I know then that Alyx is this assassin's weakness.

"I will take her to my room. Call the healers at once, all of them," I order. "And gather all the guards. I want her protected while she is weak."

I stride away, and they fall into step next to me. "My king," Orion hisses. "We killed the ones we found, but there could be more. You should wait—"

"And waiting might kill her!" I roar. "Crux will stay with me. Go, Orion. That is an order."

He nods and bows, then he hurries away as Crux paces at my side, his eyes darting to her every few seconds. Mine drop to her as I walk, finding her silent and pale. I almost stumble.

Alyx is a force of nature.

She cannot die.

I begin to run, Crux keeping pace beside me, his blade out and ready. We burst into my palace, and uncaring about the horrified looks from the staff, I lay her on my bed, covering her to warm her up.

"We should strip her," Crux says, taking charge. "Get her warm and staunch the bleeding."

Nodding jerkily, I pull the covers back, and we work together silently to strip her, neither of us focusing too much on what we expose. Crux gently lifts her, leaning her against his chest, and I press a pillow to the jagged, bleeding wound as we lay her down and cover her once more.

"Tell me what happened," he demands, his voice hard, but when I glance at him, I see the terror on his face.

"She threw me into the water, and she was hit while we were in it. We bound the arrow, but she was dragged out by an assassin. I heard her fighting. She would not let me come up." I felt so weak in that moment, so filled with shame. "When she came back, she was like this. I think it's blood loss from the wound."

Crux nods, but he doesn't seem sure. He melts into her side, holding her tightly, like he may never let her go again. "Stay strong, they are coming. Good job you have a king on your side, eh? He won't let anything happen to you."

For some reason, those words only fill me with more shame. She was hurt protecting me, and now she lies deathly still, and I hate it.

I pace before the bed. After what seems like forever, but must only be minutes, the door flies open. Orion's there, surrounded by healers. They hurry into the room, and I jerk my head at the door. He quickly gets everyone else out and shuts it to give her privacy. I hate the jealousy and anger I feel when they strip the covers back, but they remain professional, which is good since Crux looks like he's waiting for one of them to twitch to kill them. It's clear they feel it, all of them terrified, but they work swiftly to check her over. When they roll her to the side, I watch with narrowed eyes as they treat the wound, making sure they do it right.

It's too quiet, and I know we are making them tense, but I do not care.

When they lay her back and cover her, I wait, my hands fisted at my sides. They busy themselves in their bags, except for the head healer, who glances at me, clearing his throat. He's an older man with a long white beard and hair. He's supposed to be the best in the kingdom, hence why he serves the king. I've never had any problems with him, but I hate him at this moment. I hate that we're here and that being with me put her in danger.

The head healer bows his head as he moves closer. "She will recover now. She lost a lot of blood, and she will need to rest. We will keep checking on her for any signs of infection, which is highly likely due to the water she was in. I have given her some herbs to help combat any early signs. She should be okay in a few days, though she will need to be careful of her movements, lest she reopens the wound," he explains calmly.

"You are sure?" I ask as I lower my voice, stepping closer to him. "If she dies, healer, then so do you."

The healer's eyes widen. "My king?" he whispers, true fear in his gaze. I have never made any of my subjects fear me before, but I do not care.

I arch an eyebrow, and he pales.

"I swear it, my king." He falls to his knees, bowing before me. "We will ensure she lives."

"You better," I warn as I look at them all, "or I will have all your

338

heads." I step around him and sit at her side, taking her hand as I brush her hair back from her face.

"I'm here. You're going to be okay. Just rest, and we will watch over you," I promise as I kiss the back of her hand. I wish I could see her flashing green eyes as she sasses me. "It's my turn to protect you."

ALYX ISN'T GETTING BETTER. In fact, she is getting worse. The healers do not leave her alone. They keep checking on her, and they seem worried, but they do not speak about it. She is sweating, her eyes twitching in her sleep, and occasionally, a rattling cough escapes her lips.

Even Orion is worried, though he will not admit it, but when I went to speak to one of the healers, I came back to find him holding her hand and whispering softly. Crux has not left her side, and when he shares a look with me, it's obvious he feels the same.

She isn't healing.

"Call the healers again!" I demand. It's the middle of the night, but I do not care. I will go and wake them myself if I must.

"My king," Orion says sadly, "they said there was nothing else they could do—"

"Then call other healers!" I roar as I turn to him. "She is not getting better. Something is wrong, I know it."

He looks at her, his face clouding as he rolls his shoulders back. "I will find every healer. I will send out a message to the kingdom, and we will fix this."

I turn away, taking hold of Alyx's hand again as we wait. It doesn't take long. The head healer appears and checks her over as we watch anxiously. He even checks the wound, and when he looks at me, he seems terrified.

"What is it?" I ask.

"I believe the arrowhead was poisoned to ensure even if they did not land a killing blow, their target would die either way. Since it was inside her body for a while, the poison has taken hold. I don't even know which poison it is, not without the weapon—" He pales as I snarl, dropping to a bow.

"What can be done?" I demand.

"I—" He lifts his head, swallowing hard. "I don't know. I do not specialize in healing poisons—"

"Then who does?" Crux asks. "Tell me their name."

"There is one, Master Yiel, but I heard he was taking a boat in the morning. He might have left already." Crux is on his feet, and he glances from the healer to me before a blade presses to the man's neck, silencing him.

"You will keep her alive until I am back with him. If not, I will kill your entire family while you watch, and only then will I end you." He glances at Alyx once more before meeting my eyes. "I'm trusting her to you both while I'm gone. Do not let me down. Crown or no crown, I will destroy this kingdom if she dies."

He departs as quickly as he came.

CHAPTER
FIFTY-THREE

CRUX

As I move through the city that I know like the back of my hand, my dark cloak flares out behind me as I run. No one bothers me—not the brutes in the Lowers, nor the guards in the Uppers. They take one look at me and see their deaths reflected back at them. An aura of danger seeps from me, warning everyone away from me. Even the very shadows themselves seem to move, making room for me to pass.

I do not hide, not tonight. There is not enough time to skulk in the darkness, not when Alyx is dying. No one will admit it or say the words aloud, but I have seen enough death in my time to recognise when the reaper comes knocking.

As soon as I parted with the king and Orion, leaving the reason for my existence in their care, I tracked down one of my little rats, giving him a message. He scurried away, spreading the word to the other rats in my employment, ensuring the whole city knows who I'm looking for—Master Yiel.

In addition to my network of little rats, I called in every favour I am owed. Money is one way to pay for my services, but for some, I demand a future favour as payment.

Of these, most of them are regular townsfolk who needed protection and couldn't afford to part with their coin. However, many of those who owe me a favour are from the Uppers—lords who have gotten into trouble after one too many drinks and needed assistance. Often, blackmail is a strong motivator for hiring my services. When the noblemen are caught doing something they shouldn't, that person will then blackmail them. That's where I come in, making sure there are no loose lips.

Other than this, I have links with some of the other criminal groups in the city. They are nowhere near as large and organised as my assassins, but they have sway all the same. While I try to keep separate from them, I acknowledge that I need all the help I can get.

Wherever Master Yiel is, I will find him. Half the city is now looking for him, and I know it will not be long until he's tracked down. I will take him to heal Alyx, and she will be fine. I have to believe that because if I do not, then my reason for living is gone. If she dies, then so does everyone else in this kingdom, innocent or not. Even just the thought of Alyx not surviving fills me with horror and rage, making me want to tear the palace apart brick by brick and find out who was behind the attack. I try not to think about that though, as blinding rage could cause me to make a mistake, and Alyx can't afford for me to make a mistake right now.

While the city searches, I have been focusing on another task.

The bag thrown over my shoulder is full of every herb, potion, and antidote I can find. Apothecaries, hospitals, healers' homes, market stalls, herbalists, you name it, I am raiding their supplies. There has to be something in this city that can help Alyx. I don't stop to ask for permission, simply helping myself, and the few people who stumble upon me raiding their cupboards leave me in peace as soon as they see my face.

They will all be compensated at a later date. Right now, Alyx is my top priority—no, my *only* priority.

I'm filled with a deadly calm, my purpose clear—get the potions, find the healer, and fix Alyx.

The first part is complete, the gentle clink of glass vials knocking together as I hurry through the city. Now I need to get to the dock and see if I can help find this master.

"My king," a small, hissing voice calls.

Stopping, I glance over my shoulder and find one of my rats hovering in the mouth of an alleyway. He looks anxious, his eyes shifting around as though he's expecting to be hurt. This might make some worry, thinking the behaviour is because he has bad news to share. I don't bother to assume, knowing my little rats always cower before me.

"Tell me," I demand, knowing he must have news. They would not dare to disturb me otherwise.

"We found the healer at the docks."

A weight lifts from my shoulders, and a wave of relief so strong washes over me that I almost sag and shout my thanks to whatever gods are watching. I don't let him see any of this though. Never show any weakness—that is rule number one in surviving in this shithole.

Keeping my shoulders back and head high, I give him a curt nod. "Good. Secure him and get him to the palace."

The rat scampers off, disappearing into the darkness faster than the eye can see. It's only as I stand in that deserted street, knowing we now have a healer who can fix my love, that I can admit to myself just how terrified I have been at the thought of losing her. Anger is a good mask for hiding emotions, but it seems that mask was so good that it even fooled me.

Releasing a long, shaky breath, I turn in the opposite direction of the docks and look up the street towards the palace.

I'm coming, Alyx. Hold on, my love.

THE NEXT SEVERAL hours are torturous. The king, Orion, and I observe as Master Yiel attempts to heal my girl.

We all watch in complete silence while the healer does his work. I might have little healing experience, but even I can tell the expert is struggling, working his knowledge of poisons to the extreme.

When I arrived back at the palace, Alyx looked grey, all the colour drained from her skin. I had not been gone long, so I knew we were almost out of time. Thankfully, Master Yiel was delivered shortly after, carried over one of my rat's shoulders and dumped at our feet, swearing and scared. All it took was one look at our faces for him to pale and get to work without another complaint about being kidnapped.

Sighing, the master sits back on his heels and begins to put everything away. "It was touch and go. She had almost run out of time," he explains, his voice loud after such a long time without any other sounds. "If you had not found me when you did, then she would be dead by now."

His flat, matter-of-fact words hit me in the gut, making me realise just how close we were to losing her. Standing, he brushes down the front of his dark blue robes. His long black hair is pulled back into a sleek bun, but several strands broke free during such a long healing.

Turning from Alyx, he faces the three of us, his neutral expression going tight for a moment as he clasps his hands in front of him.

"Your other healers don't believe in using certain techniques and potions, especially if there is an unknown substance affecting the patient." Disapproval rings in his voice. "I do not have those qualms. If the patient is going to die without treatment, then using something that might save them seems like the most logical course of action to me."

"She's going to survive?" Joha asks with disbelief.

The healer looks at the king and dips his head. "Yes, Your Majesty."

My eyes squeeze tightly shut as pure and utter relief fills me. I knew she would survive, she *had* to, but hearing those words from the healer's mouth . . .

If the worst had happened, then I do not think I could have controlled myself. I would have stalked through the city and made others hurt like I was, killing Queen Mother and everyone associated with her. The only reason I have any sense of restraint is because of Alyx. She is the better half of me and my very reason for living. All of this is pointless without her. If she'd died, I would have taken my revenge, and then I would have ended my pitiful existence and hoped that we could be together in the afterlife.

"Why is she so still?" Orion's deep voice snaps me out of my morose thoughts. It's the first thing I've heard him say in hours, his gaze locked on the limp body of the woman we love.

"I gave her a sedative," Master Yiel explains patiently. "Her body needs to rest so it can heal from the infection and let the herbs work."

It turns out that my little raiding party in the city for anything that might help the healer was actually fruitful. There was a type of dried grass I found in one of the apothecaries I raided. I had no idea what it was, but I took it anyway, just in case. It turns out that I was right to take it, as it helped save her. Since we had no idea what poison was used, we could not use an antidote, but this herb was some type of rare seagrass from another kingdom with the ability to draw out poisons from the body. This way, we didn't need to know the specifics of the poison, as the seagrass absorbed it like a sponge. Once that was removed and burnt in the fireplace, Master Yiel worked on the infection itself, cleaning and packing the wound.

"It will need to be stitched once the infection has cleared," he continues, his gaze flitting between the three of us, obviously unsure whom to give his instructions to. "Rest and hydration are the most important things here. She came close to death, and her recovery will reflect that."

Joha steps forward and takes the healer's hand, kissing the back of it in a display of gratitude. "Thank you, thank you so much."

The master is clearly surprised by the gesture and awkwardly pats the king on his shoulder. "You are welcome, my king. I am glad to care for your betrothed. It is not as though I had a choice though." His eyes slide to mine, his tone shifting as his face twists slightly.

I am not sorry in the slightest, but I allow a slightly manic grin to pull at my lips. He looks mildly disturbed, but to his credit, he does not look away.

"Next time, just ask me. You don't need to tie me up like a hog." Shaking his head, he takes a deep breath and glances at the clock on the wall. "I must go. My ship will be leaving soon."

"Of course. Let me escort you to the guard house, and I shall arrange for a carriage to take you to the harbour." Orion immediately jumps into action, the large man needing something to do. It must have been difficult for him to be left behind when I went into the city to look for the healer.

As soon as he leaves with the master, I take the seat placed near the top of the bed, slipping Alyx's cold hand into mine.

"She almost died saving my life," Joha comments quietly, taking a seat on the other side of the bed.

"I know." My response is curt. I do not have the energy for niceties, though I suppose I never did.

Do I blame Joha for her getting attacked? I'm not sure. My mind is a mess. If he hadn't hired her, then she never would have gotten involved. Because of that, I want to throttle him. She's put in even more danger by being with the king.

However, she's an assassin and in control of every job she takes on. It's dangerous work, and we know the risks of dying every time we leave the base—not to mention, she would kick my ass if she found out I killed the king because she got hurt.

So, no, I don't blame him specifically. That does not mean I am happy with him or want to become best friends though. I won't kill him, and that is the best I can offer him at the moment.

Joha has been quiet, sensing my animosity towards him right now. He seems to have a point to prove, though, because he clears his throat and leans forward. "I love her, you know."

"I know," I reply, seemingly unable to force any other words through my clenched teeth. Her brush with death seems to have brought a sense of clarity to the king, who has been dancing around how he feels, much like the brutish guard who does not seem to even notice how he cares for her.

"We all do," Orion grumbles as he strides back into the room, his face set in a frown. Maybe I was wrong. It's about time he realised it because those two have been clashing heads more than her and I do. "The healer is with some of my trusted guards, so they will see he's returned safely."

Joha nods and returns his attention to me. "Thank you for finding him."

He's making it difficult for me to keep my newly made promise to myself not to kill him when he keeps talking to me. All I want to do is sit in silence and watch my girl.

"Do I want to know how you found him so fast?" The corner of his mouth twitches, and I realise he's doing it on purpose. Is he trying to rile me up to get a rise out of me, or does he find something about the question funny?

I'm about to snap at him, but I understand what he's doing when I notice the fear in his eyes. He's terrified. This is his attempt to calm himself and deal with what almost happened. While I need physical contact with Alyx and silence, he needs to air his concerns.

Pushing my annoyance to the side, I think about his question and chuckle darkly. "No." I grin with my reply, meaning it. He might think the healer was joking when he mentioned he was tied up like a hog, but he wasn't far off. I needed to make sure Master Yiel came to the palace, and the easiest way to do that was to make sure there was no way he could refuse.

Some might call it kidnapping, but I call it saving Alyx's life.

"Usually, I would protest," Orion grumbles from where he's

leaning against the wall. "But the less I know about this, the better. She was saved because of your actions."

"She has us all wrapped around her little finger." Joha chuckles, and it's not really funny, but both Orion and I crack a smile.

"That's my girl," I mutter, shaking my head as I watch her unmoving form. "She's had control over my heart since the day I met her."

"Tonight showed me how easily she could have been taken from us, so I am not going to deny my feelings for her any longer despite my misgivings." Orion's declaration changes something about the atmosphere in the room. This is more than just discussing our feelings. He's making his intentions clear, and he is not going to step back. "She has my heart," he continues, "and she will for as long as she wants it."

I hate hearing this, and I'm a jealous man, but I can't deny him this right. My girl is hypnotic and has caught all of us in her snare.

Joha clears his throat and looks between us. "You both know I've been obsessed with her for months. I will not lose her."

Another declaration, a line drawn in the sand, and something we are all going to have to decide how to deal with.

"So what do we do?" Orion asks with a heavy sigh, looking to me for answers.

I am secretly glad they do not ask me whether or not I would be willing to step back and allow Alyx to be with one of them, as I do not think I could control my behaviour. Alyx is mine, and I will never give her up, so there is no point in even trying to deny me.

"She cares for all of us, that much is clear." I look at her as I speak, her face still the most beautiful I have ever seen, even when she looks so pale. It's our turn to care for her now.

There is only one way I can see us all getting what we need and Alyx being able to see us without the restraints of a relationship. I have seen her confusion and flashes of guilt she feels over the situation. She loves us all, perhaps in different ways, but I have seen the look in her eye on several occasions now.

"None of us are going to step back and risk losing her, so we'll let her choose. We'll let her decide if she wants one or all of us," I begin, wishing I had a better way of explaining myself. "Forcing her to choose is only going to hurt her. She has experienced enough pain in her life without us adding to it."

Orion sputters at the idea of Alyx being with all of us, but I continue as though I didn't hear him. The king is watching me intently.

"Sharing is not in my nature, I am possessive and jealous, but if this is the only way I can be in Alyx's life, then so be it. We don't push the issue. This is her life, her heart, so she gets to decide," I explain, although there is no room in my words for their hesitation or stipulation.

We all need to agree or this will not work, and I will not allow her to get hurt because of it. I will not lose her over my own petty jealousy, so if this is what she needs, then I will give it to her.

"Are we in agreement?" I look from Joha to Orion, taking in their expressions. As I expected, the guard is frowning, but he wears a thoughtful expression rather than one of disagreement. The king is leaning back in his chair, resting his chin on his hand as he considers everything I just said, and I see his mind turning.

He comes to an answer faster than I expected though, sitting forward and meeting my eyes. "We will have to discuss how it would work with her being my betrothed, but essentially, if that is what she wants, then I agree."

The man is right. We will have to be careful with our affections when in public, as I cannot imagine the nobility approving of the king sharing a lover with anyone else, especially not a guard and an assassin. This could work though.

I turn to Orion, expecting to have to convince him that this is the best option, but he surprises me. Huffing a sigh, he looks to me then his king, and then he finally lays his gaze on Alyx.

"I do not believe she will not pick me. However, if she chooses, then I am hers." Something in his face changes as he watches the woman he loves, his expression softening.

That decided, I nod to myself and fall back into a state of silence, ignoring the other two and allowing Alyx to become my entire focus.

Now I just have to wait for her to wake up.

FIFTY-FOUR

ALYX

I am furious. In fact, I am ready to murder someone, and if I won't be allowed out of my rooms soon, then it will happen sooner rather than later. The large male currently leaning against the doorframe would make the perfect victim.

It has been days since I woke up. *Days*. Not to mention the fact I was sick for days before that. So much wasted time.

The rest of the palace knows I am unwell with an infection and that I became ill when the king was attacked, yet they have no idea how close I came to dying. Apparently, the attack was on such a large scale, there was no way of hiding it. Plus, there were witnesses when the king carried me back to my rooms, unconscious and bleeding.

Orion is currently my minder for the afternoon. He, Crux, and Joha have been taking turns spending time with me, but it has turned more into guard duty, making sure I do not leave the safety of my rooms.

"Will you stop pacing and sit down?"

It's phrased as a question, but I hear the order in his voice—an order I am going to continue to ignore. I have done nothing but sit and lie down for over a week, and I need to be *doing* something.

"If you tell me to sit down one more time," I grumble, my voice dark with my frustration as I grab the closest thing I pass, "then I will jab this candlestick holder so far up your ass, you'll choke on it."

He snorts and continues to watch me with a raised brow, clearly not worried about my threat in the slightest. "I see you're in a good mood today," he comments wryly.

Making a noise of frustration, I spin around and grit my teeth, my hands balling into fists at my sides. "Orion, I'm fine! I need to get out of here. I need to investigate who tried to kill us. The longer I stay in here, the harder it will be to find any evidence."

As it is, there is probably hardly any left, which makes it all the more important that I get out there. Joha and I almost didn't survive this attempt, and I need to do something to make sure this does not happen again. Why does no one understand that?

"Alyx, you almost died." Orion strides over to me and grabs my shoulders, shaking gently until I look up at him. "This is serious," he insists, concern flashing in his eyes.

That in itself is almost enough to get me to stop pushing— almost. It is not often that Orion lets himself feel any of the more vulnerable emotions. However, I will not be swayed.

"I understand that, but I'm not dying now!" My irritation finally breaks through, and I grip his shirt to make sure he's paying attention to me. "Please, Orion, I need to do something to redeem myself!"

Oops. He's certainly paying attention now. I didn't mean to say that last part, and any hopes I might have of him missing the comment are quickly dashed as his gaze narrows on me.

"Redeem yourself for what?" He watches me carefully.

For a moment, I think about playing the *I almost died* card to get out of answering him, but I know that is a step in the wrong direction. I want him to trust that I know how far I can push my body and know what it can handle. Still in the frame of his arms, I glance away, unable to meet his eyes as I admit my faults.

"I'm supposed to protect Joha, and I got myself so badly injured that Crux had to terrorise the city to find someone who could heal me."

When I first woke up, the three of them told me what happened and how a specialist healer was tracked down, hogtied, and brought to heal me. It was almost too much to believe, but I know Crux would do anything for me, and that was exactly his style.

I haven't spoken to any of them about this, but I feel as though I failed Joha. Failure is not an option for me, not for any assassin, as it leads to death. My failure almost got Joha killed as well. I am not sure exactly when I started caring about him more than just protecting him for my job. If Joha died, I would be devastated.

"But you did protect him. He would be dead ten times over without you," Orion scoffs and shakes his head, looking as though he can't believe that I would even begin to think any of this is my fault. "You did nothing wrong, and he would tell you the exact same thing. You were poisoned *and* had an infection from the lake water," he states matter-of-factly, like he's expecting me to suddenly agree with him. When that doesn't happen, his frown deepens.

Sighing, I close my eyes for a moment, exhausted by this conversation. He doesn't get it. "I just need to do something useful," I counter, finally opening my eyes to take in his concerned expression.

He's silent for a moment, and from the look on his face, I am guessing he's thinking hard about something. I'm about to make a joke about not hurting himself when he makes a strange grumbling sound in the back of his throat.

"If I take you somewhere, will you agree to rest for the next couple of days?" He sounds unsure, and I know it's not because he's doubting if I will agree or not. No, we are past that point, and he knows to trust my word now. I am guessing he is unsure about taking me to wherever he has planned. Is it dangerous? Excitement flickers through me, my heart racing.

"Does it have something to do with the attack?" I ask, shifting from foot to foot. To be honest, I would agree with him at this point just to get out of these bloody rooms.

"Yes."

Before he even finishes speaking, I pull away and hurry over to my wardrobe, grabbing a cloak to throw over my simple blue day dress. Pulling on a pair of boots, I quickly do them up and return to my spot before him, a wide smile on my face.

"Lead the way."

STICKING TO THE SHADOWS, Orion leads me through the palace grounds, making sure not to attract notice. It would cause too many questions if anyone were to see me out in the middle of the night with Joha's head guard.

We round a corner, pausing outside a familiar building—the cells. Of all the places, this is where he chose to bring me?

"You really need to work on your date locations," I murmur wryly, following him inside the quiet building.

"This isn't a date. This is your gift." His reply is curt as he turns to me, his face softening for a moment as he reaches out and tugs the hood of my cloak up higher to conceal my face. His hands linger there, the backs of his fingers brushing my cheeks as our eyes meet and something passes between us. He steps back with a clearing of his throat. My body is too hot, my cheeks blushing from that one innocent touch. "Stay here," Orion mutters before striding forward and greeting the two guards blocking the entrance to the row of cells.

Hope and excitement flip in my stomach, taming the sharp tug of desire. If we're going into the cells, then I can only assume they captured someone who can give me answers. I try to contain those thoughts, though, because I doubt that is possible. I killed all of the assassins at the lake house.

Silent, I wait for Orion to finish talking to the two guards. They glance over his shoulder as he speaks, trying to get a look at me, so I make sure to angle my head down a little, making it next to impossible for them to identify me. I can't hear what they say, but after a few moments, Orion beckons me forward.

Not waiting for me to close the distance, he moves past the guards and works his way down the row of cells. Most of them are empty, just a few drunk males fast asleep in their own piss. At the bottom, sequestered away from the others, is a skinny male.

Orion stops by the cell and opens the door, gesturing for me to enter. As soon as I step inside, the ominous clang of the metal lock sliding into place behind me causes a chill to run down my spine. When I glance over my shoulder, my surprise must show on what little of my face is showing because Orion winces.

"I have to speak with the guards." He rubs his hand across his shaved head, his voice gruff as he stands outside the cell he just locked me in. "You're free to do what you need to. I'll be just outside."

Realisation hits me as I watch him walk away. He isn't staying with me because he's giving me free rein to do what I need to with the prisoner. His morals won't allow him to just watch if I have to get a little more . . . persuasive. Who is this skinny male, and why was I brought here?

"So you're alive."

The thick, accented voice causes my back to stiffen, and I turn to face the prisoner. His face is no longer covered, his features unremarkable, yet thanks to his voice, I know exactly who he is. He's one of the assassins from the attack, perhaps from the roof? He's thin and looks pale, yet he's on his feet and crouched in a defensive position. His ankle is chained to a ring embedded into the concrete walls, and there's a look in his eye that I recognise from spending most of my adolescence growing up in the Lowers—hunger. He looks as though he's not eaten a full meal in weeks. Perhaps he hasn't. It would not surprise me to discover they are starving him. He did try to kill their king after all.

Pursing my lips, I make an exaggerated appraisal of him then change my expression to make it clear that I'm not impressed by what I see. "I could say the same for you."

As far as I was aware, all of the assassins were killed. It seems we missed one.

He laughs, the sound quickly turning to a hacking cough. "I am the last. You killed my comrades."

"Shame that I missed one. My skills must be slipping." Glancing down at my fingers, I examine my nails as though this is all a colossal waste of my time. Sighing dramatically, I look back up at him. "Never mind, I'm sure we can fix that." I tilt my head to one side. "Or we could have a little talk, assassin to assassin."

During this time, the assassin's smirk dropped and was replaced by a glare that tells me this is not going to be an easy interrogation.

"I'm telling you nothing." He spits at me, and I watch it as it lands at my feet.

Glancing at the disgusting glob of spittle just inches from my boots, I slowly lift my gaze back to his with a raised brow. "I think you'll find I'm a very patient woman."

Pushing up my sleeves, I stalk over to him. To be fair, he does not move back to put more distance between us or try to get away. He simply grits his teeth and stands firm.

Smiling at him, I cross my arms over my chest. "Tell me who ordered the attack."

"Fuck you," he hisses, snarling at me with such force that his spittle lands on my face.

Without giving him time to prepare for it, I slam my knee up and into his solar plexus, nodding to myself as he curls up in pain. I had been expecting this sort of reaction, so I'm not irritated that he won't tell me. We still have time.

"Tell me who ordered the attack," I repeat, my order firm and promising pain if he denies me.

"Fuck you," he repeats, mocking me.

Sighing, I shift my weight and twist my torso, swinging my leg up and around to slam my foot into the side of his head, knocking him to the ground. He attempts to get up, pressing his hands to his head as he waits for the world to stop spinning.

I do not wait for that. Instead, I repeat my question, expecting the same reaction.

This goes on and on until it reaches the point where he is barely recognisable, his face swollen and bruised. It is getting more difficult for me to keep him conscious, and he is useless to me unconscious. I'm usually more patient than this, but I'm exhausted after having been so unwell—not that I will admit that to anyone. Also, I have no idea how much time I have before someone comes into the cell. Orion will give me some warning, but it could be at any time. The guards didn't want to let me down here in the first place, so I have to be quick before they come to investigate.

It's time to turn it up a notch.

Moving back from his battered form, I lean against the bars and watch him with a reluctant smile, raising my bruised fists in a show of what is to come. "Okay, my friend, tell me something," I suggest. "Anything about the attack, or I will be forced to continue."

"I'll tell you nothing." His words are slurred, but I can still hear his hatred for me.

Reaching for the secret pocket in my dress, I remove the small wallet I slipped in earlier and open it up to reveal sewing needles. I raise them so they glint in the light. "I'm sure you know this, but during interrogations, sometimes a small, sharp object is pushed under the fingernail of the prisoner. That's you in this case." I smile and shrug. "I happen to have several needles."

When I kneel in front of him, he attempts to shuffle back, fear finally flashing in his eyes. He knows this is going to be excruciating, and his body has had enough.

"I know Queen Mother ordered the hit. Just admit it," I coax, only my voice is tighter than it was before, taking away the facade that I am calm and collected.

"No," he snarls, and I know I am not going to get anything out of him like this.

I grab his hand, and we play a brief game of tug-of-war as he desperately tries to pull it back. I am stronger, though, and he is injured. Pinning his hand down on the dirty cell floor, I remove one of the needles, turning it around so he can see it. It's such a tiny object that is about to cause so much pain.

Just as I am moving to put the needle in his finger, he darts forward far faster than I thought he was capable of. He uses his free hand to grab the dagger strapped to my thigh, accessed through a slit in my pocket.

He must have spotted it earlier when I removed my sewing purse, the slit at the perfect angle for him to reach in and grab it. Cursing, I jump back, ready to defend myself, only he turns it on himself, slashing the blade across his neck.

A wave of blood bursts from the wound. Cursing, I step back, trying to avoid getting any of it on my dress, but unfortunately, it's too late. His body wobbles and then falls back as he dies in a puddle of his own blood.

Fuck, fuck, fuck.

He was the last lead we had, and now he's dead. I understand why he took his own life—no assassin worth his name would have given up the information. If only it was not so inconvenient for me. With a sigh, I press a hand to my forehead, realising that I probably seem selfish, but I do not regret it because the assassin was a risk to Joha, and I would do almost anything to keep him safe.

Orion strides down the corridor of bars, obviously drawn in by the noise. "What happened? Are you—ah fuck," he grumbles as he takes in the dead body at my feet.

Those were my exact same thoughts.

He stares at the unmoving figure and the pool of blood before turning to me. I'm expecting a scowl, since he probably thinks I killed the male, but I'm surprised to see concern for me in his expression.

"Shit." Blowing out a long breath, he nods to himself as he comes up with a plan. "Okay, we need to get you cleaned up and out of here before someone sees you."

He's right. If someone were to see me walking around covered in blood and then discover that one of the prisoners is dead, it would cause Joha and me problems.

With alarming speed, Orion manages to find me some simple but clean clothes and hurriedly escorts me back to the queen's palace. Thankfully, there is an exit at the back of the cell block, and that means we can leave without the guards seeing me in my bloodied state. Once we are back in my rooms and he checks I'm okay, he makes sure I'm not going anywhere then returns to the cells to clean up.

The assassin killed himself, and the position he died in will be evidence enough for that. Orion already told me he's going to say the knife was his and the prisoner grabbed it through the bars after I already left. I don't like it, but I admit it will be easier for him to talk himself out of it if anyone starts to question anything.

Exhausted, I move through my bedroom like a zombie, crawling back into bed and cursing my body for making me weak. While I feel a little stronger every day, I guess I'm still not back to full strength, and I pushed myself too far tonight.

I'm asleep within minutes, still sitting upright, the lights left on. My dreams that night are filled with the smug expression of the assassin as he slit his throat, taking his knowledge to the grave.

CHAPTER
FIFTY-FIVE

ORION

Alyx is still annoyed the assassin managed to kill himself before she got anything from him. It's a testament to how sick she must have been that she didn't notice him grabbing the blade. It was a mistake, one she never would have made before. It worries me, and it seems finally declaring my feelings has unleashed a torrent I didn't know existed before.

I cannot sleep, can barely eat or think if it's not about her. I stalk her day and night, even when I should be protecting the king. Nothing has ever gotten between me and my duty before, yet she has, and she is totally oblivious as she angrily stabs the meat on her plate, eating under our watchful gazes.

Maybe that is why I find myself scouting the palace and kingdom for leads that night, trying to find anything to give her purpose and see that slightly manic smile curl her lips. I just cannot see her so dejected; it makes my heart hurt. I left her in Crux's care, who was curled around her, fast asleep, when I left, something that sent irrational jealousy through me. I cannot touch her like that.

Maybe I will never be able to. She kissed me once, but she has made no such move since. It's clear she doesn't want me like she wants my king or even the assassin, and I have resigned myself to that. I know I am large and scarred, not pretty like them, and I have nothing to offer her—no name, family, or wealth, just my duty, which I live by. No, I will love her silently. I might finally understand these troubling feelings, but I will not impose them on her. She has enough going on without me declaring my intentions and her worrying about rejecting me. She needs me, she needs us all, and before this is through, she will need my sword. I will give her that, and if it's all she can accept from me, then I will die a happy man.

I never even knew I would find love, so to find it with her is a dream, one I know will be stolen away when she leaves once more. She belongs to the kingdom, to the Lowers, and I belong to the palace and the king. We are ill-fated, so I will make the most of every stolen moment from now until then.

I understand why Crux did what he did to stay at her side. I'm starting to realise I would do just about anything she asked of me just to stay near her. I know what I'm capable of deep down, the darkness I hide from my king. I am a warrior for a reason. I am good at killing, but it is more than that.

I relish killing.

The power of it, the blood on my hands from protecting my family . . . it's a high I have never found elsewhere, which is probably why I hated Alyx so much upon her crashing entry into our world. She represents everything I try to hide—my desires, anger, and arrogance. She is unapologetic in her skills and taking of lives, while I hide, working hard to remain calm and in control at all times. She is a wildfire of emotions, ones that have lived inside me since birth.

Fire and ice, yet I seem to be melting for her, and I worry what will be left.

Will I still have my careful control? Will she have stolen it all? It's too late to fight it now either way, so I focus on the man on his knees before me. My sword is pressed to his bobbing Adam's apple, a bead of blood running down his pale, clammy skin.

Something Alyx and Joha talked about yesterday bugged me. I know Joha suspects Queen Mother killed his father, but how did she get away with it? No matter how well she covered it up, he was sick, and as king, he had to be seen. It just so happens the royal healer at that time, someone I thought was a loyal friend to the king, resigned and left after his death. Everyone thought it was due to grief, since they were like brothers and best friends since childhood, but what if it wasn't because of that?

What if he knew something and was running?

Hence the sword. I need answers, and I grew tired of asking nicely.

"Let me ask one more time. You were his apprentice. You knew him better than anyone. Where did Healer Arbella go?" The man swallows hard. He was young when he was taken on and taught by the best healer in the kingdom for years. They had grown close, and then he was abandoned, just like that, but he is loyal to his old mentor even now.

"Why are you seeking him now? Leave him in peace," he sneers, defiant even in the face of death.

"It is for the king," I reply. This man owes him loyalty. He could warn the healer we are coming, but I have no choice. I need answers. "About his father."

His eyes narrow, searching mine. "He finally wants answers? He has finally taken away their bindings," he muses with a laugh. "Fine, you might not like the answers you get though. Master left years ago for a reason. He is hiding deep within Tundra Province, in a little village between the mountains called Fireheart."

There is only one reason someone as high up as Arbella would hide, and that's to escape someone's clutches. Fireheart is a small village, but it lies deep within the Tundra Mountains and is nearly impossible to get to. Those who live there are poor yet happy and survive on the land.

He went there to hide, which means I'm right.

Removing my sword, I lean down and hand over a stack of coins. "For your trouble."

I'm about to fade into the shadows when the young man's voice rings out again. "Prepare yourself, guard dog. If you dig into this, you might end up the same as the old king." I turn back to demand to know what he means, but he is gone, departed into the night along with his secrets.

🗡

"No," Joha states. "Fireheart is at least a three days' ride from here, and that is a hard ride at best. You told me that yourself. It's too dangerous. What if he knows nothing?"

Sitting back heavily in my wooden chair, I meet Joha's worried eyes. "Joha." I cover his hand on the table. "I will be fine. I am more worried about you—"

"I'm coming too," Alyx says, and my head jerks around. She has one knee pressed to her chest, her other on the floor, wearing leather breeches and a loose shirt. Crux is in the other chair at the table in her rooms, cards spread before them since they were playing before I barged in.

"No!" we all protest at the same time.

Her eyebrow rises as she glances from her cards to us. "Yes. I'm perfectly healed now—"

"You were dying," Joha snaps.

"And now I'm not," she argues. "You are right. Orion cannot go alone. If they find out where he's going and why, they will hunt him down. He needs someone to watch his back, someone who can ride hard and fast and go undetected. That is me."

"Or me," Crux reminds her.

"No, you need to stay to protect the king. You're the best—well, other than me. I'm still on bed rest," she scoffs. "It's the perfect time.

They might even try to make another move, thinking the king is weak with Orion gone, and we can spring a trap."

"Absolutely not," Joha states.

"Are you telling me what to do, my king?" Her voice is low and sultry, danger in every word. He swallows, his eyes widening with desire, not fear.

"No?" It sounds like a question from him, and we all snort a laugh.

"I hate to admit it, but she could be right. If Crux and I go, we would probably kill each other. This way, we can spring a trap and get information. We just need to plan it well," I mutter.

I'm definitely not siding with her just to spend time with her.

"I win." She lays her cards out with a wicked grin, and we groan, knowing she is going to win this argument too.

It's not in her nature to lose.

⚓

WE SPEND AN ENTIRE DAY PREPPING, every hand on deck. While I prepared two horses and supplies in secret, Crux and Alyx worked on laying a trap and planning for any possibilities—and probably fucking since he's adamant she should not be out of his sight.

It doesn't surprise me, however, when I go to find her that night and Joha has his arms wrapped around her in a tight hug. I slip into the shadows, giving them their privacy, but I end up peeking, my eyes widening as my king so blatantly cups her face and kisses her softly.

"Be safe and come back to me."

"Don't die while I'm gone." She laughs and then turns to the shadows I didn't even see. "Crux, remember, only I get to kill you, so don't die either."

"I'll be waiting." The voice comes from deep in the darkness.

Stepping from the wall, I cough to get their attention. "It's time. The changing of guards is happening soon, so we need to be gone before the new ones arrive. It's better no one knows we have left until it's too late."

She nods, glancing back at Crux and Joha. "Don't be stupid. Play it safe. We will be back in six days, and the kingdom better be standing then." She lingers for another moment, clearly worried. She turns to me and heads my way, her eyes glinting with determination.

As she walks, she tugs up her hood, the black material concealing her face. Reaching down, she pulls up her face mask, covering her mouth so only her green orbs are seen. In leather braces, boots, and a blouse, she looks like a peasant or, well, an assassin since she has blades at her sides.

She looks dangerous and fucking sexy.

It's going to be a long few days. I didn't think about that.

She falls into step at my side, and we move through the shadows to the stables where our horses wait—two black stallions, the fastest and hardiest horses I could find. Their saddlebags are filled with all our supplies. I go to give her a boost, but as I watch, she grabs the saddle and flings herself up, sitting confidently.

Shaking my head, I move closer, checking her stirrups and ensuring everything is safe, my hand lingering on her leg as I look up at her. She meets my eyes, and I swallow what I really want to say. "Stay at my side and keep up," I order before I mount my own horse as she clicks her tongue and urges hers forward.

"You keep up." She glances over at me. "If you can, big guy."

She kicks her horse into a trot, and as soon as we pass through the open gate, she sits deeper in her saddle as we urge our horses faster, speeding through the dark city, straight through Stormhallow, and towards Tundra Province.

I hope I'm right about this.

Please let me be right and my king be safe.

365

CHAPTER
FIFTY-SIX

ALYX

We ride for two days, barely taking any breaks, but the next night, we have to rest. Tundra Pass is a hard, rocky journey, and we spent most of our time walking around fallen rocks and abandoned carts, not to mention fighting bandits. It slowed us down, and I know Orion wants to push on, but our horses need sleep and so do we, so he eventually gives in when the moon is high in the sky.

We find the most concealed place we can. We are surrounded by trees, about a few hours' ride from Tundra Province. The moon is bright here, and we work silently together to lay down bed rolls, and then I build a fire while he catches something to cook. We work swiftly and well together, depending on each other.

I let Orion cook the meat as I clean my blades and get us water, then we eat in companionable silence.

The fire sits between us, throwing the shadows across the handsome planes of his face. Even now, he's in his armour, his eyes sharp as he rips into the grilled meat.

"Are you ever going to fuck me?" I ask suddenly.

He chokes, coughing on the meat as his gaze swings to me. "What? I don't—I . . . What?" he sputters, his eyes darting everywhere as I smirk.

Putting down my wooden skewer, I lay my arm across my knees. "It was a simple question. I'm just curious. You watch me like you wonder how quickly you could undress me, and you kissed me. You want me. I know it and you know it. Everyone knows it. So when are you planning on doing something about it?"

He stares at me, his mouth opening and closing for a moment before he recovers. "I have my duty." It's a lame excuse and he knows it, but I know Orion well by now. He puts everyone before him. If left alone, he wouldn't even sleep or eat for fear of leaving his station. No, he needs someone to push him, and it just so happens I enjoy it.

Besides, I've been dreaming about having this big guy between my thighs, begging for me. I'm betting it would be hard and fast, and I want it.

I want him.

"Duty." I roll my eyes and climb to my feet, then I head around the fire and sling my leg over his lap so I'm perched above him. His eyes widen as my hands hit the metal breastplate covering his skin. "There is no duty right here, right now," I murmur as I lean in, my lips lingering above his. "Your king is not here. I am. What are you going to do about it?"

"Alyx." My name is a plea, desire warring with his morals.

Smirking, I rub my lips across his and then over his stubbled cheek to his ear. "I'm your best friend's wife-to-be." He jerks, his body stiff. "I'm an assassin, a killer. You shouldn't want me. Does that about cover it?" I bite his ear until he jerks, and then I lick away the sting. "Now stop listing the reasons why not." Leaning back, I slide my hand down his armour and press against his hard cock, watching as he swallows. "You want me; I want you. Nothing else matters."

"It does," he protests, but his voice is hoarse.

"No, it doesn't. Think about yourself for once, Orion. What do you want? Tell me right now that you don't want me and I'll leave you in peace." He stares, and I wait. "Well? Tell me."

"I want you," he admits.

"Good boy." Grabbing my blouse, I slide it up and off, leaving me bare to his hungry gaze. "Then what will you do about it?"

He freezes for a moment, only his eyes moving over my chest. When he meets my gaze, I see he is consumed with desire. The heat in his eyes makes me shiver, and I know I've broken Orion's careful control.

I gasp as he rolls us and his thick fingers rip at the laces of my trousers, yanking them free before he shoves his hand inside them. His fingers slide across my slick pussy and thrust into me so suddenly, my back arches as I cry out. He swallows the sound, his lips pressed to mine. I love it, and I want more.

"Tell me you want me," he demands gruffly.

My head hits the grass as I meet his dark eyes, his broad back blocking out all the moon's rays. I slid my hands down his back, wishing it were skin. "I want you," I admit without shame, licking his lips. "Can't you feel?" I clench my pussy around his invading fingers, knowing I'm ridiculously wet.

We killed bandits together today, and that always makes me horny, but it's not just desire—it's desire for him.

I want Orion. I have since the moment I saw him.

His fingers curl inside me, demanding my pleasure. My eyes nearly cross, and when he starts to fuck me with them, I moan. He lowers his head, pressing his lips to mine. His tongue licks at the seams of my lips before he bites down, seeking entrance. I gladly give it, our tongues tangling for dominance even as I open my legs wider, giving him better access.

Humming into my mouth, he slides a third finger inside me, so thick and wide it starts to hurt, but I tilt my hips eagerly for more. Tearing from my mouth, he slides his head down, dragging his tongue down my throat. I groan as he slides lower still, across my collarbone and chest, and circles my nipple. I grab onto his neck, tugging him closer.

"Orion," I murmur, but before I can get any more words out, his mouth seals around my nipple. I cry out, clenching around him.

Such intense pleasure fills me, I almost arch from the ground. Pain mixes with desire as he pulls back, chuckling darkly before he turns his head and does the same to my other nipple.

He lifts his head, watching me pant and writhe below him. "Look at these pretty marks. I might not be able to mark you where the kingdom can see, but I can mark you where they can't so we know you're mine, even for a night." His voice is dark and deadly, and I swear I see stars. Glancing down, I see his teeth marks and swallow, clenching down his fingers. "You like it, don't you, assassin? Like me hurting you? Like me marking you?" His eyes flit across the scars covering my body. "Did it make you wet when you got these?"

My eyes narrow, and he smirks, twisting his fingers inside me until it hurts. "Answer me, assassin."

"You want my secrets?" I ask breathlessly. "You have to pay."

"Tell me and I'll make you come," he orders, then he bites down on my breast until I feel blood. The sharp pain makes me grip his fingers tighter, betraying me, and he grins. "You did, didn't you? An assassin who likes getting hurt."

"Yes," I admit. It's something I've never told another. "I like it when I get hurt. A fight or fucking, it doesn't matter. It makes me wet."

"So what you're telling me, Alyx," he murmurs as he leans down and sucks on my nipple, "is that I can hurt you as much as I want while I fuck you." Sliding his mouth back up to mine, he lays a soft kiss on my lips before whispering, "Good because I'm big, so it's going to hurt. It's going to rip you, and you're going to take all of it anyway, aren't you?"

"Yes," I beg, rubbing my breasts against the cool metal of his armour.

"Good girl," he praises, flipping my words from earlier. "Don't forget that when you're crying later while I fuck you."

"Pay the price," I demand, "for my secret."

"Gladly." He turns my head and digs his teeth into my neck, pinning me like a wild animal as his thumb presses to my clit while he fucks me with his fingers. His teeth dig deeper, and I fly over the edge, screaming into the forest as pleasure explodes through my body.

He doesn't relent, forcing his fingers deeper, fucking me through it until I slump, my eyes shut from the afterglow.

"You didn't think I was done, did you? That was just payment for your secret." My eyes open wide as he grins down at me. It's an evil smile and so out of place on his face, but fuck if it doesn't make my heart skip a beat.

"You wanted the beast, assassin," he warns, and I yelp as he flips me.

My face presses to the grass as he shoves my breeches down and off, leaving me naked while he's in his armour. "I did. I do. That's it." I push back. "Fuck me. Don't hold back, I can take it. I can take anything you give me. I won't break."

He smacks my ass, making me cry out even as I push back for more. My head hangs forward when his hand slides lower, across the mess on my thighs, and pets my pussy. "You're wet. It won't be enough, but I don't care." He forces his fingers inside me for a moment before pulling away, and I look over my shoulder, watching as he yanks down the laces on his trousers and pulls out his cock.

My eyes widen as I stare at him. Smirking, he runs his wet hand across his length. He warned me, but fuck, I didn't expect that. He's big everywhere, but there is no way that will fit inside me.

Not a chance.

He's so thick and long, it will rip me apart.

I try to scramble away, but he wraps a hand around my throat, pinning me in place as I kick. The strength in that one hand is so astounding, it makes me embarrassingly hot.

I feel him press to my entrance and try to escape, but he doesn't let me, instead pushing into me. He forces me to take him. It hurts so fucking much, I fight his grasp. It's like a red-hot branding iron is sliding deeper inside me as he forces his length into me with one hard thrust, obviously tired of waiting.

"Orion!" I scream, trying to pull away. "Please, please." Tears squeeze from my eyes.

"No," he snarls, dragging me back and impaling me deeper onto his cock. "You taunted the beast, now you get this. You wanted me, so take it all like you said. Let it hurt. Feel it."

I breathe through it, trying to embrace the sharp pain, and as he starts to move, it turns to a burning pain and pleasure, leaving me dripping and reluctantly rocking back onto his length.

"Good girl, that's it. Look at you taking all of me. Fuck, it's such a pretty sight, seeing you stretched around me like this, your pussy pink and raw for me." His dirty words go through me, making my clit throb as I clench on him, only enhancing the pain.

The pain makes me dizzy, makes me hotter, nearly makes me come.

He stops holding back and slams into my cunt in a hard, brutal thrust. The agony cascades through my body, and it gets me off.

I come with an embarrassing whine, even as it hurts so much my head goes dizzy, but he doesn't stop pummelling into me from behind, our skin slapping together loudly even over the pop of the flames.

He ruts me like the beast he called himself. His hand slides from my neck, wrapping around my hair and yanking my head back. His mouth meets my ear as he drives into me from behind. "Imagine what they would see if they caught the king's dog rutting their precious queen-to-be."

My heart pounds in my chest so hard I'm surprised he can't hear it, my moans falling from my lips even as I push back to take more of him. "I bet you've imagined fucking me in one of those dresses on the steps to the throne."

"More than once," he growls, biting the back of my neck again, "even as they watched me, horrified. It's all I could think about, ripping up those frilly fucking dresses and showing them the monster that lives inside you that loves me claiming you like that."

"Oh fuck," I cry out, clenching on his length, imagining just that.

He chuckles in my ear as he slides his tongue through his bite. "Let's see how far I can push you."

He turns us, pressing my face so close to the fire it almost burns. The threat is there, the adrenaline making me gush around him, which is exactly why he did it. He's using my secret against me, and I can't even be mad.

"Look at you." His cock twitches inside me as he hammers into me from behind. I take it, pushing back for more. I take everything he gives me, letting him know I wasn't lying. He can't break me.

I watch the flames as he fucks me, wishing they were licking across my skin, wanting to feel their burn like his hands sliding across me.

"I want to see you come. I want to feel you come on my cock, make me come. Let me watch it spill from this pretty little cunt."

"Make me," I demand, glancing back at him with my signature grin. "Make me come."

His head lowers, his nostrils flaring as he kneels behind me like a warrior claiming his prize in battle, and I love it. One hand slides down my spine and over my ass, circling my hole, and then it moves through my cunt, and he pinches my clit between his fingers, slowly increasing the pressure as he fucks me.

My brain short-circuits and I come with a scream, gushing around his length. He fights my fluttering cunt until he grunts, slams deep inside me, and bellows his release to the wilds surrounding us.

The flames flicker as I fall forward, but he doesn't release me, even as I shake and shiver from my release. He slowly pulls his length free, making me moan, and I feel his cum dripping from me. With two thick fingers, he pushes it back inside me.

"I'm going to stain this royal cunt," he warns, shoving it deeper. I love his rough, filthy treatment. I hope he doesn't close back up after this, but I know I can push him over the edge, and I can't wait to do it again.

He surprises me, however, when he quickly strips from his armour and wraps me in his arms, laying us on one of the bed rolls. My whole lower half aches in the best way and I'm sticky, but I don't move. I snuggle closer, stroking his exposed skin.

We lie like that for a while, until our heartbeats have slowed and we have recovered enough to speak.

Sliding my fingers across the brutal scar on his arm, I rest my head on his wide chest. "What is this scar from?"

He glances down, his eyes smouldering as he watches me trace his skin. "A sword meant for the king. He was sixteen at the time."

"This one?" I ask, sliding higher to a puckered scar.

"A horse kicked. I took the blow."

"This one?"

He grins. "A fire started in the kitchen after Joha tried to cook." His hand slides down my bare side, making me shiver despite the fire roaring close by. "What is this scar from?" he asks, and I look down to see the one he is tracing.

"Ah, one of my first hunts. I was too cocky. He was a loan shark preying on women. He stabbed me with a fire poker. It hurt like a son of a bitch, but it was a good lesson." I smirk.

He rubs it before leaning down and kissing it, rolling me to my back as his tongue darts out to trace a flat one across my hip. "This one?"

I bite my lip before I speak. "Crux was teaching me to fight with blades, and I was too slow." He smirks before kissing it and moving down, stopping on one just above my pelvis.

"This one?"

"Chain," I admit breathlessly.

He kisses it better, sliding lower until his mouth hovers over my pussy. "Hmm, is this as sore as those scars? Shall I kiss it better?"

"Gods yes," I reply, gripping his shoulders as I throw my leg over one, urging him on. He doesn't reply, but his mouth seals over my aching cunt.

My cries fill the mountain air, and I know we won't be getting rest tonight.

That's fine by me.

CHAPTER
FIFTY-SEVEN

CRUX

I am going out of my fucking mind from boredom. Being on babysitting duty for the king is not what I had in mind when I set up my kingdom in the underworld. The thing that is really driving me mad, though, is that Alyx is out there without me to protect her.

If she ever heard me say that, she would kick my ass. She does not need my protection, yet I cannot help the urge to fight off any threat that even glances in her direction. She is *mine*, and I protect what's mine.

Yes, this plan was the one that made the most sense, but it does not mean I have to be happy about it. She needs to get the information, and while she is away, the king needs protection. I happen to be the next best person for the job, which is why I'm here and not with her, even if I think he's a pampered moron.

I am not sure how I ended up in this situation. Everything had been going well. Alyx had been looking at me in a new light, and then the king stumbled into her life. Now I have gone from king of the underworld to babysitter and harem member.

How the mighty have fallen.

Walking a step behind Joha in my stiff military jacket, I glance around the empty hallway. I'm close enough to pull him out of the way and protect him in a way the others cannot. We're surrounded by his other guards who all stand in a circle around us, with several paces between us. Rookies. There have been multiple attacks on their king, and they stand too far away to do anything should someone try again. They may be loyal, but they need more training. Slipping into their ranks was easy. One word from Orion and I was one of them. Others from the outside watch us closely, though, looking for weaknesses, and I have to make sure I am acting exactly as a guard would so no one has any reason to doubt that I'm supposed to be here.

I wonder where Alyx is now and how her mission is going. The one thing that stops me from dropping everything and going after her is knowing that the king's guard dog, Orion, is with her. Begrudgingly, I can admit he will help keep her safe.

The stomping of staffs against the stone floor brings me back to the present, and I swallow back my sigh as we walk into the main room where the council meets. As usual, everyone is already here, and they stand as we enter, bowing their heads to the king.

Something is wrong.

I couldn't tell you what or how I know, but over the years, I have learned to trust my gut, and right now, it is telling me that something is about to happen. While I do not think it is a threat to the king's life, I'm instantly on alert, my eyes scanning the room. These people are vipers in human skin, all waiting for Joha to put a single foot out of place so they can strike. The atmosphere is heavy, but as I pay more attention, I notice a few smug looks on the faces of the councilmen. They try to hide them and probably think they have gotten away with it. What they didn't count on was me.

Of course, Queen Mother is here, looking demure and the picture of innocence when she is the worst of them all. Standing from her curtsy, she clutches her hands before her and smiles politely at the king.

"Your Majesty," she greets, her smile never reaching her eyes. "How is your betrothed faring this morning?" The spark of interest in her voice tells me that she's asking because she wants to know every detail about Alyx, not because she's concerned. My girl is an enigma, something Queen Mother cannot control, and that drives her mad.

Joha moves farther into the room, pulling back his chair at the head of the table, and glances around, taking in who is in attendance. To my amusement, he doesn't even look at her until he is comfortable in his chair and everyone else has sat.

Glancing over, he smiles slightly and tips his head in acknowledgement. "She is slowly recovering, Queen Mother, but she will need longer to rest until she can return to her duties."

From my position directly behind the king's chair, I have the perfect view of everyone in the room, making sure to note everyone's expressions. My instincts still tell me something is not right.

"I see. That must be stressful for you," Queen Mother continues. The insincerity in her tone is enough to make me want to roll my eyes. She is laying it on thick. Does she really think Joha would take her words as sincere concern?

"Quite," he spits out, struggling to play his role as pliant puppet king. "Shall we begin so I can get back to her?"

She places her hands on the table, palms down, and glances at the men on either side of her before turning her gaze back to the king. "There is one very important thing we need to discuss with you before starting council business."

"Oh?"

I hear the surprise and wariness in his voice, and I do not blame him for it. Whatever I was sensing is about to happen. I brace myself, my hand hovering over the dagger hidden in my uniform, ready to move should I need to. The fact that she told him that "they" have something to discuss tells me this was planned beforehand. They met without him and only now decided to involve him. This could very quickly turn into a treasonous meeting.

"The attempts on your life have increased exponentially, and we are worried." Speaking with what many would see as sympathy, Queen Mother smiles with fake concern. I happen to be an expert in reading people, though, and she is lying through her teeth. This woman is the one we suspect organised the attacks, and here she is, talking about it as though the attacks are causing an inconvenience to them.

Surprisingly, I find I'm annoyed on behalf of the king, which is something I never thought would happen. I must be spending too much time with him. That or I just have a low tolerance for two-faced liars.

"I can assure you that I am just as concerned," Joha replies wryly.

"Good." She smiles and leans back in her chair, gesturing to those around her. "Then hopefully you will agree with our decision."

Joha seems to have the same realisation I do in that moment, freezing in his chair, his body stiff. They came together without him and planned against the king. Damn it. Hovering on my toes, I prepare to react should I need to.

Without waiting for him to recover, Queen Mother continues. "We have decided, as a concerned council, that for your safety, you should be confined to the king's palace. Guards will be stationed outside to protect you at all times and make sure you are kept safely within."

There is a long pause as Joha absorbs what she just dared to propose. The fact that the rest of the council went along with this is surprising, and I am sure he feels betrayed by this decision.

"You want to lock me up?" he asks slowly, seeking clarification. His jaw is tight, and I see anger working through him. "I am the king."

"Which is exactly why we want to keep you safe," she replies smoothly with a saccharine smile, moving her arms wide to gesture to those in the room. "We worry for you, my king. This way, no one can get to you. As the council to the king, it is one of our duties to keep you safe, even when you do not want us to."

It is pretty clear what she's saying, and I feel the frustration of the king's guards behind us. They are just as angry about the whole situation as Joha is, and I cannot say I blame them. This decision has already been made and taken out of Joha's hands.

The king places his hands on the table before him, and I don't know if he's bracing himself for an argument or getting ready to leave the room before they can try to "assist" him out of here.

"No, I will not be chased into hiding by whatever coward is hiding behind assassins." His voice is like ice, and his eyes are locked on Queen Mother, recognising the real threat in the room.

Sighing, she rolls her eyes, losing patience with him. "I do not understand why you are making this difficult, Joha. You will be resting in luxury in your palace."

"A gilded cage is still a cage," I murmur, momentarily drawing the attention of the Queen Mother. She frowns, her eyes flitting over my face as she tries to work out if she's seen me here before.

"You forget your place, Queen Mother. It is not your job to tell me what I should or should not be doing," Joha snaps, making the woman pale and lean away from the rebuttal in his voice. Several of the council members in the room look uncomfortable with this display, and I make careful note of their faces for future reference.

"My guard is correct. It doesn't matter where you lock me away, you are still stealing my liberties. You are taking away all of my power. Let me guess, you will run the country in the meantime?" Anger starts to lace his words as I look down at the king in surprise. Perhaps he has a backbone after all.

He nailed the issue on the head and made it clear that he knows exactly what they are doing. This has nothing to do with protecting him and everything to do with getting him out of the way. Some of the same advisors who looked uneasy before look outright uncomfortable now that their king is fighting back.

Alyx told me that Joha let his advisors and Queen Mother treat him like a puppet king so he wouldn't meet a sudden and unfortunate end. That way, Queen Mother still made decisions and Joha was king in name only. While I understand his reasoning, it's the logic of someone who hasn't had to fight for their life every single day. It seems the king has decided to finally fight back. They are already trying to kill him, so at least he's regaining his control.

Still surprised and recovering from the king's rebuttal, Queen Mother presses her hand to her chest and shifts in her chair. It is the most genuine expression I've seen on her face since we arrived here.

"The council and I will act in your place. Temporarily of course," she reassures him with a tentative smile, unsure of her place but slowly trying to recover the control in the room. "You are still king. We just need to take measures to assure you survive until we can find out who is behind these attacks."

Sneaky. The woman is a good actress. If she didn't try to kill my reason for existing, then I might try to recruit her. I imagine she has this whole room wrapped around her little finger thanks to those skills.

Joha looks around the table, meeting each set of eyes of his so-called supporters. His expression is flat. "All of you agreed on this?"

There are several calls of agreement, the loudest of which come from the males closest to Queen Mother. Most of the advisors in the room, however, look uncomfortable, mumbling their answers and lowering their gazes to the table. They might have agreed initially, but they are second-guessing themselves now that they've seen the king. There is also the possibility that they were coerced into making this decision. With what I just witnessed here, that would not surprise me.

He could fight the decision, but without the support of the council, he has even less power than he does now. The assassins managed to slip into all areas of the palace and the grounds, so locking him away in the king's palace isn't going to keep him any safer. It is just an excuse to get him out of the way, and Joha knows it.

"This is just to keep you safe, Your Majesty," one of the advisors comments, his expression firm but his voice tight, giving away his discomfort.

"Why don't you return to your palace now, Your Majesty, and I will send someone to update you on what is discussed in the council meeting?" Queen Mother smiles sweetly, but I see the predator in her eyes. If Joha tries to protest, she will find a way to have him dragged out.

"Leave with dignity, my king," I whisper into his ear.

I don't know why I do it, I don't really care if he gets dragged out or not, but something moves within me as I watch his supposed supporters turn on him. I feel him hesitate, but eventually, he must see it as I do.

There is no choice.

"I expect to be updated on what's happening in my country and to be consulted about any changes before the council makes any decisions. Remember that I am your king." Bracing his hands on the table, he pushes up to his feet, staring down the table as authority rings from his voice. "Find whoever is behind these attacks," he orders, sounding more like a king than I've heard from him before.

Spinning on his heel, he strides towards the door, his guards jumping to attention and opening it quickly. We fall into formation around the king and leave the room full of traitors behind us.

CHAPTER
FIFTY-EIGHT

CRUX

"I am sorry, my king. I do not agree with this plan, but it was put to a vote, so there is nothing I can do," the older male explains, his hands open wide in a gesture of helplessness. He wears the same robes as the other council members and advisors, yet he seems genuinely apologetic about what happened.

The king's smile is tight, but there is sincere warmth in his eyes as he reaches out and touches the man's shoulder. "Thank you for coming to see me, Advisor Perin. Your support means a lot to me." Glancing over the man's shoulder, he looks at the guards and frowns at their restlessness. "You better return before you get locked in here with me."

One council member a day has been given permission to enter the king's palace to update him on everything that was discussed in that day's meetings. Advisor Perin volunteered to be the go between and is the only one who seems to have stayed loyal. Even though this meeting is council approved, the guards hovering in the doorway are not from the king's personal protection unit, and they are making it clear that the advisor is taking too long.

Bowing his head in respect, he gives his king a quick, apologetic smile that looks more like a grimace and leaves the room, escorted by the guards.

I wait until I can no longer hear their footsteps, then I ditch my guard position and extend my arms above my head, jumping up and catching one of the ceiling beams. Swinging, I pull myself up and perch on a beam where it crosses with another, giving me something to lean against. With one of my legs propped up, the other dangles down as I carve a small piece of wood. It has only been a day since the king was confined to his palace, and he is already going stir crazy. I learned the art of patience as an assassin, so I'm not bothered. Rushing into any situation is a surefire way to get yourself killed.

Watching the king with a smirk, I count his steps as he paces—ten, pause, and then ten back—a habit I find is impossible to break, but a useful one nonetheless. I continue to whittle my piece of wood, the shavings falling from the beams and landing on the floor, looking like snow floating through the room.

"Can you not find somewhere else to do that?"

The king's annoyed voice brings a smirk to my face, but I feign innocence as I glance down at him, raising a brow. "I promised Alyx I would keep an eye on you, and that is what I'm doing."

I'm fairly sure he knows I'm only doing this to annoy him, but if he admitted that aloud, it would prove that it's working.

Gritting his teeth, he huffs out a frustrated breath and runs a hand through his long, sleek hair. "Well, do you have to do it from the beams?"

Leaning back, I take up whittling once more. "It's easier to hide if I'm up here, plus I find it comfortable." While what I say is true, I find pleasure in sitting up here because I know it annoys him, especially now that I've picked up a new hobby.

Scowling at the wood shavings on what I'm sure is a priceless rug, he takes a moment to gather his thoughts, most likely to bite back a cutting remark about my presence.

After a moment, he looks up at me with a scowl. "What are you even making?"

I flash him a grin with entirely too many teeth. "That's a secret."

Truthfully, I have no idea. Turns out I am really bad at whittling, but it keeps my hands busy, and I am less likely to kill the king out of pure boredom. The benefit of it annoying the crap out of him is also a strong motivator for me to continue.

Joha drops it and returns to pacing. I have no idea how long he's planning to do that, and I don't really care, but I know that Alyx would be worried about him. The king's mental state is not something I care a single iota about, but if Alyx comes back from her trip and Joha's mind is broken, it will hurt her, which I won't allow to happen, meaning I have to pander to the needs of the puppet king.

I must be getting soft.

I hold out for as long as I can in the hopes that he will magically sort himself out, but eventually, I have to admit I need to step in. I can practically see the king's mind unravelling by the minute. He needs something to focus on that isn't related to the council that betrayed him.

Sighing quietly, I stash my blade and piece of wood away in my secret pockets and drop down from the beams. I land silently, but Joha catches my movement and narrows his gaze on me, recognising the determined look in my eyes.

"Let's go for a walk," I say, not waiting to see if he'll listen to me or not before I cross to the door.

"I'm not allowed out, remember?" Mirth colours his words, but I don't let that bother me.

"You have this whole palace to yourself." Glancing over my shoulder, I raise my eyebrows and give him a smirk. "You should take me for a tour."

The king snorts. "I am sure you have been in every room in this building and don't need me to show you around."

He's right, I have the entire place mapped out in my mind thanks to a few reconnaissance trips. "Maybe the place will look different with the lights on."

His mouth drops open, and he shakes his head as though he can't believe I just admitted to searching his palace. I'm not sure why this seems to come as such a shock to him when he already guessed this was the case. I was not about to let Alyx in here without checking the layout of every building on the grounds.

I have never quite understood why the two separate residences for the king and queen were named palaces. I always assumed the larger, more ornate buildings where the court meets and business happens were the palace. From what I have gathered while I have been here, all of the individual buildings make up "the palace," while the king's and queen's palaces are where they can conduct their own business should they want to.

"I really need to get the guards trained better," Joha mutters to himself, shaking his head. "Assassins just keep wandering in like I left the front gates open."

What doesn't help is that he has a huge target on his back and someone with a grudge. If we find the person arranging the attacks, then hopefully fewer assassins will have a reason to enter the palace grounds. However, if he thinks that training his guards will keep assassins away, then he will be sorely disappointed. Assassins are trained for exactly this type of thing, and those who fail die.

Leaning against the doorframe, I cross my arms over my chest as I wait for him to join me. "You will never be able to keep the best of us out," I chime in, breaking through his mutterings. "Sorry."

Sighing, he covers his face with his hands and takes a deep breath. When he opens his eyes again, the panic seems to have faded, and he meets my gaze. "Okay, let's go. I need to get out of this room for a while."

THE DINING HALL in the king's palace is beautiful and has been kept in immaculate condition, but it is clear it has not been used in years, like most of this place.

"You have all of this space, yet you never use it," I observe, trying to keep the judgement from my voice.

So far, the only rooms that appear to see any use are the bedchamber, adjoining bathroom, and a small study. The music room has a beautiful piano positioned in front of a large window overlooking the wildflowers in the back, the snowcapped mountains in the background. A look of sadness passed across his features when he looked at it, and he quickly led me onwards.

He has all of this unused space and luxury, when children and vulnerable families are dying in the slums. You can barely move in the worst parts of the slums, the habitats so close together, the paper-thin walls only offer the pretence of privacy. They certainly don't provide any warmth.

Joha's expression shifts. "That will be different once we are married. My queen will move in, and more of the rooms will be in use then, hosting dinner parties, caring for our children ..."

He slows to a stop as he realises what he said and that I am no longer at his side. He turns, his expression tentative as he waits for the backlash of his words, yet there is no apology in his eyes.

Alyx. He's talking about Alyx—married, moving in, and having children.

I've frozen in place, the walls of the huge hall suddenly feeling too small, as though they are closing in on me. They constrict around me, my body motionless but begging to be released, to jump into action and do something, *anything*, to ease the pain his words cause within me.

"What is the plan once we stop the person behind the attacks?" I snap, needing to know the answer. Why didn't I ever ask this before? I was so confident in my relationship with Alyx that I didn't think it was even a possibility that we wouldn't end up together.

"What do you mean?" Joha takes a tentative step towards me.

Frustrated, I growl low in my throat. "When does this end?" I snap. "Alyx isn't going to pretend to be a princess forever. Someone will eventually work out the truth. When do I get my Alyx back?"

"Crux, I love her, and I'm pretty sure she loves me too." Although he looks uncomfortable, he shows no signs of backing down.

Although the words strike a bolt of pain through me, I can't deny that there is truth to what he says. "Okay, yeah, fine, whatever, but you would see her as a concubine, right?" I ask, needing the answer. "You can't possibly think you can actually marry her and make her your queen."

Frowning, he pulls back slightly, pursing his lips. I've offended him with my question. Good, he needs to think about this carefully. Glancing away, he pretends to look out of the hall window, no longer able to meet my eyes. "Once we are married, it will be too late, and no one will care about her background."

Snorting, I cross my arms over my chest. "I'm pretty sure someone will have something to say about the fact that your queen is an assassin."

Does he really think he can get away with this plan? If his council doesn't have trust in him now, then they will have a fit once they discover who Alyx really is.

Throwing his hands up in the air, he spins around to stare at me. "I thought we spoke about this. None of us are giving up on her, so why is this such a shock to you?"

"Because she is *mine* and you are going to take her away from me!" The anger I have been keeping a tight lid on until now bursts out. "I don't have titles or crowns to give her like you do!"

"She is not just yours anymore. She—"

I don't know what he's about to say next, but a flash of movement in the corner of the dining hall catches my eye. I just notice as a figure dressed in dark clothing lifts a bow, the quiet telltale twang of the string being released my only warning.

I fall into assassin mode, grabbing the king by the shoulders and throwing him to the ground, narrowly avoiding the arrow that was aimed at his chest. Unfortunately for me, the movement throws me forward, and I twist just in time to avoid being impaled. The arrow catches my cheek instead, grazing the skin, but the burning pain is barely noticeable as adrenaline pumps through my body.

Notching another arrow, the assassin aims at the king, his obvious target, but I'm already racing towards the figure. The arrow fires just as I leap forward, and I have to pray that it missed Joha, my full attention on the assassin.

Tackling the male to the floor, I rip off his head covering in the process. I don't recognise him, but that is no surprise. Alyx already told me what happened with the last assassin and the cyanide pill he was hiding in the back of his mouth, so as I manage to pin him to the ground, I shove part of the bow into his mouth, stopping him from biting down. He bucks and tries to throw me off, knowing what I'm doing, but I'm too quick for him. Sticking my fingers in his mouth, I scrabble around until I find the tablet. I throw it onto the ground beside us, then I reach back in to make sure there isn't a second.

"Who sent you?" I demand, moving around to keep him down.

He has dark hair, dark skin, and a fine powder on his clothes. He's one of the assassins from the Burning Lands. Narrowing his almost black eyes on me, he gives me a look full of hatred. "I do not answer to you."

"Then whom do you answer to?" I counter. "You're clearly not from around here."

He grins at me, winding me up. This guy is not going to tell me anything, so I smash my fist into his face. His head slams back against the marble flooring, and he grunts with pain, yet he still says nothing, so I hit him again and again.

"Crux, stop. We need to question him," Joha calls out from behind me, shock lacing his voice.

"What do you think I'm doing?" I snarl, not having the patience to pander to him right now. "Go back to your chambers and lock the doors. I won't be long," I tell him, keeping my eyes locked on the assassin. His head lolls to one side, and a small puddle of blood pools beneath his face, his eyes fluttering as he fights unconsciousness.

I don't have anything to restrain the assassin with, so I'll just have to make sure he can't run away from me. Standing, I take advantage of the fact he's dazed, and I stomp down on his left leg. The bone snaps beneath my foot.

This wakes him up. His body jerks, and I watch without an ounce of pity, aiming a kick to his ribs. "Tell me who ordered the hit on the king." I kneel by his side.

"Never." The assassin smirks up at me despite his pain. "Does it annoy you that assassins are getting into your city and there is nothing you can do to stop us?"

Yes, it does, but I'm not going to tell him that. I don't want this type of scum in my city, and I will go hunting to make sure none of them are bunking down, otherwise they will spread like mould.

Nodding as though he told me something interesting, I stand again and move over to his right side. I stretch his arm out, stepping on his fingers to keep it in place as I stomp again. He screams in pain.

This is obviously going to take a fair amount of convincing, so I need to disable him so I don't have to worry about him escaping. Grabbing his right, non-injured leg, I twist it roughly so I can see his heel, then I pull my dagger from my jacket and stab it straight through the skin. The effect is immediate, the blade severing the Achilles tendon from the heel, causing the tight bundle of fibres to spring up and bunch by the back of his knee. I've been told the pain is immense, and there's no chance he will be able to walk now, having lost the ability to point or lift his foot.

Any assassin worth the designation is trained to resist torture, and so far, he's done well to keep his information to himself. He's never come up against me before, though, and torture happens to be my speciality.

As I toss my knife and catch it by the hilt, I allow a chilling smile to pull at my lips as I stare down at him. I am not a good man, and I will do what I have to when it comes to protecting my family. Somehow, Joha is included in that now, and this assassin just tried to kill him.

It's time for me to get to work.

CHAPTER
FIFTY-NINE

ALYX

We reach Tundra Province by mid-morning. The small village, Fireheart, is bracketed by the mountains, cast in an almost constant shadow. The temperatures are cold, and the land is even harder to live on, meaning those that do are strong, smart, and determined. It also means they are not used to visitors, especially ones dressed like us. Here, they are cloaked in furs, their hands and faces covered in oil and coal. We stand out even after riding for days, their suspicious eyes following us as we move through the village.

Taking the main road, we dismount at the tiny stables, and I let Orion pay the unfriendly worker there. I push back my hood and eye the village, noting all possible threats—a habit I will never be able to break. It has saved my life on countless occasions.

The houses here are not like those in the Uppers nor the Lowers. They are made of stone and wood, scraped together by whatever can be harvested and found. Drying racks sit out front, and fires burn brightly within the walls. I don't see any children playing, nor any animals scampering about. Most of the houses are empty, and it's clear everyone is busy at work.

It's eerily quiet, and the stable hand is about as hospitable as the land as he spits on the floor after following Orion to my side.

"He's not here, apparently," Orion offers, his eyebrows drawn together in anger. Both of us know how precious our time is. I turn my attention to the man, running my eyes from head to toe, noting his tattered and worn clothes. His hair is long and shaggy, his face is streaked with dirt, and his eyes are hard.

Pulling out a bag of coins, I toss them to the man, knowing that is how you get someone like this to speak. He catches it, weighing it in his hand as he eyes me. I arch one eyebrow, my own eyes hardening, and he glances away for a moment.

"You will not find the healer here. He's an hour's ride north. He has his own compound there, which is where most of the elderly and sick are treated. They don't take kindly to outsiders, and the road is hard. Maybe it'd be best if you head back to where you came from," he says, spitting once more on the hay-covered dirt.

I understand the mentality. The Lowers are like this. We protect our own, and we do not trust outsiders.

I incline my head in acknowledgement of his warning. "Either way, we will go. Is it sign posted?"

"Nothing out here is." He chuckles before ambling away. Clearly, that is all we will get from him.

Striding to my horse, I mount it and turn to Orion. "What are we waiting for?"

He sighs deeply but follows suit, and we trot down the main street. Once at the end of the village, we cross a stone bridge that seems to signal the end of humans' reach. A huge forest engulfs us as we follow a thin trail only wide enough to walk in a line. I hear wolves howl and wild animals within their depths, and every now and again, we have to dismount to clear the way.

"This might be a trap," Orion cautions.

"Maybe," I reply, my eyes sharp as I scan our surroundings. "Or maybe it's not. I guess we will find out."

I steer my steed over increasingly rougher terrain as we wind through the forest.

Orion sighs deeply. "This was not a good idea," he finally says, grumpy as hell.

"Where is your sense of adventure?" I grin at him.

"Back with civilisation and beds." He smirks, making me laugh.

We continue on for at least another hour, and the forest opens up, flattening out. Lingering on the edge, we eye the wooden compound built into the side of the mountain. There is a tall, wooden fence with an open double gate, allowing us to see multiple structures inside and people hustling about. There is not much else out here, so this has to be it.

I share a look with Orion, and then we kick our horses into motion, covering the distance. When we reach the gate, I dismount and lead my horse over to the tether, my eyes on the structures I can see beyond.

Orion appears at my side, his hand on his weapon.

"Remember, we need his help."

He nods and drops his hand despite it clearly being a habit.

Leaving our horses tethered to the thin wooden pole, we stride towards the open gates and into the compound.

It's a hive of activity despite its solitude. Women and men in robes and aprons hurry between patients spread out across the buildings. One to my left clearly houses a small kitchen, and there is an outhouse to my right. The buildings between them are open, with no sides or doors, just poles holding up a peaked wooden roof. Beds cover every inch, filled with the elderly and sick. There's a courtyard in the middle with a huge well they pump water from, and at the very back is a small building, the only one with walls. Three wooden steps lead up to it.

"Excuse me." I catch the arm of a nurse hurrying past. "We are looking for Healer Arbella?"

She eyes me and then Orion. "You do not look sick. You'll be waiting a long time. We have many dying to tend to first."

"We are not sick," I admit. "We come to talk, that is all. We are old friends."

She eyes us once more. "He is not here right now. He is with an aide, collecting herbs deep within the mountain to treat the sick. He will be back by nightfall. You can wait here, though it might not be pleasant."

I nod in thanks, bowing my head as she hurries off. "So many sick."

"Out here, even a cold is deadly," Orion remarks.

"Then let's make ourselves useful while we wait." Throwing off my cloak, I lay it over a wooden barrel and push my sleeves back as Orion eyes me. "He's much more likely to talk if we are being helpful. Besides, they clearly need it."

"You continue to surprise me," he says, sliding his hand down my arm in a quick stolen touch before he nods. "You're right. What can we do to help?" He catches the arm of a passerby.

"The well needs pumping, the outhouse is clogged, the roofs are leaking, bandages need to be changed, and medicine has to be passed out. Take your pick," he scoffs, hurrying away.

"Not the outhouse," we both say at once, sharing a look before we laugh.

CHAPTER
SIXTY

ALYX

rion straightens, one leg on either side of the peaked roof. His shirt and armour are gone, exposing his built chest to the late afternoon sun. I watch greedily as he lifts his thick arm and wipes at his sweaty face before he continues fixing the roof.

"He's handsome. Is he your husband?" the lady I am tending to asks.

Grinning at her, I finish tying off the bandage and sit back. "Maybe one day," I reply.

"Good catch."

I wink at her as I move on.

We have been helping as much as we can. It's clear the place, although staffed, is in disrepair, and there are more patients than nurses and healers. They do not complain, though, not once. Kneeling at the side of a frail man, I go to change his bandage, but he grabs my hands, his grip strong despite how weak he looks.

"It is messy and nasty. I wouldn't," he cautions, shame colouring his words.

"I have never minded messes." I smile as I unwind the bandage. "My name is Alyx. What's yours?" I speak as I work to distract him, and reluctantly, he lets go of my hand. He's right. His arm is a mess of sores and infection. The smell hits me instantly, but I do not wrinkle my nose or react. I have seen much worse in the Lowers.

"Kelam," he replies. "I worked as a merchant between here and the palace until I fell ill."

"A noble profession," I murmur as I clean the wound and dress it once more. That is all we are able to do, which makes me sad. When I sit back, it's clear Kelam knows he will die from this wound and has accepted it.

"And you?" he asks. "I have seen many, and you do not walk like a healer."

"That's because I'm an assassin." I grin, putting my finger to my lips. "But don't tell anyone."

He chuckles before it ends in a cough, and I help him drink some water before laying him down on the thin sack and covering him to keep him warm. "Thank you," he says softly, "for treating me like a human being and distracting me for a moment."

It disgusts me that he is thanking me for that, but I force a smile onto my face, and I sit with him for as long as I can before moving onto the next person.

By the time the sun starts to set, I am covered in sweat, and Orion is helping me dress wounds and hand out food.

"What is the meaning of this?" a strong voice demands. My head jerks up to find a grey-haired man glaring at me, his beard reaching mid-chest. His robes are covered in dirt, and there is a basket at his side, overflowing with herbs. I did not even hear him arrive, but it's clear who he is.

"Healer Arbella, I take it?" I ask as I stand, wiping my hands on the cloth as I move closer.

"Who is asking? You are not from here." He eyes me warily.

"No, I'm not. I'm from the Lowers." His jaw clenches. "Your old apprentice told us where to find you." That makes his frown deepen. "We are here on behalf of the king."

He eyes me for a moment, clearly debating if I'm telling the truth, then he glances around, noting the prying eyes, and he jerks his head at the closed building. "In my office." He hands his basket to someone and strides over, moving fast despite his age. Orion and I follow, and when the door is shut, he sits heavily before a square wooden table. There is not much else in here besides some books and a bed.

"I suppose I knew this day would come." He watches us as we kneel on the other side of the table from him. "How is the king?"

"Facing daily assassination attempts," I admit, "but you probably already knew that."

He nods, pursing his lips. "I thought if I left and took the truth with me, it would keep him safe. I believed keeping him in the dark would protect him, but it seems I was wrong." He sighs, looking tired. "What do you want?"

"Your truth. We need it, and the king needs it. He deserves answers about his father's death, and with your confession, we might just be able to turn the tide and save everyone," I answer.

"It will change nothing. I tried back then, but it didn't work. Nobody wants the truth. Everybody has their own hand to play," he snaps. "It is why I came here, to escape the backstabbing and games and grieve the family I lost. Despite what you may think, the old king was my best friend. We grew up together, and he was the only family I had."

"Yet you left his son surrounded by enemies." I refuse to sugar-coat it. He flinches, lowering his eyes in shame. "He needs you now. We are here to take you back with us and fix this once and for all."

"What can I do? I am nobody," he murmurs.

I see a defeated man. It is clear he loved his friend dearly and his death broke a part of him. I understand his reservations, since I've seen the workings of the palace, and I have not been there long.

Imagine working there day in and day out. It would be enough to exhaust anyone, but without effort, there will never be change.

"You will come with us or else," Orion threatens.

Arbella's eyes narrow, and I sigh, forcing his gaze to me as I try a softer approach. "You loved your best friend, and you loved Joha. You left to keep him safe, and I'm asking you help keep him safe again before we lose another king and the last of their line—not to mention the last one who truly cares for this kingdom."

"I wish I could save him," he starts.

"So do it. I will be blunt, since we are running short on time and patience. You failed his father, your best friend. If you don't do this for your own honour or the future of our lands, then do it for your friend, for the old king, and help save his son."

He watches me with a closed expression before he smiles softly. "The king would have liked you. You're stubborn and outspoken—the perfect match for his son."

"Yes, well, I like his son a lot, and I plan on keeping him alive. So are you coming with us voluntarily, or do I need to kidnap you?"

"I would ask if you're joking, but I fear you are not."

"She's not," Orion adds helpfully.

Arbella laughs, wiping at his face. "Yes, I will come. You are right. I owe him this much. It is time to face the past. Nothing good has come from it being swept into the dark. Let me gather my things and leave instructions. We will leave at first light. It may not change anything, but I will try for my brother and his son."

SIXTY-ONE

ALYX

Leaning back against the rafters, I peer through a gap in the curtain, watching the comings and goings of people on the street below us. It is just after midday, and the city is alive with noise and movement. No one can see me at the top of the building, and the window I'm looking through is dirty from disuse and covered by a tattered curtain. The people who pass the alehouse we currently hide in would never guess that an assassin, a healer, and the head of the king's guard are in the attic.

"You are sure we are safe here?" Arbella asks me for the third time, his voice tight with emotion. He's clearly anxious about being back in the city, and honestly, I don't blame him. If Queen Mother gets word of him being here before we can expose the truth of how the old king died, then she will have him killed and all of this will be for nothing.

Glancing over my shoulder, I meet his tired eyes, my tone steady as I reply, "I trust the landlady here implicitly, and no one could track the message back to me here."

When we reached the outskirts of the Lowers after a few hard days of riding, I quickly tracked down one of Crux's little rats and gave him a message to pass on. It was a single code word, one that has no significance to anyone other than Crux and me. When used, it lets him know I need to meet with him in a pre-established location. The network of rats works together, passing the message along until they find him. The process is far faster and subtler than if I went stalking through the city.

It never fails to amaze me just how many people Crux has under his control. He has a way of finding the downtrodden and making them loyal to him, any sign of betrayal quickly eliminated.

We are now hidden in a room at the top of a tavern in the Lowers, close to the river but still on the outskirts, where no one could easily spot us. We used disguises and cloaks to keep our identities hidden, yet Orion is so large that no cloak could truly hide him. Plus, he walks like a guard. He is incapable of slouching or changing his posture no matter how hard he tries.

Every precaution has been taken to keep us anonymous, not to mention I was being honest when I said I trust the landlady. The only reason she owns this property is because I rescued her from an abusive marriage and she inherited her husband's hidden wealth. She owed me a debt because of this and knew that one day, she would be required to hide me, no questions asked.

There are several meeting points around the city that I have never used, but they are safe and ready should I need them. It is essential for an assassin to have somewhere to lie low should things heat up, and once a safe house has been used, it's no longer safe.

"How long do we have to wait?" Orion asks, his voice gruff with impatience. "Why can't we just storm the castle and tell them what we know?"

Orion is perched on the edge of an old suitcase, his knees almost up to his chin. At one point, I didn't think we would get him in through the hatch, but after some manoeuvring, he managed to squeeze through. He looks miserable and clearly uncomfortable.

Tilting my head to one side, I meet his angry eyes. "We have been gone for too long. We don't know what has happened since we have been away." I do not mince my words or bother trying to ease his worries, simply telling him as it is. "We need to know what Crux knows. We have one chance at this, and we cannot afford to mess it up."

"She is right," Arbella comments from the other side of the attic space. "Queen Mother is cunning and will have contingency plans in place. It is one of the reasons I left in the first place." He looks sick, his face pale and clammy. Being back in the city is a challenge for him.

I need to distract him and keep him calm, but I realise this could be a rare opportunity to get some personal information about our target. Swinging my legs around so they dangle from the beam, I brace my hands on either side of my hips and give Arbella my full attention. "I assume you knew her well, having been so close to the old king. What can you tell us about her?"

I feel Orion's gaze on me, hot and intense, but I cannot afford to get caught up in him, not now when we are so close to getting rid of Queen Mother.

The healer seems to ponder my question for a moment. "She has always been clever and calculating. I once overheard her telling one of her maids that she should have been born a man, as she has the mind of a ruler."

Sadly, I'm not surprised by this statement.

Unfortunately, women are treated differently from males, especially within the nobility. They are beautiful objects to own, posed prettily on their husband's arm. Within royalty, a woman will be looked over as the next ruler in favour of a male. I've known Queen Mother wants to rule since I met her. She exudes that energy; she was just born the wrong sex.

It's a bullshit rule.

"She is very good at giving people what they want," he continues, "changing herself to fit their needs and seamlessly moving from one personality to another. That is how she caught the old king's attention."

"That has changed since you were last here, healer," Orion grumbles, his arms crossed over his chest. "She does not bother to hide her nature anymore, but her words are like liquor, addictive and sweet to start while damaging your body and mind in the process."

It's surprising to hear Orion speak like this about Queen Mother, but then I remember he's known her far longer than I have. He's seen her at her best and worst, along with her obvious hatred of Joha. He would defend his friend to the grave.

Humming, I sit back on the beam and ponder everything I've learned. Much of it is stuff I already knew, but hearing it all together paints a picture of exactly who Queen Mother is.

I turn to Arbella. "When the time comes, you are going to have to stand up before your peers and tell them what you know. Queen Mother will be there, but we need to do this in front of them all. We have one chance."

Although there is fear in his eyes, he stands and rolls his shoulders back. "I have hidden for far too long. I will do what is needed of me."

Good. Without him, it is just our word against Queen Mother's. However, Arbella was a well-known, respected healer. The nobility will listen to him. They have to.

Somewhere below us, a floorboard creaks, and we all freeze in place. Listening closely, I try to distinguish where the sound is coming from. Before I get the chance to work it out, there's a knock on the small hatch that separates the roof from the floor below it.

A second knock follows, then a third and fourth in a distinctive quick-slow pattern, letting me know exactly who is here.

Hurrying to the hatch, I peer through the tiny peephole and see a familiar face. Throwing it open, I step back to allow Crux to enter. As soon as he's in and shuts the hatch behind him, he wraps his arms around me tightly. Without caring that we have an audience, he presses his lips to mine, and we share a passionate kiss. I can feel how much he missed me in his kiss alone, and I make sure he can feel the same from me.

Pulling back, he ignores Orion's pointed cough as he runs his eyes over me, checking for injury. "I am so glad you're back. I have been going out of my mind. Are you okay?"

If it wasn't for everything that happened recently and all the near misses, I would be offended that he thinks I can't defend myself. I know this is coming from a place of love, though, so I keep those thoughts to myself.

"I'm fine," I promise, a smile pulling at my lips as I gesture to the other male in the room. "This is Healer Arbella. He cared for the king when he died. This is the proof we needed." My words trip out of my mouth quickly, my excitement carrying them away. My happiness slowly fades away as I realise Crux is here alone. "Is Joha okay? I thought you might bring him with you."

Grimacing, Crux releases me from his hold and steps back, glancing between the three of us. Why does he look like that? Fear twists in my stomach, and I look over at Orion to see he looks just as concerned, his hands balled into fists.

"He's been locked away under house arrest 'for his own protection,'" Crux explains, shaking his head. His eyes meet mine, intense and full of promise. "Plus, he would only slow me down. Nothing was going to stop me from getting to you."

If I were the type to swoon, I would at that statement. I consider climbing into his arms once more and showing him exactly how much I missed him.

"House arrest?" Orion barks, cutting through any plans I might have been contemplating. His anger isn't aimed at any of us, but as he stands, hunched over in the small space, he begins to pace, his emotions close to a boiling point.

Crux watches the guard with a smirk, his smile slowly getting wider. "I have a lot to update you on." Whatever he knows, he clearly thinks it will help us. "I also have some information that is going to come in handy." He rubs his hands together, and I recognise his expression. It's the one he wears when he's about to commit a new crime, his excitement flashing in his eyes. "Let's plan a coup."

SIXTY-TWO

ALYX

I dress in one of my gowns, the dirt hastily washed from my body. I'm ready for battle. Usually, these dresses feel so restrictive and unnecessary, yet right now, I wear it like armour. The dark green fabric looks almost black, covering most of my skin and highlighting the decorative daggers strapped to my waist, and my hair is pinned back and twisted into a quick braid.

I'm allowing my true self to come out. The soft expression and mindless smile the council is used to are long gone. I am fierce, I am strong, and I am about to bring down hellfire on these liars who wish to run the kingdom.

I stride through the corridors of the palace with Joha at my side. He's dressed in a smart tunic, the colour matching my dress, and a crown rests atop his head, looking regal. I have not had the chance to look in the mirror, but I can just imagine how we look—fierce and united, our fingers interlaced together.

Orion leads the way, and Crux, dressed in his guard disguise, follows closely behind us with Arbella at his side.

Once we formed a plan, we left the safe house and rushed back to the palace. Orion went to Joha, telling him everything, and Crux came with me as I got ready. The first time I saw Joha was only a few moments ago, when we met in the corridor.

Guards surrounded him, but they clearly did not stop him from leaving his palace. I imagine Orion had something to do with that. He commands the loyalty of the guards, and they have always looked up to him with admiration.

Despite Healer Arbella's reluctance to be here, his expression is determined. He's not going to back down. He will honour the memory of his friend by helping his son get justice.

Unlike the usual council meetings, this one is an open session, meaning all of the nobility are invited to listen and participate, and it is being held in the ballroom rather than the usual meeting room. It doesn't take us long to get there, and when we do, there is a row of guards standing across the entrance, the large wooden doors closed.

It looks pretty foreboding and would turn many away. Just the guards' stern faces and the way their hands tighten on their weapons make you want to turn around and find somewhere else to be.

Not us though. Not today.

Joha faces the guards, my hand still tightly clasped in his. "Open the doors."

One of the guards in the centre steps forward and clears his throat. "Your Majesty, the council is in session. The whole court is in attendance."

This was exactly why we decided to strike now—the more witnesses the better.

I arch my brow at the guard who just denied the king access in his own palace. He is either brave or stupid. Although, from what I know of Queen Mother and the council, they probably threatened the guards with harsh punishments should anyone unauthorised try to come in.

I'm not the only one surprised by the guard's gall. Scowling,

Orion steps forward until he's almost touching him. "The king and his betrothed order the doors to be open." Voice low and full of restrained anger, he stares down the male.

"But—" The guard looks over Orion's shoulder to take in the king, his face twisting with indecision. The other guards shift on their feet awkwardly, confirming they have been given strict instructions not to allow the king access.

"Whose rule do you follow?" Joha asks quietly but firmly. "Mine or Queen Mother's?"

This is a pivotal moment. Without their backing, we will not stand a chance. We are taking a bet on the guards remembering the king's kindness compared to her cruelty.

There is a beat of silence as the guard absorbs this. It stretches on, making my heart skip in worry before the guard jerks his head in a sharp nod. After saluting the king, he turns his attention to the other guards, addressing them with authority. "Open the doors."

I nearly slump in relief, but I do not let that weakness show. The guards are with us. We can do this. Thankfully, the others don't debate the decision and the doors are heaved open. I squeeze Joha's hand, letting him know I'm here to support him. This is it. This is the moment we have been waiting for. Joha looks composed and regal, but I can feel the slight tremble of his hand, giving away his true feelings.

A male voice reaches us as the doors slowly open, but he cuts himself off at our interruption. Questioning noises and low chatter start from the observing nobility, heads turning in our direction.

"What is the meaning of this?" the speaker demands, one of the many advisors Joha has on his council. He's angry that someone would dare to interrupt him while he's speaking. However, that quickly stops as we step into the hall.

"Oh, Your Majesty," he greets, dropping into a shallow bow.

We are framed in the door for a moment, both of us standing tall as we run our eyes over every single person. We do not fill the silence, letting them feel the awkwardness, and as a unit, we step forward, walking steadily down the path created through the throng. The gathered crowd's whispers die as we take our time, letting them look their fill. Ahead, on the dais, Joha's council and advisors are seated in a semicircle. Right in the centre, sitting on Joha's throne and draped in diamonds, is Queen Mother. Her eyes widen in shock before they flash with anger she tries to hide but cannot.

How dare she? Red-hot fury fuels me. This woman is going down. I am determined to see it through. I should not be surprised that she is fully taking Joha's place after what I know of her and what she is trying to do, yet to be so blatant about it . . . She's sitting on the king's throne in front of a full audience. She had to know how this would look to the nobility. Rumours would have been flying about a takeover before the nobles even left the palace.

The nobles part around us like the ocean, tracking our every movement as we head right to the dais. Joha's guards surround us, making it very clear how little we trust these people. It's a statement, a warning. Perhaps the guards can sense just how hostile those on the small stage feel towards the king and are reacting to it, but they are on high alert, their eyes sharp and commanding. Joha and I stand at the front of our little group, with Orion just off to the side, close enough to leap forward and protect us if necessary. Crux and the healer are behind us, staying close as we form a barrier before the traitors and their leader.

Staring up at Queen Mother, I narrow my eyes on her, refusing to bow or cower to her anymore. She doesn't seem flustered by our presence, which just makes me angrier. Dipping her head in a pathetic show of deference, she smiles slightly and rests her hands in her lap in a serene manner, but I see her fingers clenching as she tries to hide her irritation

"Your Majesty, it is a surprise to see you. You should be protected in your rooms," she calls, her voice filling the space. Practised, false concern laces her tone, but I see the hatred in her eyes.

She might have been able to order him around before, but that is no longer how things work. Joha is *king*, and as such, he makes the decisions about his own safety. The way she speaks to him is like he's an unruly teenager she is scolding, and even those surrounding us pick up on it, murmuring to each other.

I have no doubt her plan was to keep him locked away until he was forgotten and then get rid of him quietly, taking all his power and supporters away from him, but she failed to recognise one thing.

He has me, and I would slay this entire kingdom before that happened.

Clearing his throat, Joha steps forward. "Well, Queen Mother, it is a surprise to see you in my throne. I have only been gone a few days." His eyes turn steely as he stares at her, no hint of the puppet king in sight. "You are my father's widow and nothing else. *I* am king, and you should remember that."

For a brief moment, I see shock flicker through her eyes, but she quickly brushes it off and tilts her head to one side. "Is there a reason you have come bursting into a meeting?" Gesturing to the room and everyone watching, she gives a small, curt smile. "As you can see, most of the court is in attendance. Why don't we save this until after the meeting—"

Joha shakes his head. "No, now is a perfect time. Everyone should see this." Turning, he addresses his guards, his voice stern and filled with power. In this moment, he is a true king. "Arrest Queen Mother and take her to the dungeons."

Gasps fill the air, and not just those of the watching lords and ladies. Even the councilmen on the stage seem shocked and horrified. The guards are confused, hovering at the edge of the dais, but they make no move to arrest her, looking around for confirmation from their seniors.

"This is ridiculous!" the councilman from before blusters, his face turning tomato red. "On what grounds?"

I cannot believe how they speak to their king. Once this is all done, there will need to be a major cull of council members who were influenced by Queen Mother. Still, I say nothing, waiting at the king's side until I'm needed, keeping my gaze on the woman behind this.

She is the threat, and I know all too well what a woman like her is capable of when cornered. That's when she is at her most dangerous.

"Murder, treason, and hiring assassins to attempt to murder the king," Joha answers, his voice loud and clear, leaving no room for misunderstanding. "Take your pick. She is the one who arranged the many attempts on my life. Queen Mother has been very clever about it, not having direct contact with the assassins and using her contacts to order the hits instead, but we know the truth now, and she will face the consequences of her actions."

"What proof do you have, Your Majesty?" a councilman asks, but it's asked as respectfully as a question such as this could be. I examine the male. He's one of the older council members, his long grey beard covering most of his lower face, but he has thoughtful, pale blue eyes. This is a man who takes in all the facts before making a decision.

Crux steps forward, clearing his throat to pull the room's attention to him. "In the dungeons is an assassin who attempted to take the king's life several nights ago. He obviously failed, but he knew exactly where the king would be—locked away in his palace thanks to the Queen Mother."

"That is circumstantial, and you really believe the words of an assassin?" Queen Mother counters before turning to address the court. "Why do you think I would do something like this? As you can see, the king has been struggling recently with all the attempts on his life and it has muddled his mind. It's one of the reasons I should take hold of his position while he heals. This was my greatest fear. Much like his father, he is weak."

Gaping at her gall, I feel sick to my stomach. To lie like this and attempt to make others believe that Joha is unwell is treason, yet she keeps going. She's gotten too comfortable in that throne, and now it's time to evict her.

"She wants to be queen," I call out, interrupting what would have been a convincing tirade, my voice ringing around the room. I never take my eyes off her, finally breaking my silence. I let her see the truth in my eyes—she will pay for touching what is mine. "She knows that the only way it will ever happen is if she kills Joha before he has an heir. You are smart, Queen Mother, but not smart enough. Your strength is also your weakness—your need for power and willingness to do anything to get it."

The atmosphere in the room changes, becoming electric as debates and whispers break out around the hall. This is not going the way she wanted.

"This is ridiculous." Gritting her teeth, Queen Mother finally stands and gestures to me. "She has been twisting your mind, Your Majesty. The princess is probably trying to destroy us from the inside so her kingdom can take over."

I have to admit, she does have a way of warping things to make them work for her. It's a good excuse, and I feel the crowd's allegiances shifting back and forth. Joha squeezes my hand, kissing the back of it in a show of support. He doesn't show even the slightest hint that he's doubting me, and I know that will go some distance to proving we're right.

"This isn't your first time trying to kill a king though, is it, Queen Mother?" Joha asks loudly, returning his sharp gaze to the woman in question.

"What do you mean, Your Majesty?" one of the councilmen who used to be loyal to Joha asks, leaning forward in his seat, his brow furrowed.

Standing tall, Joha addresses the councilman, his voice loud even as he wobbles over the words a little, pain filling them. Later, he will have time to grieve the truth, but for now, he must utilise it and seize the moment before it's too late. "She killed my father."

Pandemonium ensues at the bold declaration. Shouts, questions, and bellows of treason echo around the room, and our guards have to take a step closer to us to make sure that no one can break through their circle of protection.

"Out of order!"

"Outrageous!"

"Where is the proof?"

The exclamations keep coming, the noise so loud it's impossible to make out who is saying what. I turn to face the crowd and raise a hand. Seeing the gesture, the nobles slowly fall silent, and I smile in thanks. I gesture for Healer Arbella to step forward. "Please explain who you are, how you know the royal family, and what you know about this matter."

"My name is Darus Arbella, and I was the royal healer for almost twenty years. Some of you might remember me, as I helped deliver your children into the world." He smiles, nodding his head in the direction of a few people he recognises. That smile quickly slides from his face as he moves on to the real reason he's here. He releases a long, pent-up breath. "I worked here in the palace and cared for the king as he was dying."

Pausing, he lowers his head slightly, and I can almost feel his pain at the loss of his friend.

"I know for a fact that Queen Mother was slowly poisoning the king. She was adding small amounts of poison to his tea. She was getting away with it until I queried if he was being poisoned, as no natural illness worked that way." Lacing his fingers together, he rests them on his stomach, his words factual as he continues to explain. "She panicked and gave him a strong enough dose to kill him, yet in doing that, it was possible for me to detect it in my tests." The room is quiet enough to hear a pin drop, everyone straining to hear the healer's words.

"I confronted her, and she told me she believed it to be a sleeping medicine and she would never hurt him, but I knew the truth. I had seen how she treated him when she thought no one was watching and how much she hated him. I raised the issue with the council at the time, but I was laughed at, and they wrote me off as a grief-stricken old man." Anger enters his voice as he stares at Queen Mother. "Prince Joha was never told, and I began to fear for my life, so I left and haven't come back until now."

"This is—how ridiculous!" Queen Mother protests, unable to form words. She's losing her composure, knowing there is too much evidence against her. At the very least, she needs to be questioned, even if there wasn't enough information to pin this on her.

"Arrest her. We can interrogate her in the dungeons," Joha calls, and this time, the guards hurry forward, dragging Queen Mother from the throne she has sacrificed so much for and towards the exit of the hall.

No one tries to help her, and even her most vocal supporters look elsewhere as she is taken away, unable to meet her gaze. Self-preservation runs strongly through the councilmen, and right now, Queen Mother is a sinking ship. If they were to speak up or try to fight for her, they know they will just end up in the dungeons—a dangerous place to be when you're trying to hide your involvement in a plot to assassinate the king.

"You will pay for this, Joha!" Queen Mother shouts as she is wrestled from the room. All pretence of a calm, gentle woman is gone, revealing the power-hungry person beneath. Dignity flees when faced with the truth, her face puffing red, her eyes narrowed in vile hatred as she struggles against the guards. "You and your conniving betrothed will pay!"

I feel Joha quaking ever so slightly, so I squeeze his hand. It is probably his adrenaline, but it could also be relief. This is not over yet though. We might have dealt with the most difficult part, but there is still something very important to handle. Keeping his hand in mine, I take a step forward and turn to face him. I cup his face, and when I speak next, I make sure my voice projects so everyone can hear us.

"Take back your throne, my king."

This seems to release him from whatever gripped him. Taking a deep breath, he strides forward with me at his side. Joha takes my hand and gestures towards the smaller throne beside his and helps me into it. Smiling up at him, I follow his lead, fully aware of everyone watching us. He rolls his shoulders back and slowly sits in his throne, gripping the armrests tightly.

"All hail the king!" Orion shouts out, and I'm surrounded by the echoed yells of the rest of the hall, the sound almost deafening.

"All hail the king! All hail the king!"

CHAPTER
SIXTY-THREE

ALYX

Joha stares at his people, all eyes on him. They look to him for answers, for leadership. Now is his time to become the king he always has been but they never saw.

Gone is the puppet king, and in his place is a true ruler. As my eyes rove across his face, I know it will be the last time I sit at his side like this. We are a farce after all, and he got what he needed. He's safe now, Queen Mother cannot hurt him, and the truth is out. I don't fit into his plans for the future anymore, and my heart clenches at that reminder. Grief fills me until I can barely breathe as he starts to speak, oblivious to my turmoil.

"Today has been shocking. I know you must all have questions, which I will answer in due time. For now, I believe it is best for everyone to return home. We have a traitor to deal with and investigations to conduct, but I promise I will protect this kingdom with everything I have. We will not be deceived ever again. In honour of my father and the duty I am sworn to, I vow this to you. We will survive, and we will flourish." Standing once more, he looks at his subjects. "For now, allow us the privacy to grieve for what we have lost and the treachery that has been discovered." He turns to me. "Shall we, my love?"

I swallow hard, bile crawling up my throat from the pain. My chest is so tight, it feels like I cannot breathe around it, the restriction making me lightheaded. My limbs are weak as I stare into his beautiful face, knowing he will never be mine again.

I'm happy he learned the truth, and I'm happy he's safe, but part of me is sad this is over because now that the truth is out, I have no reason to stay.

He holds out his hand to me, tilting his head as I hesitate. His eyes search mine for answers I cannot give him. I knew how this would end, I just never expected it to hurt so much, but that's my fault, not his. I should have kept my distance and not gotten romantically involved.

Standing, I lay my hand in his and force a smile. "Let's," I murmur.

Hand in hand, we leave the ballroom—a king and his fake bride.

Once we near the palaces, and I slip my hand from his. "I am tired," I tell him, trying not to let sorrow enter my voice. "It's been a hard few days' ride and now this . . ."

"Of course." He blushes in embarrassment. "Go rest. I will have some food sent to you. Everything else can wait until tomorrow."

I incline my head, acting like the perfect bride for the guards and nobles who followed us. Keeping my head high, I start to walk towards the queen's palace before I hesitate and then backtrack. Uncaring about the eyes on us, I reach up and kiss him softly.

It's a goodbye, our final kiss, although he does not know it yet.

Before he can question me, I turn and flee, unable to look at him because if I do, I might ask him to let me stay, but I can't. I refuse to let the tears fall, even as they burn my eyes.

It's over. Our deal is done, which means one thing.

It's time for me to leave.

THERE IS no point in delaying it. I will leave tonight. I'm all ready when my doors suddenly burst open, making me whirl. Joha kicks the doors shut on the shocked guards' faces and stomps over to me, not stopping until we are almost pressed together.

As I stare into Joha's eyes, grief fills me for what I am about to lose. He does not need me anymore. I have outlived my purpose, so this is over. I was hoping to leave quietly, but I should have known he would ruin my plans.

Joha is no fool, he must have sensed something was wrong, but there are some things not even a king can fix. I might be good at pretending, but he cannot make me a true lady like he needs, and I cannot ruin his future with the truth of what I am getting out of this and who I am.

I made my choice. I knew what I was doing when I agreed to this, but it's so hard.

"Joha." I trail off, unsure what I was going to say in the wake of the anger in his gaze.

He glances at my packed bags, his nostrils flaring for a moment. "No. You are not leaving. I knew something was wrong earlier."

"My job here is done, Joha. It is time for me to go home. We both knew this would end eventually. You are a king, and I am an assassin. There is no future for us." I wish my voice were stronger and full of conviction, yet I just sound exhausted from what happened.

"No." That single word is a hard order. He looks around the room as if searching for more words, and I step closer, pressing my hands to his face. I memorise his handsome features, knowing this is the closest I will ever be to the king. He has a kingdom to run, and I have lives to claim, yet here, in this moment, I wish I could stay with him, but we are too different. He has a future, a destiny, a purpose—one I was never supposed to be a part of.

"We knew this was coming," I murmur, and I cover his lips as he begins to protest. "I'll admit I never expected to come to care for you." I cannot bring myself to say love or I might lose my nerve and stay. "But it changes nothing. I don't belong here, and staying will only hurt you in the long run. This was always the plan."

"No," he mumbles, shaking his head and tugging my hands away. "Stay, Alyx, please."

I hate the plea in his voice. Turning away, I grab my bag, but when I look back, he drops to his knees, a place I have never seen Joha. His head is tilted back, and tears swim in his eyes. "I will beg you if I have to. Take my dignity, take anything you want, just stay with me."

"I can't," I croak as I reach down and tug him to his feet. "Never kneel for anyone, not even me."

I don't deserve it.

Before I can chicken out, I hoist my bag higher and push past him, heading to the door and away from the man I love. My heart breaks with each step until the shattered pieces lie between us like a tether we can never break.

He calls out, stopping me at the door. "Revenge." I hear his feet on the floor as he crosses it, not stopping until his warmth is pressed to my back. "I promised you revenge and answers in return. I intend to keep my promise, and to do that, you must stay here."

We both know it's an excuse, yet I turn around, my back pressed against the wood, a soft smirk tilting my lips. "I have to stay here to get my part of the deal?"

"Yes, unless you are going back on your word?" he counters desperately.

My lips twitch. "Never, you know an assassin's word is law." That is exactly why he's using it against me. "Which you knew. Are you using this as an excuse to keep me close, my king?" I tease.

Grinning, he presses against me, tilting his head down and blocking all the light until all I see is him. His lips brush kisses over mine as he speaks. "Yes, just like you were hoping I would, which is why you let me catch you leaving. You're the best assassin in this kingdom, Alyx. You could have disappeared without me ever knowing, but you wanted me to. You were hoping I would stop you, weren't you?"

Swallowing, I search his gaze. "Maybe." It's the only weakness I admit to, but Joha has no issue being weak for me and bridging that gap.

"I love you, Alyx. If I have to use this to keep you with me, then I will, and when that is done, I will find something else. I am never letting you go."

"If they find out what I am, they will—"

"I do not care," he interrupts, his voice harsh. "Let them make demands. I have given them everything, but they do not get to take you from me." He cups my face, and I lean into his hands, greedy for his every touch. Maybe I should worry about how deeply I feel for him, Orion, and Crux, but as I look into his eyes, I cannot seem to care. "Say you will stay." His lips ghost over mine, cajoling me. "Stay."

It hurts as much as it heals me because I know this will not end well.

This time, my tears do fall, and Joha kisses them away. "You do not get to leave me, Alyx. I cannot do this without you. They can have my mind, my body, and my future, but you have my heart, and I cannot live without it or you."

"You are a fool," I murmur, my voice thick.

"For you? Absolutely." He grins, kissing each of my eyelids before pressing a soft kiss to my lips. I don't react at first, torn between what I need to do and what I want to do. "Stay with me. Stay with your fool," he pleads, kissing me between each word.

I kiss him back, tears sliding down my face. The saltiness mixes as our tongues tangle in a languid, loving kiss. His hands tighten on my cheeks as he presses me against the door.

I grip his shirt, pulling him closer before we break apart. His desire-filled eyes freeze me in place as his hands slide down my shoulders, across my sides, and around me. I gasp as he yanks me up, lifting me into the air. He doesn't look away and neither do I as he spins and walks us across the room and lays me on my bed, crawling up my body, his lips meeting mine in a hungry, promising kiss.

My hands slide greedily down his back until they meet the strip of his exposed skin at the base of his spine where his shirt has risen, and I explore the muscles on his back as we kiss. He pushes up, pulling his mouth from mine.

"I'm going to remind you why you belong here, and I'm going to keep reminding you how much I love you until the day you believe it. You were always supposed to be mine, Alyx, just accept it."

Never one to be outdone, I wrap my legs around his waist and spin us, pinning him down on the bed. My hands grab his and hold them above his head as he grins up at me. "More like you belong to me, my king."

"Prove it," he says, twining his fingers with mine as he lies back.

Arching a brow, I lean down and bite the edge of the tie on his shirt, and then I tug it down, watching it unravel. The material parts, exposing more of his tanned, muscular chest for my greedy eyes. I lean down and place a kiss at the base of his throat, feeling him swallow against me as I move farther down and do the same.

Sliding my lips across his collarbone, I nip the skin there as he groans. I watch his eyes slide shut, his lips parting as he arches into my touch. "If they could see their perfect king now, on his back and begging for me to touch him, what would they think?"

"That I'm a lucky bastard." His eyes open and clash with mine.

Releasing his hands, I slide farther down, taking his shirt with me, and then I flick open a dagger from my side and cut it away. The material falls to my bed as I run my lips across his chest, licking and sucking his nipples. When he groans, I slide lower, kissing along his impressive abs and over his hips as I unlace his trousers. I push them down his thighs so he's naked for me. His cock is hard with precum leaking from the tip, and when I lean down and blow a warm breath across him, his length jerks for me as he moans.

"Alyx."

Keeping him trapped in my gaze, I lean down and dart my

tongue out, dragging it along his tip and tasting his desire as he watches me.

I taunt him, observing his every reaction. His hands fist the sheets above him, and his torso stretches as he lifts his hips for more. It's a fucking perfect sight.

Gripping his cock, I slide my tongue down the veiny side, tasting him as I torture him. I suck the tip as he gasps, lifting his hips off the bed as he tries to bury himself in my mouth. Chuckling, I pull back, waiting for him to slump, then I suck him again, pushing him to see how much it takes for him to break. I ignore my own desire and slick thighs as I suck on and nibble his cock until he cries out. My nipples harden, pebbling in my shirt as red-hot desire races through me. The most powerful man in the kingdom is letting me control him. It's a heady thought, leaving me wet and wanting until he finally snaps.

Jerking up, he throws me down next to him, pressing me face down into the soft bedding. His hands grip my trousers and he yanks them down, quickly stripping me until I lie naked below him. He forces my thighs open with his hand and cups my pussy, making me groan. "You like teasing me. You like playing with me. I can feel you dripping against my hand."

"What do you plan to do about it?" I ask, grinding into his hand as I widen my thighs to give him better access.

"I would tease you back," he murmurs as he leans down, biting the soft flesh of my ass. I yelp, even as the sharp pain fades into pleasure. "But I need you too much."

His fingers slide through my desire, then his thick digits thrust inside me as I cry out. It's my turn to grip the bedding as he fucks me with his fingers, curling them so I see stars behind my closed eyes. I push back for more as he bites and kisses along my ass and then lower. He licks around where his fingers spear me before his lips cover my clit, sucking and kissing. Joha adds a third finger, stretching me deliciously, and I rock into his touch, gripping the bedding as I give myself over to him.

"You taste like heaven, better than the most expensive wine. You

421

taste like perfection and all mine," he whispers against my pussy, making me groan, and he lashes my clit with that silver tongue until I reach for my release, trembling below him.

"Come for me. Come for your king," he orders.

I come apart with a muffled scream, clenching on his fingers as pleasure racks my body, leaving my legs shaking. He fucks me through it, and when I slump, he pulls back and I roll. My eyes land on him as I pant. Smirking, he lowers his hand, glistening with my cum, and strokes his cock as he watches me.

I glance from his cock to his eyes, growing annoyed. "Well, are you going to fuck me, or do I need to show you—" I scream as he grabs my thighs, yanks me down the bed, and impales me on his length.

He throws my legs over his shoulders as he kneels, my pussy clenching around his invading length. His smirk makes me all that much hotter as he watches me. He pulls from my clinging body then slams back inside me, making me arch up as I cry out. Our eyes clash as he fucks me, setting a hard pace.

Cupping my breasts, I tweak my nipples harshly as he hammers into me.

"That's it. Let me see you get yourself off on me. Let me watch you heighten your own pleasure." His jaw grinds and his eyes tighten with his desire. I watch his abs roll with each thrust, his muscular arms holding me.

"Joha." I slide my hand down my body as he watches and part my fingers around his cock as he slams into me, letting him slip through my hand with each thrust.

Groaning, he falls down over me as our lips meet, our hips rolling in a familiar rhythm. "Say my name again," he begs against my lips. "You're the only one who says it like that."

"Joha," I cry out, and he snarls, his lips meeting mine in a hard, fast kiss as my nails dig into his back as we both reach for that high.

I want this to last forever, but nothing ever does, and as our tongues tangle, he fills me with his cock, sending me over the edge with a cry. Moaning into my mouth, he follows me over that cliff, filling me with his pleasure. Our lips meet clumsily, slowing until we break apart. He presses his sweaty forehead to mine, our eyes locked as we pant. "I love you, Alyx."

I grip him tighter, hoping we can stay like this for as long as possible.

In the privacy of the palace, I let myself admit why it hurts so much. "I love you too."

CHAPTER
SIXTY-FOUR

JOHA

I wake before Alyx and I watch her, knowing I could have lost her last night had I not arrived at that exact time, but she's wrong if she thought I would let her go. I chased her through the Lowers once before, and I would do it again.

King or not, she belongs at my side, and I'm never letting her go.

I'll make her realise that, but for now, I have a reason to keep her here. It wasn't all lies, I always planned to keep my promise and help her find the truth, so when she wakes, I help her dress, and then we have breakfast together before heading out. Orion falls into step next to us.

"Where's Crux?" she asks Orion, her arm threaded through mine. Uncaring who is watching, she threads hers through his as well. He stares down at her, love shining in his eyes. He does not protest or pull away, and that makes me grin. I like seeing him happy. He deserves it, and he deserves to take something for himself when all he has ever done is live for me. The fact that we love the same woman doesn't even annoy me because I know nobody could ever

424

love or protect her as well as he will. Even if she did flee yesterday, he would have dragged her back. He's not letting her go either, no matter what she thinks.

She belongs here with us.

"I expected him to be stalking us," I admit.

"Apparently, news of what happened reached the Lowers and it's chaos. He went to help. He will be back," Orion grouses. "His exact words were, 'Tell my Alyx not to kill too many people without me. I'll be back before nightfall, where I belong.'"

She chuckles, wearing a bright smile that steals my breath for a moment. I want her to be like this always, happy and between us. It will take work, but I've never been the type to shy away from that.

She doesn't seem to understand that I would be willing to give up everything for her. She will one day, and if they try to make me choose, I will always choose her.

I sober then and look at Orion. "I need to keep my promise to Alyx. We need to find out what happened to her family."

We share a look. I know he looked into her past and already guessed, but she sighs and confirms it now. "My real name is Alexandria Stormhallow."

Orion jerks, blinking down at her. "The Stormhallows . . . They died in a fire, did they not?"

We stop, and Alyx swallows, pain flashing in her green eyes. "It was not an accidental fire. They came that night and slaughtered everyone. I managed to escape, but nobody else did. I changed my name to keep myself safe, but I have to know who was behind it and why. Someone ordered their deaths."

"Then we will find out who. We should start at the source—the old head of the guards. Wilhem is retired now, but nothing went on with the soldiers in this city without him knowing. It's a good place to start, and I know exactly where he is."

She frowns. "I tried to find him before. He's gone."

"No, not gone, hidden," Orion promises. "Trust me, I'll find him."

THE SMALL SHOP door jingles as we step into the bookshore located in the market just past Stormhallow Province. We disguised ourselves and slipped from the palace to speak to him. As the older man lifts his head behind the counter, recognition flashes through his eyes.

"The king, his guard, and his betrothed in my shop, which can't mean anything good." He sighs before stepping around the counter. "Are you here to kill me?"

"Not right now," Alyx replies, pushing her hood back. "We need answers."

"Well then, come in." He guides us to the back, locking the door after us and sitting at the square table we surround. "What answers? I have not been part of the palace in a long time."

"That's fine." Alyx looks to us then blows out a breath. "I need to know what you know about the deaths of the Stormhallow family."

He recoils, looking between us. "Why? It was a fire, a terrible accident." There is something in his voice that betrays him. Others might have missed it, but not her.

"We both know that's not true." She leans forward. "Please, if you know anything, tell me."

His eyes narrow on her, tracing her features. "You know, their youngest had hair the colour of fire and eyes as green as gems, just like you."

Alyx says nothing, and Wilhelm rubs his face.

"It's better not to know, I imagine," he mumbles before dropping his hand. "It was a fire, but it was no accident. I was ordered not to investigate it, but I did anyway, and it's one of the reasons I left."

"Ordered by whom?" she asks.

"The king," he admits, and I jerk back. "I think he knew the truth and was trying to protect me. The Stormhallows were killed due to their unwavering support of the king. I think whoever was behind it they were clearing the way, isolating him, and he knew it. Knowing that would put me in danger, and I think he was trying to protect me." He eyes Alyx. "The past is buried and best left there."

"No, it's not," she snaps as she looks at me. "They were killed for supporting your father." There is so much pain in her voice, and for a moment, I worry she will blame me, but she reaches for my hand.

I kiss the back of it. "I am so sorry, Alyx."

Our lives just keep getting more and more interconnected. We are both orphans, but as I stare into those green eyes, I know our parents would be proud of us and what we have become.

"Who killed them?" I ask as I glance at Wilhelm.

"Nobodies, hired thugs. They are all gone now, dead to cover their tracks. I do not know who ordered it."

"I can guess." Alyx shares a pained look with me. "Queen Mother. It has to be. She killed his supporters, and then she killed the king."

They say power corrupts, and I know they are right, but staring into the grief-stricken eyes of my love, I wish it didn't. I wish I could save her from what that venomous woman did to our families.

Is it really better to know?

Staring into her eyes, I am not sure.

CHAPTER
SIXTY-FIVE

ALYX

I stride through my bedchamber and towards the sitting room, my simple but elegant skirts swishing around my legs as I walk. Today I fancied a change from the stifling dresses I usually wear, and I am in a pale blue skirt and formfitting jacket. A white blouse with frilly cuffs and collar completes the outfit. My fiery hair is pulled back, half up, and a glittering tiara rests atop my head.

"Alyx, stop," Orion demands from behind me, and I jerk to a stop as his hand catches my wrist, halting my movements.

I immediately scan the area for any threats. With Queen Mother locked away, the assassination attempts should stop, but you can never be too careful. Plus, there was something about his voice that put me on edge. Assured that there is no one in my quarters but us, I let my eyes roam over his face, only to wince as I take in his expression.

I am in trouble.

His shoulders are set, and his jaw is tightly clamped together as he stares down at me. He is angry, but there is something else I cannot quite figure out, which is unusual. I am always able to read Orion. Pulling my wrist from his grip, I hold up both hands in surrender. "Whatever I have done, I—"

He cuts me off by stepping closer, causing me to bump up against the wall. "You were going to leave without saying anything."

Ah, that's what this is all about. It has been two days since the showdown with Queen Mother, and I was wondering if Orion was going to say anything about what happened afterwards. Joha was always going to tell him what happened, and I knew Orion would not take it well. He must have spent the last couple of days stewing on it and has finally decided to confront me.

Keeping my expression open, I allow him to see the truth in my eyes. "I knew you would stop me."

"Yes, I would have, and if you had left, I would have dragged you back," he snaps, tilting his head to one side like a predator eyeing up his prey. "You were going to leave us."

The hurt and accusation in his voice almost breaks me. "Because I had completed my part of the—" My explanation is quickly cut off.

"Those excuses do not wash with me. Joha told me what you said to him, about not wanting to hurt him and his duty." Anger flashes in his eyes, and darkness hovers over him. "You cannot leave us, ever." He steps closer, his body now pressing against mine as he pins me against the wall, caging me in.

I could easily escape if I wanted to, but this dominant side of him always gets me worked up. My lips turn up in a taunting smile as I feel his hard cock through his trousers.

His eyes gleam and his lips twitch for a moment before returning to a stern expression. "Do you understand?"

"I am not sure. You might have to explain it to me in more detail," I tease, pressing my hands against his chest to feel his muscles moving beneath my fingers. I fucking love how strong Orion is and how firm he feels when I touch him, and I am not just talking about his cock.

He stares at me for a moment, desire fighting with his anger before the first wins.

His hand slips under the waistband of my skirt and cups me through my underwear. He growls as he feels the wetness that waits for him there, then he rubs his fingers over my slick folds. Gasping at the sensation, I lean my head back against the wall. It feels so good, and he's not even fully touching me yet. As though hearing my thoughts, he roughly pulls my underwear to one side, his large hand covering me. He coats his finger in my arousal before plunging it deep inside my cunt.

I cry out at the sensation, the abrupt roughness of the action making my back arch and my nails dig into his chest. It hurts but in the best way, and I fucking love it.

His head lowers to mine. He swallows each jagged breath I release as he pushes a second thick finger inside me, curling them as he pumps into me with a ferocity that makes my eyes roll into the back of my head.

"You. Are. Mine," he grunts with each brutal thrust of his fingers. "Is that clear enough for you?"

I am his, and he is mine, whether that be as betrothed, queen, or assassin.

I'm close to coming. My breath is coming in ragged pants as I rock my hips into his touch, holding onto Orion's shirt for dear life.

The door pushes open, and Joha steps into the room. "Good morning, betrothed. Are you ready to . . ." He doesn't see us at first, but when he does, he trails off, his eyes locked on where Orion's hand is buried below my skirt.

"Your Majesty," Orion greets formally, dipping his head in a practiced greeting, his hand still moving between my legs.

I am still pinned to the wall, my cheeks red and my body aching with need. I whine as my orgasm fades away. "My king," I greet with a mocking grin as I spread my legs wider when Orion stills. I hope he'll carry on and finish what we started.

There is an awkward moment as none of us move, not sure what the protocol is here. I desperately want them both, my pussy clenching tightly at the thought. I know that Orion is going to defer to the king though. I am actually surprised he hasn't already stepped away and apologised. The three of them have spoken about all wanting to be in my life romantically, but have they discussed sharing me sexually?

Thankfully, Joha does not keep us hanging, glancing at me with a smug smile on his face. "Please, do not stop on my account. This seems important."

Orion hesitates, glancing between Joha and me as though waiting for one of us to say that we are joking before we make him wait outside.

"You better not keep the king waiting," I croak out, my voice tight with desperation as I lick my dry lips.

This seems to snap him out of his trance, his fingers moving inside me again. He's holding back, though, his movements slower and more careful as he claims my lips. We kiss deeply, fully aware of our audience, and I wonder when he is going to finger fuck me like before. It is what I want—no, it is what I need.

Biting down on his lip hard enough to draw a growl from him, I dig my fingers into his chest. "More."

This seems to snap his control, and he slams his fingers in me as I cry out, loving the feeling of him stretching me. With Joha watching every moment as his best friend pleasures me, it is not long before I am on the brink of orgasm once more. Orion must feel it, as he slides another finger into me, pushing me over the edge.

I do not bother to hold back my cry of pleasure as the orgasm slams through me, making me shudder with each pulse of my cunt clamping down on Orion's fingers.

"Good girl. Next time you try to leave, I won't let you come," he grumbles, his eyes sparkling. He knows the effect those words have on me. Pulling his fingers from me, he lifts them to his mouth and sucks off my arousal.

All I can do is lean against the wall as I attempt to catch my breath and recover from that earth-shattering orgasm. I reach up and start to unbutton my jacket and blouse, watching as Orion silently strips too. A silent message passes between us. We aren't going to stop, and we aren't going back. There is no going back. We want each other, so despite the fact that our king is here, we will not hide.

The two of us are naked, precum glistening on the head of his cock. The only thing left to remove is the tiara resting on my head. As I reach for it, there is a movement out of the corner of my eye, stopping my action.

"No, keep the crown on."

Joha's sharp command makes me shudder in pleasure, and I smile as I hold my head high, the jewels glistening in the light. Orion finally steps back, his possessive stare on me the entire time, and I am able to see Joha.

He takes up residence in the high-backed armchair in the corner of my room, looking like a king on his throne. My skin erupts with goosebumps, all the hair on my arms standing on end as I stare at his magnificence. He truly was born to lead, and now he's actually been given the chance, he is rising to the challenge.

Joha watches me with a hunger that lights a fire inside me once more. I do not know what awaits us in the future or how much longer we will all be together, so I am going to make the absolute most of the time I do have.

I take an involuntary step towards Joha, unable to resist him, and Orion's warm body slips in behind mine, his heat radiating against me despite the fact we're not touching. "Go to your king," Orion orders in a low, quiet voice that leaves no room for argument.

I spare Orion a heated look over my shoulder before I turn back to our king. I walk over to Joha, swaying my hips more than I need to and drinking in the way he watches my every movement. His eyes catch on my breasts, my nipples hard and desperate for his attention.

I hear heavy footsteps, Orion's presence quiet and strong behind me until his voice breaches the silence. "On your knees before your king."

With eyes on Joha, I follow my orders and don't stop until I am before him. Lowering to my knees in the open gap between his thighs, I smile up at him coyly as I wait for his next move. It does not take long for him to lean towards me, spreading his legs wider to give me space, and then he pulls me up against him. It's an awkward position, but we make it work, our lips locked together as his hands explore my body. His fingers tweak my nipples, and I gasp into his mouth, resting my hands against his chest to stop myself from losing balance.

When I am steady against him, I shift one of my hands and drag it up his leg teasingly until I am at the apex of his thighs, and I find exactly what I am looking for. His cock is hard and straining against his clothes, as though trying to get to me. Just seeing how much he desires me makes me want him all the more.

Pulling back from our kiss, I grin at him as I undo the laces of his trousers, swiping my tongue over my lower lip as his cock springs free. Wrapping my hand around his length, I watch him with amused pleasure as he groans. I love the effect I have on him, on all three of the men in my life.

"My king, do you want me to serve you?" I purr, and his eyes blow with desire, his head jerking rapidly as he watches me.

I hear Orion drop to his knees, yet he does not do anything but watch as I run my hand over Joha's cock. I shuffle back a little and lean forward, running my tongue along his hard length. My hand squeezes the base the whole time, and when I am sure he is ready, I take him into my mouth. Giving a few shallow sucks, I savour his groan of pleasure. I relax my throat and take him deeper, hollowing my cheeks to add to the pleasure.

Behind me, I feel Orion lining himself up, the hot press of his cock stretching my entrance. Excitement flares through me as I realise the two of them are going to fuck me at the same time. I have dreamed about this, yet I was never sure it would happen for real, the possessive nature of my guys potentially being too much. It looks like I was wrong.

Orion rubs his cock across my cunt, bumping my clit with each roll of his hips, arousing me all the more and making sure I am ready before returning it to my entrance. The pure size of his cock could be damaging if I was not prepared for him, which is why he was so thorough when he finger fucked me. It will still hurt, but I cannot fucking wait. I bob on Joha's cock, getting into a rhythm, my eyes locked on my king as Orion starts to push inside my wet heat. His invading length stretches me deliciously, making me groan, but I don't stop sucking, my hum vibrating down Joha's length.

Snarling, Orion rocks inside me before growing impatient, and with one smooth movement, he plunges to the hilt, not giving me a chance to adjust. He is being careful not to hurt me in the process, but he's big, and the sting makes me clench around him even as I moan on Joha's cock. Pulling from my clinging cunt, Orion slams back into me, causing small noises to escape me from the force. His hand wraps around my hair, pulling my head back, and in doing so, he gains control of my actions. He directs me on how to pleasure his king as he pounds into me, my mouth sliding down on Joha's cock, and when he pulls out, I'm pulled back. My careful control is stripped back, allowing me to enjoy the feeling.

"That's it, look at his eyes, Alyx. See what you do to your king." My eyes roll up to meet Joha's, even as tears escape from the force of being used. I see what he means—the obsession, the hunger. It's stark and raw. "He loves seeing his betrothed being used like this. He enjoys watching as we share you, doesn't he?"

Orion's gruff, dirty voice fills the air, making me moan, and Joha's eyes slide to him for a moment before they drop to our joined bodies. The fire only grows as he watches me get fucked by his best friend and guard.

Oh yes, our king likes watching me get fucked, and that only heightens my pleasure as I push back, demanding more.

It is so fucking intense. Orion delivers punishing blows, forcing me to take more of Joha's cock into my throat, yet I know he would not let anything happen to me. He would never give me more than I could handle.

Joha is practically quaking beneath me, and I dig my nails into his thighs to hold on, knowing it will leave marks. If I could smirk right now, I would. I could bring this man to his knees, I can make him weak, and that thought is heady.

I'm his, but he's all mine.

"Our good, proper king loves watching his assassin being fucked," Orion snarls, fighting my cunt as he speeds up. "Don't you, my king? You act innocent and regal while sitting on your throne, but how many times have you imagined bending her over it? I know I have."

"Alyx," Joha groans, lifting his hips to bury himself deeper in my throat, his jaw grinding. "He's right. You look beautiful on your knees for me with him deep inside you. So beautiful—I—oh gods!"

He suddenly stiffens, thrusting into my mouth and calling my name as he comes down my throat. I swallow the salty taste of him, licking every drop clean from his cock before I rest my head on his thigh and smile up at him. He's watching me with pleasure-hooded eyes, an adoring smile curling his lips as he reaches down and strokes my hot cheeks.

"So beautiful and all ours." He lifts his head, his eyes meeting Orion's. "Now, my guard, make our girl come for your king to see."

"Yes, my king," Orion mocks as he presses my head deeper into our king's lap and tilts my ass higher into the air.

Now that I'm all Orion's, he decides to take it up a notch. He no longer has to worry about choking me, so he pounds into me, straddling the line between pleasure and pain. I moan as I grip onto Joha's knees and hold on. With each thrust, he bumps against my G-spot, the size of him stretching me to my limit. I wish I could freeze this moment and relive it whenever I pleased, remembering the love I felt in their every movement.

It doesn't take long, his sharp thrusts bringing me to a frenzy. I try to say something, to warn him that I'm about to come, but I find myself at a loss for words. Each thrust gets faster, harder, losing finesse as he chases his own end. All of a sudden, my orgasm rips through me, just as rough and explosive as the act itself. I have to bite down on my scream, holding back my noises of pleasure. The last thing I want is my guards running in. They have probably been able to hear much of what we were doing anyway, but a scream is something they could not ignore, especially knowing the king is in here too.

Pleasure rips through me so fiercely that my vision goes white, and I have to simply hold on and ride out the sensations until my vision returns. Orion roars behind me, his movements faltering as he gives one last punishing thrust. He pulses within me, and although I can now see, that does nothing to dim the second round of pleasure, my pussy milking him dry.

Once the orgasm releases us from its grip, Orion pulls out from my greedy cunt and gently helps me into a sitting position on the floor, almost falling to the ground next to me. He looks exhausted but happy, and I glance up at Joha to find him watching the two of us with a smile.

"Well," he drawls, "this was not what I was expecting when I came to your rooms earlier."

"You have to admit it was a nice distraction though." I grin up at him, my hand rubbing his knee affectionately. As I move, I realise how sticky and sweaty I am now. "Ugh, I am going to need a shower before we do anything else."

Orion stirs beside me, pulling my chin up and pressing a kiss against my lips. "That is something we can arrange." Without saying another word, he pulls me against his chest and stands, cradling me against him. I laugh in surprise, but I do not struggle, because I know he would never drop me.

He carries me to the bathroom, and over my shoulder, I watch as Joha stands and sheds the rest of his clothing, following us with a grin.

CHAPTER
SIXTY-SIX

ALYX

N ow washed and fully dressed once more—though we did have to rewash since they got handsy—I am ready to tackle the day. The space between my legs aches in the most pleasant way, reminding me of how I spent my morning. Joha and Orion devoted our shower time to making sure I was clean and not feeling any discomfort after our session in my bedroom. I was very happy to allow them to fawn over me.

However, there are other important jobs that need our attention today, like what we found out, and that thought sours my good mood.

Surrounded by guards, Joha and I walk through the palace grounds. We take the long way around so we can be seen together. It is important to show a united front after everything that happened. Support for the king has been stronger than we thought, the treachery of Queen Mother making others realise that they have all been fed lies about him over the years in her bid to take over.

Orion leads the way, looking out for any threats and giving me a great view of his ass at the same time. With the three of us together, there is only one person missing.

"Where is Crux?" I ask Joha quietly, making sure we are not over-heard by anyone. Orion handpicked these guards and promises they are loyal, but it is better to be overly cautious.

"I am sure he will turn up. He is always lurking around some-where." Although Joha's reply is said dryly, when I glance at him, I see a smile playing on his lips. The three of them might not be best friends, but they all seem to respect each other's decision to be with me.

He's right. Crux is probably tracking our movements at the moment, or at least has eyes on us reporting back to him at all times. For this next job, we are going to need him and his particular skill set.

After passing a set of long, low buildings, we pause as we reach the entrance to the prison block.

Turning from his position, Orion looks at Joha. "Are you ready for this?"

We're about to question the former Queen Mother. She's been interrogated by the guards, Crux being one of those involved, and now it is our turn to see what truth we can get out of her before deciding her punishment. She has committed treason of the highest order, so there will be no court case here. Joha's decision is law.

My eyes roam over his face, and I look past the controlled mask he's wearing and take in the turbulent emotions beneath. Although the former Queen Mother was working against him, she has been a part of his life for a long time, and it is only recently that he suspected she was involved in his father's death. It was a huge blow for him to learn that someone who was supposed to be supporting him and a part of his family did something so heinous. This is the final face-off, and I can only imagine the mess of feelings he must be experiencing.

My own emotions are all over the place. Queen Mother is finally getting what she deserves, and that fills me with a grim sense of satisfaction. I will not shed a tear when she is finally gone, and I would be happy to do the honours of taking her life. While I may be dressed in finery and draped in jewels, I am an assassin underneath it all. I never proclaimed to be a good person.

I'm also filled with nervous excitement. This is my chance to find out about my family.

I am sure she is behind the orders to kill my family in that fire. I want to hear her say it though. I want those words to pass her lips as I stare her in the eye and tell her who I really am.

I need to know the truth about what happened, not just guesses and rumours.

I cannot have closure until then.

Squeezing Joha's hand, I wait for his answer. Whatever he decides, we shall honour.

I lower my voice so only he can hear me. If anyone were watching, they would assume I was whispering sweet nothings into his ear. "If you need more time—"

Shaking his head, he cuts me off. "No. I am ready. Justice needs to be served."

Orion nods, and with a simple hand gesture, the guards around us break formation, two of them entering the prison before us to ensure the way is clear. They are quick and thorough, and we walk into the dark building, guards ahead and behind us.

A narrow walkway through the length of the building is bracketed by cells on either side, with guards stationed on either end. Most of the cells are empty, with only one other actually occupied, and from the smell of the man within, I would guess he got too drunk and needed a place to sober up. The pathway is too thin for Joha and me to walk side by side, so I step back to let him lead the way.

Stopping outside one of the final cells, I look inside to find the former Queen Mother huddled in one corner of the dingy room. She has a ratty blanket wrapped around her and appears to be asleep. All of her jewels have been stripped away, and she's in nothing more than her stained dress, her unbound hair falling around her in a knotty mess. She looks so much younger and weaker, but I know that is just an act. A viper lives inside this woman.

Joha kicks one of the bars with his boot, a metallic clang filling the air.

"Constance." He barks the name as an order, and I realise this is her name. I never thought to ask it before, though it makes sense, since she has no longer has a title.

She jerks awake, looking around with confusion, as though she cannot remember where she is. I see the exact moment she remembers, her eyes hardening. I would feel pity for her, since her life has drastically changed, but no, I could never feel pity for *her*. She deserves everything she gets.

Climbing shakily to her feet, she uses the wall behind her to keep herself steady, wrapping the blanket around her shoulders like a stole. She may be in a jail cell, but she's still determined to look her best. She's wearing the same dress she was when she was arrested. It must be uncomfortable, although from the odd shaping of the bodice, it looks like she removed the corset beneath it.

Clearing her throat, she brushes her hands down her skirts, taking her time before slowly turning to us. "Well, well," she begins, her voice scratchy from disuse. "Look who has deigned to see me."

Joha stares down at her, his body tight with tension, yet I can tell he's trying not to show any reaction to seeing her for the first time since she was arrested.

"It has been several days since your arrest. Are you being treated well?"

This is typical Joha, checking that she's being looked after despite the fact that she killed his father and attempted to kill him. I would not extend such courtesy.

"Has it only been that long? It feels far longer." She appears mournful, releasing a long sigh as she leans against the wall for support. "Are you here to let me out so we can move past all this silliness?"

A laugh escapes me. I knew she was conniving, but this is a whole new level I didn't think she was capable of. Ignoring me completely, Constance keeps her gaze on Joha, waiting for his reply.

Joha simply stares at her, shaking his head at the audacity of it all. "You killed my father, and you have tried to have me killed on multiple occasions. You cannot talk your way out of this. We have proof, so there is no point in trying to deny it. I know you believe I am a weak fool, but you cannot think I will let you go."

As he stands up to her and shows how he has grown without her constantly putting him down, he finally looks like a king. He no longer has to hide his intelligence or interest in ruling the land for fear of her killing him, and without constantly having to pretend, he is growing into the person he always should have been.

Constance realises this too, knowing she no longer has control over him and cannot talk her way out of jail. In a flash, she loses the mournful expression, her face transforming into a snarl as she stalks forward and grips the bars that separate them.

"The throne should have gone to me," she growls, looking more animal than human, her knuckles white from gripping the bars with such force. Orion steps forward, ready to jump between them despite the barrier keeping Constance back.

"I know you believe that, but that is not how things work. You could never rule. You are not family." Somehow, Joha is able to keep his temper in check as he talks to his would-be killer. There is a glimmer in his eyes, though, that tells me he's finally seeing the other side of her.

"If you died before having an heir, the throne would have gone to me!" Hatred practically oozes from her, her sense of self-righteousness clear. She feels like she has been cheated out of what should have been hers. "After your father died, I realised I could manipulate you into agreeing to my whims. You were young and didn't know enough, so I was able to mould you." Her gaze suddenly turns to me, even though her words are still aimed at Joha. "However, you grew up and started to have ideas of your own.

I needed you out of the way. Things only got worse when *she* arrived."

There it is, the confession we need. However, I have something to say that Constance needs to hear, something I have been looking forward to telling her since the day I met her.

I place my hand on Joha's shoulder, silently asking for permission. He glances at me, emotion brimming in his eyes, and I can see this is a good time for me to take over and give him some time to collect himself. Nodding, he takes a step back so I can move closer.

Looking at the woman who has caused so much pain, I am unable to hold back the air of smugness that surrounds me. "Do you know who I really am, Constance?"

She scowls and releases the bars, taking a step back in an attempt to compose herself. Her eyes run over me critically, and she purses her lips as she clearly finds me lacking.

"You are not a princess, of that I am sure."

I want to laugh at her prim assessment of me, quite certain that she is trying to insult me with her words. If I were a lady, this might wound me, but she has no idea how lowly I am in comparison.

Clasping my hands in front of me, I tilt my head to one side and let the mask of the king's betrothed drop so the cold, calculating killer rises to the surface. "I am an assassin. Joha hired me to help protect him because someone was trying to kill him. I adopted the position as his betrothed and helped him regain some of his power that you stole."

Constance pales, yet I get the impression it's not due to her fear of me. Instead, she seems more offended by the fact I am no lady from a noble house.

"An assassin!" she exclaims, turning her outrage to her stepson. "Is that how far you have fallen, Joha? Your father would be disgusted."

Finally losing control over his temper, he storms forward and confronts her, furiously jabbing his finger in her direction.

"Do not speak of my father, you witch," he snaps, taking her by surprise. This is certainly not the placid, easily manipulated man she thought she knew. Widening his stance, he gestures towards me. "I love this woman, and she has helped bring peace to the kingdom, something you were determined to destroy. I think my father would be happy with my choices." He takes a deep breath. "Alyx, you had some questions."

He steps back to allow me to move forward, but I can see his body shaking, showing just how much all of this is affecting him. This is the woman who murdered his father, and he is only just getting the chance to properly grieve that fact.

I want to get him out of here as quickly as possible, away from the woman who tore apart his remaining family so he can begin to heal. Clearing my throat, I wait for Constance's attention to return to me.

"What do you know about the deaths of the Stormhallow family?" I ask calmy, not wanting to show my hand just yet.

"Stormhallow?" She frowns, scrunching her nose in confusion. "They died years ago, before my husband's death."

"You mean your husband's murder," Orion corrects, his voice low with anger.

"They were the former king's biggest supporters, and they mysteriously all died in a fire," I continue, not about to leave without answers. "You and I both know it wasn't an accident. Tell me what you know." Despite my heart pounding in my chest, I am able to keep my voice even yet firm. This is an order, not a request.

The former king ordered his guards not to investigate, even though he knew the fire that killed them was deliberate. He knew his guard would be killed if he started digging around, so he kept him from danger. I understand why he did it, especially when he was losing his supporters left, right, and centre, but he also caused the truth behind my family's murder to be washed away. They never got their justice.

Queen Mother is the only person I can think of whom the former king might have been afraid of and also had the type of power to stop him from investigating the death of his biggest supporters.

She raises a brow, but I see a flicker in her eye that tells me everything I need to know. "They died in a fire—"

I cut her off before she can deny her involvement again. "A fire that was set deliberately."

Laughing, she glances at Orion and Joha, hoping they might back her up for what she believes are outrageous accusations. "I didn't set the fire, if that is what you are implying."

We know this. She has alibis for when the fire was set. Besides, she would never do the dirty work herself.

I nod in agreement, and for a moment, she thinks that she has gotten away with it once again, outsmarting the assassin. I am about to crush those hopes. "But you ordered it."

I'm not sure what makes her finally give up the act, whether she knew she wasn't going to get away with it or so that she can brag about the crime. Either way, any sense of decorum disappears, and anger returns to her face.

"The Stormhallows were always getting in the way, constantly supporting the king no matter what he suggested. They could not be bribed, so they had to go." She looks up at me with a gleam in her eye, no hint of guilt or regret. "I ordered the fire, you're right about that, but there is nothing you can do about any of it. I am queen!"

Fury courses through me. She is so blasé about the fact she killed my entire family. With one command, she took everything from me, all for the crime of my parents following their king. My heartbeat pounds in my ears, and I have to dig my nails into my palms to stop myself from leaping forward and tearing her scheming eyes out. I should feel at peace knowing that I finally have answers, yet I feel anything but.

Joha says something beside me, but all I hear is white noise, my focus locked on Constance and hers on me. She works out why I asked quicker than I expected

"You're not just an assassin, are you? The red hair, the eyes, and the unrelenting determination . . . You're her, aren't you?" Her voice breaks through to me, and I hear the moment she finally realises who I am. "The youngest Stormhallow."

I don't bother to reply, her eyes scanning my face.

"I cannot believe I did not see it before!" She starts laughing, shaking her head as she steps back into the centre of the cell. She clucks her tongue, looking so smug that I want to knock her out. "You may have gotten me," she mocks, "but there is so much more to all of this than you know."

"Ignore her, she is trying to get a rise out of you," Orion snaps, placing a hand on my arm and guiding me and Joha away so we can discuss what we have learned. This is a smart move, as it also takes her out of my line of sight. The longer I look at her, the greater the chances are of me acting on my anger.

"What now?" I bark, needing to know what we are going to do with the traitor.

"We could execute her," Orion suggests, and from his expression, it is clear this is the option he favours. "Make it public. It would show her supporters that we mean business and won't tolerate betrayal, especially in this time of change."

Joha surprises me by shaking his head. "That would just make her a martyr." Sighing, he rubs a hand across his face. "No, I thought I wanted this big confrontation, but now I find I don't need it. She will pay for her crimes, but there is a better way than killing her— something that will make her sorry she messed with me for the rest of her existence."

What could possibly be worse than death to a person like her?

A thought hits me like lightning, and I start to see the plan forming in his mind. "You're going to exile her."

Joha looks triumphant as he turns back to look at the woman in the cell who used to have so much control over him.

"You are found guilty of murder of the former king, betrayal to the throne, hiring assassins, and attempted murder of the current king." His voice is regal, ringing out around us. "Your greed is at the heart of this, so your punishment shall follow suit. You shall be exiled from this land. If you set foot in our borders, you will be killed. We shall escort you to the border, and you can wander the wasteland beyond for the rest of your life. You shall live in fear and discomfort, alone and without any of the luxuries you pride so much."

Constance pales as he speaks, true horror hitting her as she realises what this will mean for her. Joha was right. This is a far greater punishment to her than being locked away forever or executed.

"Your Majesty." Her eyes are wide and pleading. "Please, do not exile me. I will not survive it."

It is not lost on me that we were just discussing the option of executing her. I believe she would choose that if we were to give her the choice.

Warmth appears behind me, and I know Crux has finally joined us. Glancing over my shoulder, I find him dressed as a guard. One of his little rats most likely reported to him what was happening in here, causing him to turn up at the most opportune time.

"Anyone who tries to help you shall face the same punishment," Joha continues, ignoring Crux's sudden appearance, even as the assassin moves forward, drawing Constance's eye.

"Do not think that we will not be watching. Every assassin, spy, and street rat will know your face and report back to me should you try to return." His threat is very real, and I know he's telling the truth. Crux's web of connections reaches far and wide. From the way Constance backs up, true fear colouring her face, I know she senses the danger Crux poses to her.

Joha takes my hand in his, squeezing slightly so I look at him. Understanding shines in his eyes, and if anyone knows how I feel, it is him. "Come, Alyx, let us leave this place so the guards can deal with their prisoner."

Joha and I turn to depart, leaving Orion and my assassin behind to do what is needed. As we pass, Crux takes the opportunity to brush my cheek, not bothering to hide the movement. His eyes promise more, and I know as soon as he is done here, he will find me. His touch is comforting to me, settling the twisted feeling in my stomach. He will stay here and make sure that Constance is properly prepared for her exile.

"Guards. Prepare the former Queen Mother for exile," Orion calls out, and prison guards jump forward to follow their commander's orders.

It is the last time that title will be uttered in regard to her. She will be banished, a bad memory and, in time, a story. While she suffers, the kingdom will move on.

I link my arm with Joha's, my mind spinning with what I have learned. Although I know Constance was behind my family's demise, I cannot help but ponder her last words. *There is so much more to all of this than you know.* Does she mean my family's deaths or the attacks on Joha?

I should be happy, but my instincts are telling me that she's right, and we are about to be hit by a storm we are fully unprepared for.

CHAPTER
SIXTY-SEVEN

ALYX

The night is alive with excitement and a kaleidoscope of colours, and I know Joha was right—the kingdom needed this. Rumours have spread far and wide about Queen Mother's betrayal and plans, and everything is unbalanced, most waiting for it to fail. They needed hope, a new start, and so did we.

Sang Pram is a celebration of life, of welcoming in another year. It's a huge gathering, and everyone from the kingdom is welcome. There are fireworks, parades, dancers, and feasts being held across the kingdom. It's a perfect diversion, and this year, I am part of it, not just sitting on a roof in the Lowers with Crux watching the fireworks from far away. No, this time I am in the midst of it, and it's far different in the Uppers than in the Lowers, but the feeling it gives me is the same—hope.

These last few days have been stressful, and everyone needs this, including Joha. We needed to show the kingdom we are united and stronger than ever.

Fireworks shoot into the sky, discharged from the boats in the harbour just out from the docks. The explosions fill the air with bright colours, forming shapes, a story being told of our kingdom. People turn their eyes up in awe, and kids laugh and clap, demanding more. Even I am not immune, a smile on my lips as I watch flowers explode in the sky before I turn my eyes back to the road we are slowly making our way down.

Joha's subjects line each side of the street, some peering from houses and shops windows or perched on roofs to get the best view of the parade as it follows us. We are slowly making our way through the Uppers towards the docks where Joha will welcome in the new year for everyone to see. It's tradition, one I am happy to be a part of. I smile and wave alongside him, throwing out traditional flowers for the crowd, a sign of prosperity and happiness.

Joha holds my other hand, shooting me a wide, unchecked smile. His robes catch the light, a deep flowing purple that fades to a pure white at the end, embroidered with flowers and fireworks of all colours, and his crown sits perfectly on his head. My dress is a reflection of his, only inverted. It begins white over my chest and stomach and fans out to a full, deep purple skirt.

Orion walks at the side of our palanquin, scanning the crowd, and Crux is on the other side dressed as a guard. Neither of them is willing to put the king or me at risk.

Despite everything that has happened, I find myself enjoying the night. I grin and wave to the excited crowd, spinning and dancing with Joha on our open-top palanquin.

My eyes catch on something shiny, and my smile drops as Joha spins me again, my head jerking around to seek out that light.

There.

I stumble from Joha's arms, squinting to see as we draw closer. When my eyes finally make sense of what I am seeing, my heart lurches and then stops. Terror races through me, flooding my veins with adrenaline.

Sitting atop a balcony of the last large house before the street turns left towards Cairns is a wooden crossbow. It's massive, the size we use to take down ships, and it's armed with a metal bolt aimed right at us . . . at Joha. A cloaked figure holds it, blending into the darkness. The guards are absorbed in the frivolity, the crowds too much for them to handle.

They do not notice the threat aimed at their king, but I do.

"It's not over," I whisper in sudden understanding as everything Constance said comes back to me. I glance at Joha, my eyes wide as he frowns at me even as he waves.

"What, my love?" he asks happily.

"It's not over. Whoever is behind this . . . It wasn't just Constance. It's a trap. This is a trap!"

Grabbing Joha, I throw him towards Crux, letting gravity take hold. I am trusting him with one of the most precious things in my life. "Get the king to safety!"

I duck under the arrow that flies through the air, imbedding where Joha just was, and then I gape in shock. It would have speared him to the wood, and he would have been dead on impact. They planned to kill him in front of his people and display his bloody corpse for all to see.

This isn't over.

I can sense the attacker readying another arrow, so I take a running leap from the palanquin, rolling across the packed dirt. I ignore the screams and chaos erupting around me as I run to the closest horse. Yanking down the guard with an apologetic look, I throw myself onto its back. My dress spreads out around me as I kick the horse into action and gallop towards the house. I hear Orion and Joha yelling after me, but I am focused on the assailant as another arrow is released. I jerk my horse to the side and narrowly avoid it. Unable to spare a look back, I send up prayers that no one is injured as I bear down on the house. I speed up, then I clamber to my feet on the horse's back, crouching as we gallop. When we reach the balcony, I push myself off its back, leap up, and catch the railing. My legs swing before I use my upper body strength to yank myself up and over. I tumble over the rail in time to see the attacker racing towards the back window before throwing himself out of it and into the chaos of the streets on the other side. It will take Orion or the guards too long to get here, so I push off, racing towards the open glass.

I throw myself out, landing with a groan on a cart below. As I roll from it, my dress catches on the wood, so with an annoyed snarl, I tear off the skirt, ending it just above my knees so I am free to run.

My head jerks up, and I see the dark shadow moving quickly through the screaming crowd. The chaos of not knowing what's happening causes people to run in every direction, making it impossible for the guards to get through the masses—me included.

I scan the area for a faster option before I see the pitched roofs of the shops to the left. Racing towards the wall of the first house, I jump up and catch the edge, throwing myself up and over. I flip and land on my feet, and then I race across the joined roofs, light on my feet so I do not slip off. I ignore everything, my eyes focused on that cloaked figure as I reach the last shop and throw myself off, diving into the next street after them.

It's an empty row of shops, since everyone is at the parade, and the sudden silence bar the random fireworks makes my breathing seem loud.

The figure glances back, showing slitted, dark eyes between the gap in the cloak and the mask. Grabbing a crate from the empty stall next to them, they turn and fling it at me.

I lift my arm and block the box flying towards me. It shatters, making my arm throb, but I keep moving, refusing to let it slow me down.

What they don't realise is this street ends in a dead end, and as they reach it, they glance back, noticing I'm getting closer. With no other choice, they rush at the eight-foot wall.

The figure leaps over it. Stepping back, I take a running jump at the wall and hit the side of a building to the left, using it to push off and then flip over the wall. I land on my knees on the other side, now in Cairns Province, and jump up into a run.

We duck and weave, taking all the side streets in Cairns Province, which tells me they know exactly where they are going. It's probably a trap, but I have to stop them or they will just come back and try to kill Joha again.

Constance was right.

It's not over, but it will be tonight.

CHAPTER
SIXTY-EIGHT

ALYX

My breathing is loud, controlled but loud, as I dash after the robed attacker, gaining on them with every winding street. We suddenly break out onto the front of the docks, the crashing of ocean waves reaching us as they race across the concrete edge. The ships to our left set off more fireworks, throwing embers down around us as I race after them. The whole place is abandoned and empty, waiting for the celebration to reach it.

Pulling a dagger as I run, I hurl it with all my strength. They must sense it because they weave at the last moment, and it catches their side, making them stumble. I leap, and we tumble across the concrete, my head dangling off the edge of the dock as they pin me, but I kick out, and they fly back.

I flip to my feet and pull another dagger, moving away as we circle each other, neither of us flinching as fireworks explode above us.

"Well, I'm waiting." I smirk, and they rush me. I duck under their arms and kick out their legs, but they manage to get back up and spin. They fist my dress and yank it, and it almost rips, exposing my shoulder as I snarl.

"You asshole!" I spit.

They glance at the now exposed mole on my shoulder, one I've had since I was a child, and they freeze. I use the opportunity to spin out of his grasp and kick out, sending them flying backwards a few steps.

Panting, I brandish a dagger as I stare at them, waiting for their next move, but I don't expect them to just stare. They reach up, and I prepare to react, but they press their fingers to their eyes, pulling something free, and I blink. Suddenly, bright green orbs stare back at me from under that cloak as he yanks down his mask to reveal pouty pink lips and sharp cheekbones dusted with freckles.

"What are you doing?" I hiss in confusion. Why isn't he trying to kill me?

Why is he unveiling his face? That's something no assassin would do willingly.

Reaching up slowly, he pushes his hood back, and bright red hair springs out in every direction as he combs his hand through it, a cheeky grin tugging up his lips as I stumble back in horror, gaping at his pale face, green eyes, and red hair.

The same as mine.

"Hello, sister. It's been a long time. It is you, isn't it? I knew the king had a red-haired protector, but I never imagined it was you. You always hated that mole. I told you it was a sign of strength. It's you . . . You're my little sister. My Alyx."

I stare at the face that is both familiar and not. He's older, with burns down the left side of his face and neck.

It's him though.

If he had grown up, if he had gotten older, then this is exactly what my brother would have looked like—a mix of my mother and father.

"How?" I whisper, my heart lurching as I stand frozen to the spot, scarcely able to believe it nor comprehend how this is possible. "I saw you die."

"No," he snaps before he blows out a breath. "You saw the fire starting to consume me after I ordered you to run. I managed to free myself and climb out of the back window. I did not die in that fire like our parents." He takes a step towards me. "I thought you were dead as well. I searched for you, but I couldn't find you anywhere. I thought they found you and killed you like our parents and staff."

Shaking my head, I stumble back a step, swallowing around a lump in my throat as we stare at each other.

"Alyx . . ." He steps closer again, and I remember why we are here.

The king, the attack . . .

Is he behind it all?

Is my brother the one Constance mentioned? A ghost, forgotten and left to wander through these lands and cause havoc? Was he pulling her strings all along? Was he the brain?

But why?

"Why? Why did you do this?" I croak, confused and hurting. I thought my entire family was dead. I have grieved them for years. Every day, I grieved my brother, my best friend, and here he stands, alive and well. "Our family is loyal to the king—"

"Was loyal! Look what it got them!" he shouts over the crashing waves as another firework explodes overhead. He takes another step towards me, his hands spread carefully. "Don't you see? I did this for us, for our family."

Tears burn my eyes as I stare at the desperation in his gaze. They slide down my cheeks as my lip quivers, and he softens his voice.

"Being loyal got our parents killed. They took everything from me. Yes, I did this. I was giving the orders, manipulating everything, and playing the game they started, not me. I just joined in, knowing it was the only way. Don't you see, sis? I did this for us, for our family, to get revenge."

Shaking my head, I waver as I stare at him.

"It's almost over, Alyx," he begs. "I did what I had to for us, for our family."

"No." I stumble back in horror, and he rushes closer. I hold up my hands to ward him off. "You're not him. My brother died that night. He never would have done anything like this. He was kind and soft—"

"And weak," he interjects, arching his eyebrow. "Like you back then, but look at you. I guess we have both adapted to survive."

I lift the dagger and point it at him, nearly touching his chest even as my heart breaks. "You killed so many people. Tell me it wasn't you. Tell me it was all her. Tell me!" I scream, the horror of everything he's telling me building up.

Please, please don't let me have loved a lie all this time.

"Her?" he scoffs. "She was a means to an end and useful to a certain extent. We understood each other."

"Because you both wanted the same thing," I whisper in horror. "Power, rank, money. This isn't about revenge. It never was." I see the truth in his eyes he tries to hide.

I was right. My brother died in that fire. This isn't him.

I still cannot bring myself to bury the dagger in his heart. He wears my brother's face. For so many years, I dreamed of a moment such as this, wishing I had him back with me. Somehow, this is worse.

"Alyx, it's me," he pleads. "I read you stories every night when you were scared of the dark, remember? I wiped your tears and patched up your knees when the other kids bullied you. I protected you. It's me. It's still me, your big brother."

Swallowing hard, I lower my dagger.

I can't do it.

He smiles softly and steps closer, his arms spread like he's going to embrace me. "That's it. It's me, it's me." I nod, unsure what to do, and his hand abruptly moves. He grips the sharp edge of the dagger, cutting his palm as blood spills down the blade.

I blink, frowning at it and then him. "Atlas?" I whisper, not understanding.

His eyebrow arches, his lips pursing for a moment.

"I am sorry, Alyx, truly, but I cannot let you stop me, and there can only be one of us," he explains, sounding like it should make me feel better, and suddenly, he yanks the dagger from my grip, spins it, and slams it into my chest, plunging it in deep as my eyes widen in shock and agony.

I stumble back, and he watches me. Horror fills me as I stare at him.

"For what it's worth, I am sorry, Alyx," he says as agony rips through me. My legs become weak, almost failing me. "It will all be worth it in the end. When I sit on that throne, it will be because of our family's sacrifice. I'll make sure they remember them and you."

It was all a lie.

I fell for it.

I let down my guard, and now I'll pay the ultimate price for my weakness.

I stumble back another step, my body turning cold and weak as the backs of my feet touch the edge of the dock. I glance back to see the crashing waves before I turn my head to see him once more. He's tracking me with his head tilted as he watches. I feel my organs shutting down, my body giving up to the blood loss as it puddles below me.

So much blood.

The knife is still in my chest, and my lungs are not getting enough air. My head is turning fuzzy, and my ears ring as more fireworks explode overhead. I jerk in shock.

"Goodbye, Alyx," he says, waving with his fingers.

My body gives in, and I stumble from the dock.

My arms spread as I plummet, tumbling and crashing into the turbulent waves below before they swallow me. They close above me, my blood turning the water red as I sink, my gaze on the figure standing at the surface, watching me.

My eyes close as the darkness claims me.

My last thought is of them, of Joha, Orion, and Crux.

I love you.

I hope I haunt them. I hope they know I love them with everything in me.

I hope they know this is not their fault.

SIXTY-NINE

One week later

ORION

T am worried about the king.

Something inside him broke, leaving him silent and hurting, and I find myself with nothing to do but hover around him like an anxious nanny. This is what my life has boiled down to—worrying and planning for the worst. All my years of training and working my way to the top mean nothing now that we are on the run.

That awful night just seven days ago, although it feels like a lifetime since it transpired, changed our lives completely. Alyx is dead, and Joha was chased from the palace. These are facts, but even thinking them leaves me panting in agony.

Atlas has taken over, claiming an old rule that means he should be the rightful ruler. He took the throne by force, and now the king is hiding in the maze of tunnels under the city like a criminal. If he were to step outside and be recognised, he would be killed on the spot.

Everything we have worked for is gone, but worse yet, so is Alyx.

Alyx . . . Even her name makes the broken shards of my heart rip into my chest until I can taste blood. The only thing keeping me together is my need to protect my best friend and Crux, knowing that is what she would want.

I am organised and logical, making sure I have contingency plans in case something doesn't work. This, however . . . I never expected anything like this.

The former Queen Mother ordered the deaths of Alyx's family, and now Alyx's brother, who was believed to be dead, appeared from nowhere, apparently the mastermind behind the plot to kill the king. He was working with the very person who killed his family and took everything from him. It makes no sense. Then, he killed his sister and took the throne.

My throat tightens up at the thought, and I have to cough to clear it, moving away from the open doorway to sip a glass of water. The cool liquid helps wash away the pain and focus my mind on my purpose—keeping Joha safe and returning him to his rightful place on the throne.

I cannot afford to break now, not until everything is right. I will shatter into a million pieces and allow myself to grieve, but until then, I have work to do.

The restless anxiety that has become my almost constant companion twists in my chest, and I return to the doorway, leaning against the wood and staring into the room. It's small, only just fitting two single beds and a tiny wooden table holding a lantern, but it is safe, and that is what matters most.

Lying on one of the beds, Joha stares up at the ceiling. As soon as I see him, some of that anxiety in me eases, helping me breathe and stay focused. It has been like this since that awful day, this compulsion to make sure I know where the king is at all times, meaning I am by his side constantly. If I am away for even a couple of minutes, that terrible feeling takes over again.

I cannot lose anyone else. I would not survive it.

It's strange because while I am relieved to see Joha, looking at the shell of the man he has become makes my heart hurt. He has not left the underground series of rooms that we now call home in a week. In fact, ever since we moved to this safe house, he has hardly left the room the two of us share—although calling this place a home is a bit of a stretch, considering it feels more like a series of interconnecting burrows, much like the ones the rabbits behind the palace like to dig.

This is one of Crux's hideouts, and he has been moving us around to keep us safe. Apparently, he has several throughout the city, the locations of each only known to a select few. It is much better than some of the hovels we were initially hiding in, yet it is still not ideal. The lack of windows and fresh air is getting to me, and I can almost feel the weight of the earth above us pressing down on me. Even so, I ignore those feelings, as I know we are safest here. This current location is only known by one other person—*was* known. Alyx knew.

Alyx.

My heart clenches painfully in my chest at the abrupt reminder, and physical agony racks my body so hard, I stumble against the doorframe. My breath is stolen from me, the weight of her loss a burden I cannot carry.

It is funny how the grief comes and goes. The smallest thing sets it off, shattering me to pieces and making me useless, which is why I have to hold myself together. I cannot think of her or allow myself to acknowledge the fact that she is gone, as it will tear me apart. Everyone thinks I am strong, and physically, I am, but her presence made me weak. I would gladly accept this one weakness, though, if it meant that I could be a part of her life. She was not just mine, however, and once I realised I did not have to give up my love, I dove in headfirst. The king, the guard, and the assassin all in love with the same woman.

She was everything I ever wanted and didn't know I needed.

461

Without her, I don't feel whole. If I didn't have Joha to look after, then I honestly do not know what would have become of me. My focus needs to stay on him so I don't get distracted with the past. Return Joha to the throne, his rightful place, and kill the bastard who dared to take what was ours.

Anger smoulders in my veins, lighting me with purpose and burning away all other thoughts. Yes, I am used to anger, and I can use it as fuel to get us through this. It's this feeling of desolation that I cannot seem to get past. It seems to hide in the shadows of my mind, appearing when I let my guard down for even the slightest second. If I let it take hold of me, I will never be the same again. I lived a good life before her, and I can do that again once I help Joha.

Who am I kidding?

My whole life changed the day I met Alyx. I just didn't know it at the time.

⚓

Joha

THE WEIGHT of Orion's gaze only seems to grow heavier as the days drag on.

I want to shout at him to stop looking at me like I'm an injured animal or treating me like a child, acting more like a nanny than my head of guards. There are so many things circling around my mind that I want to say, but I know anything that comes out will just be ragged wails of loss. Even if I could form words and say how I'm feeling, I cannot find it in myself to lash out and tell Orion to give me space. I cannot find it in myself to do much of anything.

If I open my mouth, it will not be words that escape, but pain.

I am drowning in grief, and I do not know how to get myself out of this, as if the tide of despair is trying to drag me further out to sea.

Physically, there is nothing wrong with me, since all of my pain is internal. When I look at my reflection, I expect to see scars or wounds, some sort of proof of my agony, but there is nothing. I look as perfect as the day I met her, yet there is nothing left of that man she loved. It all left with her. She took all my goodness, my heart, my power, and my strength with her. I am a shell of a man.

I try not to look at my reflection, as I just feel sick. I should have seen this coming. I should have protected her, but I failed, and I am the one who is safe and alive. When Alyx died, she took my soul with her, and now I feel more like a spectre wandering the land, soulless and broken. I had finally removed Constance from my life and was beginning to rebuild my kingdom with Alyx at my side, our future so close I could taste it . . . only for both of those things to be ripped from me.

She was everything to me. The loss of her is far heavier than the loss of my throne, something I feel disgusted about. Perhaps it is because I know I will get my throne back, but I will never get to see her beautiful face again. My whole life was mapped out in my brain with her at my side, and now I am not sure how to go on. When I became king, I made a vow to put my people before all else, but she worked her way into my heart and became my world.

My people are now suffering though. Crux and Orion think I cannot hear them when they discuss the state of the kingdom in the other room. Really, I am absorbing every word they say, cataloguing Atlas's sins. No matter what he has done, I am still king, and this is my kingdom. Failing my kingdom means failing Alyx, something I must not do. It has only been in the last day that I have been able to think about anything other than her and my pain. It is funny how guilt and shame have a way of piercing their way through my thoughts. They are fierce motivators.

I need to make this right.

I sit up in bed, my body screaming and aching from disuse, but I do not let that stop me. I have been locked in my devastation for too long. Turning to look at Orion, I find him watching me. Concern and grief line his bloodshot eyes, even though he's trying to hold himself together for me. We all have our ways of coping.

Crux is out and has been most days, determination written into his every stride. He does not tell us where he's going, but I am sure it has to do with the usurper on my throne.

Alyx would not want me to waste away, especially not because of her. I can almost hear her scolding comments in my ear.

I shall keep fighting, and I will make sure her brother pays for what he did.

I shall be king again, and when that crown sits on my head, I will spend the rest of my life wishing the matching one was upon hers.

CHAPTER
SEVENTY

CRUX

Today is the day. Alyx will be avenged.

While the others were hiding and grieving, I was working—anything not to feel or think.

I have spent the last two weeks haunting the city, looking for those who are still loyal to me. Because I spent so much time in the palace recently, some of my rats shifted allegiance, but I tracked them down and quickly beat some sense into them. Every favour owed to me has been called in with the crime bosses in the city, and when that didn't work, I bribed the rest.

I created an army.

An army for her.

Finding those among the nobles who still support the king was easier than I thought it would be. These people should really be careful because if I can track them down, then others will be able to as well. Orion gave me the names of lords and other noble families who always supported Joha. To my surprise, I was able to convince them to help me without even needing to bribe them. Even those who weren't originally a fan of the king want to help, as Atlas is destroying the city. He doesn't know how to rule, simply ordering people to change things on a whim. The rich are being affected as much as the poor, meaning they are prepared to work together.

Usually, that would piss me off. The rich only help when things get bad for *them*, not caring about what is happening in the Lowers. In all honesty, I couldn't give a fuck, my whole focus on getting back at the fucker who took away my reason for living.

Alyx.

My heart constricts painfully in my chest, making me pause for a second as I steady myself against a wall. Everything I have built here, my whole underground empire was for her. My entire life was built for her. Now that she's no longer here, everything has lost its meaning. I could easily just disappear into the sea with Alyx, but her king and guard are useless without her. She would be devastated if they were killed because she was not here to protect them, so I have taken over that duty. It is what keeps me moving—get the king back into power and get my revenge on Alyx's brother at the same time.

What happens to me after, I don't care, but I suspect the pain of losing her will finally consume me.

Maybe I will fall into the waves that stole her from me and let them consume my wretched, broken soul so we will be together again.

I still remember that night vividly. Every element has been etched into my mind, and when I close my eyes, it all plays out in agonising detail. I was too slow, caught up in protecting the king, and I did not get to her in time. I was just entering the docks when Atlas stabbed her, pushing her into the sea with a careless shove.

A ragged cry escaped me as I watched her fall, my heart going with her as her limp body hit the water. I have never run as fast as I did in that moment, not caring that it was dangerous or that the bastard who just stabbed her could attempt to kill me next. No, my only thought was to get to Alyx. She would be okay if I could reach her. She *had* to be okay. Sprinting to the edge of the dock, I leaped into the water, diving deep. The water was stained red, but the churning sea soon diluted it. I searched the water for her for what felt like an eternity. She was not there. I searched and searched, my lungs screaming for air until I realised the futility of it. She was not there. I can only assume her body was washed out to sea.

I did not even get to say goodbye.

Even just thinking about it now makes my knees feel weak, and I want to fall to the dirty ground and scream out my anger and pain for all the world to hear. That memory plays out in my dreams, and I wake up screaming. It is safe to say that I have not been getting much sleep since that day. Exhaustion plagues me, but I have my purpose to keep me going. Entering the secret entrance to my current safe house, I climb the steps down to the tunnels beneath the city. I have lived underground for so long now that it does not bother me to be far below ground. Passing through the various hidden doors, I finally get to Joha and Orion.

They both sit at the wooden table in the centre of the main room, looking over at me in expectation. It is a surprise to see the king up and out of bed, some light returned to his eyes.

Good, he will need that to get us through today.

I cannot and do not have the energy to force him to live when I am barely doing so myself. It does not matter if he doesn't want this because it's what she would want. This is all for her.

"Get ready," I snap in greeting, throwing two bundles onto the table without explanation. "We're going out."

Orion frowns, his previously shaved head covered with hair, catching the light as he leans forward and opens his bundle of fabric. He arches an eyebrow at what he finds inside, but he says nothing, instead glancing at Joha.

The king looks at the bundles and then back to me, his confusion evident. "Where are we going?"

A grim smile takes over my expression, and I have no doubt it is evil and bloodthirsty. "To take back your throne."

Dethrone the false king, kill him, then put Joha back into place.

It's all that repeats in my head as they share a look.

I am nothing more than a weapon.

⚓

We move through the city like wraiths in the night. The moon is low in the sky, meaning we only have a few hours before the sun rises and takes away our advantage as we hug the shadows of the buildings. The tunnels only take us so far, and the rest of the journey is going to be above ground. We are now in the Uppers, and we just need to get to the palace walls without anyone seeing us.

The king and his guard are silent behind me, following my lead. It took less convincing than I thought it would to get them both on board with my plan.

It seems none of us care if we live or die anymore.

Getting into the palace grounds should not be too difficult, but Atlas has massively increased the number of guards that patrol inside the wall. This is going to make it more challenging, but not impossible. Reaching the wall, we circle our way around to the secret entrance I discovered when I was first stalking Alyx here.

"This is not going to work," Orion grumbles, his body stiff with tension. "There are too many guards. We will never get past them."

He is right, and I know he's been taking in the changes Atlas made. While he and I could sneak past, the king does not have the same training we do and would bring attention to us. I enjoy his discomfort and I smile, knowing my expression disturbs him. The king just watches us silently, glancing between us.

"It is a good thing that I planned a little distraction."

The three of us slip through the secret entrance, staying low in the shadow of the abandoned building built against the wall. It is the perfect place to sneak in, and I am surprised the guards have never thought of that and blocked it off.

I sit in the shadows and watch the patrolling guards when a huge boom shakes the ground under our feet. Shouts and sounds of panic fill the air as guards run towards the front of the palace and the main gates. It seems that my old friend, Mr. Singe, has pulled through with his end of our arrangement.

Mr. Singe used to be a medic for the palace and enjoyed experimenting with different remedies. He was discharged by the former king when he managed to create a chemical that exploded on impact. Several guards raided his stash and managed to blow themselves up in the process. None of that was Singe's fault, but he was discharged anyway. When I offered him a chance to get some payback, he was up for the challenge.

"That was your distraction?" Joha asks with a raised brow. "To blow up the front gates?"

I simply grin in response, loving the fuck out of causing mayhem as part of my revenge. Orion looks as though he cannot decide between wanting to strangle me or feeling impressed.

"You have been busy," is all he says, begrudging respect in his voice.

Usually, I would be crowing with victory at making Orion actually compliment me, but we don't have time for that. Besides, that is not why we are here. We are here for Alyx, and I am not about to waste this chance, as it might be the only one we have.

"Come on, we need to make the most of the distraction."

Sticking to the shadows, we run through the grounds. I don't bother to check if they are keeping up with me. I have revenge to get, and I will not let anything stop me from having it. I scan the main palace before my eyes shoot over to the smaller but no less grand king's palace where the bedrooms are situated. It stands to reason that Atlas would be asleep at this time, yet he could still be working in the main palace. We cannot risk choosing the wrong one.

Out of nowhere, a small shape appears and runs up to us. Both Joha and Orion reach for their weapons, but I put up a hand to stop them. I know exactly who this is—one of my little rats. Scurrying forward like the creature they are named after, he whispers a few quiet words into my ear. I nod in acknowledgement and dismissal, then he quickly disappears into the shadows.

Blowing out a breath of relief, I feel a knot of tension leave my shoulders. "Atlas is holed up in the office in the palace. He heard the explosion and called all of his guards to block the door."

We may have a wall of guards to deal with, but I would rather face them any day than go into a situation without knowing exactly where I am going.

"Then let's go pay him a visit." Joha's eyes narrow as he turns his attention to the palace, as though he can see through the walls directly to where Atlas sits in his office.

With a new sense of determination, we bolster ourselves and sneak into the main palace. Most of the guards are guarding the office or the main gates, so it is easy to get in unnoticed. It feels strange to be back in the palace grounds, knowing Alyx is no longer here. Once I avenge Alyx and get Joha back on the throne, I will never come here again.

I cannot. It is too painful.

I know the layout of the palace like the back of my hand, so I push down the emotions that threaten to overwhelm me and focus on leading us through, not needing to check for directions. I make it my business to know the layout of my enemy's base.

As soon as we reach the long corridor that leads to the king's office, the whole atmosphere changes as we are hit with a wave of nervous adrenaline. The guards stop us immediately, since there is nowhere to hide in this large, open corridor. Their weapons are quickly pointed towards us, and they tighten their formation to make it impossible for us to pass.

One of the guards moves forward, a mark on his shoulder indicating he's of a higher rank than the others. "Stop. Under the orders of King Atlas, you cannot pass."

My brows rise at the king comment. It seems Atlas did not waste any time asserting his dominance. However, legally, Joha is still the king, and Atlas is simply playing pretend.

Orion shifts his weight beside me, moving closer and pulling down his hood so they can see exactly who is before them. "Stand down, Captain Leon. The true king is here at my side. You know that." Orion gestures to Joha next to him, his voice steady and even, expecting them to follow his orders.

The captain winces, clearly wanting to listen but torn about his current orders. "Please, sir, do not do this. I do not want to hurt you."

There are some quiet noises of agreement from the other guards, none of them stepping down. Orion's presence has shaken them. This is a male they all look up to, who has trained with them, worked with them, and would have died with them.

"You swore a vow to protect the king and the Crown," Orion reminds them, his voice deepening as he gestures towards the closed office doors. "That usurper in there is *not* the king. For as long as Joha lives, he will have the crown, whether that madman in there wants to accept that or not." Frowning with disappointment, he crosses his arms over his chest, not bothering to hold his weapon in front of his soldiers. "You used to be loyal to the king and to me. Show that loyalty now by stepping down. I do not expect you to join us in this fight, but for your king, put down your weapons and let us through."

There is a long, heavy pause, and I watch as the guards exchange glances, clearly torn by the decision. I would have been happy to cut my way through them to get into that office, but if this works, then it is certainly an easier way to go about it.

"Yes, sir," the captain states, snapping into a salute. "Long live the king."

It only takes a heartbeat before the rest of his soldiers do the same thing, dropping their weapons on the floor. Their loyalty to Orion is surprising, and it makes me look at him in a new light. Perhaps he's not as bad as I thought. Now is not the time for these thoughts, though, and I need to focus.

The guards step away, leaving the doorway clear for us. The three of us look at each other, swapping shallow nods to show we are ready. There are only two ways out of this now—success or death—and for Alyx, only success will do.

Orion steps in front of his king, protective to a fault, and kicks the door in with one powerful smash of his boot. Stepping into the room with his sword raised, he holds up his other hand, palm out, towards his guards in the gesture to hold off. Incredibly, instead of jumping us the moment we step over the threshold and into the room, they follow his silent order, hanging back with their weapons raised.

The room is full of guards, all of them looking anxious and uncomfortable as the rightful king steps into the room. Bringing up the rear, I am the last to enter, scanning everyone who stands as a threat and planning how I will disable or kill each one.

Atlas sits in a large wingback chair behind a huge desk, watching us with raised brows. He hides his surprise well, but I am an expert in reading people. He is shocked that we managed to get this far, and he knows this is not because of our superior skills, rather that the guards are still loyal to the former king and not him.

"Well, well, I *am* surprised," he drawls sarcastically, leaning forward in his chair, placing his hands on the desk. "I did not think you had it in you, Joha."

"That is king to you, scum," Orion barks out, reminding everyone in the room who the true royal is.

Anger and annoyance flash across Atlas's face, bringing a dark spark of joy to my withered soul. Whatever he has been doing for the last decade or so has twisted his mind. He might be smart, he would have to be to pull all this off, but I see the madness in his eyes that he tries so desperately to hide.

"You really think the three of you can take me?" His sneer quickly shifts to a maniacal laugh. "The guards will stop you before you take a single step forward."

I'm not so sure about that, asshole.

Joha chuckles, and although I can see a slight tremor in his hand, he does a good job of hiding it. "Do you think I would only bring two others with me? I brought a couple of friends who will be here soon."

As if on cue, a guard runs into the room, his appearance dishevelled and face red with exertion. I spin, ready to attack, but it quickly becomes clear that is not needed. "Sir! There is a riot on the grounds, and they are making their way towards the palace."

Panic flickers on Atlas's face, quickly morphing into rage. Slamming his fists down onto the desk, he pushes up from the chair, a vein pulsing in his forehead.

"Shit!" His shout makes the guards flinch, which only makes me wonder what it has been like here the last two weeks with him in charge.

"Kill these three and then deal with the peasants outside." He spins on his heel to stare out the window. It's obvious he expects his orders to be carried out without delay. This is not what happens though. The guards turn to Orion, looking for guidance, and I know the tides have turned.

Stepping forward, I pass Orion and the king, placing myself in front of them as I stare at the back of a killer. My heart was previously racing in my chest, but now it settles. I know exactly what I need to do next and how this is going to go. For Alyx, it is all worth it.

"You killed your own sister. Do you really think the guards will be loyal to you?" My question makes Atlas freeze. I hit a nerve. Perhaps he does have a heart after all. Is it the fact he killed Alyx that is hurting him or the knowledge that no one is following his orders?

"Enough," he hisses, looking at me over his shoulder. "Kill them now!"

Again, the guards flinch and shift their weight from foot to foot as they continue to look to Orion for guidance. We have their support, and Atlas is only making things worse for himself. A grim sense of excitement moves through me as I realise that the moment I have been waiting for the last two weeks has finally arrived. I am going to kill him.

I will wear his blood like a mark of honour as I go to my grave with her.

I reach for my dagger, anticipation thrumming through me as I stare into the eyes of the man who killed the woman I love.

"You started a rebellion without me?"

The sarcastic words fall into the tight silence of the room.

That voice. I know it like I know the sound of my own, but it can't be. She's dead. It's my mind playing tricks on me, it has to be, but that doesn't stop me from spinning, my breath catching as I find a figure framed in the open doorway. Guards reach for their weapons, unsure who is a threat, but all I see is her.

"Alyx." Her name is a strangled whisper, and my knees threaten to give out. From the corner of my eye, I see Joha and Orion staring at her in shock, attempting to deal with this huge revelation.

She's here. She's alive.

She's real.

Stepping into the room as though she owns it, she tilts her head in that familiar way as a wicked smile tilts up her lips. She looks the same, with her long red hair plaited back and pale skin touched by freckles. I'm silent, staring at her as she heads our way. Her familiar scent wraps around me like a promise and an apology. She brushes a hand over my shoulder in reassurance as she passes. The physical contact is almost my undoing. I nearly crumple before her, everything else forgotten, but her eyes are for her brother. No matter the joy in my heart or the ground moving under my feet at her sudden appearance, I have to keep it together. We're about to engage in a fight to the death, but damn does she have good timing.

Walking up to the desk, she places her palms down on the surface and leans forward with a quirk of her lips, looking as though she is about to tell a secret. Everyone else in the room is forgotten as she peers at the remaining member of her family.

"You did not really think you could kill me that easily, did you, *brother?*"

CHAPTER
SEVENTY-ONE

ALYX

His eyes are wide, filled with horror and shock and maybe a dash of relief as he stares back at me.

My brother, the boy I loved more than anything in this entire world.

He's the man I grieved for years, dreamed of, loved, and sought revenge for, and here he stands behind my lover's desk—no, behind my king's desk, Joha's crown on his head. He stands in Joha's palace like he owns it, as though he deserves it after spilling my blood to get it.

Me, his sister.

"How?" His whisper fills the room, and I know my men are wondering the same. I can feel their eyes on me, but I cannot bring myself to look or I will break.

I have missed them so much, and even though my chest aches with the healing wound, I knew I had to be here when I heard of Crux's movements.

"I saw you die," Atlas whispers.

"No, you saw me fall. There is a difference. Here is a tip, brother. When you try to kill an assassin, make sure they are really dead. We have a terrible habit of surviving anything and coming for the ones who tried to end us."

"The blade—your chest . . ." He shakes his head, stock still as he stares at me.

"Ah, yes, I'll admit even for me that was a tough one to come back from." I part my blouse to show the wicked, raw scar covered in an assortment of herbs and pastes thanks to the sailor who saved me. "I washed up on the southern shore, half dead and broken. An old sailor found me and saved my life, nursing me back to health." I glance at Joha.

"I promised him a title. I hope that's okay." I grin before I glance back at my brother, and it drops. "When I woke up a few days ago, all I could think about was you and what you did to me. I came back here and planned while I healed. I learned that one from you. Nobody looks for you if you're dead, and it makes your enemies lower their guard. I suppose I should thank you for that lesson." I keep my eyes on his as a grin flirts on my lips. I'll never let him know just how weak I am and just how close to death I was. I know I should be resting, since I am not out of the woods, but when I heard . . . well, I couldn't let them have all the fun. Besides, a few snorts of that sailor's old telf weed—a stimulant sailors used to keep themselves awake and alert—and I was good to go.

All I could think about was one thing—revenge.

"I was going to break in and kill you myself, but it seems someone else had the same idea," I say with a suffering sigh. "You had to go and spoil my plan, didn't you?" I wink at Crux, and he grins.

"Sister, you have to understand," Atlas starts, his voice silky and cajoling. It's the same one he used on me as a kid.

It used to comfort me, but now all it does is infuriate me.

He falls back into his chair from my sudden kick. "It's Alyx to you.

We stopped being family when you nearly spilled all the blood from my body. I hope it was worth it. I hope this was all worth it," I tell him. "And no, I don't understand. I don't understand your greed or your madness, but you know what I realised as I lay there with nothing to do but look back on everything? I don't need to understand. You made your choice, and now you must live with that for however long I allow you to."

"Alyx, I did this for us, for our family, to make them all pay."

"Really? Still pushing that one, are you?" I remark as I lean my hip against Joha's desk. "Try again. It isn't working." I arch a brow and wait.

His face pinkens slightly as he watches me, the cogs in his head turning as he tries to think his way out of this one, but he is a fool if he thinks I would ever take his side.

I loved him once, and it made me weak. Never again.

I do not need his love, not when I have three men ready to go to war for me.

I don't need him, maybe I never did, and I think that scares him. I think he knew that, and he decided to get rid of me before I saw the truth and turned on him.

"Join me." He holds out his hand, his expression hopeful and shrewd. "Look at what we can accomplish together. We have all made mistakes—"

"I call plunging a dagger into my heart more than a mistake. You are even more of a fool than I thought you were if you think that blatant manipulation will work. You care for no one or nothing. You do not want someone at your side. You want everyone under you. You want to control them, own them. I should have seen it when we were kids, your need for power and station, but I was blinded by love. Not anymore. Call this what you want, but it is not revenge and we both know it. Drop the act, we both know how this ends. One of us will die, and it will not be me. Not this time."

He stares at me for a moment before he blows out a breath. "Fine, then let us do this."

Relief fills me that he will not try to convince me, that he will not lie to me anymore. This is almost over.

He brandishes a dagger, but before he can thrust it towards me, I fling myself over the desk, uncaring about my wounds, adrenaline pumping through me. I want to end this quickly, so I kick out, sending the dagger flying into the air. Catching it, I arch my brow at him as he sits down heavily in his chair once more and peers at me.

"You won't kill me," he says, and everything else fades—the guards, the palace, the coup, even my men.

All I see is him, the perfect mix of my mother and father.

Once, he would have been right, but he threatened my men, the people who have been by my side through it all.

They are my family, not this traitor.

I was desperate for answers and revenge once, but everything I needed was right there beside me all along. They took the broken pieces of me and put me back together, and he tried to take that from me.

He tried to steal the only goodness I have found in this world.

"I might not have been able to kill you that night out of love, but not this time. All that is left in my heart for you is anger. You are not the boy I loved and idolized. You are not my brother. You are simply someone standing in my way, an enemy, and do you know what I do to enemies? I destroy them." I point the dagger at him as he watches me, searching my eyes and seeing the truth.

"Alyx, let me," Crux begs behind me. I do not spare him a look, knowing better than to underestimate this man like everyone else did.

"No, this is my fight. This is my family and my problem. I love that you want to protect me from this, but you can't," I tell him as I push from the desk, my booted feet hitting the floor. I expected a fight, I expected it to be a bloodbath, but as I press the dagger to his chest, he tilts his chin back, challenging me.

"Then kill me, little sister. If you can do it, then do it. It's the only way I will stop. If you truly hate me that much, kill me."

He's gambling on my love for him.

Doesn't he realise he carved that from my heart with one strike of his blade?

I see it in his eyes, the confidence that I will not be able to do it and he will win once more—right up until I push the sharp edge into his chest. I cut through his skin and slowly press it deeper.

He glances down at it then up at me, disbelief in his eyes. I do not look away, not even as I push it deeper, knowing the agony all too well.

As I split his heart, I split my own, and I know this is a wound I will never heal from, but I do it.

I spill my brother's blood to protect the ones I love. I break my heart and soul to keep them safe.

Despite my bravado, it hurts as I plunge that dagger into his chest, like slicing open my own wound. I stare into my brother's eyes, a man I loved, as I bury it to the hilt. Tears blur my vision and fall down my cheeks as I stand above him, my hand wrapped around the hilt still plunged into his chest.

His eyes widen, his lips parting on a gasp of agony as blood bubbles there. "Alyx, I'm sorry." He lifts his hand and brushes away my tears softly, like he used to when I was a child.

"I know," I murmur. The words are choked from me as my tears fall for everything we have lost, for the innocence that was stolen from us both, and for the fire that changed us. I cry for everything that could have been and what will never be as he starts to die.

Power corrupts, but it doesn't mean he didn't love me, even if it wasn't enough in the end.

"I always loved you," I whisper as I stare into his rapidly blinking eyes, his blood pumping over my hands, staining us both.

We both should have died that night in the fire, yet as the light starts to dim in his eyes, I know I survived for a reason, even if it hurts.

Pressing my forehead to his, I stare into those familiar eyes. "I'm with you," I murmur. "I love you, brother."

"I love you," he chokes out, his voice thick as his body jerks and the light dies in his eyes, his body going limp.

He's dead.

My eyes close for a moment, my throat thick as I swallow around my agony. "Goodbye," I whisper just for him. Sniffing back my agony, I pull away, and with bloodied fingers, I slide his eyelids shut before I stumble back, hitting the desk.

I feel movement at my side, but I do not look away from my brother. I can't.

"Alyx." My name is a whisper.

"It's done, it's over." My voice sounds strange, even to me, and when I turn my head, I see three worried faces. "He's dead. I killed him." I hiccup over the words. "It's done."

"Shh." Crux wraps his arms around me, and I stiffen, fighting back the agony wanting to splinter me. I cannot fall apart.

"Leave us," Orion orders, and there is shuffling and the sound of a door shutting, and then he holds my side. "It's just us. They are gone."

"You can break, my love," Joha promises as he presses his head to mine in an echo of what I did to my brother. "We have you. We have you."

I break, sobbing into their arms for everything I have been forced to do and everything I have endured.

I grieve the loss of my family, my innocence, and my soul.

They hold me through it, putting my pieces back together again, being strong when I can't.

My eyes find my brother over their embrace, and I know the price I paid was steep, but if it lets me keep them, then it was worth it.

Everything was worth it.

CHAPTER
SEVENTY-TWO

ALYX

The sun is barely over the horizon, but we have things to do, even covered in blood. I follow my men through the palace. Doors have been broken and buildings are half burnt from the riot. I find it strange that to get peace, you have to incite violence. They stand there, waiting, as everything ended when they realised the truth—the king is back.

The crowd parts for us as we head towards the throne room, and when I glance back, I see everyone falling into step behind us.

The palace is damaged, but it will heal. Everything is as it should be.

Why do I feel hollow?

This time when I enter the throne room, I do it as me, Alyx the assassin. All my secrets and scars are bare for them to see and judge. I hide nothing.

This is who I am.

This is who they made me.

Joha stops before his throne and turns to face the crowd of lords

481

and ladies, scholars and soldiers. Uppers and Lowers stand as one, nervously staring at their king. I step back to allow him his moment, fading into Orion's and Crux's sides. My secret is out. I am not their princess.

Everything will change, but it doesn't matter.

My eyes go to Joha once more. It doesn't matter, not as long as he's safe and where he should be—leading our kingdom.

He clears his throat, drawing every eye. Dressed in clothing from the Lowers, he should look out of place, but if anything, he has never looked more like a king. Without a crown, he stands tall, his enemy's blood on him.

Gods, I love this man.

"There has been a lot of upheaval and unrest within the kingdom. I am here to assure you of our prosperity and the righting of wrongs. The throne is once more mine, where it belongs. The usurper is gone and will never threaten this kingdom again. Blood has been spilled, lives have been lost, and we will mourn for what has been taken, but just as the sun rises once more this dawn, so shall our kingdom. I stand with you, every one of you, and once the debris and death has been washed away, we will be reborn. Our kingdom is strong, our people are even stronger, and I thank you all for coming to my aid. I will spend my life repaying that and being the best king I can be, but I could not have done it without those standing at my side." His eyes move to me, then Crux and Orion. "Without my family. Without my love."

Joha moves over to me. "One thing I have learned from this is how important the truth is, how important it is to hold those you love close and never let them go, as well as the importance of change." His eyes meet mine boldly as he carries on talking. "It is time for new traditions, new rules, and new rulers." Their king, too proud to kneel even in the face of death, drops to his knees before me.

He looks up at me, hopeful and worried, his lips pressing to the back of my hand.

A killer's hand.

"Be my queen? For real this time. No lies, no sham. Stay with me forever?"

"They will never accept me," I say only for his ears. I hear the crowd moving, whispers spreading. "This was always just a deal—"

"It was never just a deal. It was always more. We belong together, Alyx. You keep me grounded and humble, and you are the only person to ever bring me joy, to love and accept me. If they cannot accept you, then I will banish them or worse, but it is time for a new age in this kingdom. Who better to be queen than someone willing to die and bleed for this throne? You deserve it more than even me. These are your people, Alyx, and together, we can unite the Uppers and Lowers. Together, we can heal the kingdom, but I cannot do this without you. I do not wish to do this without you. This power, this station meant nothing until you came along, so stay with me. Be mine." He kisses my hand again. "Be ours." The last is whispered, but I understand. He's not asking me to leave Orion or Crux. He's asking me to stay with them all.

My family.

My eyes move to the crowd. I see confusion, but also hope and relief. Joha is right. This has brought our kingdom together. I might not be who they would have chosen for their queen, but I would do anything to keep this kingdom and its king safe.

It's terrifying to shine the light on those who live their lives in the shadows, but when I glance back at Crux, he smiles and nods at me, encouraging me. My eyes find Orion, and he presses his fist to his chest, hope in his eyes.

Dragging my gaze back to Joha, I find my heart making the decision before I can.

I fall to my knees before him, grip his hair, and kiss him deeply for everyone to see. He kisses me back, and when I pull away, I rest my forehead against his, searching his beautiful eyes.

"Yes, yes, I'll stay. Yes, I'll be your queen."

We stay like that for a moment, soaking each other in. He's right, it's time for change, and there is nowhere else I would rather be in this world.

All this time I was searching for answers, for a family and a home, and now I finally have one.

Rising, I let him lead me towards the throne, and before our people, I slowly sink into the throne next to Joha's.

I wear a wide smile on my face as the crowd erupts in applause and celebration.

It will not be easy. When everything dies down, there will be questions, but as I look to those I love, I know I can weather it and endure anything as long as they are with me.

I might be a Dagger and Joha might be the Crown, but they are my heart.

CHAPTER

SEVENTY-THREE

Four weeks later

ORION

Although we are surrounded by guards, I am still on alert. Having both the king and his new bride wandering through the city is risky, even when everything seems relatively calm. Their reception has been surprisingly warm, the nobility from the Uppers and the Lowers appreciating their backgrounds and strengths. Besides, after the coup, support for the king has been pouring in.

I am not on duty, but I stand with the guards, glancing between the king in front of me and Alyx in a clearing. She looks so regal in her gown, which is simple in design but well-made and easy to move about in, just in case.

The last four weeks have been . . . intense. Figuring out who was loyal to Joha and Alyx was a long and arduous job, and there were several unpleasant instances. Thankfully, Alyx's training meant that

485

she and Joha were never really in danger. I am never far from them, and Crux is always hiding in a dark corner somewhere.

They married last week.

It was simple for a royal wedding, in part due to preference, but mostly because of how quickly it was thrown together. Many of the king's advisors tried to convince him to wait, but neither of them wanted to. I do not blame them after everything that happened. None of us take anything for granted anymore, particularly how much time we have together. What made the wedding so special and different to previous royal weddings, though, was that the whole city was able to play a part. Joha and Alyx walked through the city after the ceremony to meet their people—the whole city, not just the Uppers. I think that was the moment they fully won over the people.

Alyx was born into nobility but grew up as an assassin in the Lowers. She has brought the two into a strange, tentative harmony that no one else would have managed. She is a queen of the people. News of who she really is travelled fast around the city, and now she seems to be loved by all. They appreciate the fact that she gets involved in their lives, not just sitting in the palace all day surrounded by nobility.

Of course, it was a nightmare to keep them safe with an event on such a large scale, but everything worked out well.

Standing back with the semicircle of guards around us, I focus on Alyx. The queen. *My* queen. She wanted some time to herself. Standing in a beam of sunlight, her head tilted back and eyes closed, she looks as though she is praying. I wish I could see inside her head and know what she's feeling right now. There is a broken piece inside her thanks to her brother's betrayal and her actions to keep us all safe. Joha, Crux, and I are trying to heal that wound, but it will take time.

I can give her that. I may not have the charm, looks, or skills like Joha and Crux, but I am strong and dependable. I love her with every fibre of my being and will remain with her always. She is my best friend's bride, but she will always be mine. I will never betray her, and I will carry her damaged heart with mine to shelter it from the guilt and grief in her mind.

CRUX

Perched on the edge of a roof, I stare down at the scene before me.

Alyx looks radiant as she clutches a single flower against her chest, her head tipped back and eyes closed. She looks like she is in pain, and that makes me twitchy, wanting to do something to help. She wouldn't appreciate that though, not when she is trying to work through the demons in her mind.

Ever since that awful day when Alyx killed her brother, everything has changed mostly for the better, but it changed her, damaged her in a way none of us can heal.

Alyx and I had a conversation about how our relationship was going to work going forward. A queen cannot be seen having a relationship with an assassin. I would give up my life for her in a heartbeat, but that is not what she wanted. She knows me too well and understands how trapped I would feel in trying to live the life of a noble. Being in the spotlight and attending balls is my idea of a nightmare.

This meant that I needed a reason to be around the king and queen, but not constantly, so I blend into the shadows as their spymaster. This gives me close access to my Alyx, but it also means I can come and go as I please. My criminal empire mostly runs itself now, yet I put in an appearance now and again to make sure they remember who is in charge.

I am not a good man, and I don't pretend to be. Alyx knows this and does not expect me to change who I am.

Staring down at her, I shake my head in disbelief. How is this my life? I just wish she was not hurting so much and that I could do something to help. Instead, I hang around and get information for them, waiting for when she's ready to talk to me about her brother.

She always comes back to me. It is just a matter of waiting.

Thankfully, I am a patient man and she is more than worth the wait. I have been in love and waiting for her since we were kids. This world has tried to tear us apart time and time again, but we will always find our way back to each other. Alyx is the love of my life, and she holds this assassin's heart and always will.

JOHA

I am the luckiest man in the kingdom—not merely just because I am king, but because I have the most amazing woman at my side, one who would do anything to keep us all safe. She did the impossible and put us before even her family. She did not just save us that day, but the whole city.

Slowly but surely, we are making changes by bringing people together and trying to shrink the gap between the Uppers and Lowers. There is a lot of work to do. The former Queen Mother did a lot of damage to the royal family's reputation, and those years where I was simply a puppet are difficult for people to ignore. Now that I have Alyx by my side, though, they can see how I have changed and how determined we are to make the city a better place. Alyx is seen as a hero for killing Atlas, and I have already heard songs being sung about her bravery and beauty, even though I know they wound her, a reminder of what she lost.

A gentle breeze tousles my hair, the air warm and sky bright. My gaze isn't on the sky, though, but the gorgeous woman standing by the ruins of her family's estate. The sunlight filters through a cloud and seems to shine directly on Alyx, like a heavenly spotlight. My wife is beautiful, but in sunlight, she is exquisite.

My wife. I am still getting used to that, and it always brings a smile to my lips, even on a day like today when it is shrouded with sadness.

She was the most beautiful bride, and the memory of it is engraved into my mind. That was the best day of my life, and I will never forget it. Every time I close my eyes, it replays through my thoughts, and I am transported back to that moment.

The cathedral was bedecked with white lilies, the aisles full to bursting as everyone tried to get a glimpse of the new queen. When she arrived, wearing the traditional dark colours we favour for weddings, I was dumbstruck.

She might have gone for a traditional colour, but the dress itself was anything but. The fitted bodice displayed her curves, the black fabric glistening like stars. The skirts bloomed out at her waist, trailing behind her in an explosion of sparkles and stars. Her gorgeous red hair was pulled back in a complicated braid, and she wore a silver band upon her head, with spokes fanning up and outward like sunbeams. Diamonds and silver flowers were woven between the spokes, making it glisten with every movement. To finish it off, her see-through black veil rested on the headdress and was also adorned with sparkles. She looked like a walking star, and she was mine.

Even now as I look at her, watching from a distance, I swear I can see an outline of her wedding dress. I don't, of course, as it is the light playing tricks on me.

I am obsessed with her and utterly in love. Things have not been easy, but we are working together, all four of us, to create a kingdom that is safe and happy. She has helped shape me into the man I am today, giving me the confidence to finally take my rightful place.

Today is a difficult day, though, as it is the anniversary of her parents' deaths and she is grieving. Given the circumstances, it is especially difficult this year, her brother's betrayal making every-thing sour. I am glad we are able to give her the space to do so while also keeping her safe though, as I have no doubt she would have come here alone if we did not arrange this. When we left the palace, she insisted that we walk and not take a carriage. She wanted to feel the breeze in her hair, and it was not far. Besides, it is good for the people to see us, as she reminded me.

Yes, today is a hard day, but tomorrow will be better. Everything is better now with her at my side.

My queen.

My love.

ALYX

Gathering the courage, I open my eyes and stare up at the wreck that once was my family's estate. My heart aches as I take it in. I have not returned here since that fateful day, as it was always too painful for me, but I knew it was still here.

I always wondered why it was never torn down and turned into something else, but now I know the truth. Constance insisted that it stay in its burnt, destroyed state as a constant reminder of what can happen at any time. She was trying to control everyone with fear.

The city is healing from her and Atlas's betrayal, and change takes time, but I can already see a difference.

I am a queen now. I sometimes wonder if I would have still ended up with Joha, Orion, and Crux if my family wasn't murdered and I was introduced to society as a lady. There is no point in thinking like that now though. Everything is so different, and if the last year has taught me anything, it is that we have to make the most of every moment.

Marrying Joha was one of my happiest moments, but that was for the kingdom, since they needed a queen. Officially, Joha is my husband, but really Orion and Crux are just as much a part of my life. The last month has been a crazy whirlwind, and we have been so busy that this is the first chance I have had to take a breath and properly grieve.

In my mind, Atlas still died the night of the fire. The man who stabbed me and took control of the city was not my brother. The man who did all of that was sick and twisted. He might blame our trauma, but I went through the same event and did not turn out like him.

Staring at the wreckage, I let the painful memories and guilt move through me, not trying to stop them. This needs to happen for me to move on. I cannot keep living in the past.

My throat tightens up, and my eyes sting as they fill with tears. "I'm sorry, Atlas, for how everything happened," I croak out, feeling that damaged, fractured part of me shift. Pressing my hand against my chest, I push past the feeling and finally allow a few tears to fall. "I hope you are now at peace with our parents."

Would they be happy with my life now? Have I made them proud despite the lives I have taken over the years? No, I cannot think like that anymore. They are dead and have been for years. I cannot live in the shadow of ghosts any longer. That is why I am here today, on the anniversary of their deaths—to take back control and release myself from the weight I place on my shoulders.

"It is all over." I am not sure whom I am talking to. Myself? My parents? Either way, every word I utter is filled with the truth. "I have been ruled by my grief ever since that day. I spent all of these years trying to get revenge, and it is finally time for me to be happy." Several more tears break through, but I do not bother to wipe them from my face or hide my pain. "I will always love you, and I hope you are proud of me, but I have to live my life now." Taking a deep, shaky breath, I prepare for the hardest part of it all—walking away.

Striding up to the wall that separates the estate from the street, I place my hand against the scarred brick and squeeze my eyes closed for a moment. This is one of the most difficult things I have ever done, but I meant what I said—I cannot live life searching for revenge.

I have to *live* it.

I can feel the weight of Joha's, Orion's, and Crux's gazes as they stand back, giving me the space I need. Their support gives me strength, and I know they are the path I am supposed to be on.

Opening my eyes and taking a deep breath, I bend down and lay a lily at the entrance to the estate. The flower was in my wedding bouquet, and I wanted to bring it here for them.

Straightening, I smile at the burnt house even as a tear rolls down my cheek. "Goodbye," I rasp.

Turning around, I walk towards the three men who make my life worth living, leaving my painful past behind me. I step forward to embrace my new life. I will never forget who I am or where I came from, but I was being held back.

I smile at Joha and Orion, and Crux. All of them wait and watch. They are three men who never should have been mine but are, and I thank the gods for letting me meet and keep them. I do not know what the future holds for us. No doubt it will not be easy, but we have endured much worse, and I know we can survive anything as long as we are together. Our kingdom will prosper. We will make sure of it—as one.

ABOUT K.A. KNIGHT

K.A Knight is an USA Today bestselling indie author trying to get all of the stories and characters out of her head, writing the monsters that you love to hate. She loves reading and devours every book she can get her hands on, and she also has a worrying caffeine addiction.

She leads her double life in a sleepy English town, where she spends her days writing like a crazy person.

Read more at K.A Knight's website or join her Facebook Reader Group.
Sign up for exclusive content and my newsletter here http://eepurl.com/drLLoj

ABOUT ERIN O'KANE

Erin lives in the UK with her cat and works full time as an independent author. Now a *USA Today* bestselling author, she began writing in 2018 when she published her first book, *Hunted by Shadows*. She specialises in writing fantasy and reverse harem paranormal romance.

Previously to writing, she worked as an intensive care nurse. Despite having to now use a wheelchair, she doesn't let it stop her and loves to travel the world.

She met K.A. Knight in 2018 when they became partners in crime and began writing together. In 2019, she became co-authors with Loxley Savage, writing fantasy reverse harem.

She's Disney obsessed, loves to read, craft and snack, and is always planning her next story.

Make sure to follow her on her social media pages for updates on what she's currently working on:

Facebook group: https://www.facebook.com/groups/ErinOKanesShadowRealm

Facebook author Page: https://www.-facebook.com/ErinOKaneAuthor

Newsletter: http://eepurl.com/gJhSd9

Instagram: https://www.instagram.com/erin.okane.author

OTHER BOOKS BY K.A. KNIGHT

CONTEMPORARY

LEGENDS AND LOVE *CONTEMPORARY RH*

Revolt

Rebel

Riot

PRETTY LIARS *CONTEMPORARY RH*

Unstoppable

Unbreakable

PINE VALLEY COLLEGE *CONTEMPORARY*

Racing Hearts

DEN OF VIPERS UNIVERSE STANDALONES

Scarlett Limerence *CONTEMPORARY*

Nadia's Salvation *CONTEMPORARY*

Alena's Revenge *CONTEMPORARY*

Den of Vipers *CONTEMPORARY RH*

Gangsters and Guns (Co-Write with Loxley Savage) *CONTEMPORARY RH*

FORBIDDEN READS *(STANDALONES)*

Daddy's Angel *CONTEMPORARY*

Stepbrothers' Darling *CONTEMPORARY RH*

STANDALONES

The Standby *CONTEMPORARY*

Diver's Heart *CONTEMPORARY RH*

DYSTOPIAN

THEIR CHAMPION SERIES *Dystopian RH*

The Wasteland

The Summit

The Cities

The Nations

Their Champion Coloring Book

Their Champion - the omnibus

The Forgotten

The Lost

The Damned

Their Champion Companion - the omnibus

PARANORMAL

THE LOST COVEN SERIES *PNR RH*

Aurora's Coven

Aurora's Betrayal

Book 3 - *coming soon..*

HER MONSTERS SERIES *PNR RH*

Rage

Hate

Book 3 - *coming soon..*

COURTS AND KINGS *PNR RH*

Court of Nightmares

Court of Death

Court of Beasts

Court of Heathens - coming soon..

THE FALLEN GODS SERIES *PNR*

Pretty Painful

Pretty Bloody

Pretty Stormy

Pretty Wild

Pretty Hot

Pretty Faces

Pretty Spelled

Fallen Gods - the omnibus 1

Fallen Gods - the omnibus 2

FORGOTTEN CITY *PNR*

Monstrous Lies

Monstrous Truths

Monstrous Ends

SCIENCE FICTION

DAWNBREAKER SERIES *SCI FI RH*

Voyage to Ayama

Dreaming of Ayama

STANDALONES

Crown of Stars *SCI FI RH*

SHARED WORLD PROJECTS

Blade of Iris - Mafia Wars *CONTEMPORARY RH*

CO-WRITES

CO-AUTHOR PROJECTS - *Erin O'Kane*

HER FREAKS SERIES *PNR Dystopian RH*

Circus Save Me

Taming The Ringmaster

Walking the Tightrope

Her Freaks Series - the omnibus

STANDALONES

The Hero Complex *PNR RH*

Dark Temptations *Collection of Short Stories, ft. One Night Only & Circus Saves Christmas*

THE WILD BOYS SERIES *CONTEMPORARY RH*

The Wild Interview

The Wild Tour

The Wild Finale

The Wild Boys - the omnibus

CO-AUTHOR PROJECTS - *Ivy Fox*

Deadly Love Series *CONTEMPORARY*

Deadly Affair

Deadly Match

Deadly Encounter

CO-AUTHOR PROJECTS - *Kendra Moreno*

STANDALONES

Stolen Trophy *CONTEMPORARY RH*

Fractured Shadows *PNR RH*

Shadowed Heart

Burn Me *PNR*

Cirque Obscurum *PNR RH*

CO-AUTHOR PROJECTS - *Loxley Savage*

THE FORSAKEN SERIES *SCI FI RH*

Capturing Carmen

Stealing Shiloh

Harboring Harlow

STANDALONES

Gangsters and Guns *CONTEMPORARY*, IN DEN OF VIPERS' UNIVERSE

OTHER CO-WRITES

Shipwreck Souls *(with Kendra Moreno & Poppy Woods)*

The Horror Emporium *(with Kendra Moreno & Poppy Woods)*

⚓

AUDIOBOOKS

The Wasteland

The Summit

The Cities

The Nations - *coming soon*

Rage

Hate

Den of Vipers *(From Podium Audio)*

Gangsters and Guns *(From Podium Audio)*

Daddy's Angel *(From Podium Audio)*

Stepbrothers' Darling *(From Podium Audio)*

Blade of Iris *(From Podium Audio)*

Deadly Affair *(From Podium Audio)*

Deadly Match *(From Podium Audio)*

Deadly Encounter *(From Podium Audio)*

Stolen Trophy *(From Podium Audio)*

Crown of Stars *(From Podium Audio)*

Monstrous Lies *(From Podium Audio)*

Monstrous Truth *(From Podium Audio)*

Monstrous Ends *(From Podium Audio)*

Court of Nightmares *(From Podium Audio)*

Court of Death *(From Podium Audio)*

Unstoppable *(From Podium Audio)*

Unbreakable *(From Podium Audio)*

Fractured Shadows *(From Podium Audio)*

Shadowed Heart *(From Podium Audio)*

Revolt *(From Podium Audio)*

Rebel *(From Podium Audio) - coming soon*

Also by Erin O'Kane

The Shadowborn Series:

Hunted by Shadows

Lost in Shadow

Embraced by Shadows

The Shadowborn series- the boxset

Born From Shadows Series:

Demons do it Better

THE WAR AND DECEIT SERIES:

Fires of Hatred

Fires of Treason

Fires of Ruin

Fires of War

Fires of the Fae:

A Lady of Embers

A Spark of Promise

A Legacy of Hope and Ash

THE CURSED WOMEN UNIVERSE:: VENOM AND STONE

Betrayal and Curses

Fractured Wings

Bloodlines series:

Midnight Magic

Midnight Trials

Midnight Deception

Midnight Conviction

Midnight Ascension

The Complete Bloodlines Series – omnibus

THE BRIDES OF DARKNESS – INTERCONNECTED STANDALONES:: A KINGDOM OF BROKEN BONDS

A City of Embers and Brimstone – coming soon

Standalones:

Second Chance

Love Bites

<u>Co-writes</u>

By Erin O'Kane and K.A Knight

HER FREAKS SERIES:: CIRCUS SAVE ME

Taming the Ringmaster

Walking the Tightrope

The Wild Boys:

The Wild Interview

The Wild Tour

The Wild Finale

The Wild Boys Series- The boxset

STANDALONES:: HERO COMPLEX

Dark Temptations

By Erin O'Kane and Loxley Savage

Wicked Waves duet:

Twisted Tides

Tides that Bind

FIND AN ERROR?

Please email this information to thenuttyformatter1@gmail.com:

- *the author name*
- *title of the book*
- *screenshot of the error*
- *suggested correction*

Printed in Great Britain
by Amazon